Trinity

Written by:

DISVON RAYFORD

BOOK SERIES READING ORDER:

GODLY BEGINNING: SEBASTIAN'S STORY

TRINITY

GIRL WITH THE SWORD

Table of Contents

CHAPTER 1

The Smartest Man In Dasha

SCION: It almost seemed too good to be true. Dasha had become one of the most highly technological kingdoms on Plinth. Most of the other kingdoms gained the knowledge of how to harness the planet's energy from us. We developed most of the stuff that aided in the endeavor. It was discovered by accident. A man, who had been digging a new plot for his cottage, was zapped and fried. At first, it was viewed as dangerous. Queen Micka had closed off the area. But Princess Calypsa, at the age of seven, saw a good use for it. The girl was twenty years old now, and most people knew her as the spoiled brat of Dasha. She was cruel, and always gave the villagers a hard time. She picked on the women and bullied the men because she knew she could. Her mother, Queen Micka, was very ignorant to her daughter's behavior, though it is said that the queen beats her. One of the reasons we didn't see much of her as a child. Calypsa was a very beautiful woman, though. She had long flowing purple hair like her mother's, and hosted a very pretty face. Which is why I didn't get why she was so cruel to the other women, when she was far prettier than them. I was what you might consider an engineer. I worked on products that ran on the planet's energy. I put wires back the way they were supposed to be and often welded certain devices. I was considered to be the smartest man in Dasha. My parents were very poor. We didn't have much when I was growing up. Food was hard to come by and my father would often steal from the market. Most of this changed when Micka took over. She had developed Dasha into something impossible. Homes were remodeled and there were places that harnessed PE and used it to power certain parts of Dasha. In people's homes, those that could afford it, people were able to connect to the PE and use it for everyday conveniences. Along with homes that ran on PE, there were also schools. Queen Micka introduced the educational system to Dasha. She started up schools where kids could learn and get free food, provided by the Government of Dasha. The Government of Dasha was started seventeen years ago. It's sole purpose was to oversee the growth and development of our kingdom. Queen Micka, of course, was head of the government and had the final say on things. It was said the government system was adopted, though, from Nasher. Thanks to the education system, I was able to get a good job and start making good money. There were cottages being built that were for those who could afford them. Most of the trees that were outside of the gates were cut down to make more space for new cottages. Life had become easier indeed. Where I worked, we had a room where we kept track of how much PE was being used. Not just in Dasha, but in other kingdoms as well. The other kingdoms paid to use our PE. That was, of course, until Princess Amana discovered her own conduit. This sparked what most would call a technological war. Every time we advanced, somehow, Kindy would either catch up or pass us. One thing Kindy had on our advances was medicine. Princess Amana was a genius. She created vaccines for every known Plinthinian disease. Our medications came from there. As well as certain inventions. One invention was a device that used PE and allowed you to communicate with someone who was far away.

We called it the receiver. It was created by none other than Amana. Calypsa had some kind of hatred towards Amana, but I just chalked it up to princesses not liking other princesses. Or at least it seemed that way. Kindy used more of the PE than Dasha. And Nasher used less of it. Nasher had developed as well as Dasha or Kindy, but the people there were more moderate. They weren't trying to invent or keep up with the innovation. They were content with just buying our inventions and spending money to have cottages built for their people. Nasher was ruled by King Tig and Queen Tisiphone. They had a son who was named Nigel. Nigel was a smart one as well. But his smarts were in business. He was the one who rode to the different kingdoms to cut deals and do business. He was the one who brought PE to his kingdom, as well as the receivers and the medicines. When he came here for the first time five years ago, Princess Calypsa was only fifteen. Nigel was quite taken with her. It was said they secretly were seeing one another but those were just rumors. On the other hand, Nigel was also quite taken with Princess Amana, but she was not the type to be bothered. She was more focused on her creations and bettering her kingdom. The truth of the matter was, there was no telling what was true and what wasn't. One rumor that I found hard to believe was that Sebastian himself had appointed Nigel's parents the King and Queen of Nasher. Sebastian was something I had a hard time believing in, period. Although I was here for the Dasha Massacre, I was very young and hardly remember it. My parents said my brother died that day. We mourn him on the day of. Of course, most of Dasha have someone they mourn on that day. It was considered the most horrible day in history. Not just for Dasha, but for the other kingdoms as well. Kindy and Nasher had been attacked by an army of undead, and Queen Alisa, Queen Micka, the Nashin royalty, and even our old prince, Caprius, who nobody had seen or heard from in over twenty years, had all gathered to fight our god's dark half. In the end, our god saved us and went back to Heaven. This was the story they told in the churches that started to pop-up all over Plinth. The story of how a boy had grown into a god and saved a planet. They even say the PE we use is just left-over energy he left behind. I chose to believe the opposite. People like me were considered blasphemers. Even Queen Micka didn't like blasphemers. She often would preach herself. Calypsa was very non-religious. I knew this because she showed no signs of respect towards the church. She didn't go with her mother and she often took time to let whoever she could, know exactly what her feelings were toward Sebastian. I liked that about her. Her will to be stubborn. It reminded me of myself. I am also a stubborn ass. They call me Scion. And much like the rest of Dasha, I just wanted to be of use. That was the new thing. All the creation of all these technologies were something that people were trying to be part of. Everyone was looking to come up with the next best thing. It was at this time that I had gotten arrested. I was working on something amazing. So far, everything was on paper. Which made it easy to lose track of things and information. I was working on a device that would allow you to save information without having to write on paper. A system where you could just say what you're looking for and it pops up. Unfortunately, I was arrested for…yes you guessed it, blaspheming.

I had taken a good swig of my drink. A woman who I worked closely with, was complaining, as she often did, about our dear princess, "…has the nerve to tell me to put on more makeup. Said I wouldn't look so much like a dog.", "I don't think you look like a dog.", I told her. "Yes well, unfortunately I was born in a place where the princess, even though she looks nicer than me, still rubs it in my face. Fuck her.", "Yes, and fuck Sebastian for creating the bitch.". While I'm quite sure she agreed with me somewhere in there, she didn't appreciate the fact that I said, fuck Sebastian. The guard arrested me and threw me into this cell I was sitting in. I sat, just thinking things over, wondering if I shouldn't have let myself get carried away. There was a loud clang at the end of the hallway. The next thing I knew, a young woman was standing in front of my cell. "Are you, Scion? Smartest man in Dasha?", "Depends on who's asking.". The girl was wearing a hood. Upon removal, "Oh my…". It was Calypsa. She had come to me and was smiling at me. Princess Calypsa was smiling at me. "So, here's the thing, I'm taking you from here. But under certain conditions. You must come and work for me in my lab. Is that okay with you?". I nodded. Anywhere was better than here. She opened the cell and directed that I follow her. As we left the dungeon and entered the sunlight, it burned my eyes. Calypsa noticed and gave me what appeared to be glasses. "They are for deflecting sunlight. I call them sunglasses.", "How original.", I said, sort of sarcastically. Even though she realized I was being sarcastic, she laughed it off, "Don't think I came up with a cool enough name?", "I would have called them sun deflectors.". We both laughed as we made our way to the castle. "So, did you hear what I did?", I asked, hoping that she wouldn't care. Of course, she didn't. This showed before she even answered me, "I don't believe that rubbish. Sebastian is just somebody that someone made up to make us more docile.". I was so happy to hear someone finally say it. Feeling like I could ask anything, I decided to clear something up, "So, you and Prince Nigel…". Calypsa looked at me out of the side of her eyes, "What about Nigel?", "Well, there are rumors that you two…well…", now I didn't want to finish what I was asking. "There is nothing between us. Not even friendship. I hate that insufferable man. Always thinking he's Sebastian's gift to women.". I let out a laugh at this. There were so many women I knew that wanted Nigel. When we finally reached the castle, we went into a door that was on the side. Inside was a huge lab the likes of which a man like me can only imagine. There were all sorts of contraptions, all running on PE, of course, and there were also beakers filled with different colored chemicals. I followed Calypsa, as she led me to a station. The station was titled 'computer'. "This is where you will be working and here is a bluescript.". I looked at the bluescript and realized immediately, "This is mine. Where did you…?", "When I heard what you were working on, I knew it would win this techno war against Kindy. So, I sought you out. Then I heard you'd been arrested. Now personally, I don't care what you say about me, or

Sebastian, but if you can create this thing, then you will be honored above all geniuses in this kingdom.". I beamed and started working right away. Sometimes, I would stay all night working. I was trying to make it where you could speak into a system and the words would appear on the screen, but this was proving extremely difficult. No matter what method I tried. I tried crossing the wires, placing them straight, and I tried all the components. It was a matter of getting the system to react to the vibration in a voice. I didn't know if I'd be able to pull this off.

One day, I received a call from Calypsa, "How is everything? Are we there yet?", "Not yet, but I'm getting close.", "Well, whatever you do, don't let Amana beat us to it. Okay?", "Sure, sure, but I need concentration, can I call you later?". I hung up and continued working like a man possessed. Finally, there was a breakthrough. I found that instead of making a device to speak into, why not make a device where you can write out the letters without having to use ink? That's how the alphabet board came into creation. And it worked. You just 'type' the letters you want, and they appear on the screen. "I DID IT! I ACTUALLY DID IT!". The other scientists were looking at me. Calypsa came into the lab and came to check my work. "You did it. I knew you could do it!". I felt so proud of myself. Of course, I didn't realize I had created more than what I had bargained for. But more than that, there was that feeling I had as I walked through the village. People knew I was the one who created the computer. I was the one who made things that much easier. Computers were the most expensive thing to buy. As usual, a bloke from Kindy showed up to view our new advances and brought one hundred computers. They were to be delivered via carriage. I laughed to myself, because I remembered when the carriage was the most inventive thing we created. Prince Nigel showed up as well, much to the annoyance of Calypsa. "Oh, dear, fairest Calypsa, how I haven't been able to...", "Please just stop before I puke, Nigel. What do you want to purchase?", "Well, my lovely lady, I was hoping to pick up about two hundred of those computers. If that's possible.", "Of course it is.", "And what about the offer I discussed last time?". Calypsa turned away and ordered for someone to help Nigel, who just smiled handsomely. I was jealous. He was handsome after all and a prince. But, Calypsa truly had no interest in him. Queen Micka had arrived. "Nigel, don't you have someone else's doorstep to darken?", "Queen Micka, it is always a pleasure. You look more and more lovelier with each visit.", he said, bowing, "By the way. My father says hello, and that he misses you, and would like to visit with you soon.". Queen Micka waved her hand and turned around. I was checking components and making sure the system was fine. Each computer linked up to one major system. We were installing them in the other kingdoms, but they weren't fully prepared yet. Our system was almost set up. But I had to ensure that there would be no crashes. Queen Sheena had arrived from Kindy and after greeting Nigel, made her way up towards the shop, "It's good to see you, Calypsa. Think you can provide us with more wires? We have a short supply and we're working on a new school building.", "Another school? Really? How many do you Kindins need?", said Queen Micka, ordering someone forward to take the order. "Well, as our princess says, you can never have too many. We still have children who want to come, but we don't have space. That's why this school we are building now will house over three-hundred children.", Queen Sheena was saying. Calypsa gave me a small smile. "Well, if there isn't anything else, I believe you are done here, Nigel.", "Are you quite sure that's all you want, Calypsa?", Nigel asked, stepping closer towards her. I felt a small roar in my heart. "I'VE TOLD YOU TO STOP DISRESPECTING MY DAUGHTER!", yelled Queen Micka, and I loved her even more for that. Nigel looked hurt, but none the less, backed away, "Well, thank you anyway. Until next time.", "Next time, I cut your tongue out. Tell your father THAT, boy!". Nigel rode off in his carriage. Calypsa looked at me and smiled brightly. I smiled back.

The next day was a strange one. I had been greeted by a strangely cloaked girl. "I'm trying to find Calypsa. I understand that sometimes she works out of here.", "Well, she is the princess. She comes and goes as she pleases. Is there anything I could help you with?". The girl looked disappointed. "No, I don't think so. Thank you anyway.". She walked away sadly. I wondered who she was and why she didn't really want to show her face. It was gorgeous. Her eyes had the same… I trailed off in thought. That girl had eyes like Calypsa's. As I pondered on this, Calypsa came into the shop, "Hey, you, how is my favorite genius?", "He's wonderful!". We both smiled at each other. I had this strange feeling that Calypsa liked me. As the day passed us by, Calypsa stayed in the shop to help me. She was helping me check components in the system. "I think if I readjust this one, it should boost the signal. Give that a turn.". Calypsa turned the component, and it did boost the signal. We smiled at each other. "I don't usually get hands on like this. But I like working with you.", she said. She reached over and kissed me. I felt like I had just died and joined my brother. "CALYPSA!", Queen Micka had just walked in and ruined the moment, "We need to talk. Excuse us.". Queen Micka grabbed her daughter and led her away. I knew right then and there that she was in trouble for kissing me.

The next day, I didn't see Calypsa, but that same cloaked girl with her face hidden came back, "I heard I missed Calypsa yesterday.". Being that I was not in the mood for this kind of crap, I snapped at her, "What the hell do you want with her anyway?". The girl stood there, looking like she was thinking of an answer to this. "Never mind, just tell her that Ko-e is here to see her. If she doesn't know who that is, tell her to seek me where she first met Amana.". The mysterious girl turned and left. The day after, Calypsa came back into the shop. She had a mark across her eye and seemed as if she was avoiding me. "I was worried about you.". She tried moving away from me. "Did your mother do that to you?". She turned and faced me, "WHAT THE HELL DO YOU CARE?!", she yelled at me. I stood there in shock. I placed my arm around her, "I do care.". She leaned in on me and placed her head on my shoulder, "My mother says I can't be with you because you're just a villager.", "Well, who would she prefer? Nigel?", "My mother hates Nigel. But she'd like you if she gave you a chance. My mother doesn't want me to be happy. She wants me to be as miserable as possible.". I felt for her. Then I remembered, "There was a strange girl in a cloak who came here looking for you. She said her name was Ko-e.". Calypsa didn't recognize this name, so I gave her the rest of the message, "She said if you don't know that name, go to where you first met Amana.". At this, she left my arms and stood before me, "This girl said that? You're sure of this?". I didn't understand. Princess Amana was in Kindy, and I didn't understand what she had to do with this. "Calypsa, what's going on?". Calypsa didn't answer and instead kissed me and left the shop. The next day after that, Queen Micka came into my shop. "I understand you like my daughter.". It was more a statement than a question, "Well I'm here to let you know you won't be seeing her for a while.". I felt my hands starting to shake, and in a small tone I asked, "What did you do?", "Excuse me? What did you just say to me?", "I SAID WHAT DID YOU DO TO HER?!", I yelled at her. Queen Micka smiled, "I think some alone time will do you good. Yes. That's what you need. Some good alone time, in a Dashin cell. GUARDS!". Then, I found myself in a cell, again. But this time, I was worried about Calypsa. What had Micka done to her and who was this strange girl? Well whoever she was, she was standing right in front of my cell, "What do you want?", "I'm going to free you. And… Calypsa if I can manage.". I sat up at these words. I was so happy to hear someone would help me. "Do you know what Queen Micka has done with her?", I asked hopefully. "She's locked her in her room.", "Why?". This seemed really strange. All this because she didn't want us together? "Well, it's sort of my fault. I should have known Calypsa would be harder to get to than Amana. Amana is just as difficult.". Amana? "What does she have to do with any of this? Why are you looking for the princesses?". She removed her hood, and I saw the most beautiful woman I had ever seen. She was way more beautiful than Calypsa. She had long black hair that shined, even in darkness. Her face was pale, but she had powdery lips, and a perfect nose. Her eyes were lined with red, but her pupils were gold. "Well, because they are my sisters.".

CHAPTER 2

Alisa's Worst Fears

ALISA: When Amana was five, she met her sister, Calypsa, for the first time. It was then at that moment that I began to think we were making a huge mistake. I remember pleading with Micka then, and telling her that the girls shouldn't be separated. There was a part of me that just always figured that in the end, Sebastian would come and be with his daughters. But whatever fantasy I had of that was now gone. I was now Queen of Kindy. My parents had retired to the fields and had built themselves a nice cottage. Now that PE had come into existence, it allows us to live more easily and leisurely. When Amana was ten, her and Calypsa tried they're second daring escape. I awoke one morning to find Amana was nowhere to be found. She wasn't in her room, she wasn't at the horse stables, she wasn't in the new lab we had just built, nor was she in any of the schools. I knew right away, she had run away again. What truly gave her away was the fact that the day before, we had argued about why she wasn't allowed to go and hangout with Calypsa. It was her birthday and she had said that the greatest present would be for me and Micka to allow her and Calypsa to play together. I knew that no reason I gave her was good enough. Amana is a genius. She wasn't going to just accept the crap I was feeding her. The first time she went missing like this, I cried in her room. But this time, I was more prepared for it, and I took out a horse from the stable myself, and rode to find her. Sure enough, on the edge of the Dark Wood, I found both girls. Calypsa begged me not to return her to Dasha. To just let her run away. But I knew the better thing to do was take her back. If I didn't, it could piss Micka off, and she was unpredictable. She had been unstable ever since I had first met her. Then, Falsa went and made her the queen. Now, I knew that she was abusing her daughter, but it wasn't my place to really tell her how to handle her daughter. Even if her daughter's father is my daughter's father as well. Amana and Calypsa's connection scared me the moment it became a thing. Alex was connected to Bastian and I'll never forget how she would get angry whenever you did something that she felt was insulting towards Sebastian. She would even attack me if I said something she didn't like. She would have strange tantrums that didn't really match the mood she was in less than two minutes ago, and she was very obsessed with Bastian. I saw a similar situation with these two girls. Both somehow sensed their connection, and both were fighting like mad just to be within close proximity of one another. Sheena had always told me that we wouldn't be able to keep them apart, but we can never tell them about their father. Alex had come to me in a dream and warned me as well. She told me the girls can never know Sebastian is their father. Interestingly enough, I didn't think they'd believe that anyway. Sebastian had become a figure. Someone that either you believed in, or you didn't. People who were really shaken by the last war, started churches that preached how Sebastian wants us to live. There were other churches as well. Some of these other ones were more along the lines of absurd. Making up stories about Sebastian as they go. Abusing the truth. Sebastian was one of the greatest friends I've ever had. Looking back on all the stuff that happened all those years ago, all seemed so small. They barely ever spoke about my role in the war. Although, all of us were considered legends; Sheena, Micka, Tig, and Tisiphone. We were all there in the last war and we all fought. Now it just seemed so far away.

Amana, tired of running away, instead found a new way to discuss stuff with her sister. They had started to secretly send letters. When I first found the letters two days ago, I was pissed. I was going to yell at her, and remind her of the rules, and tell her how she was being reckless. Until, I actually read what they were discussing. Everything that we had now, all the nice homes with the cool stuff like the coldbox, and receiver, Amana and Calypsa planned it out. Amana created a place to store cut meat. Even keep beverages cold. But while Amana created the coldbox and the receiver, it was Calypsa who learned to harness PE. It was Calypsa who was developing certain other technologies, while Amana either perfected what she had created, or created something herself. Like medication. One of the greatest things that I've ever seen. A miracle that helped either to ease or cure diseases. These two girls have been secretly working together to advance and improve the planet. Sebastian would be proud if he saw how they went behind our backs to aid the people of Plinth. I wondered if Micka knew about this. I was too afraid to ask. I didn't want to ruin what these girls had done. I found another letter. This one scared me though;

My dearest Amana,

I've concluded that they will never tell us the truth. The only way to get what we are looking for, is to force it from them. In the past we tried to find Father ourselves, but now I think that we should make Father find us. If you agree, please send your reply, asap.

With love, your sister
-Calypsa.

I read and re-read the letter. Not too far from that letter was another one, but this was Amana's reply. She hadn't sent it off yet;

Dear Calypsa,

I do hear what you are saying, but trying to force it from them could prove to be just as bad. We do not want to push them away. I know you are angry and have more reason than I to be. But we are very close to our technological breakthrough. We will soon have the information we have been searching for. Please just try and be patient.

With even more love.
-Amana.

The scary part to these letters, was the fact that they have been communicating for years. Behind our backs, these girls have done amazing work and I could not deny it. I heard noises moving towards me. I made to hide the letters, but I was too slow. Amana came into the room. She saw what I had in my hand and froze. "Amana, I want to talk to you.". At the moment, that was all I could think to say. The truth was, she wasn't a little girl anymore. She was twenty years old now and too smart for me to just tell her something. As much as I wanted her and Calypsa to have a true sisterly relationship, I was told by a goddess, not to tell them their true parentage. "I'm not angry with you. I'm actually proud more than anything else.". Amana just stood there, staring at the letter in my hand. "Listen, I know we've been tough on you girls, but this is...", "So, now that you know the lengths in which we had to go behind your backs...", she was saying, anger in her voice, "...now you think that we made the right choice?". I was lost. I opened my mouth to say something, but Amana cut me off, "You always wanted us separated. Now you see the stupidity in all of it. Well I don't care!", she yelled, casting a dark look towards me. "Amana, if it were up to me, the two of you would have been together every day, but…". She cut me off again, "Whatever! You always have kept us separate. And you refuse to tell us who our father really is. Unless you'd like to save us the trouble and tell me that answer now.". I watched her face to see exactly what she was trying to pull. Then it dawned on me, "You wanted me to find these letters. You wanted me to tell you who your father is. And if I don't, what then?", "Then me and Calypsa will find out on our own! I was just giving you a fair warning.", "We told you, when you were little girls, that you do not have the same…". Once again, she cut me off, "DON'T GIVE ME THAT SHIT! I know that we are related. We've tested our blood!". Now I was panicking. I had no idea she knew how to do that. It was obvious certain breakthroughs she kept between her and Calypsa. "When did you do this?", "It doesn't matter.", Amana said coldly, "All that matters, is I've done the test, and me and Calypsa share the same blood.". This was unexpected. Amana was usually very well mannered. Unless, of course, you're speaking of the reasons why her and Calypsa can't see each other. This whole conversation was reminding me of Alex's tantrums. "Amana, you need to listen to me. I WANT to tell you everything. It breaks my heart that I can't, but you must realize we have a good reason for it!". I had used my last hope. If I could convince her to stave off this quest to find their father, then maybe things can be fixed. It didn't matter if they know they're sisters. Besides, they both still didn't know about their third sister. Thank goodness she was far, far away and I didn't have to worry about her. Or so I thought.

That very same night, I had a guard stationed near Amana's quarters. I was not going to allow her to run away again. After our conversation, she had, of course, chosen to hold a grudge against me. At dinner, she was very quiet. Sheena, who had just returned from a business trip in Dasha, could sense we had one of our many, YOU CAN'T SEE CALYPSA, arguments. "So, the schools are going to be fine, Amana. I've ordered more wiring. We should be able to get the third district children into the school. It might be a good idea to have the adult schools separated from the children.". Amana just nodded and said nothing. "Alisa, how was your day? Did you miss me at all while I was gone?". I could see Sheena was trying to lighten the mood. I decided to oblige, "Yes, dear, I did.", I said with a smile. I looked in my daughter's direction and she was still just focusing on her food, not saying a word. "Me and Amana had a certain talk today, didn't we?". Still nothing. "Sheena, apparently, Calypsa and Amana know they are related. They have been sending each other messages, and guess what the best part is. They've been playing us.". Amana looked up, "Perhaps we wouldn't have to, if you and Micka just admitted what you two are too afraid to admit!", she said through gritted teeth. "Well I also informed her that maybe we have a good reason for it.". Sheena was looking back and forth between us. She was starting to feel uncomfortable. Knowing she wasn't Amana's real mother, never stopped her from being her mother. It was apparent right when I gave birth that Sheena loved Amana. When she was a baby, Amana was the biggest handful there could be. She did things a little bit extra. She wasn't a regular baby. It was good to have Sheena helping me along the way because Amana had different bodily functions than most Plinthinians. She pooped more, and vomited more, and urinated everywhere. Once she had showered Sheena in poop when she was playing with her. That never stopped Sheena from loving her. When Amana ran away the first time, Sheena was just as worried. She led search parties trying to find her. But we should have known back then how it would be. "What do you mean they've been playing us?", Sheena asked, looking at Amana for an answer. "Well, why don't you look at these?", I said, handing her the letters Amana left out on purpose. As Sheena read the letters, she grew more and more weary. She looked up at me with fearful eyes. Eyes that even Amana noticed, "Can you please tell me why I can't just be with my sister? Why all this mystery concerning our father? What is it?". Sheena looked as lost as I was earlier. "Perhaps, we can talk about this later, yeah?", Sheena asked. Amana just nodded and continued to eat dinner.

Later that evening, I received a very unexpected visitor. As Amana and Sheena had gone to the garden, I was approached by a woman who looked vaguely familiar. She had long green hair and her eyes were a sharp hazel. "ALEXA?!", I asked in shock. Alexa removed her hood. "It's been a long time, hasn't it?", she said, giving me a warm hug, "I wish I was here under better circumstances.", "What do you mean? What's wrong?", "Ko-e has run away. Caprius has determined that she will try to seek out her sisters.". All my fears were realized in one day. I didn't know how to tell Alexa that Calypsa and Amana have already figured out they are sisters. I also shuddered at the thought of what would happen if they met Ko-e. And I really didn't want to tell her that Amana and Calypsa have found a way to figure out who their father is. "We have to find her. She can't be that difficult to find. I'm sure someone has seen her.", "I'm sure, too…", said Alexa, "…because I happen to know that she has made her way to Dasha. I've been following her trail. She makes it quite easy really. She is a very beautiful woman now, and not many forget seeing her.". Not wanting Amana and Sheena to overhear us, Alexa and I secretly made our way towards my guard house, where I sent out a few good men to try and locate Ko-e, before things got out of hand. I sent a messenger forward to Dasha to warn Queen Micka of Ko-e's possible presence in Dasha. I hoped that we could stop this before it started. Only thing was, I still didn't know what I was protecting these girls from. It felt like the only thing we were keeping them from, was being in the same area. Like if they all came together, they would explode like some kind of bomb. Alexa looked anxious now. "I really hoped you'd have found her first. I'm afraid of what Micka will do if she finds her.". In truth, so was I. Micka had been beating Calypsa since she was a little girl and I didn't want to think about what she would do to Ko-e. I knew she wouldn't even think about hitting Amana. But, Ko-e's mother is dead. And as for Caprius, I had no idea what he'd been up to. "What is Caprius doing these days? Why didn't he come looking for her?", "Well nobody really knows me, so it was easier to get around. If Caprius came, he was afraid people would get in his way of finding her. Plus, one of us had to stay behind and it might as well be him.". While I tried to guess what that meant, my messenger had returned with a message from Micka. Messengers these days weren't people on horses, but rather mechanical birds that had been trained to deliver quick messages. Another lucrative business began by Amana and Calypsa. Micka's reply was quite clear, and frightening;

Alisa,

This is an outrage! These girls were supposed to be kept separate! Now you tell me that Falsa's daughter is running around my kingdom when she is supposed to be in Alexandria! What is Caprius doing? Why is she here on Plinth? You had better find out what is going on before I do!

-Queen Micka
Ruler of Dasha.

After I had re-read the letter for the third time, I turned to Alexa, who was watching anxiously, "We need to go to Dasha. Now.", "So, you'll be coming with me, then?", Alexa asked in a hopeful tone. "Yes, I don't want Micka dealing with this on her own. I don't trust her to handle it properly.", "What if she finds her before us?". I hastily wrote down another letter and sent it off. "I've told her to detain her and nothing else. I've told her you've come to fetch her, so we will arrive together.". Alexa nodded. Alexa and I proceeded to the horse stables. "We'll take two horses instead of the carriage. The carriage would be too obvious.". As we prepared to leave, Amana came into the stables. She didn't notice us, and I grabbed Alexa and pulled her down, so Amana wouldn't see her. I watched to see what she was doing. I had assumed she was running away again and that was the last thing I needed. But she only came in and put food in the horse bowls and then proceeded out. "Whew, that was close. Let's leave before she comes back.". We boarded our horses and proceeded to the gate. "Soldier, you are to tell nobody that the Queen has departed.". The soldier nodded and me and Alexa rode out of Kindy.

As we reached the field, Alexa came up next to me. We had stopped near the Jasmine to let our horses re-fuel on water. "There is something else I need to tell you…", she said in a scared sort of tone. "What is it?", I said impatiently. I had had enough bad news over the last three days. What with learning about Amana's deception, and Ko-e being in one of the kingdoms, I didn't think I could take it anymore. "Well, it's about Sebastian.", "What about him?", "We think he's been in contact with Ko-e. You know, speaking to her in her dreams.". I felt frozen. I had prayed to Bastian so many times over the past twenty years. Not once has he ever answered me. I always just assumed that he had become busier with his ascension to Heaven. But now I saw a selfish bastard who blatantly ignored his other two daughters for a daughter created out of hate. It must have shown on my face because Alexa quickly said, "But I don't think it's because he favors her or something. She is closer to him than the other two and has less people around her. She understands how important it is to keep the secrets of Alexandria.", "If that's true, then why is she searching for Amana and Calypsa? She knows they can't know who their father is, right?". Alexa bit her lip, "Well, no. She does not.". I rounded on her, "WE WERE ALL TOLD! ALL THESE YEARS I'VE BEEN CRUEL TO MY DAUGHTER FOR NOTHING?!". Alexa folded her arms and replied, "Perhaps you have forgotten what Alexandria is like! Do you truly think we could have kept it secret from her? There are literally pictures of past goddesses and not to mention a picture of her mother, who by the way, WAS a GODDESS!". I hadn't been thinking about that. "What have you and Caprius told her?", "We told her that there was nothing below us, and I think that is where we were wrong. We should have told her the full truth. Then she wouldn't be here. The only reason she is, IS because we lied to her. We told her all her life there was nothing beyond the cliff. But she decided to see if it was true or not. I don't know. Maybe Sebastian told her. But, as you said, we had better find her.". I became quiet. I was so angry with Sebastian, I wanted to rip out my soul just to find him and give him a thrashing. Ko-e was given everything anyone could want but it wasn't enough. Like her sisters, she felt something, and she had to go after that feeling. Part of me understood. But the part of me that didn't was the part of myself that just wanted to choke the life out of Bastian. We got back on our horses and rode on. We were nearing Dasha and I knew that soon, really soon, things were about to become more hostile. In a way you could feel the problem getting bigger. I just hoped that whatever was on the cusp of happening, I could keep Amana far from its clutches.

CHAPTER 3

Scion Meets Amana

SCION: "Scion, we must hurry up. We are wasting time!", Ko-e was yelling at me. We had been trying to find a way into the castle for the past day and a half. Micka had the castle heavily guarded and it was obvious that the security had been amped up so Calypsa couldn't escape. But then, I noticed something else as well. Queen Alisa and another woman came riding in on horses. Queen Alisa was trying to conceal herself, but I knew what she looked like and felt I'd never forget. She was a lovely lady. The girl riding behind her with the long green hair was fair as well. Both seemed to be looking for somebody else. We watched as they rode up to the castle and were greeted by Queen Micka. They proceeded inside. "Well, that is that. Come on, we'll go to Kindy and contact Amana.", "Um, I don't think I'll be joining you for that one.". Ko-e looked at me confused, "But, I need your help. Please, I can't do this alone.", Ko-e wrapped her arms around me and started to sob into my chest. I didn't know what to do, so I patted her head. "Who was that woman with Alisa? Do you know her?". She broke her head away from me and looked me in my eyes, "She is from my kingdom. She is the Queen of Alexandria.". If there was ever a time where I thought someone mad, this time would be on the top of the list. Alexandria was a fictional kingdom, said to be in the clouds. It's also said to be Sebastian's main dwelling. It's his kingdom here on Plinth. I tried not to laugh, seeing the look on her face. I started to open my mouth to say something, but then, Ko-e grabbed my hand and led me away on a run. I looked to see who was behind us and it was a group of guards. As Ko-e continued to pull me, I wasn't looking where my feet were going and I fell. Ko-e, who was holding my hand tightly, stumbled as well. The soldiers nearing us, I didn't want Ko-e to be caught, so I pushed her hand away from mine, "GO! GET OUT OF HERE!". Ko-e watched me for a few seconds then turned and ran. I was right. The soldiers ran right past me and proceeded after Ko-e. I got up and tried to think how I could possibly help. As if I was meant to, I saw a horse nearby. I jumped on it. I felt someone's hands try to snatch me off, but I had kicked the horse and was chasing down the guards. They had finally cornered Ko-e, "Now just come with us. We don't want to hurt you. Your sister-in-law is here to take you home, okay? Just come with us.". I didn't really think about what they were saying. I grabbed something above my head and sent the horse on its own, charging at the group of guards. Right away, Ko-e used the distraction to escape. "YES!" I shouted, unable to contain my happiness with my genius. Then I felt myself being taken to the ground.

When I came to, I was once again in the dungeon. I felt like this place was becoming my second home. There were voices nearby, "…Calypsa's friend.", "Why did he help Ko-e? Perhaps, he just thought her a girl in distress? We can't assume he was helping her for THAT reason.", "YES, BUT SHE COULD HAVE TOLD HIM!", Queen Micka was shouting. Told me what? I thought. Then I remembered Ko-e telling me that Calypsa and Amana were her sisters. Queen Alisa was here, along with this mystery woman, and Queen Micka also was taking this seriously? What if Ko-e was telling the truth? What if Alexandria was real? What if Calypsa truly was her sister? As I placed my hand to my head, "He is awake now. Let's ask him. Excuse me, young man, your name is Scion, correct?", the woman with the green hair addressed me. "I'm not telling you anything.", I said right away. Queen Micka put her face to the cell, "You, boy, will start telling us what we need to know, or I will cause you so much pain, that you will wish you'd never gotten involved.". I wasn't scared of Queen Micka, I was only worried about Calypsa. "There is no need to threaten him, Micka. Let's just tell him the situation. I'm sure he'll cooperate if we do.", Alisa was saying. "NO ONE IS SUPPOSED TO KNOW THAT, ALISA!" Micka yelled at her. Alisa stood her ground and got in Micka's face, "I've turned a blind eye to your cruelty against your daughter for the last fifteen years, now I'm telling you to let me take care of this!". Micka opened her mouth, then closed it again. I admired Queen Alisa right away. "Scion, I am Queen Alisa, and I'm here looking for the girl, Ko-e, because it involves the safety of the planet.". I couldn't understand how the whole planet could be in danger, but something in her voice made me trust her somewhat. "So, what threat does Ko-e pose exactly?", "Well, that's a bit harder to explain.". Alisa looked like she was wrestling with herself on what to say, "Our daughters have responsibilities, and right now, Ko-e is interrupting those responsibilities. That's all. So, if you would kindly tell us where she is hiding…", "I'm afraid I don't know. I only caused the distraction to help her get away.", "When did you first meet her and what info has she given you?", Alisa asked me. "Well…it was two days ago. She came to mine and Calypsa's shop looking for Calypsa. Then she told me that her and Calypsa were sisters.". I didn't tell them everything. I had questions myself I wanted answered. There were rumors about Amana and Calypsa being secret lovers, but that sounded like nonsense. Especially now that I knew Calypsa liked me. But the rumors were believable because it's said that every time the princess ran away, she met Amana. They had been doing this since they were little. But it didn't occur to me that maybe they knew they were sisters. Even then, if that's the truth, what man could have Queen Micka and Queen Alisa together? Secretly, I gave the mystery man props. But I still needed to know the truth. Not to mention who Ko-e's mother actually was, because it couldn't be this woman with the bright green hair. "Listen, Queen Micka will release you from here, but you need to go home and forget about this. Forget about whatever you thought you had with Calypsa, and forget about Ko-e. We will handle this from here on out.". Although I nodded and agreed, I was far from going to forget. Micka let me out, grudgingly, looking murderous. I could tell that she didn't like Queen Alisa very much. That night, as I was lying in bed, I wondered who the girls' father was. I started to dream that I was with Calypsa. We were in the woods, lying naked on a blanket. As I laid there, holding my girl, and not thinking about all the craziness, I felt completely at peace. That was until Ko-e was standing there, smiling at me. I quickly wished there were clothes on me and clothes appeared. Calypsa was still sleeping and I looked up at Ko-e. "Ah, I am quite sorry. This seems like a private dream. But I had to communicate with you.". I looked around. It felt like I was wide awake, but looking at Ko-e, I knew I had to be sleeping. It didn't make any sense for me to be here. Or her for that matter. "Where are we?", I asked her. "We are in your dream. I had to find you and tell you what happened.", "I want some real answers! Who is that woman with the green hair? And also, why is it such a big deal you get brought back to Alexandria? Tell me what's really going on.". Ko-e stared at me for a while, "Well, you see, I've told you that I was from Alexandria. My brother is the king there. His name is Caprius.". I knew that name, but it was impossible. "That would make you Falsa's daughter!", I found myself shouting. As much as I didn't believe in the stories of Sebastian, Falsa was indeed the previous Queen of Dasha. She wasn't very nice from what I remember. But neither was Caprius. There were stories that the war changed him. Made him into a much better person, but there is no telling if this was true or not, for nobody had seen him in over twenty years. As for Falsa, she had been killed. Rumors circled her death like vultures. One rumor was, Micka killed her for the throne. But that wasn't true. Micka had built a statue to honor Queen Falsa. When Ko-e and I had passed it a day ago, she had stopped at it and admired it. I didn't give a shit about it, but now it made sense why Ko-e did. "But, this whole time, you've been in Alexandria? Is that what I'm to understand?". She nodded. "Why are you barely showing yourself now?". Ko-e's small smile she had been wearing slid off her face. It had been replaced by a look of great irritation, "I grew up in Alexandria. It's a planet all to itself. It sits above the clouds and from way up there, you would never know that there was anything beneath us. My whole life I was told there was nothing but Alexandria. All the planets my father created were far away.". Her father? "Who is your father?". Ko-e's smile returned. "Why don't you guess?". I thought about who it might be. But I found one answer in my head, and it was preposterous, "Sebastian? Is that your father?", "He is mine, Calypsa's, and Amana's.". I felt my jaw hit the floor. Not really, but the weight of it might as well be. Sebastian had always been made up to me. Then I started to think, I am speaking to Ko-e in my dreams. I looked at Calypsa, who had covered herself with the blanket. "It's her dream as well. She pulled you here. She doesn't realize she can do that. But that's because she has been lied to as well. She doesn't know who her father is. That's why I've come. I want to know my sisters and enlighten them.", Ko-e said, with a bright smile spreading across her face. "And Queen Alisa, Queen Micka, and that other woman, don't want that?", "Right!", she said, beaming at me. Just then, I felt another presence. I looked, and Alisa was standing nearby. She hadn't seen us yet. Ko-e disappeared, and I woke up in my cottage. The next day, there was a knock at my door. When I went to open it, Calypsa was standing outside. "May I come in?". I considered it, then stood aside. Calypsa looked around my cottage. I had just moved in here a week after I started working in her private lab. "Quite nice.", she said. I noticed a small cut above her eye. "Your mother, she still hits you?". She turned to me and I noticed her eyes were shining with tears. She ran into my arms. "Scion, take me away from here! Take me anywhere! I want to just be with you! I never want to return to that horrible woman in that miserable castle!", she cried. She continued to sob into my chest. I wrapped my arms around her. I considered telling her what I knew, but decided against it. Despite what Ko-e had told me, I felt that Alisa may have been right. Ko-e didn't fully understand what she was doing and there was some danger in the girls finding out the truth. I knew this was especially true for Calypsa. Calypsa pulled me into her dream without realizing it. This meant she had abilities. If she learned about them, what would she do with them? Would she help take care of her people, or would she use them to kill her mother? There was also the possibility that she just might run away. While I tried to secretly ponder what she might do, Calypsa asked me, "Did you see Alisa? What was she doing here?", "They were looking for someone. She's left, then?", "Well, for now, yes. But, I hate her.", "Why? I didn't know you had a history with her.", I lied. I knew some of it. But I wanted to hear the full tale. She told me about her and Amana's attempts at trying to run away. Told me that they were sisters, but their mothers won't admit it. And they refuse to tell them the truth about their father. I felt bad listening to her. I knew who her father was. And I know she wouldn't believe me if I told her. "…Alisa and all of Kindy. Scion are you listening?". I came to. I had totally been lost in thought. "What did you say?", "I said it would be nice if I could leave this place behind with Amana. If she left her mother. But…", she paused for a bit, "…she loves her mother.", she said in a scathing voice, "If it were up to me, I'd just kill her and be done with it.", "You don't mean that. Alisa is a nice woman. Sure, a bit edgy, but very nice still.". Calypsa watched me. She seemed to be waiting for something. When it didn't come, she spoke, "I heard a rumor you were arrested yesterday. You had been seen with a woman.". I became stony. Not like the sweet treat, but just completely frozen. I didn't know how to tell her about Ko-e. Part of me was starting to see why Alisa told me to back out. "Well, it's not what you might be thinking.", "And what do you think I am thinking?", she asked, her voice starting to get shaky. "Well, she was trying to help me get to you.". She sat there considering this. "My mother and Alisa were after this woman. They questioned you in the cell. Why?". This was not what I was expecting. I figured she thought I was sleeping with Ko-e, but she was already putting pieces together I hadn't thought she would. She then took out some parchment and wrote on it. She then took one of her delivery birds, automated systems that fly where you direct them, and tied the parchment to it and sent it out. "Where did you send that?". She looked at me and considered. "Do you trust me?", she asked. "Yes, I do. Now where is that bird going?", "To Kindy to tell my sister what has happened here.", "What if your mother finds out?". Calypsa laughed at this, "We've been communicating like this for years! Neither Alisa, nor my mother, ever knew about it.". Calypsa and I had taken to my room. We fell on my bed, kissing one another. She stared into my eyes and I stared into her golden ones. I remember thinking then, she must be a goddess, because who else has eyes like this?

When I awoke, Calypsa was gone. I realized that I should bathe and get ready to head towards the shop. As I had finished bathing and decided to eat something, there was a bang on my door. When I opened it, it was none other than the lady with the green hair, accompanied by Alisa. They both forced their way into my home and both stood blocking the door. "So, even though I told you to back out, you still think you have a role to play here.", Alisa said, brandishing something at me. It was the letter Calypsa had tried to send to Amana. "Read it.". I took the letter in my hand and opened it;

Dear Amana,

You will not believe what is transpiring here. A strange girl has gathered the attention of our mothers. Yours' travels with a stranger. I have a feeling this may be what we have been waiting for. The other element you mentioned. Please respond as soon as you get this!

-Calypsa

As I finished reading the letter, I felt the shock go through my bones. "What did you want me to do? She turned up here this morning!", "YOU IDIOT BOY! YOU HAVE NO IDEA WHAT YOU ARE DOING!", the girl with the green hair bellowed. For a minute, I stared at her in disbelief. She then pulled her hood down and I stared at her much harder. She looked vaguely familiar in a way, I just couldn't put my finger on it. "This girl who you THINK you are helping, is going to be your downfall. You are inadvertently bringing the end of the world.". I hardly felt this situation was that serious. How could three girls finding out they were sisters end the world. As if we would blow up at that exact moment. I felt they were being silly. Then I thought about Calypsa's power to pull me into her dream, and I shivered. Alisa noticed and looked me in my eye, "This isn't going to be easy, Scion. For whatever reason, you've been chosen.", "What the hell are you talking about?", I said breathlessly. The woman with the green hair looked shocked as well. Suddenly I knew her face. It was a face I hadn't seen in four months. My mother's face. She didn't look exactly like her, but she looked as if she could be a relative. Before I could say anything about that, "Scion, I came here to find Ko-e, but instead found a young man who is in over his head. Your situation reminds me of someone else's. It isn't by mistake that Calypsa has become taken with you. Alexa, I fear we may be fighting a Dattur on this one.". A Dattur was a small creature that, for one, nobody had ever seen. At least not that I knew of. But they are the most dangerous creatures on Plinth. "Alisa, I know what you are insinuating, but we can't base this situation around that. We are supposed to prevent it, not allow it.", "CAN SOMEBODY PLEASE TELL ME, WHAT THE HELL YOU ARE TALKING ABOUT?!", I shouted. I had enough of this. Calypsa and I liked each other. If she wants to run away and be with me, so what? I was starting to like the idea. Alisa gave me a sad look. I took it as pity. But I didn't need pity. I was going to be with Calypsa. That's all that matters. "Listen, Alexa, can you explain to Scion, why we don't want our daughters to come together?". I looked at the woman that resembled my mother.

The reason I hadn't seen my mother in four months was because we weren't on talking terms. She was angry with me and I was willing to let things stay that way. Alexa moved closer to me. "If the daughters of Sebastian come together, something bad will happen. It was predicted long ago. Alex, the goddess, told us to never tell them who their father is. So, we thought the best thing to do was keep them apart. But, Amana and Calypsa found each other unexpectedly.", Alexa finished, and looked at Alisa. Alisa carried on, "So, from that point on, we told them that they were not sisters and that they did not have the same father. We told them to stay apart and never see each other. But they kept trying. I recently found out they have been writing to each other, and now, Ko-e has gotten involved. Then, there is you.". Alisa said, pointing her many ringed fingers at me. I stood for some time, trying to understand all of this. Part of me knew I had to accept that Sebastian was the girls' father, but I also had to accept what I was being told now. None of this explained how I fit into the story. As if she had read my mind, "You are the catalyst. You see, Calypsa was the first, now, Ko-e is attached to you somehow. I don't know exactly how yet, but if you meet Amana, I'll know that I'm right in assuming. You see, I was in your dream.". I froze. Then she saw us. But what did that mean? "How were you able to enter into my dream?", "Well, I didn't do it on purpose. I was born with a certain gift. Lucky for me, I saw what I saw. So, Scion, you must stay away from ALL three girls. Alexa and I are willing to move you, so we can prevent what I think I see coming.", "And what do you see coming?", I asked in a mocking sort of tone. "I see another war coming. And you, dead.". I didn't know what to say. "Why would there be a war? We've been at peace for so long. Who would even want a war?". Alisa didn't answer this. "So, you will come with us.", "Where are you going to take me?", "Somewhere we can ensure you won't come into contact with the girls.". I wasn't too sure I agreed with any of this, but decided it best not to argue with a queen. The women led me to a carriage that was waiting not too far from my home. I felt bad. Calypsa would come searching for me, and I wasn't going to be there. I'd be gone. Specifically, to get away from her. I kept telling myself it wasn't just Calypsa, but she kept popping at the top of my head. When I thought of Ko-e, I became upset. I felt like this was all her fault. So, Amana and Calypsa were in contact, big deal. The real problem was the girl who wanted to tell them too much. "Why not just take Ko-e back to Alexandria? That would end all of this, right?", "If it were that simple, don't you suppose that's exactly what I'd do?", Alexa answered angrily. I decided to be quiet and say nothing else. As the ride continued, we had left Dasha and were in the fields now. I tried imagining what Calypsa would say once she realizes I'm gone. Will she come searching for me? Will she just have assumed I abandoned her? I didn't know what to think. I wanted to jump out of the carriage and run back to Dasha. As the fear started to settle on me of the unknown, we had finally arrived. We were on the edge of a very dark looking forest. The queen took out one of those portable homes and pushed the mechanism that blew it up. I walked inside and found a bed that was attached. "If you can be a bit patient, we can get a coldbox out here for you. Maybe even a cooker. We can set you up and you should be good. Until further notice.", said Alisa. I looked around and figured, what choice did I have? I nodded. The women turned to leave, and I watched them walk out of the PH and step into the carriage and depart. Living on the edge of the wood wasn't so bad. I was able to feed myself and things were a bit easier. No hustle and bustle of citizens looking to upgrade their cottages, I haven't had to stress on the computer system, and I couldn't stop thinking about Calypsa. Everything was perfect, I thought sarcastically. Calypsa would run wild in my dreams. But they weren't happy dreams. I was right to assume that she would think I left to get away from her. Her mother had been informed of my departure and she delightedly told her daughter. Calypsa was unable to believe it, so she went to my cottage. When I wasn't there, she waited for me to come to work. When I didn't show up there, she began to realize her mother was probably right. She banged on my door. She cried outside of it until the guards came to collect her. The only reason I knew all this, was because somehow, connecting with Calypsa's dreams, gave me insight into her memories. Even the foulest ones. There was never anyone I had felt more for than Calypsa. She suffered so much at the hands of her mother. I was on the verge of going to her one night. Since I had left, she had become less vibrant. My guess was this is how she usually was when she wasn't writing or working with her sister. Her mother had become tired of this attitude and tried to solve it with the usual beating. Calypsa was a bit smaller than her mother, but I felt she could fight back. Maybe she was just so scared of her mother now, she wouldn't dare. I had prepared myself to travel to Dasha, when Alexa had arrived with my coldbox and cooker. "What do you think you're doing?". I didn't answer because I knew she had already guessed. She forced me to put everything back, then left me with these words, "Queen Micka has guards on the lookout. If you return to Dasha, you die. Queen Micka's decision, not ours. So, if I were you, I wouldn't risk my neck.". She rode off, leaving me in my fury. A couple days later, I was being awoken by somebody. All I saw was bright red hair and assumed it was the Queen. "Alisa, what are you...?", but the person covered my mouth and ordered me to be quiet. Outside of the PH, I could hear voices. They sounded like men. I could hear the clinking of armor and the sound of swords being unsheathe. "What is going...?", the hand covered my mouth again. This time, one of the men outside said, "I can hear, but I can't see. Do you think there are ghosts around here?", "Don't be daft! There isn't any ghost. You heard what Queen Alisa said. Amana has tech that isn't out yet. She could be using it to hide her and the guy.". The situation started to dawn on me, I looked up and saw a young beautiful woman with flaming red hair and red golden eyes. She removed her hand from my mouth and I stayed quiet. The men searched for twenty more minutes, and then finally, "They aren't here. Let's keep looking.", "They have to be near! This is where Queen Alisa said he should be!". The men turned on their horses and started riding off. I backed away from the girl who was no doubt, Amana

Tia. She was just as gorgeous as Calypsa or Ko-e. "Listen to me, you are in grave danger. My sister has told me who you are and I'm sorry you've been dragged into this game.". She got quiet again, listening for the soldiers. "Okay, here's the plan…", "NO MORE!", I found myself yelling. She pressed her finger to her lips and looked out of the entrance. "YOU NEED TO STAY QUIET!", she hissed quietly at me, "Those soldiers were given orders to kill you. Which I must admit, is my fault. My sister begged me to find you and well, my mother didn't believe me when I said I was going to check something out. She quickly alerted Micka, who felt the best way to deal with this…was to kill you.", "Great, so now my queen wants me dead. Should have known this is what I'd get for falling for a princess.". Amana looked for a second like she might say something serious. Then she started to laugh, "Did you really expect any less? I mean, given who her mother is and all.". I smiled. Amana was lively. A lot like a little girl. But she was very smart. She led us away from where I'd been camping, and I found that she was very pleasurable company. Often, we would abuse Queen Micka, while at the same time talking of the injustice of her and Calypsa never being able to play together. While all this was very interesting, it had occurred to me that what Alisa said would happen was happening. I had met the final sister. But seeing as how I had no idea where Ko-e was, and I knew Calypsa was in Dasha, the sisters were still very far from meeting each other. "Scion, there is something I need to know.", Amana said, after two days had passed of us traveling and avoiding soldiers together. "What exactly did our mothers tell you? I mean, I get the feeling you aren't being fully honest.". I know who your father is. I felt myself beginning to say that, but caught myself, "Oh it's not anything we haven't already discussed.". Amana looked at me thoughtfully. Lying to her wasn't so easy. It was like she was a Plinthinian lie detector. She watched me for a bit longer, me trying to match her gaze without looking guilty. "No. You aren't telling me the truth. It's fine. Maybe Mother and Sheena were right.". I watched her for a moment. In the sunlight, her hair glowed, and it looked magnificent. Another thing

I noticed about Amana, was that she was a lot more cheerful than Calypsa. She didn't seem to be bothered by her mother like Calypsa was. "Calypsa really doesn't like her. Are you aware of that?". Amana let out a sigh and for the first time made a really long face, "I know. It's because of Queen Micka. I hate her. She has always ruined my sister's life!". It was funny to hear her talk about her this way. It was only a week ago that I found out that they were sisters. I had never met Amana, now, Calypsa sends her after me. "Are we going to meet Calypsa at some point?". Amana nodded. "Don't worry...", she said, "...we will somehow get into Dasha without being noticed.". I highly doubted that. I was to be killed on sight and she is the Princess of Kindy. If there were ever two people who should avoid Dasha for their own goodness sake, it was the two of us.

Ko-e's Journey

KO-E: When I had left Alexandria, it was with one single goal in mind. A goal that my father unintentionally planted into my head. For over fourteen years, I questioned my brother and Alexa if I ever would see Plinth. Or even Dasha, where my mother was a goddess and a queen. I often would complain about the somberness of Alexandria. Sure, it was close to Heaven and all that good stuff, but once you've done everything there is to do, you grow very bored. I frolicked in the fields of Kindy flowers and I've tried every cuisine. I've learned to do battle like a goddess, and I've taken every possible mind test there is. Being this close to Heaven allows you to experience things that they definitely do not have anywhere else. I've learned that since I've left. Almost nothing is the same. And the people are terrible. Many times, I've fled from persecution. And even worse, my journey has been made difficult by the fact that my sisters are royalty. Alexa was always great company. She was originally from Plinth, but was found by the goddess before me. She was brought here and brought up as the younger sister of Alex. Now, she remained to help my brother and my great-grandmother raise me. But being older than me and also being sort of bossy, made me grow tired of her. I found solace with Grandma. She was always telling me stories from her childhood and making me laugh. Unfortunately, I had heard all the stories, and Grandma's adult life was too miserable to speak of. So that's when I studied. I studied what goddesses were capable of. Parnim told me that once, there used to be a kingdom that taught the goddesses how to protect themselves, but that it ended up being an evil kingdom, and Father had to destroy it. While I knew I was greatly loved and all, I didn't really like my home. I wanted to experience something great. Something different. In my dreams is when I'd see my father. "Ko-e, how is everything? Are you okay?", my father asked me. "Well, I was wondering if you could tell me about Plinth?". My father, as he often does, became quite nervous and grasped for something else to talk about, "You should see this other planet called Noxxer. They've learned how to travel to their moon. It is a lot more amazing than Plinth. Here, let me show you.". My father led me to a room with globes. In the room, I saw what my father spoke of. A green man was wearing a strange suit as he walked out of a strange vehicle he had used to travel to the moon. He took something from out of his suit and waved to the device. "Father, this is beautiful and all, but what about Plinth? I want to see where my mother is from.". Once again, he hesitated and then I woke up.

Sebastian always did this. He would show me everything else except for Plinth. I didn't know why Plinth was off limits. I couldn't understand why the place my mother and father both lived, I couldn't visit. "There is no reason. One day you will. But for now, just focus on your studies.", my brother was telling me one day. My studies involved learning to harness my power and learning what to do in a situation that I might have to use it. This all seemed pointless at the time, because there was nobody in Alexandria that would want to harm anybody. The boringness I lived with daily was getting to me. All day it was the same. I'd wake up in the morning, with my little pet Dattur, Casian, and we would make our way to the rose fields, where she would roll around and play. Then I would have my studies taught to me by Losa. Losa is a nice girl. She is Parnim's sister and has always delighted in teaching me. "What's that face?", she would ask me whenever I wasn't really feeling happy. "It's my father and everyone else. Everyone refuses to tell me about Plinth. I don't understand why.". Losa gave me a reprimanding look, "There must be a good reason. Why else would they keep it from you?". As I pondered what the answer to that might be over the next couple of days, I found myself having a strange dream. There were two girls. One with vibrant purple hair and the other red flaming hair. Both girls resembled the other. As I looked closely, I realized that we all resembled each other. My first thought was that these were my daughters in the future, but that seemed too strange. Then I noticed my father was admiring the two girls. He hadn't seen me, and I hid. But there was no hiding from him. He looked in my direction and I forced myself to wake up.

I awoke with a start, and I immediately felt love. A strong love that I couldn't fight against. The two girls I saw, they were the ones doing it. Somehow, they were communicating with me. I wondered if they realized they were doing it. I started to see them more often in my dreams. And what was really interesting was that one day, the red-haired girl looked in my direction. She blinked, and I realized she was seeing me. At that moment, I woke up and suddenly, I had a feeling that I needed to see her. As the days rolled on, I didn't have any more dreams, but the two girls from my dreams continued to haunt me. Once it had gotten to the point where I could no longer ignore it, I felt I had to ask Caprius, my brother, if what I was seeing meant anything. "Caprius...", I called out to him, "...there is something serious I need to talk to you about. Do you have a moment?". At that exact time, Alexa and Caprius were spending their usual time in the garden. He had been kissing her cheeks softly when I approached. I had never known that feeling with a man. Perhaps that's the reason why when I met Scion, he seemed to make me want to kiss him. I couldn't explain that feeling. At this time, I didn't know anything about what that feeling would feel like, and at the time, I was more concerned with the girls who wouldn't leave my head. "Sure, what's bothering you?", Caprius answered, although he did look annoyed. "Well, I've been having these strange visions. Usually, Father tells me what my visions mean, but he won't say anything about this one.", "What is the vision of?", Caprius asked, suddenly more serious. "There are two girls that keep appearing…". Caprius cut across me, "FORGET THE DREAM! FORGET THOSE GIRLS!". I was confused. Caprius has never gotten this upset before. He'd always been positively happy, but now he was shaking. Alexa, too, was looking upset. She stared from me to my brother and then stood up and placed her hands on my shoulders, "You have to try and move on. If you seek those girls out, it could be bad.", "But how would I seek them out? I don't even know who they…", something started to dawn on me, "They are on Plinth…aren't they? And Plinth is close, isn't it?", "Ko-e, listen, you need to trust us. Going down to Plinth isn't a good thing!", Caprius tried convincing me, but I felt the damage was done. "IT'S BEEN THERE THIS WHOLE TIME?!", I shouted, pointing downward. I ran off, with Caprius and Alexa on my heels. I didn't stop until I had reached the edge of Alexandria. I looked over the cliff and all I saw were clouds, but I got the feeling if I jumped, I would survive. Caprius had always said I'd be diving to my death, but somehow, I knew, Plinth was right beneath us, and there in that land, were my sisters. For now I realized why my father was admiring them. Because they were his children. I felt something on my leg and looked down to see Casian. She was looking at me rather sadly and was obviously trying to stop me from going. "I'm sorry, girl, but I need to do this. Please understand.". I picked her up and kissed her little snout. At that moment, Caprius, Alexa, some guards, and Penelope, my great-grandmother, all came running towards me. Seeing all of them, I felt compelled to stay and stop this. But the red-haired girl was still fresh in my mind, so I let myself fall. I didn't even realize I was still holding Casian.

It had been a month since my grand escape, and still I was no closer to my sisters than the day I found out where to find them. When I landed, I was in a field. I looked up, but could not see Alexandria. Casian jumped from my hands and ran off. "Casian! Casian!", I tried to call the creature back to me, but it was gone. I had no idea what had gotten into her. As I proceeded through the field, I found myself in the midst of trees. I continued through for a day. Finally, I decided to rest. This whole land was new to me, but I knew I must be on Plinth.

I awoke, or at least I thought I had. My father was sitting against a tree. He was wearing his diamond armor and his sword had been placed in the dirt with the end pointed down. "Well, I always knew this might happen, but I've come to do the right thing. Turn back, Ko-e. Go back to Alexandria and forget your sisters.", "So, you admit they are my sisters?!", I shouted back at him, with no desire to return to Alexandria. My father gave me a sad look, "Well, if you must, I can't stop you. But please understand, their mothers are not going to let you walk into their kingdoms and request to meet them.", "Why not? Why are you keeping us separated?". My father looked even sadder, "Some things, Ko-e, are best left unsaid and unchanged. Please, consider what I am telling you.". I did consider it. The truth is, I knew there was a part of my father that was right. I understood that they most likely had a very good reason for keeping us apart. But this feeling I was feeling, I couldn't just ignore it. "I felt the same way about Alex, you know? Couldn't stop thinking about her. Dreamed of her all the time. I thought I was going mad. Is that what you're feeling?". I nodded my head. Father just shook his head and the next thing I knew, I was awake.

While still trying to make sense of what my father was hinting at last night, I finally heard voices. I hid nearby to overhear what was being said, "...got it. I mean the whole thing hooks up to your cottage.", "I don't know how I feel about a thing that can do that. If you ask me, this whole tech war is scary. And I've heard some really nasty things are going on.", "Like what?", "Well, there is supposed to be some genius in Dasha, and from what I heard, he is really close with the princess.". I perked up my ears when I heard Dasha and princess. "…ridiculous thing really.", "But I heard he is mighty cute.". I looked to see who was talking. One girl had black hair and the other girl's hair was orange. Both girls seemed to be resting next to what looked like a pond. "Is he really? Wouldn't think a princess would go for a villager. I'd think she would want Nigel. He is something special.". I listened to the girls talk about men they thought were cute for over half an hour. It was at this time that I first heard the name, Scion. The black-haired girl had mentioned him. I found myself thinking, so this is what it's like on Plinth. Women just talking about which men they found good looking, and so far, since I hadn't seen any men, I had no idea what men were like here. There were some noises a few hours later. Both the women were sleeping. I awoke and listened to the sounds. Three men made their way from out of the trees. I watched to see what they were doing. "Pretty things, huh? What you think, Hoss?". Hoss looked like a cross between a hippo, a creature on one of Sebastian's other planets that was known for its fat stature, and a man. He looked the girls over and one of them woke up with a start. They covered her mouth, so she couldn't scream and started to haul her into the forest. The other woman started to wake and discovered Hoss hanging over her. Before she could scream, Hoss had bent low and covered her mouth. From my hiding spot, I could see him beginning to drool over her, "I haven't had a girl like you in a long time.", he said, holding her to the ground and starting to feel under her shirt. I heard the other woman scream from beyond the trees. I knew now why Caprius didn't want me to come here. I was terrified. I wanted to jump out, but I was afraid they'd capture me as well. Just then, I heard the other woman scream again but followed by one of the men who had taken her running out of the woods, "Hoss, we need to get…", he never finished saying what he was saying, unfortunately, because Casian had torn a hole in his neck. Hoss looked at the creature and stood up with his knife in his hand. Casian launched at him, and just like that, Hoss fell to the floor. He was still breathing. The girl in the woods came out. Her clothes had been ripped but she seemed okay. The other girl with the black hair was getting to her feet and started to kick Hoss. Both girls turned to look at Casian who had jumped at the girl with the orange hair. She screamed and both girls ran off into the woods. I stepped out and picked up Casian. "Casian, good girl. Why did you run off earlier?". The black-haired girl had come back. She stared at Casian in my hands, then looked at me, "Princess?", she asked. At first, I didn't know what to say, then I understood that she was confusing me with one of my sisters. "No, I am Ko-e.", "Oh…", said the girl with the black hair, "…I am Mileeda and this is my sister, Corsa. We are from Dasha. Why are you out here? And what is that thing?", she asked, pointing at Casian, who stared at the girls. "This is my pet, Casian. She is a Dattur.". Both the girl's mouths hung open. They had obviously never seen a Dattur before. I was surprised by this. "Aren't there Dattur's here on Plinth?", "You say that like you aren't from this place!", Corsa, the girl with the orange hair, exclaimed. Both girls gave each other a certain look. Hoss's blood was starting to flow from underneath him. He was still breathing and awake but was unable to speak. "Well I am not from this planet. I'm from Alexandria.". Once again, the girls looked at one another and exchanged looks. "Uh, do you two think you could take me to Dasha?". Mileeda walked towards me and fell to her knees, "If you truly are from Alexandria, then that means you know him.". I was confused. I started to think I should have stayed home, when Corsa, too, came before me and fell to her knees, "You know our god!", she said. "Your god? You mean my father?". Both girls started to kiss my feet. "Please stop! I don't want this sort of attention!", I yelled, hoping they would cease. They stared up at me, confused. "But you have to be a goddess!", yelled Corsa. "Well, I am! But that doesn't mean I want you to kiss my feet.". The women got up, looking embarrassed. "That Dattur saved our lives. We thought for sure we'd be raped, but we knew the danger when we started this journey.", sighed Mileeda, "You see, me and my sister are spreading the good word!". I didn't know what that meant. "Say, why don't we get out of here? I don't like being here with this guy.", I said, pointing towards Hoss's body. They both nodded, and we started to move away. I noticed Corsa's ripped clothes and I snapped my fingers and they returned to normal. "HOW DID YOU DO THAT?!", she exclaimed. "You mean you couldn't? I just assumed you wanted to stay that way.", "You are very strange, Ko-e. You don't seem to understand a lot.", said Mileeda.

Mileeda and Corsa were the best thing that had happened to me so far. They were leading me to Dasha and telling me of Plinth. They told me about my sisters and how they were in what was called a 'tech war', and I guess neither side was winning. To me, it sounded like my sisters were using this war as a cover to improve Plinth, while keeping their mothers in the dark about their communication. I started to realize how different Plinth was from Alexandria. People here were either mean, or nice, or just didn't want to be bothered. Mileeda and Corsa were very interesting. They had been raised to honor my father and his sacrifices. Some parts of what they told me didn't sound right, but I didn't correct them on account of I found them as interesting as they found me. Casian had taken to the two girls quite nicely. At night, she would often lay with Corsa, who was younger than Mileeda by three years. Mileeda and I would often lay awake, and she would tell me about Dasha. "…so, I've only ever been this close to Calypsa.", she was explaining to me one night. We were camped in a clearing and we were somewhere near Dasha. You could tell because not too far away were bright lights. I was mesmerized by them. "They are the lights from the cottages. My parents grew up before we had PE. Would have really been a bummer to have that kind of life.", "I wouldn't know. I've always had everything I wanted. Except for the fact that I'm not supposed to be seeking out my sisters.". Mileeda looked shocked and confused, "But they are your sisters! Why shouldn't you be allowed to have them in your life? I couldn't even imagine never knowing Corsa.". I looked over at Corsa. Her lovely orange hair glowed in the light of our fire, and Casian, with her white fur and blue dots, passed out with her. "I wish I knew my sisters. I've only seen them in dreams.", "Well, they are the two princesses of our land. Personally, I don't know how you think to get to her. Queen Micka keeps Calypsa well-guarded. And I've never even seen Amana, only heard of her.". I secretly was jealous of Mileeda and Corsa because they had always been together. I looked over at the lights coming from Dasha and was ready to begin my journey into the city.

When morning arrived, we went down to Dasha. Outside of the gates were rows of Cottages. "You have to have a lot of coins to move into one of these.", Corsa was explaining. Kids were coming out of their homes carrying bags with books. They all seemed to be going to a study session. I recognized that because I, too, had to carry a lot of books often, when Losa was schooling me. As we made our way down to the gate, an old man approached us. He was wearing what appeared to be a guard suit and was watching us closely. I noticed he was mostly watching me. "Hey! You there! Come here!", he shouted at us. We made towards him, making sure to keep Casian hidden because nobody on Plinth had ever really seen a Dattur, and pretty much would cause a commotion if they saw her. "Now, you two look like Taxin's daughters, and you look like...", the man trailed off. He stared at me for some time, then motioned for another guard, "Say, who does she look like to you?", he asked the new guard. The new guard wasn't as old as the first guard, but he looked at me the same way. He looked terrified. Mileeda and Corsa were watching the scene, wondering if we were in some kind of trouble. Feeling like something may be wrong, I decided to ask, "Can we go?". The men both just stared at me, until the older one finally spoke, "Falsa...", "What?", I asked, confused by why he would say my mother's name. "You... you look like Falsa...", the older man repeated, clearly unnerved. The younger guard was transfixed. "You look just like our old queen! But, then that makes you…", as I started to catch on, I realized I didn't want these people recognizing me. I snapped my fingers, "Oh, what were we doing? Oh yeah, Taxin's daughters. Well you go ahead and be on your way. Have a very pleasant day, and make sure to tell your father that Fod says he will be in his sermon tonight.", "Thank you!", said Mileeda, looking at me from the corner of her eye. When we had passed into the village, more people stared at me. "They all recognize you!", exclaimed Corsa. I quickly found a cloak and pulled it over my head. "Good idea. I didn't think people would react to you like this.", Mileeda was saying, as we passed a gaggle of children. The children all tried to stare into the hood of my cloak. As we continued walking, a young man grabbed Corsa's hand, "Well that was a lot quicker than I thought. I thought you'd be gone longer!", the young man said, pulling Corsa toward him and kissing her. Corsa, looking embarrassed, mumbled something that sounded like, see you later, and left with the young man, taking Casian with her, who was still concealed. I watched as they walked away and looked to Mileeda, "That is my sister's mate, Dony. He's okay. He's always treated my sister with respect, and she really likes him. How about you? Do you have anybody you like?". I knew I couldn't answer this question, because I had never known a man who I could fall for. Just then, I saw a man being led by guards. He was a very handsome man, who had hair that touched his shoulders and a slender but muscular body. I watched as they pushed him, and he swore. "Who is that guy?", "That is supposed to be the smartest man in Dasha. Your sister is quite taken with him.", "HE KNOWS CALYPSA?!", I yelled, forgetting myself. People stopped and stared for a bit. Mileeda pulled me closer, "He is her lover. They work together in the main shop.", Mileeda said, pointing to an area that had a large sign that said, 'COMPUTER MAINTENANCE AND SHOP'. It was from this point that I told Mileeda I wanted to be on my own and started to do reconnaissance. I watched the man in the shop for three days. Finally, Calypsa showed up. I watched her for a long time. She WAS my sister. Her face had a bruise on it. I wondered where she had got it. I watched her leave the shop to go back to the castle. I followed her. The castle of Dasha was a lot smaller compared to the castle in Alexandria, but it still had a luxurious glow to it. I had found that what interested me the most about Dasha, was the statue of my mother right outside of the castle. I loved it. I also saw how much we looked alike. I had seen pictures of my mother, but this was the most glorious thing ever.

I had fallen asleep under my mother's statue and my father had chosen this time to enter my dreams again, "Hello, Ko-e, I see that things are going smashing for you, huh?". I didn't appreciate his sarcasm. "Ko-e, go home. Look at yourself!". My father passed me a mirror. In the mirror, my face was sort of dirty. I looked wild and uncared for. My father was watching my face. "I'm not going till I talk to my sisters.", "Ko-e, this is only going to be harder on you. Please just go home. You don't realize what is going to happen if you keep this up.", "I thought you said that I should continue if I must?", I asked, looking at him in disbelief. "There are things that will take you out and throw you and everything you love away. I've seen it. Ko-e...trust me, I know what I'm talking about. If you stay here, you will endanger your sisters. Is that what you want?". I didn't know how I could be endangering them. "If you aren't going to talk plainly, then just go away!". He did, and I woke up. When I awoke, I knew I had to try. I went to the shop and talked to the handsome man inside. When he told me Calypsa wasn't there, I decided to go back to watching the shop. I watched later as Calypsa arrived and entered the shop. I watched her kiss the handsome man and I felt jealousy. I watched as she left again, being dragged by her mother away from the shop. I knew that I would have to reveal myself. Just so I can get this man on my side.

Later that evening I had a dream of two little girls meeting for the first time. They knew something was different but similar about each other right away. I recognized the area as the field underneath

Alexandria. They played near the Willet. The girl with the red hair was suggesting they go to her kingdom. She wanted to protect the girl with the purple hair, who had the same eyes as her. They rode off together, and the red-haired girl fell and hit her head. There was blood and the purple-haired girl took her and placed her on her stomach on the horse, and climbed back on and rode off. When I awoke, I realized that I had been reaching into Amana's dream. I went back to the shop. After the man, Scion, was rude to me, I revealed to him that Calypsa is my sister.

Now I was trying to survive, because there was nobody to help me. After I watched Scion get arrested, I watched Queen Alisa and Alexa head towards the dungeons. I thought about breaking Scion out again, but realized it would be too risky. As I was trying to figure out what I was going to do, Corsa and Dony were passing by, "Ko-e, what are you doing? Do you need help? Let me help you.", Corsa pulled me to her and led me to a two story cottage. Inside was a man sitting at a table with two women. One who I recognized as Mileeda. Mileeda stood up and gave me a huge hug, "It's dangerous for you right now! I've been hearing rumors of you in the village. I think you should go back to Alexandria.", Mileeda said, as she looked from her father to me. Her father stood up and held out his hand, "I'm Reverend Taxin. It's good to meet you. Well, I should say it's an honor. And this is my wife, Floris. When my daughters first told me of you, I didn't believe them, but your eyes tell me everything. I saw your father many years ago.". I sat for some time, listening to Taxin tell me of my father. I was quite surprised with everything he was telling me. At the end of his story, I felt there was a side of my father I never knew. There was a lot my father had told me of, but he left out parts about his dark-half and some of the other things. My mother, according to Taxin, was an evil woman, "She executed people just for wanting to leave. Her son was just as evil, the spoiled little-shit.", "You mean Caprius? Surely he wasn't that bad.", "Oh no? There was a family that had two daughters. The mother had passed away when the girls were young. Caprius walked right into their home, raped their oldest daughter, and placed his seed. The girl was so distraught that she killed herself. Now you tell me how that isn't that bad.". I had stopped asking questions. Later that night, I kept going over it, over, and over again in my head. How could Caprius do something like that? When I saw those men about to have their way with Mileeda and Corsa, I was too scared to do anything. It was so frightening, that the thought that my brother would do the same, killed a part of me. And learning the truth about Falsa as well, had hurt more than I thought anything ever could. I cried a bit into my pillow that night. I had been staying with Mileeda's family. Mileeda had heard me crying, "There, there. Please don't cry, Ko-e. I know how hard it must have been to hear all that.". Although she said she understood, I didn't think she did. I couldn't fall asleep, but I knew the main person that could help me understand was my father. But no matter how much I prayed, he wouldn't come.

So much time had passed now. I found myself caring less about finding Amana and Calypsa, and caring more for the family that was supporting me. Floris had taken the time to show me how to cook. I enjoyed listening to how when she was younger, they had to start fires manually. Now thanks to my sisters, you just push a button. Taxin was taking every opportunity to let me know that he respected my father. Taxin was a priest at the church and loved giving life lessons using my father as an example. Corsa spent so much time out of the house, that I was quite sure she didn't live here. "Of course, she does. She is just spending time with Dony is all. That's what love does.", Mileeda was explaining to me one day. When I wasn't learning to cook, I spent time with her. She was a lot like a sister to me now. We would often go and collect things Floris needed for dinner, or often just abuse Corsa and Dony's relationship. I had been using less of my power because a huge part of me enjoyed all the work. I was finding it hard to believe I'd been in Dasha for two months and still had only spotted Calypsa once. To be the sister of the princess, but not be able to get close enough to her to tell her was torture. I started to put it behind me until Corsa brought something home. "Look what I found in the market. They have these posted everywhere!". I looked down at the paper that Corsa just handed me;

Wanted: Scion Tin

Believed to be traveling with Kindin Princess Amana Tia.
If seen, please notify Dashin or Kindin authorities.

Under the writing was a picture of Amana and Scion. Scion looked particularly suspicious, while Amana looked as fair as ever. At the very bottom were the words, "Dead or Alive: Scion Tin only. As I examined the paper again and again, I realized my troubles were far from over. At the very bottom was a side note:

There is also an intruder within the kingdom. Her name is Ko-e and she, too, is wanted. If you see her, only report to soldiers who will alert Queen Micka. It is very important that this girl is captured. Anyone found aiding her will be executed.

I felt horrible. I looked at Mileeda, who was able to tell what I was thinking, "No, don't even think about it. You are staying here! Nobody knows that you are here, so you don't have to worry.", "But, I will not risk you and your family. I have to leave.", I said, giving her a very stern look. "Listen, we are best friends, right?", Mileeda asked me. I had never had a best friend before. I found it strange that this girl would call me that. But at the same time, I was overjoyed, "All the more reason for me to leave, then.", "Ko-e, I don't want you to feel like we don't want you here.", said Floris, entering the room followed by Taxin. "That's right. You're living proof of our god, and Queen Micka wishes to silence that fact!", said Taxin, flaring up, "I mean it doesn't surprise me! She has always been ignorant of him! She chased him out twenty years ago! Now that I know why, it only makes her look worse!". Taxin was losing himself in his rage. "Love, please, relax. Let's just worry about Ko-e, okay?", Floris said, rubbing her husband's back. "For starters, we shouldn't call her Ko-e anymore, there is no picture, so nobody knows what you look like.", said Mileeda. "We can also get those pupil changers from the market to hide your eyes!", said Corsa. I was overwhelmed with how much they wanted to help me. I had always known such love, but never from strangers. Part of me understood why my father loved this planet above others. The people here can be cruel, but those with the proper hearts, are willing to share, even with those they don't know.

After dinner that night, I decided that I wouldn't allow them to risk themselves. I walked out of the house in the middle of the night. As I was walking, I spotted a familiar figure. I watched as the figure made their way across the open path towards the shops and went into the computer shop. I followed at a slow kind of pace but not losing the figure. As I peeked into the shop, I saw Calypsa. I hesitated, then entered. "Hi.". Calypsa froze and before I knew it, had the sharp end of a sword pointed in my face. She stared at me for a long time before finally lowering the blade. "...you've been looking for me...", she said slowly. "Yes, I have.". Now that Calypsa was right in front of me, I didn't know what to say. There was so much I wanted to tell her but didn't think this was the right time. Then I got to wondering why she was here in the middle of the night. "Your eyes...they are like mine and Amana's. You are the one Amana told me about. The girl she saw in her sleep.". I nodded. "Well, you need to get out of here. My mother is looking for you and when she finds you, I don't know what she'll do. Things have been sort of chaotic here, or maybe you haven't noticed?". Calypsa was sporting a black eye and a bruise on her face that looked menacing. I raised my hand and placed it on her face. I stared into my sister's eyes and for the first time since Casian saved Mileeda and Corsa, I saw terror. My sister was truly afraid of her mother. Seeing this made me realize what Father was telling me.

Why Caprius and the rest wanted us separated. Calypsa was angry. She was the one thing between the three of us that had known only hate. Perhaps Scion was her one chance at having something else, and now, because of me, Scion can't even come home. "I'm sorry.", I said without really thinking. Calypsa had a tear that rolled down her eye. "What are you doing here anyway?". She looked at something that looked like it might have some major importance. "I've told my mom to take away this foolish bounty she has placed on Scion and Amana or else I unplug the system. This will disrupt everything Amana and I have built.". Part of me agreed. "But what about the innocents?". Calypsa looked at me cross, "They will just have to suffer. I'm done playing by my mother's rules. It's time she abided by mine.". She reached for the object and I immediately thought of Mileeda and her family and how they would be paying a price for something they haven't done. I grabbed her wrist. "Please, I'm begging you, I don't want my friends to suffer.", "How can you have friends? Oh, I see now. You just want Scion all to yourself. People have told me how you were latched onto him. Didn't bother you that he was with your sister, did it?". I was lost as to what she was referring to. I did like Scion. I knew I did. But I wouldn't have done anything with him. "You don't truly believe me capable of that, do you?", "I don't know what I believe, but I will not let you stand in my way.". She brandished the sword at me again, but this time, she came at me. I snapped my fingers, and the sword disappeared. Calypsa stared at her hand in disbelief. Then she whispered, "How did you do that?", "Because we both are special. You don't need to live like you have been. You can be free.". I placed my forehead on hers and got flashes. I saw Micka grabbing her by her hair and slapping her when she accidently went to sleep in her princess dress. I saw, as she was terribly beaten at the age of fourteen for trying to fight back against her mother. I saw as she cried and wrote a letter to Amana. I broke apart from her, tears in my own eyes, "You wanted to kill yourself. You were going to do it before you freed Scion.". Calypsa nodded. She looked down and then charged past me out of the shop. When I ran out after her, she had gone.

CHAPTER 5

Calypsa Awakens

CALYPSA: Ko-e was not at all what I expected, but then again, neither was Amana. Both girls were always putting something before themselves and it was annoying. Couldn't they understand that my mother had to pay? Didn't they agree that my mother was evil? Amana has said she hates my mom but refuses to aid me in her death. If Mother was dead, I could become queen and rule this place differently. Scion would be my king and I wouldn't have to suffer anymore. I could have children and do all the other things that other women, NORMAL women can do.

I felt a sharp jolt going through my body since Ko-e touched me. The jolt was changing me somehow, making me more powerful. I fell behind a building, clutching my chest. It felt like it was on fire. I let out a scream that brought people from out of their homes. "IT'S THE PRINCESS!", I heard someone exclaim, and I knew it was time for me to get moving. As I got up to run, a man placed his hand on my arm, "Princess, come with me, I'll help you.". Without looking to see who it was, I pushed him away and the man flew further than I would have expected him to. I expected him to be forced back a bit, but he flew into the next building, hitting a wall, and not moving afterwards. I realized it was Fod. I ran up to him and he was still breathing. I looked around and everyone was watching me. I felt the eyes of the crowd, waiting to see what happens next. My first thought was to go back and look for Ko-e and ask what she did to me, but then I realized something. She is my sister, and she might know our father. Perhaps, this was something to do with him. Maybe, this power is something I inherited. But more than that, I realized what I could do with this ability. The thought of putting my mother's head in the dirt, while she kicks and screams, brought me great delight, but I knew it was too soon. I needed to take my time. I couldn't immediately let her know I had this power.

I went home, feeling invincible. The guards that had allowed me to escape were doing their very best to find me before my mother realized I was gone. Trus, a very stout and unattractive guard saw me and huddled my way, "Princess…" he panted, "…we have been looking all over for you! Please don't do this to us again. You of all people know how your mother gets when…", he stopped talking. Fear had spread across his face. He looked up and realized my mother was right behind me. I turned and faced her. Remembering I didn't want her to know about my power, I looked frightened as well. "Do you have any idea how worried I have been?", my mother asked, with that scary silent voice that was particularly partial only to her. I tried to think of a lie on the spot, but before I could, my mother had slapped me. I staggered somewhat but turned to face her none the less, "I'M NOT AFRAID OF YOU ANYMORE!", I shouted. Trus was looking even more uncomfortable. "Well…mam…your Highness, so I'm not needed anymore, so…". Trus turned to get away, "TRUS, why don't you show my daughter…the courtyard? You might find what I've been working on out there really interesting, Calypsa.". I gulped. Whenever my mother took that calm tone, it was never anything good. Trus reluctantly led me to the courtyard, where I saw the most horrible scene. Trus, who had led me here, fell to his knees before my mother, "PLEASE, YOUR MAJESTY?! PLEASE?!", "Stop your pathetic begging and join the rest of your men.". The men had been lined up along a wall. Each had been cuffed and had their armor and shirts removed. A strange machine, with what appeared to be a long belt of whips, was placed behind them. It was a wide machine and it looked like it ran on PE. My mother had been quite inventive indeed. She had created a device designed for punishment. But it was the worst kind. After Trus joined his men and another guard handcuffed him, mother walked behind the machine. "I call it the whipping hour. Because from now on, when my men fail to keep my daughter safe, I will whip them for an hour. Or rather, this machine will do it for me.". She handled the lever and the machine whirred and the belt began to turn at a rapid pace. The whips started hitting the men, who all cried out and wailed. I listened to the wailing of the soldiers, who all stared at me when they could, with hate in their eyes. "STOP THIS!", I pleaded. "Well, you're the one with the power to prevent this. All you have to do...is STAY IN YOUR PLACE!", my mother yelled. She cut the machine off and the men fell to the floor, gasping, and crying, and staring daggers at me. My mother threw the key to Trus, "Unlock yourselves and return to post. If any of you attack my daughter out of anger, you will face worse than this.". She dragged me from the scene and led me to my room. After throwing me in, she faced me, "You think I don't know, but I do. You went to disconnect the PE tonight, and in the process, you've met Ko-e. Tell me where she is hiding, and I'll forget all about tonight.". It was funny, now that I think about it, how my mom thought she still held all the power. "Oh, and don't think I haven't heard about Fod. I know your powers have awoken.". I stared at her in disbelief. "How...?", "Well, you see, let's just say I've got my ways of knowing. Did you really think something like that would happen and I wouldn't know? You are the PRINCESS for god's sake. You really thought I didn't have spies tracking you? I'm quite sure one of them was smart enough to follow Ko-e when she departed.". The one good thing about that, was that Ko-e had the power to protect herself, too. "All I want is to know who mine and Amana's father truly is. Why do you refuse to say anything about that?", "Okay, I will tell you who your father is. Your father is Sebastian.". When she said it, I didn't believe her. "Fine, continue to play this game.". I undressed and put my sleeping gown on. My mother was still standing there. "So, you don't believe me? So be it.". She walked out of the room. I laid down feeling angrier.

That night, it felt like I had been woken up, but I was in a forest. A familiar one. I saw Scion there and I ran to him. I couldn't speak for some reason. Then I saw Amana. I knew the two of them were traveling together. I had asked Amana to go and find him before my mother's men did. My mother had decided to kill Scion. Something about how Alisa had told her not to, made my mother decide to do it. Scion and Amana were looking over something. I got close and realized it was a map of Dasha. Of course, leave it to Amana to go all out. Now that we were older, getting away seemed easier. But I stayed for Scion. I noticed that Amana was looking at Scion a certain way. Then the two kissed. I stood frozen for some time. I continued to watch, as Amana started to undress. As I felt my eyes burning, I felt a hand on my shoulder, "It isn't real, Calypsa. This isn't really happening.". I turned, and Alisa was standing behind me. The scene suddenly changed, and we were in a room. "I know what you saw is hard, but that was your subconscious creating that scene. I guarantee, Amana isn't kissing on Scion.", "What are you doing here? Where are we?", "You are asleep. And I'm communicating with you this way, so your mother doesn't know.". I had never experienced anything like this. Amana had told me she had dreams like this, but I had never put any thought into them. "Why are you talking to me in my dreams?", "I wanted to let you know I am allowing Amana to escort Scion. I just wanted to tell you.", "Allowing?", I said. Alisa just stared at me. "You remind me so much of him you know.", "Of who?", I said, trying to contain my anger. I'd always hated Alisa. Ever since she had abandoned me to my mother. She allowed my mother to beat me and never tried to help. Now she shows up in my dream, acting like I'm supposed to be appreciative of what she is doing. "Your father. You remind me of your father. A lot more so than Amana, or even Ko-e. Listen, I'm not supposed to tell you who he is, but I can't do this anymore. You deserve the truth. When I was a bit younger than you are now, I was raped by your father. He didn't do it intentionally. It's hard to explain, but that's how Amana was born.". I didn't know what to say. Now it made sense that she was a lesbian and still had gotten pregnant. "Falsa, the former Queen of Dasha, raped your father, and that's how Ko-e was born. And you, you out of those two had the only consensual birth. Your mother and father were together for a time. That's how you were born.", "You were raped? I never knew.". I was starting to realize that maybe she was how she was because of that. "Yes. It obviously isn't something I talk about, and Amana is a constant reminder of it.", "But, you don't beat her like my mother beats me. Why does she hit me?", I wondered. Alisa bit her lip, "Well, your mother isn't a very happy individual. She has kind of always been this way.", "Then what did my father see in her? And how are you all connected? I don't understand why Falsa would rape him, while he would rape you, but choose to be with my mother.". None of it made sense. Alisa was looking regretful. "It's hard to explain. I guess the best way to know is to give you your father's name. Sebastian.".

I woke up in the morning with a slight headache but I still remembered mine and Alisa's conversation from the night before. Sebastian is my father. This wasn't a lie. My mother told me the truth last night. But she knew I wouldn't believe her. I went into the market with the hopes I'd find Ko-e, but I couldn't find her, and nobody knew where she was. It wasn't easy for her to hide with her golden eyes that me, her, and Amana all share. Unless she had changed her appearance. I moved around the village and got a lot of angry eyes on me. "HOW DARE YOU SHOW YOUR FACE?!", somebody shouted, and they threw an apple at me. The apple bounced off my face and landed with a small thud. "WHO THREW THAT?!", I demanded. The people grew quiet. Then from out of the crowd, a young man appeared. "HOW DARE YOU SHOW YOURSELF AFTER WHAT YOU DID TO MY FATHER?! HE WAS ONLY TRYING TO HELP HER!", he shouted, pointing at the crowd of angry people starting to gather. It was no secret Fod was a huge deal in the church. Fod was here for the last war and witnessed things that changed his life. It was unfortunate he was the man who had tried to help me. "It was a mistake. So, this is uncalled for.", "You are a monster. Just like your mother.". I felt that jolt going through my body again, and I knew I shouldn't, but I was so angry, "How dare you compare me to her?", I said, almost in that same scary tone my mother uses. The young man looked at me and knew he had done something terribly wrong. I lifted my arm and the young man began to lift into the air. I didn't know how I was doing it. The young man started to scream, and I could feel something creeping down my spine. It was his fear. I continued to psychically keep him in the air until I decided to let him down. He clutched his stomach and everyone else looked on in fear, "DON'T EVER COMPARE ME TO HER!", I yelled. I looked at the crowd of on-lookers and walked away. I had almost forgotten I was looking for Ko-e, but I didn't care about that right now. What was that? I kept asking myself. I thought I was just stronger, but do I have that kind of power as well? I believed I truly was the daughter of Sebastian, and that now I was realizing this, I was getting stronger. I couldn't wait to tell this to Amana. Then I remembered where she was and who she was with. I knew the time had come. These people believed I was like my mother. Well it's time I show them the difference.

CHAPTER 6

Amana Vs. Calypsa

SCION: Amana and I finally got to Dasha. We managed to sneak past using Amana's void disruptor. It was the device that allowed her to turn the whole PH and all the stuff inside invisible. I had to hand it to Amana. I thought there was nobody smarter than me or Calypsa put together, but I was wrong. Amana was twenty times the genius. She was smart enough to keep us hidden for over two weeks, and somehow, still managed to sneak us into Dasha while we were visible. Once inside, we started making our way to my cottage, when a certain scene had met our eyes. Calypsa was standing in the middle of a crowd. They all seemed really angry. As we got closer, we discovered the reason. Duson, Fod's son, was upset about something Calypsa did to his father. Whatever it was, we didn't know, but Calypsa raised her arm, and I watched, as Duson was lifted into the air, and started to scream. I looked at Amana, who was watching Calypsa like she had never seen her before. When Duson fell to the ground, Calypsa yelled, "DO NOT EVER COMPARE ME TO HER!". We watched as she walked away, with a very strange smile on her face. "I need to go talk to her.". I made to walk away from Amana, but she grabbed me, "No, we can't, something isn't right.

Calypsa would never have done that.". I didn't want to tell her that she was wrong. I had seen what Calypsa could become if pushed. It seemed like with me gone, she was becoming just that. But where did the power come from? She wasn't able to do stuff like that before. I should know. But it didn't make sense, until I saw Ko-e. Her eyes were different, and she was wearing a tulsa(Wig), colored green. I watched her for some time, because she slightly threw me off. But there was no mistaking that pretty face. Ko-e was standing in the crowd as well, looking horrified. She was standing next to Mileeda. An old acquaintance. I walked away from Amana, who was still in shock, and walked towards Ko-e and Mileeda, "Well, didn't expect to see you today, Mileeda. Finally came out of the prison you call home?". Mileeda looked at me with disgust. Ko-e on the other hand, hugged me, "It is really good to see you, Scion, but you can't be out here. Let's go to Mileeda's home.". Mileeda, not looking too happy about this, led the way. When we reached the house, Amana had taken the first seat she could find. Ko-e was watching Amana. I just remembered, she hadn't met her yet. All three sisters are in Dasha now. "Calypsa… Why did she torture that young man like that? Why did she do that, Scion?", Amana asked me. Ko-e took a deep breath and went into explanation on how she and Calypsa met. She explained that she might have gained her powers when her and Calypsa touched. Amana was watching Ko-e closely. She stood up and walked right up to her, "I know you. I've seen you somewhere before.". Ko-e blinked her eyes, and the false color she had faded, and the golden eyes returned. Amana sat down in the chair again.

I had decided to leave. It was becoming too crowded in that house. Amana and Ko-e now realized they were sisters and wouldn't stop talking. Mileeda's parents had come home and were overjoyed to learn the Princess of Kindy, was also a child of Sebastian. They were feasting and having a swell time, while I was brooding over the scene earlier in the village. I couldn't get over what Calypsa had done or that smile she wore as she walked away. I was walking without even realizing it, straight to the computer shop. I walked inside, and there were only a few people working. I made my way to the back, nobody saying anything to me, and discovered Calypsa sitting in the back. She was deep in thought, with her eyes closed. She sensed my presence and opened her eyes. "Scion…", she said slowly. I tried to grab her, but she held her hand up. "Scion, I truly did miss you. I know why you left.". I looked at her beautiful form. I wanted her badly. But she just kept sitting there, as if she wasn't even thrilled to see me. "Calypsa, what happened earlier? Why did you torture Duson?", "I thought you would be more interested in HOW I did it, not the fact that I did.". She seemed cold. I didn't know why she was being so sideways with me. All I wanted was to be with her. "Calypsa, you do know that I love you, right?". Calypsa made no acknowledgement of what I had just said, and instead stood up with anger in her eyes, "Oh yeah? Then why were you with Amana?", "Because she saved me from your mother's soldiers. She said you sent her to!", "Well, the truth is I did. But I saw you two. I saw you two kiss.". I had never kissed Amana. But believe me when I say, I definitely wanted to. She was gorgeous. I still felt Ko-e was the best-looking sister, but at the same time, my heart belonged to Calypsa. I started towards her and she raised her hand. I felt an invisible force in front of me, stopping me from touching her. "I don't want you anymore, Scion, you're just like other men! You just want to be with any woman you want!", "Calypsa, that isn't true! I've never kissed your sister!", "Just like you didn't know my father is Sebastian?". I felt cold. I knew. Alisa told me, but I chose to keep it quiet. For fear of what Calypsa would do with this info. "How did you find out about your father?", I asked, hoping I could confuse her. "My mother and Alisa told me. Plus, I met Ko-e. She is the reason I have these powers now.". I shot for her while her guard was down, and I wrapped my arms around her and kissed her. For a minute, she forgot what she was doing and was kissing me back. When we had split apart, she was crying. "What is it?", "It's you! I told you I don't want this anymore!", "Then why are you still holding onto me then?". She released me.

She stood awkwardly, then charged out of the shop. I followed her, and saw she was running towards the castle. I continued to follow her. I told myself I wasn't letting this go. I loved her and there was no reason why we shouldn't be together. Before I could even set foot on the stairs to the castle, I was taken from behind by a guard, and even worse, Queen Micka was glaring down at me.

AMANA: By the time Ko-e and I finished our really invigorating conversation about Alexandria, I realized that Scion was gone, "Mileeda, did you see where Scion went?", "I think he walked outside.", "AND YOU LET HIM?!". Mileeda just shrugged it off as if this wasn't that much of an issue. "You do realize he is to be killed on sight, right?". At these words, she looked up at me and shook her head. I understood right away. "You had past relations with him, didn't you? You used to sleep together.". Mileeda turned scarlet and did not face me again. "We have to go rescue him!", I said, looking at Ko-e, who was looking at Mileeda with disappointment. She followed me out of the house and we went into the village looking for Scion. Ko-e pointed me in the direction of the computer shop and we went inside. It looked just like Kindy's, which makes sense, considering that it is copied from the same bluescript. I walked to the back and found the main server, but nobody was there. A young-looking woman rushed to the back and started working on the server. "Excuse us, we are looking for a young man…", "If you are talking about Scion, I saw him with the Princess, they left. Probably went back to Scion's cottage, most likely.", the girl said, blushing. It was obvious that a lot of women liked Scion. Ko-e led the way to his cottage, but nobody was there. That's when I knew there was one other place to check for sure. The castle. The likelihood that he had been arrested was very high. Ko-e, although a bit frightened at the idea of approaching the castle, mainly because she has been hiding this whole time herself, followed me up the stairs. Guards made way for me as I walked past. Finally, I made my way into the throne room of Queen Micka. "Princess Amana. Wow. I must admit, I never thought I'd see you in my kingdom. What a surprise indeed. And you've brought the fugitive known as Ko-e to me. Well, you can return to Kindy. I'll take everything from here.". I stood my ground. Queen Micka looked into my eyes and I glared into hers, and it was instant hate. I could see all the emotion she had towards my mother in her eyes. "Where is Scion?", "Scion, is a Dashin citizen and will be executed for breaking Dashin law. Is there anything else I can help you with?", "And which Dashin law has he broken?", I asked. I could see she was enjoying the fact that I was worried about Scion. She truly was as Calypsa had always described her. On a note to myself, who gets off on other's suffering? Micka does. "You needn't worry, Princess. Last time that I checked, you weren't this kingdom's princess, that would be MY daughter. You belong in Kindy with YOUR mother. So kindly, return there.". Micka was wearing a very cocky smile that was pissing me off. Ko-e, who sensed my anger, stepped in, "Uh, Queen, I mean, your Highness, I just wanted to say…that I'm sorry for coming into your kingdom. I'm sorry for the trouble…". Micka held up her hand, "Listen to me and listen well. It is now too late for apologies. You've already set in motion events that the both of you will later learn was better to leave alone. You two, will hate each other. You don't see it now, but you will. It's already happening to my dear Calypsa.". At this point, Calypsa came into the throne room. When she saw me, she glared and came towards me. "Traitor.", she said, once she was close to me. "Traitor? How? What are you talking about? I brought Scion back to you. Where is he?", "Scion is paying for his crimes.". I could hear a faint scream. "What did you do? Where is he?", "Why are you so worried about him, Amana? Do you love him?", "Funny, I thought you did.". Calypsa got angry and waved her arm at me. "No! Amana!", Ko-e screamed, as I flew back and hit a wall. "HOW DARE YOU?! HOW DARE YOU?!", I could hear Ko-e saying. She threw herself at Calypsa and the two began to fight using their powers. Ko-e throwing blue energy at Calypsa. I decided to use the distraction. I made my way towards the screaming, which was getting louder now. I finally found the source and was horrified by what I was seeing. A machine designed to whip. Although the machine was designed for multiple people, it was only Scion getting whipped. I ran to the machine and pulled down on the lever. The belt stopped moving and Scion's back was a bloody mess. I ran up and placed my hands on the cuffs. They shattered in my hands, but I didn't stop to think about this. I was more concerned with the bloody mess in my hands. I laid Scion on his stomach to keep the dirt from entering the cuts on his back. I pulled out my dittany and began pouring it into his wounds. The cuts would heal but he would be weak for some time. Micka had found me. She had used the distraction as well to come after me, "Did you really think this was going to be easy?", she said, gesturing to someone behind her. It was a crowd of Dashin soldiers. "You have one chance, Amana. Leave the boy, go back to Kindy, you can even take Ko-e with you. But get the hell out of my castle.". I looked at all the soldiers. I knew I stood no chance. But, Sheena had always taught me to stand up to any kind of oppression. "No.", I said flatly. Micka put her face in her hands, "I am really trying here. What do you think will happen if I kill you, Amana? Your mother will rain fire and brimstone upon me. Yet you continue to push me? Even though this WILL bring war to Dasha. All those innocent people, suffering. And why? Because you want to take Calypsa's boyfriend.". This wasn't true. Sure, I was saving him, but who would save him if I didn't? "I WILL NOT LET YOU KILL THIS MAN!". I stood up and held my hands out in front of me. I didn't know what I was expecting, but I watched, as Micka disappeared, and all her men were tossed askew. Taking the chance, I grabbed Scion and placed him over my shoulders. Once again, I didn't stop to think about how I was able to carry Scion so easily. I entered the throne room, just in time to help Ko-e. Calypsa had her against a wall, and looked like she was going in for the kill. I waved my hand and she flew away from her. "COME ON!", I shouted, and we ran out of the castle. "SEIZE THEM!", I heard Calypsa shout, and sure enough, there were soldiers behind us. We continued to flee, Ko-e grabbing my hand and leading me through a back way. Ko-e had been hiding for almost two months in Dasha and had found all kinds of routes and shortcuts. She had led us out of Dasha. We were running through the outside cottages. Finally, we made our way out of there. I immediately activated my void disruptor and turned us all invisible.

Scion was out cold. It had been two days since we had escaped, and I didn't know what this might bode. Ko-e was worried about Mileeda and her family, "Mileeda was going to let Scion die. I'm not wishing bad on them, but they weren't very nice. Or maybe it was only Mileeda. She WAS sleeping with him.". Ko-e blushed and looked the other way. I could tell she really liked Scion. "Well I can tell you this, he is definitely going to be free when he wakes up. I'm sure he doesn't want anything to do with Calypsa anymore.". I knew he was finished with her, because so was I. I couldn't believe she had tortured that boy, Duson, and condemned Scion to death. I couldn't understand why she would do that all of a sudden. What was the truth? Ko-e had told me Sebastian is my father. She also told me that me, her, and Calypsa are goddesses. While this explained our abilities, what it didn't explain is why my best friend just turned on me. I wanted a better explanation, but Ko-e didn't have one. "When I first came here, I feared everything. Now, I just wish I had stayed in Alexandria period. Why I felt like I needed to meet you two, I don't know. Maybe it was just being lied to for all those years.", "What is father like?", I found myself asking before I could stop myself. Ko-e smiled but then removed her smile. "Father is no better than the rest of them. He is a liar and he will do whatever he needs to protect his secrets.", "That sounds like a person who could make my mother not tell me the truth for my whole life.". We laughed it off.

That night when I was sleeping, I had a strange dream. I was walking in the field where we had been camping. I could hear a strange whistle behind me. I turned to see who it was, and I saw a man standing there. He had messy brown hair but when he faced me, I saw myself in his eyes. "Father...", I said breathless. "Hello, Amana Tia. I would say I'm happy to finally meet you like this, but it's not the best time. You girls have really messed up, you know?", "No, I don't know, so why not explain it to me?!". My father smiled, and then began to laugh, "Man, it is so crazy how much of your mother you have in you! I love all you girls. But I'm afraid that what I need to ask you to do is not going to be easy. In fact, it will be positively the hardest thing you've ever done.", "What?", "I need you to kill your sister Calypsa.". I didn't answer right away. "Kill her? But, whatever she is going through right now, it'll pass.", "No, it won't. If you don't kill her, someone else will. Someone worse. It must be you. I know you love her, but she has her mother in her. And her mother mixed with all that power, isn't a good thing. You have to, Amana. It has to be you.", "Why not Ko-e? Why do I have to do it?". My father lowered his head, "Because, Ko-e has too much love in her. She isn't going to do it. She isn't capable. Not like you.", "Her mother was Falsa! Why can't she?!", "Because you saw her. She wasn't even trying. She wouldn't kill you, your sister, or anybody. She is not weak, but loving. She is too loving. She has more of me in her than her mother. You, Amana, grew up in the real world, you understand things that Ko-e doesn't. That is why it must be you. It just has to be.". I woke up to tears falling down my face.

I didn't know how to explain to Ko-e that our father had asked me to kill our sister. It was hard enough trying to figure out why Calypsa had betrayed everything she cared about, without wondering why the first time I met my father, he asked me to kill my sister. Ko-e was wiping Scion's forehead. I watched for a time. She was lovingly dipping the cloth in the water, and placing it on his head. She turned him on his side to check his back injuries. They had healed, but the scars would remain, perhaps for the rest of his life. Ko-e was sensing something wrong with me. I had been avoiding her gaze and trying not to say anything. We had been living in the PH my mother had given to Scion. I looked at him occasionally, to check and make sure he was breathing. One day, he began to cough, and Ko-e had rushed to his side and was giving him water. I, on the other hand, was thinking of the best way to kill my best friend. Ko-e was so occupied caring for Scion that she wasn't really noticing the looks that were crossing my face. But I knew I could only keep her off my back for so long.

"Amana, why have you been so quiet?", Ko-e finally asked me on the third day. "There isn't much to say.", I said, hoping she wouldn't question what was really going on. "You're lying. I can tell. Just tell me what it is.". I decided to tell her about our father's request. "You can't be serious. Just like that, he wants YOU to kill her? But what about the fact that she has been suffering at the hands of Micka? That's who he should be asking you to kill!", Ko-e said angrily. I felt where she was coming from. Micka was the one who started all this. It made no sense why Calypsa had to suffer. "Father said if I don't kill her, someone worse will.". Ko-e was thinking about what that probably meant, when Scion coughed and blinked his eyes, but they did not open.

SCION: I was in a weird room. Amana and Ko-e were there, but they seemed to not be able to hear me. A man in fancy armor made of diamond was watching me curiously. "I'm sorry, Scion. This really isn't how I intended this to go.", "Who are you?", "I'm Sebastian. I wanted you and Calypsa to be happy, but it looks like the prophecy is coming to pass. I only hope that I can convince you.", "Convince me of what?", "Amana is going to kill Calypsa. I know, you don't want this, but I need you to convince her. She will be convinced by you.". I didn't understand why this man, who claimed he was Sebastian, was suddenly asking this much of me. "Listen, I don't really know you. And as far as I'm concerned, you don't need to ask me this, I'll gladly kill Calypsa myself!", "Well, I'm surprised to hear that. But I know this anger you feel will pass. You will want to be with her. And you will have to remember this, she isn't going to stop.

She will not be what she was when you met her. Trust me, she is my daughter, I know.", "No, you don't. Because you have never been there for her.". I felt my blood starting to boil. How dare he try to tell me about Calypsa? There was no way he understood. "I've been there her whole life. Just because I wasn't there physically, does not mean I haven't been here. I'm here now, right? Aren't we talking?". I thought about the answer to this, "Sure, now that it's too late to stop whatever is happening. Why not make a grand appearance?". I was realizing that Sebastian was overrated. "Scion, when the time comes, you will convince Amana. I won't need to be there for you to do that. But I'm just trying to prepare you. There are some very bad things on the horizon and you could end up dead if you aren't careful.".

When I woke up, Amana and Ko-e were asleep. Ko-e was lying next to me. From the looks of things, she had been caring for me. I realized right away that we were inside the PH that Alisa had given me. I knew I shouldn't, but I decided to step outside. Outside, there was a nice clean field. Only a few trees stood in the area. My guess was we were somewhere near Kindy. I heard movement from within the PH. Ko-e emerged from inside looking worried. When she saw me in the field, relief spread across her face, "I'm so happy to see you're awake, but you shouldn't be out here.", "I felt like I needed the air. I didn't mean to frighten you.", "Oh, I wasn't frightened, I was just wondering where you had left to. You've been asleep for four days after all.". Four days? Suddenly, the fullness of what had happened dawned on me. Calypsa betrayed me to her mother. And Queen Micka had me chained and whipped with a most horrible machine. I felt on my back and could feel the markings. Ko-e touched my hand and placed her other hand on the middle of my back. I could feel her fingers running across the scars and I winced some. Ko-e came around to face me. She placed her hand on my face and I felt compelled to kiss her. As we were about to, a strange rustling sound was made nearby. Still holding Ko-e in my arms, we both looked down and Ko-e broke apart from me, "CASIAN!", she exclaimed, picking up a strange creature I had never seen before. Looking at it closer, I realized it resembled a Dattur. The description of Datturs are pretty detailing. Seeing one up close was something different. This particular Dattur was Ko-e's pet. She had been the Royal Pet of Alexandria for centuries. I was fascinated by the beast. It was so small and could fit in the palm of your hand, yet was so deadly you wouldn't want to piss it off. Insects were similar. But no insect compared to Casian. She was truly a marvel. When Ko-e told me how old she was, I couldn't believe it. "So, this creature was around when your father was walking this planet?", "Oh yes. She is very familiar with my father's scent. He has always been very kind to her. But I suppose she really misses Alex.", "Who is that?", "The goddess before me. She lived in Alexandria and ruled over it. She ascended to Heaven with my father twenty years ago.", "You mean she died?", "No. I mean she lives in Heaven as a goddess with my father. She is his wife.", "Really? Well that must be awkward. I mean with you three girls and all.". I felt like I might had overstepped. But, Ko-e was wearing a very funny smile. "I always wondered. But he never explained. I don't know why we all exist. Technically, you're right. Alex is his wife, so why do I, Amana, or Calypsa exist?". As Ko-e tried to think about that, I fell back on her beauty. When she noticed me staring at her, "What?", she said with a small giggle. I reached in and kissed her. When me and Ko-e kissed, I felt like she wasn't holding back like Calypsa had done. I embraced her, and we laid there, kissing under the moonlight.

When we awoke, we had totally forgotten why we were hiding in the PH. Dashin soldiers had found us. Leading them was Calypsa. Of all the people to discover me laid up with a woman, it just had to be Calypsa. "Well, this doesn't surprise me. I had a feeling one of my sisters was screwing you.". I jumped to my feet. Ko-e stood up but did not look worried. "You gave him up when you decided to torture him!", Amana shouted, emerging from what looked like nowhere. Calypsa, surprised by her arrival, immediately raised her sword and charged at Amana, who in turn took out her sword. Although there were other men that Calypsa had brought with her, they were too busy paying attention to Amana and Calypsa. I felt the uncomfortableness of the situation. They were sisters and had loved each other for years. Now they were locked in combat. The kind of combat that one person had to die. Ko-e was watching her sisters fight with fear etched all over her face. In the end, it was little Casian that jumped into the fray. "Casian, no! Come back!", Ko-e shouted, but it was too late. Casian had run between the two. Both Amana, and Calypsa stopped fighting to stare at the little creature between them. Both had a strange confused look. Casian had started to settle on Calypsa's leg. "What is this thing? Shoo!". Calypsa kicked her leg, but Casian did not let go. As Calypsa aimed her sword at it, Amana jumped and scooped Casian in her hand and threw her, while in the process, Calypsa stabbed her straight through her shoulder. "AMANA!", I heard both me and Ko-e shout at the same time. Calypsa staggered away, mumbling to herself, "Amana… I didn't… What have I done?". She watched, as Amana laid there bleeding. She looked at her men, who didn't know what to say either. Ko-e ran and fell on top of her sister, "HOW COULD YOU?! SHE IS YOUR SISTER! YOU ARE EVIL, JUST LIKE YOUR MOTHER! YOU ARE A HORRIBLE SISTER!". She waved her hand and sent Calypsa flying ten feet back. She turned Amana over and held her in her arms, "Please, stay with me, Amana, please.". Amana was coughing blood now. I looked at Calypsa, who was getting to her feet. I was so stunned, I didn't know what to say, but I knew whose side to take. I picked up Amana's blade and charged after Calypsa. Right at that moment, a horse stood in my path. On the horse was the girl with green hair, Alexa. "THIS IS OVER! EVERYONE, RETURN TO YOUR PROPER KINGDOMS! Yes, this includes you, Calypsa, NOW!", "I don't know you, and don't see why…", before Calypsa finished saying what she was saying, Alexa jumped off her horse and started to attack Calypsa. She punched her, and she fell to the ground. "How…?", "I WAS RAISED IN ALEXANDRIA! YOU DIDN'T THINK

YOU'D BE ABLE TO JUST BEAT ME DID YOU?! Now, return to Dasha, or there will be hell to pay for you!". Calypsa, without another word, got onto her horse and commanded her men to do the same. She looked at her sister, bleeding in Ko-e's arms, then they rode off, leaving us, and a dying Amana. Casian settled up to Amana's side and was weeping into her shirt. "Amana, please, don't die like this! Please!", Ko-e shouted. Amana was starting to fade, and I felt my eyes burn. I knew her for only a month, and now she was dying. I bent down over her, and her eyes were still open and blinking rapidly. She looked at the creature she had made this sacrifice for. "I know where we can save her.", said Alexa. Ko-e reached into her sister's pocket and pulled out a small vial. She opened it and started to dab some of the substance inside the vial onto Amana's wound. Then, Alexa hoisted her up on her horse and rode off. Ko-e and I stared at one another before we followed. We walked at a somewhat brisk pace. After about six hours, we arrived in Kindy. Where Ko-e was led away, and I was seized, and taken to the dungeon.

After waiting for I really didn't know how many hours, Alexa came to fetch me. "Sorry you were locked away like this. Alisa is not very happy.", "Neither am I. How is Amana?". Alexa looked worried, "She is alive, but things are not looking too good. With this latest attack, Alisa feels that Micka has finally overstepped.", "What?! But it was Calypsa that did this!", "Yes, Calypsa did this, but the thing is, it was on Micka's orders. I had just come from Dasha. And things there are going insane. There was a family that was arrested recently. They've been accused of harboring Ko-e.". My stomach made an uncomfortable noise. "Who has all been arrested?", "Well, from what I can make out, it was a mother, a father, and their daughter.", "I'm going to Dasha.", "LIKE HELL YOU ARE! You are going to stay here! You have personally caused all this.". I was angrier than Micka whenever she was in her 'my daughter pissed me off' mode. "HOW COULD I HAVE?! I AM JUST ONE MAN! I DIDN'T ASK FOR THIS!". I felt my chest rising and falling. The weight of the world was falling around me. "I know you didn't ask for all this. But until further notice, you are to be detained. Now that can be within the castle, a nice room for you can be set up, or you can stay in here. What's your choice?". I finally decided to ask, "Alexa, where did you hail from originally? You can't have been born in Alexandria.". She stared at me for a few moments, thrown off by the change in topic, "I was from Dasha.". Now I had finally put the pieces together, "We are cousins, then. I mean, your mother was my mother's sister.". My mother and I haven't spoken since she kicked my father out of his home for her new husband. That was six months ago. Looking at the surprise on Alexa's face reminded me heavily of my mother. "I vaguely remember my parents. Falsa killed them when I was younger for wanting to leave Dasha.". Ko-e walked in at that moment and stood rooted. "Ko-e! I didn't want you to…", Ko-e had run off. "I'll go after her, okay?". I followed her to a nice artificial pond. It was really beautiful. Ko-e was sitting next to the water crying. I came and sat next to her, "Mothers, who needs them? Just ask Calypsa, she…", "I always thought that Alexa just grew up in Alexandria. She never, not once, mentioned her actual parents. Now I know why, but I wonder…", "Wonder what?", I asked. "Why didn't she kill me? My mother killed her parents, and she never wanted revenge? She should have just killed me. Then, Calypsa would have never tried to kill Amana.". She started crying again, "My father told me that if I come here, I will be killing my sisters. I didn't know what he meant, now that I do…", she stood up and stared at the lake morbidly. Sensing what she was thinking, "No, don't do it. You have done nothing wrong, do you hear me? You haven't done anything.", "YOU'RE WRONG! YOU JUST DON'T GET IT! The truth is, I had responsibilities, and so did my sisters. I messed everything up by coming here. If I had just listened…", "NO! THAT'S ENOUGH!", I yelled, "Listen to me, no, listen…", I grabbed both her arms, "…you had no way of knowing all of this. You couldn't have known.", "Scion, I think I might be in love with you, but I don't think we can be together. We are too different. I'm a goddess. And you are just…", "Just what? Just a man? I don't care about any of that!", "That's my point. You don't care. I know you are a good man, but you don't realize the game you are involved in.". I didn't know how to answer her, or how to try and convince her that I did feel something for her. "I think, Mileeda and her family are in trouble.", I said, and I explained what Alexa told me. Ko-e looked faint. She looked me in my eyes, then kissed me. When she finally broke away, she walked away from me, "Where are you going?", "I'm going to Dasha to save my friend and her family. You are to remain here. Do not leave Kindy. Okay? Do not leave Kindy.". And just like that, she was gone.

CHAPTER 7

Mileeda's Fate

CALYPSA: I had killed Amana. There was no other way. At least that's what I kept telling myself. I jumped from my horse the second we crossed the Dasha boundary. I ran to my mother. These days, I found more comfort in her than I had my whole life. She was waiting for me. In her hand was a letter. She looked morbid, but ushered me in. "You didn't kill Amana. She is still alive.". Relief had settled over me, although I knew that Amana would never forgive me for today. "This is a letter from Queen Alisa. Perhaps it's best if you read it.". She handed me the paper and I began to read;

Dear Micka,

Let's face it. We both knew it was coming to this. Ever since the day you betrayed us in the past. Now you've gone and allowed your daughter to seriously injure Amana. We were told what would happen if our daughters learned the truth, but I should tell you, Calypsa knows. She knows about her birth, and her sister's. I told her. I thought she would use this info in a good way, but she has decided that she would rather war with me. Her hate is so strong, it reminds me

heavily of you. If this is the path we must take, then so be it.
As of right now, Dasha and Kindy are at war.

-Queen Alisa Tia

The fear that was settling over me wasn't the kind of fear that you would think. It was rather a fear of what I was going to have to do. A fear that I had always been afraid of. War. I've never experienced it. And now I was going to have to participate in one. With both my sisters as the opposition. "Have you at least tried to persuade her otherwise?", I asked my mother. I couldn't imagine my mother wanted war any more than I did, but in the end, she wasn't known for backing down. "I'm sorry, Calypsa, but I'm afraid that what you read in that letter, I wholeheartedly agree with. The truth is that me and Alisa hate one another, and this war will balance things out.", "Like what? What are we even going to war over? Why can't Amana and I just settle this ourselves?". It wasn't that much of a stretch that my mother had some other ulterior motive for wanting to go to war with Alisa. And sure enough, I guessed right away, "The kind flowers. You want the whole field.", "Kindy is the only place they grow. I have plans for those flowers. Come. I want to show you something you might like.".

My mother had led me down to her vault. I had never been inside of her vault. Once, I had attempted to break into it, and see what she had in there. I had thought she might have some mystical item that would help me escape her. Unfortunately, she had caught me though, and punished me severely. My mother's vault was hard to get into. I remember trying all sorts of ways. But for the first time, I was seeing how you open it. She placed her hand on the door, after she pricked her hand for blood to come out. The door slid to the side, and I dropped my jaw. It was a vast collection of things I'd never laid eyes on before. There was one contraption that was constantly spinning so fast, I couldn't see what it was. There was a strange mirror that didn't show the person's reflection. There was what looked like a chemical station with all sorts of beakers containing strange colored liquids. But my mother had led me to a dirt patch. In the dirt were flowers that I had never seen before. They were green and shining, but the center was red. "These are called revealers. When I was young, I had the pleasure of partaking in the juices these flowers produce. Do you see the red center? It is supposed to be green. But this red stuff…", she led me to a room that had been located at the back. It was a cell. In the cell was a young man I recognized. Duson. Mother had chained him up. "Mother, what have you…?", before I could finish my question, Duson awoke and tried to come at me, but the chains didn't let him get anywhere near me. He was acting mad, and rabid, and was foaming at the mouth. "What is wrong with him?!", I asked incredulously. "This is what the revealer juices do in their current state. They turn people into these creatures. This is a perfect weapon to use against Alisa. But even more importantly, I want the revealers that existed twenty years ago. I need the green liquid. Not this one, even though, it shall have its uses.". I had no idea that my mother was such the mad scientist. "How long have you been trying to get these flowers to go back to their original color?", I asked, becoming intrigued by the whole experiment. "Well, ever since your father ascended. I don't know what made them turn red, but I figure that Alisa may have chemicals I could use to return it to its natural state.", "You didn't just think to ask her this?", "Calypsa, use your brain, dear. Do you really think Alisa would want me resurrecting the flower that gave me my insight? They only grew these in the Dark Wood. Only gods and goddesses are supposed to drink from them. But, Falsa told me to do it. She told me that it would make me wiser than I could know.", "Why did Falsa give you the kingdom and not her own daughter?". I had begun to wonder about the answer to that since I had met Ko-e. Ko-e was Falsa's daughter, so why would she give my mother Dasha? "Well, at the time, Ko-e wasn't even made yet. Also, Falsa had adopted me as her daughter. There are things I've learned about Falsa since then. Things that if I had known, things might have been different.". My mother laughed. I just continued to watch Duson. "What has Fod said about his son missing? How long have you had him here?", "Only a week. He came here trying to stir trouble. He said some very disrespectful things about you and that just made me angry.". She gave me a small smile. Then she led me to another cell. "This prisoner has been given something different. It is revealer juices that I came close to bringing back the green color to. It had turned blue. From there, I knew I had to see what this blue liquid would do. Perhaps, you recognize this girl?". When my mother opened the door, a girl with black hair and a very pretty face was lying on the floor. "Please help me…", the girl was saying. Her skin was doing a strange dance between a normal complexion and a strange blue tinge. "I'm still trying to see what's happening to her, but she just seems to be in some sort of pain. To be honest, for what she is guilty of, this is getting off easy. Her parents faced much worse.". I did know her. Her name was Mileeda, and she was hiding Ko-e, along with her family. I knew her father was a priest. I also knew she had a sister, but apparently, my mother hadn't caught her. "I plan on publicly executing the parents so that they can be an example. I want you to start being queenlier. I know you have never been a fan of your role…", "Okay. I understand. I will be queenlier. You're right. I've been a fool.". My mother looked stunned to see me agree with her. She beamed and pulled me into a hug, "I never thought I'd feel this with you. All you've ever shown me is hate.", "Well, who's fault is that?". We both laughed. Mileeda tried to stand and was barely able to hold herself up. She once again pleaded, "…help…". My mother went and grabbed the spinning object, which stopped spinning at her touch. It was a strange metallic contraption that had two large balls revolving around what looked like a strange green shard. "This, my daughter, is the last of the revealers in its pure form. I've been containing it in this ionic energy void. Let's see what happens when I expose her to it.". She threw the gem in the room and closed the door. You could hear Mileeda screaming on the other side. As terrifying as it was, I was interested in seeing what would happen. When the screaming stopped, mother opened the door. Mileeda was holding onto the wall with her back facing it. "Mileeda, how do you feel?", I asked. Mileeda looked up, and the next thing we knew, she had tried to attack me. She was extremely strong. My mother managed to pull her back and close the cell. She banged on the cell and dents showed on our side. I looked at my mother, "Incredible.", I thought, feeling on the dent and listening to Mileeda's crying. "Mother, would you indulge an idea I just came up with?", "Yes, by all means.". What I had planned was sinister, but I believed Mileeda could be used, just like our other experiments.

I proceeded into the village. I knew it would only be a matter of time before Ko-e showed up. Sure enough, she rode into the village on a thunder-horse(A single rider machine designed for faster travel). "Where is Mileeda and her family?", "Well, why don't you come this way and I'll lead you to them?". Ko-e looked uneasy. I didn't blame her. I felt different these days and I wouldn't trust me either. After all, I did have something nasty planned. Ko-e followed me none the less, and we ended up going to the castle, of course. "How did you like the thunder-horse? Only royalty can use one. You obviously borrowed Amana's. How is she? Is she healing?". Ko-e stopped and pushed me up against a wall. The guards that were nearby all pointed their swords at her. "Now you listen, I came here to take Mileeda and her family away from here. That is the only reason I am here. As far as I'm concerned, you are no sister of mine.". She released me, and I stared at her. She was not the same girl who I met in my shop. She was angered by the events of late. Before, she probably would have given me a straight answer to my question. Once we had arrived in the castle, I led her to the dining room. "Are you hungry, Ko-e? We have many new fruits that I and Amana have dreamt up. Try this one, it's called starlond. A fruit made from the dust of a star Amana...", "Stop it. Stop trying to distract me. Where is Taxin? Where is his wife and daughters? Tell me, now.", "The interesting thing about this fruit, is that it can sometimes cause hallucinations. Interesting, huh? That is the reason we both a…", she grabbed me by my throat. I in turn grabbed her, and we started tussling around the dining area, knocking things over. "You are the most sickening creature I've ever met!", said Ko-e, throwing me into a table. The guards ran in and surrounded Ko-e, who snapped her fingers expecting something. When nothing happened, she looked confused. She did it again, and this time, one of the guard's swords disappeared. "Ah, I see now. You're losing power. Been away from home for too long. Well, that makes what I have to do easier. Seize her, please.". As the guards started in towards Ko-e, she jumped behind one of them and knocked him across his head. He quickly fell out and she dashed around, quickly incapacitating the guards. When there was one guard left, he looked at me and ran. "Tsk, I will have that man whipped for his desertion.", "Are you really that far gone?", asked Ko-e, who was looking at me like she was barely seeing me. "How is Scion these days? It must be nice to be fucking the man your sister once fucked. It doesn't matter to me, I don't mind sharing. Tell Amana as well, I'm sure she would like to know what Scion is like.". At this point, I wanted to see how angry Ko-e could get. Ko-e smiled at me, which I wasn't expecting, "Well, I can tell you, he is definitely glad to be rid of you.". I felt a lump in my throat. Despite how much I told myself I didn't care, the truth was, I still felt something for Scion. Before I knew what I was doing, I was rushing towards Ko-e, with my dagger in my hand. I felt a hand wrap around my wrist, and I looked, and it was my mother, "Girls, this is quite unnecessary. If she wants to see what's become of her friend, then take her.". Mother smiled that evil smile she does when she is feeling happy for somebody else's misery. I allowed my mom to lead us to her vault, where she was keeping the 'special prisoners'. Ko-e watched as my mother pricked herself and used her blood to open the vault. "Micka, who are you really? A blood door can only be opened by those WITH god blood.". My mother didn't answer and just smiled. I hadn't given it any thought, but my mother did seem different. She wasn't like Queen Alisa, or King Tig, or Queen Tisiphone. She was somehow stronger, smarter, and faster. She seemed to have some kind of link to things I couldn't understand. Such as her knowledge of the revealers. I wondered what else my mother was keeping from me. We were standing outside of Duson's cell. My mother was going through with my plan. "Well, open the door, Ko-e.". Ko-e could sense that something was on the other side of the door, and that she shouldn't open it. But she did anyway, and Mother pushed her in, and closed the door behind her. Ko-e, on the inside, had screamed, and then, silence. My mother wanted to open the door, "No, we will come back later. I think there are more important things to do.". My mother nodded.

Later that evening, I was in my room and had received a letter from Amana. I was surprised to see that she was capable of writing in her condition. It was my impression that she would still be recovering. I looked at the letter and the writing suggested she was strong. I wondered if maybe her goddess blood healed her faster. The letter read;

Dear Calypsa,

We were best friends. We were sisters. By blood we still are. We have known for a long time that we were related. But now, I feel like my world, as I've known it, has ended, because you are no longer a sister I look to for comfort. You've tried to kill me, and for that, I don't know if I could forgive you. I live in Kindy, and you live in Dasha. We have known each other since we were little girls. You have tried to flee your mother's abuse several times. I have pleaded with my mother to save you. Now we both know the truth about ourselves and I wonder, what in that truth, could have turned my sister against me? Why must I sit up and cry and wonder will we ever have what we had? We built Plinth into what it is now. My mother respects what we have done. Now she is claiming war against your kingdom. I've told her there must be other ways, but she says

your mother intended this. Calypsa, I write to you not out of anger, but to plead with you to speak sense into your mother. This war will kill innocent people and there is no need for that. Please do this favor for me.

-Amana Tia

P.S

Ko-e has left to find Mileeda and her family. Can you at least insure their safety? Then I know, you are still there.

As the letter ended, I felt a dark place in my heart. Mileeda and her family were already suffering. Ko-e as well, was being either torn apart by Duson, or she was already dead. Ko-e was my blood-sister just like Amana. But figuring on how I hadn't met her until recently, I didn't care much for her. I knew that Amana would be angrier. I knew she was going to react in a way that if she didn't want to kill me before, she will now. I thought about it. Why am I doing this? Why am I doing all these things? At first, I was angry about Scion. Now, I realized it was more than that. Curiosity. That's all it really boiled down to. Seeing the result of everything. Seeing how it all turned out. I suddenly found myself outside of the castle and was staring into the face of Falsa. Her statue was glittered with small diamonds that were all different colors and the features of her face were really detailed. My mother hired the best sculptor in Dasha. Lincoln Tin, who just so happened to be Scion's father. What I knew of him was that he had found his wife with another man and being thrown from his home soon after, drove him to kill himself. This wasn't too long ago. I was sure this was the reason Scion didn't speak to his mother. Then the most clever idea came to me.

I went into the village looking for Scion's mother. Surely, she understood the amount of trouble he was in, and would most likely want to get him out of trouble. But for what I was going to need, it was going to take a lot of convincing. Even if it was doing something for her son, what I needed her for was going to be a rough agreement. I finally found the cottage. It was a small cottage. You didn't see very many of these now. It was mostly a poor thing. It was amusing. Scion had lots of coins, and yet, he allowed his mother to live in this squalor. I didn't feel sorry, but I wondered if she would aid her son. Before I could knock, the door opened, and a gruff looking man stepped out. He held a bottle of only what I could assume were spirits, and he didn't look very happy. He looked in my direction and a smile spread on his face, "Now what we got here?". His voice was slurred, and he was walking in a horizontal line towards me. "Very pretty.", he said, placing his hand on my face. I grabbed his hand and squeezed till I felt the pop. He screamed and backed away, clutching his hand, "YOU BITCH!", "If I were you, I'd sober up immediately.". The man looked like he would murder me, but was still in too much pain. A woman was now stepping out of the house. She wore what looked like a long shirt over a very nasty green pair of pants. "WHAT THE HELL IS GOING ON HERE?!", she yelled, as she made her way outside. She looked over the scene, then anger spread on her face, "YOU DAFT IDIOT! THIS IS THE PRINCESS! GET IN THE HOUSE!", she slapped the man on his head hard, and he stumbled, but went into the cottage grumbling. "What do you want? I would love to hear about you and my son. I assume that's why you are here. I always said he was too handsome for his own good.". The nerve of this woman. Speaking to me like I was some commoner. "Well, I am here because of your son, but the reason isn't what you might think.", "You want to save him from your mother, right?", she asked, placing her hands on her hips, and giving me an irritated look. "No, actually. I was hoping you could bring him to me and my mother.". She looked taken aback, "I'm sorry, I'm confused. You want me to condemn my son to his death?", "No. I want you to bring him back here and make him realize he belongs here. This is his home, not Kindy. Which I'm sure you haven't heard, but we are going to war with them.". Now she looked serious. Before, she was annoyed that I would come here, now I could see the worry creasing her brow. "You want to have him on your side, because he is smart, like his father was.", "He wasn't too smart, obviously.". I smiled to infuriate her. She ignored my sleight about her husband and continued, "I'm not telling him anything. My son and I may not be on talking terms, but it doesn't mean I'd betray him.", "Sad, I figured you'd say that. But what if it was for your niece?", "My niece? Is this some game to you, Princess? My niece and her parents were slaughtered by Falsa.". I laughed inside. The first time I had seen Alexa, I knew she was a Dashin. She may have grown up close to Heaven, but there are some things you can tell right away. "Would I mention her, if she were dead?", I asked, watching for an expression on her face. The man poked his head outside, "Lona, I need more stony.", "Get inside the house…now!". She was in control of this gentleman. He listened without arguing. I admired her. "Listen, my sister was executed. I don't appreciate you coming here and dragging all this up. I am now, kindly asking you to leave, Princess.", "Well, I guess if you don't want to know the truth, that's up to you, but I on the other hand will now go about my way to secure the safety of this kingdom.". I started to walk away. Then I felt a hand on my shoulder, "Prove my niece lives, and I will aid you.". I stared Lona in the face for some time, and then we grabbed each other's hand and shook.

I decided to go check on Ko-e and see if she was dead yet. I made my way back to my mother's vault. I did the blood prick and it opened for me. As soon as I entered, I knew something was wrong. Mileeda's door was wide open and she was nowhere to be found. I quickly went to Duson's cell, and put my hand on the door, which flew open at my touch. Standing inside was a pissed off, bloody Ko-e, and a dead Duson, with his neck completely snapped. "So, this is how you treat your blood? This is how you repay me for wanting to free my friend? Calypsa, I will not attempt to kill you. You will meet a very sad ending. And I will watch with great pleasure.". She stepped out of the cell and then I felt that jolt rush through me again. Ko-e was doing something. She had taken something inside of me. I felt it. "I bet Scion was mad when you left him in Kindy. But you should be careful, Amana wrote to me, which means she is probably well enough to take him off your hands.". Ko-e stopped and turned to face me. In her eyes was pure hatred, "Goodbye, Calypsa.". With that, she turned and walked out, closing the vault door. I stood up, brushing myself off, then I was knocked out.

When I came to, I found myself in a very precarious position. Mileeda had tied me up. When I tried to snap the ropes, I found it impossible. "Gold makes you weak. You can't break that.". How she suddenly knew this, I didn't know. I struggled more, but to no avail. "I honestly used to think you were different. That Calypsa is not her mother. When I saw how you stood there, with that disgusting look of happiness, I knew…that you are your mother.". I felt angry. I couldn't argue that my actions of late did make me in my mother's image, but there were things that I still didn't understand. Like, why I was doing all this. "So, you're just going to keep trying to free yourself? You're not even going to answer for this injustice?", "What the hell do you want me to say? You don't matter, Mileeda. Your whole family will soon be dead.", I said, trying to keep her off balance. But she looked at peace. Even with the strange blue tinge her skin now had. "I had a really nice time in my cell. I learned new things about myself. Like the fact that your mom…will regret what she has done. She will regret everything that she has ever done. All the evil she has committed. She will know fear.", "You don't think she ever has? What do you know about my mother? If it wasn't for her, your family would have died twenty years ago!", "YOUR MOTHER IS AN EVIL BITCH!", Mileeda suddenly shouted, losing her cool posture. "My mother was and is the best thing for Dasha! I may not have realized it before, but I do now. What my mother has turned you into is beautiful.", "And what about what she turned Duson into? Was that meant to be beautiful? SHE TURNED HIM INTO A MONSTER!", "Well then, maybe Duson should have been taught to watch his mouth!". Mileeda slapped me so hard, the chair I was sitting in fell over. My jaw was in agony. Injecting her with the revealer fluid has made her very strong. She lifted my chair and got in my face, "I'm going to let you live, Calypsa, because my friend has asked me to, but after I'm gone, you will realize I haven't really left.". I was hit again, and then I was out.

This time when I came to, my mother was untying me. "Calypsa, we need to stay in here for the time being. Things are a bit chaotic out there.". I was still groggy, but I was awake enough to ask, "What do you mean?". I could hear shouting in the distance and what sounded like battle. There was a bang on the vault door. "Do not worry, they can't get in.". The banging on the door continued, until I finally heard an awful scream. Then the door started to open. My mother grabbed me and led me to one of the cells. She closed the door and told me to stay inside. Standing at the vault was a young man. He was very smug looking, but he wore what looked like royal armor made of gold and silver. He strode into the vault and his eyes found my mother, who I noticed looked slightly worried. I had never seen my mother look this scared before and was shocked to see her act this way. "Where is Ko-e, Micka? What the hell have you done with my sister?", "Caprius, I wasn't expecting you. I thought you were quite busy in Alexandria.", "No, as a matter of fact, I've been worried sick about Ko-e. Alexa has informed me that Calypsa has tried to kill Amana. And has made attempts on Ko-e as well.". My mother looked like she was going to piss herself. I couldn't understand why this, Caprius, had this effect on her. Then I remembered exactly who he was. "Caprius, I can't be expected to…". Caprius cut my mother off, "You can't be expected to what? To actually give a shit? I told Sebastian not to trust you with any of this.", "Falsa, your mother, gave me Dasha! Who is Sebastian to take that away?!", "Well, for starters, he is OUR creator. He deserves respect. Speaking of respect, you now have a choice, give up Calypsa, now, or give up your kingdom.".

My mother looked torn. She wasn't giving away my hiding place, but rather was starting to get her momentum. "Give up Calypsa? To whom?", "Give her up to me. I am now the liaison between this planet and Bastian. And he says Calypsa needs to be dealt with.", "Well, I can handle my own daughter.", "She is HIS daughter as well.". Now my mother looked more nervous, and she spoke in a voice I had never heard, "Caprius…please…she is my daughter. She is all I have! I don't want to lose her! Please tell Sebastian! Please!". Mother was on her knees at Caprius' feet, begging him not to take me. It was such a pitiful scene for a woman who I used to fear. "There is no negotiating on this. If you truly wanted to keep your daughter, you would have raised her better.", "LIKE HOW YOU RAISED KO-E?! SHE IS THE REASON FOR ALL OF THIS!", "And Ko-e will be taken home as well, when we find her.", "I had her here, but she escaped! Now you want to punish me?", "This isn't your punishment, even though you deserve one. My mother would be ashamed if she knew how you raised your daughter and how you treated her's.". My mother quickly grabbed one of her beakers, filled with the red liquid, and broke it upon Caprius' head. He stumbled, and within that time, my mother wrenched the door open of the cell I was hiding in, "RUN!". I didn't think about it, I rushed past Caprius who was still recovering and ran all the way out of the castle. Only then did I see what was happening. Men in the same colored armor but more meager looking than Caprius', were battling Dashin soldiers in the streets. It was a bloody battle, and in it, I saw bright green hair rushing towards me. Before I could move, Alexa was on top of me. She had me pinned to the ground. "Well, I was hoping I'd catch you. Time to pay up for what you did to Amana!", "That was an accident!", I yelled, trying to break free, but I was still weak from when Mileeda had me tied. Then, as if it was meant, Alexa was pulled off of me by Lona, who was holding her by her neck with both arms and was giving me the nod to get away. I ran off to the stables, where I could find my thunder-horse and hopped on. I turned the mechanism to start it, and rode out of Dasha as fast as I could. The battle was taking place outside of the kingdom gates as well. I found myself pushing forward. Once I had got out of Dasha, I didn't know where I was headed, but I knew that it had to be worse than where I just left.

CHAPTER 8

Alexa's Trip: Tig's New Problem

ALISA: Amana was still weak, but still managed to boss and order people around. She was dealing with all the war necessities. She made sure there were more men than usual stationed at regular posts throughout the villages, she made sure that I took out all the extra stationary weapons and placed them at entrances and outer viewpoints, she had made sure to tell Sheena to keep her special guard ready at all times. She was, herself, prepared. She was barely able to hold a sword, so she was working in the lab on some new weapon that she would be able to hold and use easily in her condition. I decided I'd go check on her in her lab and see how she was doing. The lab was busy. Workers moving all over the place, trying not to bump into each other. I stopped a young girl with white hair and asked, "Where is my daughter?". The girl pointed to an area where all I saw was a mountain of raw materials. Then, moving closer, I saw that Amana was working behind this wall. She had pieced together what looked like a hand-held cannon. It all seemed so complicated to look at. I remember my days of just mixing chemicals. But my daughter could do that and create all sorts of easy things to use. "Mother, you really shouldn't come in here without the proper wear.". I noticed everyone was wearing a gown. "I didn't have the time. Look, I wanted to talk to you about all this prepping you are doing. I think you should relax. You still aren't fully recovered from…", "Mom, I just need some time right now. I need to work to clear my head.". I looked down and saw she had a letter. The letter was from Calypsa and it was short;

Dear Amana,

I'm not going to even try and do anything you've asked. My mother is going through with this war and I agree with her. I'm sorry that it has come to this, my sister. But in the end, we both realize, I'm sure, that being children of Sebastian, only one of us can rule this planet. And that's what this is all about. Who will rule. I don't know about you, but I look forward to the day we find out who that will be. You, me, or our dear Ko-e.

-Calypsa.

I knew right when I finished reading that this was the cause of Amana's new vigor. She was terrified of what Calypsa was going to do, but at the same time, she was hurting from losing her best friend. "Amana, I know what you're feeling, but you need the rest.", "What I need is peace to work.". The message being quite clear, I let her get on with her work. Coming out of the lab, I ran into the least of all people I wanted to see. "Where is Amana? I have questions I know only she can answer.". Scion had been circling Amana like a vulture. There was a huge part of me that did not like Scion. I often saw how he stared at Amana and it only angered me more. I saw him kissing Ko-e, and now he was eyeing Amana. "Amana is busy and doesn't even have time to speak to her mother, Scion, so why not leave her alone?", "You don't understand!", "Actually, Scion, I do. You are wondering what your role in this whole thing is.", "Damn straight!", "But, you need to be patient. There are still things I'm trying to figure out, too.", "Well, Sebastian came to me, and he told me that I was a part of this. That I was supposed to be with Calypsa and that he didn't intend for me to be in this position.". Scion was a pain in my ass. But once he told me Sebastian had come to him in a dream, I forgot all of that, "Sebastian came to you? What did he say? Did he mention me?". Scion eyed me with a very surprised look. I felt my face burn and I quickly tried to look down, but the damage was done. "So, you still want him? That's funny. After how he abandoned you with his child, all you can worry about is if he mentioned you?", "It isn't like that, and I wouldn't expect you to understand. And I don't care how close to this situation you are, you do not get to talk to me like that!". I felt like I used to feel when I'd tell Amana she couldn't play with Calypsa. Scion was right. My feelings for Bastian were overtaking the fact that I should be concerned with the upcoming battle. I walked away from him, before I could embarrass myself some more. I was extremely angry with Sebastian. He visited Scion, but not me. I had the ability to enter people's dreams, but Bastian couldn't be bothered to check on me. If I found out he had been contacting Micka as well, I was ready to shout him down here.

The days had passed by quickly and I had gotten word, from Caprius of all people, explaining that he had attacked Dasha under orders from Bastian, and that Micka was being held. I thought to myself that this should be the end of this. Unfortunately, the letter went on to explain that Calypsa had gotten away and that I should be on the lookout. This was far from over. Alexa had been missing as well and nobody knew where she was. This was getting tense. I had sent out some scouts to help in the search of Alexa. I wasn't the only one either. Tisiphone had arrived in Kindy, with a satisfied look on her face, "I knew this would happen one day, I just knew it. Bastian is finally coming to his senses about Micka.", she said, greeting me in my throne hall. "Let's go to my private meeting room.". Upon entering, Amana was already waiting inside. "Tisiphone, it's good to see you.", "Likewise, Amana! You are so beautiful now!", she replied, pulling Amana into a very hard-pressed hug. "Listen, there are some things that your mother...". Amana cut her off, "I know that my father is Sebastian.". Tisiphone looked shocked at this revelation, and so I had to bring her up to date, "I don't understand... You're telling me that Ko-e's presence here on Plinth, somehow has affected Calypsa's mind, and now she has gone mad?". I nodded. "So, Calypsa is missing, and nobody has seen Alexa? Have you considered they might be together somewhere?", "I don't think so.", Amana replied, "Alexa went to capture her after she tried to kill me.", "But, why would she try to kill you in the first place? I thought that you two love each other?". I was surprised that Tisiphone knew this much, but of course, I had told Tig, who in turn told his wife. "Where is Nigel?", I asked, changing the subject. Amana was looking rather upset by Tisiphone's question. "He is helping to search for Alexa. I haven't told him everything, but he chooses not to question. Do you think I should have told him?", "No, you made the right choice by not telling him. But we need to worry about Calypsa. She is the real threat. If we find her, then maybe we can end this war.". Amana, and Tisiphone both nodded.

Later that evening, as I was walking on my garden path, I was approached by a strangely cloaked individual. I looked around for guards, but there were none and I knew something was off. How did this person get into the castle? I watched them, and they just stared back at me. Finally, they removed the hood and I saw pink hair, with a glowing individual attached to it. "ALEX!", I shouted, and I rushed forward and embraced her. She hugged me, too, and then pushed me away, "It's good to see you, too.", she smiled. "Why are you here, Alex?", I asked, suddenly realizing she wouldn't have just come to visit. "I'm sorry, Alisa, but I need Amana to come with me.", "Why?", I asked. The look in Alex's eyes wasn't exactly uplifting. "We can't let what's about to happen come to pass. We need to stop it. If Amana comes with me, there just might be a chance we can prevent this.", "Where do you want to take her?". Alex glared hard into my eyes, "Alexandria. We need her to stay there until we find Calypsa and end this.". I considered it. But looking into Alex's eyes, I knew there was more. "Alex, what are you trying not to tell me?". Alex turned her back on me and stared at the hedges shaped like kind flowers. "I can't explain everything, but if she doesn't come with us, something terrible is going to happen.", "Who is us?". Someone else appeared, also wearing a cloak. Once they removed the hood, I realized I had never seen this person before. He looked like he didn't really care for his surroundings, and he had the same red rim and gold eyes as the girls. "Listen, Alisa, I don't want to be here any longer than I have to. So, let's just get this over with, shall we?", he said. Before I could think of an answer to that, he pulled out a sword that looked vaguely familiar, "If you don't bring her, we shall take her.". I looked to Alex for support. "Brixin, there is no need for this, put that away, Alisa is going to cooperate.". Brixin looked me over and then sheathed his sword into what looked like thin air. "Alex, what is going to happen to my daughter if I let her leave?", I asked, not taking my eyes off Brixin. "Well…". Brixin cut her off, "She will die. All of them. They are abominations that must be rectified. Perhaps except Ko-e.". I felt numb. I looked at Alex, who was suddenly stone quiet. My mouth starting to dry, I answered, "No. I will not let you take my daughter like this. What the hell is wrong with Sebastian? You tell that son-of-a-bitch I want a word.", "My father doesn't have to answer to you, and you will show him respect!". So, Brixin was Alex's son. I saw the resemblance. He had short hair that he seemed to have shaved, but it was pink colored, and he had his father's face. He was Sebastian's twin. "I knew your father way before you were even thought of, you disrespectful little shit! How dare you come into MY kingdom and demand something like this? Alex, how could you?". Alex turned back to face me, "Alisa, let me ask you, would you rather your daughter destroy this planet, or would you rather let her die to protect that from happening?". I thought that was an impossible question. Amana would never destroy the planet. She loved it and the people on it, then I remembered something, "Alex, I want to talk to you, in private, please?", I asked, looking at Brixin, who was giving me the most hated look he could muster. Alex walked away with me, giving her son only a nod. "Alisa, I understand, it is a lot, but Bastian isn't the one giving this order. Believe it or not, we have those we must answer to as well.", "But, Bastian created us, he is our god. I don't understand who he has to report to.", "Have you ever thought about who created Bastian?". I hadn't ever thought that far ahead. "There is something I never told you, though, Alex, I've seen Amana. In the future.", "I remember, you told us.", "Yes, but not everything.". I explained when Desian tried to kill me, and I was transported to the future, Amana explained it had been three-thousand years and that she would take care of this war. Alex was angry with me. "Why didn't you ever tell me this?", "Because there was so much already happening at the time, I wasn't worried about a second war.". Alex considered this for some time, then nodded, "If this is true, and she really did tell you that, then perhaps, you might be right in saying we shouldn't get involved.". Alex said, with that same thinking face she always made. I noticed that she looked the same and showed hardly any signs of age. I, on the other hand, felt like an old tomato, even though, neither me, nor Micka, had signs of age either. "Okay, it's settled, then. Amana will handle this. Brixin, we are going.". Brixin was admiring the garden when Alex called out to him. "...okay.", he said, breaking away from a rogue kind flower that had grown in the garden. They just seemed to disappear. "Mom, who was that?". Amana had come out into the garden. "Nobody special.", I replied, knowing she would know I wasn't being truthful. But she didn't need to know how close to death she was.

ALEXA: I had been dragged to someone's house. I had no idea where I was. I had been knocked out, and the last thing I remembered was being taken by a strange woman with teal hair. Food was brought to me regularly. It was pushed through a hole in the door, but I could never see who was passing it to me. One day, the door opened, and a man holding a bottle was standing in the doorway. He walked in and closed the door and stared at me. "Who are you? Where the hell am I?". The man didn't answer, and he set the bottle down. "Lona isn't here now, sweet. Let's have some fun while she is gone.". The man made for me, and I quickly twisted his arm behind his back. He yelled in agony. "I SAID WHERE THE HELL AM I?!". The man was too busy yelling to answer. The door busted open, and the strange woman, who for some reason looked familiar, was standing there. She made for the man, and grabbed him from me, and broke the bottle over his head, "I TOLD YOU TO NEVER COME IN HERE! OUT! GET OUT OF THE HOUSE!". The man cowered away, and the woman turned towards me. I guessed right away who she was, "You're Scion's mother, aren't you?". She nodded. She came and ran her hand across my face, and tears rolled out of her eyes, "You are my sister's daughter. I can't believe this. I thought you died with your parents...". She continued to look me over for another minute. "Listen, this little reunion is fun and all, but I need to get going. I have respon...". She cut me off, "Listen, you are to remain here. It's too dangerous out there right now.". I was confused on how she didn't understand what my situation was. "I am the Queen of Alexandria. I need to go.", "You are my family and I will protect you. And my son.", "Scion is safe in Kindy.", "He isn't safe anywhere. You don't understand. If Micka doesn't get him, then Calypsa will. That girl wants to kill my son. I saw it in her face.". I knew this was true, but I didn't have time. "My husband will be searching for me.", "He is, and we have already pointed him elsewhere.". This woman was impossible. "Why are you doing this? What do you even expect to happen now?", "I just want the chance to understand why my niece lives.". I started to remember her. Her and my mother had a close relationship. But one day, my father had crossed Falsa and was to be executed. When my mother decided we should all flee, my parents were captured, and I managed to get away. I was found by Alex, who took me to Alexandria, and there I've been for the past twenty years.

After I explained all this to my aunt, she cried at the part when I told her how I married Caprius. "You do realize exactly who he is, don't you?". It suddenly dawned on me why she was keeping me here. "He isn't what he used to be. He is different. He only looks out for the good of everyone.". As I spoke more with my aunt, she was convinced that Calypsa was deranged, "She is obsessed with my son, and she may not be able to see it, but I can. She will get him killed.", "I can protect him. I grew up close to Heaven and I was trained to battle with gods. I must go. But I promise, I will come back and see you.". She smiled at me and nodded.

As I proceeded out of the house, the grumpy man who tried to assault me was sitting against a barrel. I hadn't asked Lona who he was, but decided I'd go and try to find my husband. I didn't have to search for long because I found him inside of the castle. When I walked in, the men rushed me to him. "Alexa, I have been worried about you.". He embraced me, and I kissed him. "I was worried about you. Don't worry, I've been safe, I was just with family. I'll explain later.", I said, because I saw the look on Caprius' face, and I knew what he was going to ask. "We have Micka locked up, if you would like a word with her.". I noticed my husband had a strange scar on his left temple. "Sweet, what is this?", I asked, touching it. He grabbed my hand, "Why not ask Micka?". I had a soldier lead me to where she was being kept. She looked unhinged. She had been writing on the walls. I recognized the writing as Godlic, the language of Sebastian. "Micka, what is all this?", I asked, looking around the cell. Micka's eyes fell on me and she stood up straight. "Well, it's just a story.". The circles within circles covered half her cell and she looked positively proud of it. "Micka, are you feeling alright? What did you do to Caprius?". Micka looked at me sharply and then laughed, "Has something happened to him? Is he different? Please tell me?", "What has happened to you? You look mad.", "Mad?", Micka repeated, "Not mad, just awake. I can see where all this is going, hehe. And as for Sebastian, well, tell him I'll be waiting for him, just like last time.".

She started to laugh, and I realized I wasn't going to get anything out of her.

"She is mad.", I told Caprius later, as we laid in the bed of the royal guest chambers. "She has always been. Part of me thinks my mother knew that about her. Why else would she put her in charge of the kingdom?", "Yes, but there is more to it than that. Like how is she able to read and write Godlic? We can't even do that, and I grew up in Alexandria. We have always been as close to them as the stars, but we don't know how to speak their language. Micka does, and Falsa couldn't have taught it to her. So, what do you think?". Caprius was deep in thought on this subject. I knew that Sebastian could tell me. He knew the answer to this mystery. I decided to go to sleep. As I was sleeping, I found myself in a strange land. Everything looked new, and fresh, and the buildings were made of metal and stone. Plus, they were as tall as the turrets to the castle in Alexandria. I marveled at what I was seeing. Then I saw a house, not as big as the buildings it was surrounded by. It was a three-story house, painted black, and if you were to not be looking for it, you'd miss it. As the door opened, out came a familiar glowing black hair individual. She was looking at a small object in her hand and looked up and noticed me. "Alexa...? But that can't be...". She looked around, then pulled me into the house, which was a lot bigger on the inside. I knew that there was godly magic involved. "Alexa, how did you get here?", "I don't know, where are we, Ko-e?". Before she could answer, there was a bang on the door. "You need to hide. She can't see you here.". Ko-e put me in what looked like a huge closet filled with all sorts of clothing I'd never seen before. I could see through a small hole in the door and I was shocked at what I was seeing. "Where is it, Ko-e? The energy signal stopped right outside your door.", "Amana, I've told you already, I want nothing to do with this craziness. Trust me, if something showed up here, I would just tell you.", "You know what? I'd like to believe that, but certain things you've kept from me in the past, say otherwise.". Amana was wearing a leather outfit with a strange emblem on the shoulders and on her chest. There were two others with her. A man and a woman, and their uniforms were black but looked like cotton, and they had the same emblem. They wore berets as well that also had the emblem, but written underneath were the letters; P.E.D. "I know that I haven't always been honest, but really, this was no reason to show up with your two cronies.". The man and the woman looked at each other. "Do you know what a level-six threat is?", "No. You know good and well I never looked into your complicated system of rules.". The two glared at each other, and Amana continued, "A level six threat, is a time displacement. Someone from the future or the past becoming fluid in the present. P.E.D watches for these things. And one of those things, just spiked outside this residence.", "Well, I didn't see anything. So, you can rest easy.", Ko-e said, glaring daggers at Amana. "So, then you don't mind if we search your house, then, right?", "Actually, I do mind. Because I have just as much right to my privacy as you have, Amana.", "Mam, the energy is headed in a different direction.". Amana looked at something in the woman's hand and nodded. "Well, Ko-e, it appears that whatever it was might have nothing to do with you after all. Listen, you two are taking over this situation. I need the both of you to get a time displacement team over there and inform me of the secondary threat level once you arrive on-site.". Amana looked at Ko-e, nodded, and then departed. Ko-e waited until she was sure Amana wasn't coming back, then came and opened the door. I knew where I was, but not when. "How many years have passed?", I asked as soon as she opened the door. "It's been over three-thousand. You died three-thousand years ago. I don't understand how you got here.". I explained to her what was going on where I had just come from, and that I went to sleep and suddenly was here. "That's why you disappeared for some time. Nobody knew where you were. Then you showed up and…", "And what? What happened?". Ko-e looked morbid. "Alexa, my brother is sick. Micka did something to him. When you get back there, you need to stay away from him. You can't cure him.", "What did Micka do?", "I can't explain it to you. Just trust me. As for the war, you don't need to worry about that. It'll end peacefully. It's what happened after that, that was evil.". I listened to Ko-e's story. P.E.D is Amana's secret army. Plinth is now made up of multiple nations, all with their own armies. They've attacked each other a few times. And amid all the killing and suffering, Amana uses the cover to send people on missions of the highest importance to protect the planet. Amana doesn't try to stop the other fighting. She doesn't care about Plinthinians killing each other. All she cares about are the threats that could kill all of us. Ko-e was considered a threat in Amana's eyes, but was forced to treat her equally. Unless she wanted another war on her hands like before. Listening to Ko-e made me realize that things weren't going to get one-hundred percent better, but they would transform into craziness. "Ko-e, what about Micka? Do you know anything about her?", "All I know is that she…".

I never heard the answer, because I was woken up by a strange sound next to me. I looked over and Caprius had gotten out of the bed. "Sweet, what's wrong?", "Kill…kill…kill…". I got out of the bed and grabbed my blade nearby. I watched him closely to see what he was doing exactly. I moved slowly around to face him, and saw that his eyes had turned red, and blood was running out of them. "CAPRIUS!", I shouted. I moved towards him, but he grabbed me, and threw me away from him. "KILL ME! ALEXA, KILL ME NOW!". I started to cry. Ko-e told me something was going to be wrong with him, and now I see what it is. The scar on the side of his head had a strange red glow to it. It seemed to be coming out of his head. "Caprius…don't ask me that. Please.". Caprius fell to the floor and looked like he was wrestling with himself, "Alexa, I don't want to hurt you, I love you. Please, kill me.". I stood over him with my blade, and was about to plunge it into him, when he suddenly growled and pushed me. I hit the wall and felt the back of my head starting to bleed. When I woke up, Caprius was gone and I had no idea what I was going to do.

TIG: Being the King of Nasher had all the perks you could want. Food whenever, every woman wants you, and even better, is everyone listens to you without question. Over the last twenty years, Sebastian's daughters have transformed Plinth into a paradise. PE made living so easy. My son, Nigel, tries his hardest to have Sebastian's daughters. Calypsa is his prime target, but Amana has really held the candle. Unfortunately, neither want anything to do with poor Nigel. Not that he hasn't had his share of women. Calypsa being Micka's daughter, I always felt sort of kin to her and would love her as a daughter-in-law. But the letters I've sent to Micka, hoping she might indulge this idea, have fallen on embers. Micka has decided to close everyone off. Calypsa, from what I understood, had a very troubled childhood. And now from what Nigel has told me, she has gone and given her heart and body to the man who created the over-glorified computer. Of course, the recent news was more troubling than that. Calypsa tried to kill Amana. Stabbed her straight through the shoulder. And, Ko-e, Falsa's daughter, was here somewhere, and even worse, is now, Kindy and Dasha are going to war. I'm expected to take a side, but I don't see why I should. Micka is an old friend, and Alisa isn't really somebody I've been close with. I was more for Micka, but Tisiphone, my wife, has a hatred so deep for Micka, I'd be a fool to side with her. Micka had killed her father, and that was, of course, a good enough reason to want to kill somebody. She has had to make due with the fact that because Micka is Ruler of Dasha, she couldn't make a move on her. And because she was the mother of one of Sebastian's children, that has kept her from raising a sword to her neck. This never stopped her complaining about her. But now, Micka has started a new war, it felt like things weren't going to get as crazy as they got last time. There was no Desian to go around killing everyone, and there was no Falsa to keep playing or tricking people. I figured this war would end easily. After all, it was really based on how much Micka and Alisa hate each other. Both are moms with the same father for their children. I was glad Tisiphone only had Nigel, and none of Sebastian's kids. Although, I feared that she would have gladly had one of his children. "My king, there is something you must come and see!", one of the men was calling to me. I left my seat to find out what he was talking about. Nigel had beaten me to the scene. A man was lying on the ground just outside of Nasher. He had a crowd of soldiers surrounding him and one of them was already dead. His neck had been bitten. "What the hell is going on here?", "Father, I don't know what is wrong with this man, but he's one of our soldiers. He's been infected with something.". The man stood up and lunged at another soldier. Quickly, the soldier stabbed him with a sword, but the man was still trying to get him, foaming at the mouth. As crazy as the scene looked, there was also the fact that this man was familiar to me. "HALT!", I yelled. The men backed away to allow me to view the man up close. The man was named Cecil, and I knew him to have a wife and son. I looked him in his eyes and they were blood red. He seemed to be calming down, but then he lunged at me once I had gotten a bit closer. I took out my blade and stabbed him through the top of his head. "I want someone to find out what the hell happened to this man. Whoever can bring me any info will get thirty pounds of coin. Spread the word. Nigel, we need to talk.". My son nodded his head, and we proceeded to the castle. As we entered, I rounded on him, "How long ago was he discovered in this condition?", "Twenty minutes ago. He kept trying to bite everyone, eventually biting poor Nover's neck and killing him on the spot. When we tried to stab him, he wouldn't die.". I placed my face in my hands. Cecil was a good man. One of my best soldiers. I had never had an issue with him and now all of a sudden, he became wildly sick with something. "Do we have any medication that could prevent this? Whatever IT is.", I asked Nigel. Nigel did all the business, and so I assumed he would know. "I don't think so, Father, but I can take a sample of blood to Amana and maybe she can come up with something.". I felt my stomach growl at the idea of Amana finding the cure. "Son, I don't think we need to be getting involved with them at the moment. After all, they are at war.", "But, only Amana can possibly aid us. We don't know what this thing is, but it's defint…", Nigel stopped talking, because there was a scream. We both made our way back out the castle, only to discover Nover was now walking around, and he had a look in his eyes that suggested he was infected the same way as Cecil. Nigel rushed forward and put his sword through his head and Nover fell to the floor. I was suddenly reminded of something. As I looked around, there was a girl, who was holding her hand. She looked no more than fourteen. Her mother, from what I assumed, was wrapping her hand in a cloth. The girl was looking sweaty and I knew what was coming. "Seize that girl. But do it respectfully. She is sick.", The soldier who I spoke to walked over to the woman and the girl and the woman made a scene, "…YOU CAN'T TAKE MY DAUGHTER! PLEASE NO! YOUR MAJESTY! HELP ME!". I approached the poor girl, who was looking even more sweaty. "Listen, your daughter has been bitten by that gentleman.", I said, pointing to Nover, who was now being put into a cart. "We need to at least let our med team look at her to make sure…", "MY DAUGHTER DOESN'T NEED ANYTHING BUT ME!", the woman yelled. I could see this wasn't going to be an easy parting. I motioned for Nigel to come. "Mam, I really am so humbly sorry. If it makes you feel at ease, you may accompany her.". The woman considered this, then nodded and proceeded to follow Nigel to the med area.

ALEXA: I made my way to the dungeon where Micka was being kept. I had the soldiers open the door. Micka was still insanely writing out Godlic letters on her walls. "Micka, what happened to Caprius?". Micka turned and looked at me with a smile on her face, "So, it's happened, then? He's transformed? What was it like? Was it beautiful?", "DO YOU THINK I AM JOKING WITH YOU?!" I asked, feeling my blood rise. I could feel the blood running down the back of my head, getting tangled in my hair. But I didn't care about that at the moment. "A joke? No. I don't think you are joking. But I warned him. I told him not to try and take my daughter. Now I don't know where she is.". Micka placed her face in her hands and started to shake uncontrollably. I wondered where Calypsa had gotten to as well, but was more concerned about my husband. "Micka, you had better tell me what you did.", I said flatly. "Caprius is supposed to be the King of Dasha. But instead, he became king of Sebastian's false kingdom. And married the little welch who lost her parents. I have an idea, if you let me out.". I never thought I could feel so angry. Ko-e used to ask a lot of questions, but I always kept my patience with her. Micka was tiring in a way I didn't think or imagine was possible. "I can cure Caprius, but you must let me out.", "I AM NOT LETTING YOU OUT!", I yelled at her. Micka just stood with a haughty smile and returned to her writing, "Well, do let me know when you want to have your 'sweet' again.". I stormed away, tears falling down my face. I quickly wiped them and called forth some men, "I need you to find King Caprius. He may not be himself, so be weary.", "Aye, mam, and what about the queen?", "Leave her to rot in her cell until she decides to tell us what we need to know.". I knew that I had to ride off to Nasher, because nobody there really knew the full extent of the danger now being posed. I quickly wrote a letter to Alisa and made my way to Nasher.

When I arrived in Nasher, I could tell something was off right away. "HALT, WHO THE HELL ARE YOU?!", I was asked by a Nashin guard. "Queen Alexa of Alexandria.". The man looked at me, then stared back at the other guard. "It's alright, let her through!", said Prince Nigel, who was coming to fetch me. I had never met Nigel, though, and didn't understand how he might know me. "I was asked to search for you some time back, but then we had a situation here that gained my attention. I do apologize.", he said. "What situation do you have here?". He led me to an area with tents. The tents seemed to take up a quarter of the kingdom. As we made our way through the tents, I noticed people being given medication and resting. We were in a sick med. Nigel led me to a tent all the way at the back. Inside was a man who had been chained with gold chains. The man looked very weak. But as I moved close enough, I realized it was

Caprius. "He seems to be in his right mind at times, but at others...". Caprius looked up at me, with those bloody eyes, and I saw sadness. "Please, you have to help him.", "We want to. But there is a bit of an issue. First, he bit one of my men, who turned into a creature, who bit another man, who bit a little girl, who is in a very bad state. Believe me, we want a cure. But the only one who can help in that department is Amana, and my dad doesn't want anything to do with the war.". What the hell does that mean? Just as I was pondering that, "Well, I wasn't expecting this. You've grown into quite the woman. Very beautiful. Now if you would kindly leave before some more trouble shows up, I would appreciate that.", "Tig, what are you talking about? You can't avoid the problem. Do you know who this man is?", "He looks like Caprius.", "You do know what he does for Sebastian, right?". Tig looked uneasy, but none the less, stood by his decision, "Listen, it's nothing personal against you, but I don't want that war coming anywhere near Nasher. We got enough issues and Amana doesn't need to add that to her plate. Please, if you want to ask her for the cure, then I would love that, but in the meantime, please give Nasher its space.". I was angry, but Tig would keep Caprius here and I would be allowed to make a difference by going to Kindy and hoping Amana would help me.

As I left Nasher and headed for Kindy, I found myself in a forest. I was wishing I had my Caprius with me. I remembered when I first told him how I felt. I knew it was strange coming from me, but there was this agreement that we shared. We both agreed we'd be there for Ko-e, no matter what. Caprius had a kind heart that was surrounded by mud. He was raised by a woman who was so evil, and so shameful, that I always had a hard time believing she was from Alexandria. But I guess that what happened to her was so sad and messed up, it was no wonder she turned into what she did. Falsa had been a goddess like Alex, but was killed for fear she would bring Sebastian's vengeance. I laid in the grass, crying into my sleeve. How could I have been so stupid as to allow myself to trust Micka? We all knew what she was capable of, but I thought she would be past all of that. We were trying to stop the girls from meeting. We were trying to do what Sebastian asked of us. Now I finally knew the suffering that came from it. I finally understood what Micka had done to anger everyone and make them hate her. I barely remembered the last war. How much it took. I remember I had lost Alex. She never visited. Alex was my adopted sister, and she saved my life when I was a little girl. Now she was too busy to see how I was doing. I heard a noise and a girl with strange blue skin had made her presence known. "Who...?", I started to say, then she held up a hand and pointed behind me. Ko-e was standing behind me. She was covered in dirt and blood, and looked angry. "Alexa, I would hug you, but...", she waved her arms in an up and down motion to symbolize how dirty she was. "KO-E, WHAT HAS HAPPENED TO YOU?!", I asked, looking at her in horror. "Micka and Calypsa tried to kill me.". I heard the words, but still couldn't believe it. "Did you say, Micka tried to kill you?", "Yes, both of them. They both tried to kill me, using a poor boy they've experimented on.". Ko-e explained to me how Micka had been experimenting on her citizens with this liquid from a flower called a revealer. Her intentions were to use this as a weapon against Alisa and take Kindy from her. "Are you telling me that Micka was planning this war this whole time?", "From the sounds of it, yes. And what's worse, is she has somehow turned these poor people into something else. Look what she has done to Mileeda. And we still haven't been able to find her mother and father. Her sister is hiding with her lover.". Micka had gone too far. I knew I had to tell Alisa what Micka was planning. "Ko-e, where are you going to go?", "I'm going to search for Calypsa. Me and Mileeda.", "We should get moving, Ko-e. I think I can feel her nearby, and I don't want to lose her again.", said Mileeda, closing her eyes as if she truly could sense Calypsa. "Okay, I'll head to Kindy and warn Amana and Alisa.". Ko-e went in the other direction and proceeded to look for her sister, while I went to Kindy.

I wanted to tell Ko-e about the future, but thought better of it. I didn't know who to inform of what I saw and experienced. When I arrived in Kindy, it was a crazy frenzy. People were trying to prepare themselves. Cottages had been fitted with all kinds of protections, and from the looks of things, small cannons. I saw through the crowd, a very weary looking Amana, giving directions. I hadn't forgotten the Amana in the future, nor what Ko-e told me. "Alexa, I'm glad you've returned, we can use your help.", said Amana. I remembered meeting her as a child. I was a teenager when I first came to visit. Amana reminded me of Ko-e in so many ways. But what I could always see in her was her spirit and willingness to do what had to be done. She proved this when she first ran away from home. Ko-e did the same, but not till she was much older. "Amana, there is something important I need to share with you and your mom.". Sheena had come riding up on her horse and settled up next to Amana, "Alexa, how nice to see you. Where is Caprius?". Sheena wasn't a fan of Caprius, mostly due to his past. But she knows he's only ever tried to make up for those mistakes. Sheena had a sister who was killed by a man who had forced himself on her, and knowing Caprius caused a girl to kill herself, made it a sure thing that she hated him. "That's what I've come to talk about.". They led me to the castle, where Alisa looked as weary as her daughter. "Alexa, please don't bring me any more bad news, I don't think I can take it.". I felt bad, but knew I had to tell her about Micka's plans and her experiments. I told them how they tried to kill Ko-e and how Ko-e was searching for Calypsa in the woods. I told them how Caprius is in Nasher with some kind of disease that Micka has given to him. At the end of my tale, Alisa covered her face with her hands then looked up, "Alexa and Sheena, we need to talk. Amana, just continue to help in the village.", "WHAT?!", Amana shouted, "Why do I get left out of this conversation? I thought we were past this?", "This conversation is one you don't need to hear. Just trust me.". Amana stormed out of the room. "Follow me please.". Alisa led us to a small room with just a table in there surrounded by chairs. I sat down, and Sheena and

Alisa sat next to each other. Tisiphone had also entered the room. "Listen, Alex came here.". I felt my ears perk up at the mention of my stepsister's name. "Alex was here? But I don't understand. It's been twenty years and she just decides to show up here? Why?", "She didn't come for a friendly visit, as nice as that would have been. She came here and threatened to take Amana and kill her. She wasn't alone. She came with Sebastian's son, Brixin.". Now the three of us were silent. "Sebastian was willing to let Amana die? Why would he do that?", Sheena asked. "Apparently, he has people he has to answer to, and they were the ones ordering this.", "It still doesn't make sense. Sebastian loves his daughters, why would he kill them?", I said, trying to imagine whatever reason could possibly be good enough to murder his innocent daughter. Then I remembered that Amana isn't so nice three-thousand years from now. But before I could mention that, "There is something I need to share with both of you. I have been too afraid of sharing this because it sounds too far-fetched, but I have been to the future and I've spoken to Amana. She says that she will end this war.", Alisa said more to me than to Sheena or Tisiphone. "I've been as well, and I spoke with Ko-e and saw Amana.". Alisa looked at me with shock. Sheena gasped and was looking between me and Alisa, Tisiphone was just patiently waiting to hear the rest. So, I explained how Amana was in the future, and how Ko-e had to hide me from her. "The truth is we don't know what is really happening at that time, and I don't think we can just believe that Amana is evil. I'm sure Amana is just looking out for the planet.", Alisa said, with a sharp look towards me. "Are you saying Ko-e was lying to me?". Alisa looked taken aback. "No, not necessarily, but I am saying we don't know for sure. There could be two opposing views of how they see each other.". I considered what she was saying for a minute, but then there was some commotion outside. When we came out of the room, there was a large clutch of soldiers who looked sort of weird. When I had gotten closer, I realized the weirdness that I was seeing was the red in their eyes. They were attacking servants and soldiers alike. Suddenly in the middle of it all was Amana. She was fighting the men and women madly. She dashed through the crowd towards us, "CALYPSA HAS BROUGHT THESE DOWN UPON US! SHE IS IN THE VILLAGE! I THINK SHE IS SEARCHING FOR SCION!". And with that, Amana was off. "Amana, wait!", Sheena called after her, then gave chase. Alisa, Tisiphone, and I looked at one another and began to help. I was slashing through the crowd, but the men and women seemed invincible. "Where did Calypsa find these people?!", I shouted, trying to take down a particularly large man. Alisa was handling herself quite well, but it looked like she might succumb at any moment to the overwhelming hoard. As I tried to fight my way towards her, I saw something out of the corner of my eye. Next thing I knew, I was engulfed in a white light. When I opened my eyes, it was to discover myself in the same future I had visited before, with the tall buildings, strange lights, and signs.

CHAPTER 9

Micka's Secret

SCION: It was a very strange day. I had been hanging in the fields where the kind flowers grew. I had rolled some and was smoking a kind cigar, when I noticed something flying above me. It was a female, who looked vaguely familiar. When the female landed hard in front of me, my cigar dropped from my mouth, "CALYPSA?!", I exclaimed. I stared at her and couldn't believe what I was seeing. She had changed drastically. Her hair was still purple, and she still had a beautiful face, but that face was screwed up into a look of unbearable anger. She was covered in blood from almost head to foot. She started to walk towards me and I fell backwards. The look on her face changed from one of anger to fright. She extended her arm to me. "Calypsa, what the hell has happened to you?", I asked. Calypsa didn't answer, and just continued to stare at me, as if I were some lost puppy. She moved on me, and knelt over me so fast, I didn't have time to stand or roll out the way. When she finally spoke, it was in a very somber tone, "Scion, I needed you, and you abandoned me.", "What the hell are you talking about? You almost killed Amana!". Calypsa staggered away from me. She placed her face in her hands and started to shake her head, "No, no, no, no, no. Amana wants to take you from me. But we can run away! I have a hiding place.". She wasn't acting like her usual self. Then again, she didn't look like her usual self either. I wanted to make her pay for what she did to me, but now I finally understand that she is utterly mad. "Calypsa, let me help you. You need a bath. Whose blood is this?", "My army.". At first, I didn't understand what she meant, but then I heard screams coming from the village. I looked at Calypsa again before I ran off towards the noise. There were people attacking the citizens. At a closer glance, these people were covered in blood, just like Calypsa, except I saw their wounds, and then realized these people were dead. Calypsa joined me, and I started trying to save people. Calypsa grabbed me, "No, allow the cleanse to happen, Scion. Once this world is cleansed, my mother and I can rule it properly.", "What's happened to you? You hated your mother! Stop this Calypsa!", "Scion, if you will not help Dasha, then you are against Dasha. If you are against Dasha, then I will have no choice but to kill you.". I looked around for any weapon I could find, but before I found anything, Calypsa was on top of me. She grabbed my face with her bloody hands and kissed me. It was disgusting. I could taste all the blood. "GET OFF OF HIM!", I heard someone yelling. I looked, and was relieved to see Amana rushing towards me. She hit Calypsa with her shoulder and Calypsa flew off me. Amana pulled me up from the ground, "RUN!".

I listened to Amana and took off, away from Calypsa. It didn't take long though for Calypsa to catch up to me and block my path. I tried to turn around, but with her ability of flight, she was able to be wherever I ran to. I was starting to realize I couldn't escape her. "Give it up, Scion. I'll give you another chance to come with me or die.", "Calypsa, I am never going to join you.". As Calypsa made her way towards me, Sheena came from out of nowhere and started to fight Calypsa, "Calypsa, you need to stop all of this! This is what your mother wants! You don't want to hurt anybody!", "You're wrong, I do want this. I want everything my mother wants, and more!". She stuck her blade in Sheena's gut and Sheena fell to the ground. Amana came rushing up, but it was too late. Calypsa gave a cold heartless laugh, and then flew away. All the dead people who had been attacking, stopped to follow Calypsa out of the kingdom. I watched as she flew away, then I looked around at all the damage. There were dead men, women, and children in the streets. Even worse, there were those that had gotten injured and couldn't move. I saw one man whose leg was three feet away from him. I saw a woman looking desperately for her children. But besides these scenes I was seeing, the one that hit my heart was Amana's. Amana was holding Sheena's lifeless body, but was trying to patch her up. I watched as Amana took out that small bottle she usually carried with her. She took out the paste and shakily placed some on the wound. I stared into Sheena's eyes and I saw nothing there. "Amana, she is gone.", I said, placing my hand on her shoulder. "NO! She isn't gone. She is just hurt. I will get her to the castle.". Amana lifted Sheena, and carried her to the castle. I followed. When we got into the castle, Queen Alisa was helping with the clean-up. When she saw Amana carrying Sheena inside, Alisa dropped everything she was doing. Amana placed her down and kept trying to listen for her heartbeat. But there was none. It was slowly dawning on Amana. Alisa was stroking Sheena's face with silent tears falling from her eyes. Amana stood up and ran. "Amana!", Alisa managed to say, but I could see her torn feelings. Not wanting to leave Sheena's body but also wanting to go after Amana. I gave her a nod and gave chase.

AMANA: The numbness I felt was nothing compared to the pain that was settling into my body. Sheena couldn't be dead. She was the leader of the Kindin Forces. She was the Queen of Kindy. She was my mother. I didn't know where I was going. I only knew that Calypsa just ruined my life. I found a wall to land on and fell against it. My face was burning, and I felt the tears come, but didn't remember when they started. Scion showed up at some point and put his arms around me. I remembered crying into his chest. Then my mother was there. And she was crying and holding me. We both were crying. That's when I noticed Sheena's body was among the others who had been killed. All our preparation, and we still weren't ready. This wasn't just an attack. This was a personal assault. Micka was supposedly locked away in her own kingdom, and Tisiphone was headed that way now. While I tried to figure out how I would possibly go on without Sheena, a strange woman appeared before me. She had vibrant pink hair and a very beautiful face. I had never seen her before. "Amana, it's time you and I had a long overdue conversation.", the woman said, holding her hand out for me. "Who are you?", I choked out, still unable to keep my voice straight. "A very good friend of your mother's.", "If that's true, then how come you have to approach me without her knowledge?". She smiled, "Our last conversation wasn't very uplifting. I felt I should speak with you like this. I hope you will allow me the pleasure.". I considered her for some time, then nodded. We walked over to a very quiet part of the kingdom. The fields were filled at the moment with death preppers (Funeral preppers).

When we had reached the pond near the field, the woman turned and smiled at me, "You have so much of your father in you. I have watched all of you girls grow. It pains me that things have turned out this way.", "You speak of my father, but I still don't know who the hell you are.". The woman gave a small laugh, "I am Alexandria, but you may call me Alex for short. Your mother saved my life many years ago.", "But how do you know my father?", I asked. "He is my husband.", she said, showing me a glowing green ring on her finger. "Husband? I don't understand.". Alex took a deep breath, then explained exactly who she was. She also told me how I was born. After she finished talking, I felt disgusted, "Why would my mother keep this from me? She should have told me the truth.", "Maybe. Or maybe you didn't really need to know that.", "SHE WAS RAPED! AND THAT BASTARD WHO ABANDONED ME DID IT!", I found myself yelling. My mother had always been a strong figure to me. Next to Sheena, I always saw my mother as invincible. To learn something as horrible as she was raped and impregnated hurt just as bad as losing Sheena. "Sheena was an excellent warrior, and a wonderful friend. May her soul forever rest in Paradise.", Alex said, closing her eyes in prayer. "If you are my father's wife, then where have you been this whole time?". I was finding it very hard to believe that this woman was married to Sebastian. I was finding it even more insulting that she would say these things about my mother. "I get it, you are upset at the loss of a woman you considered a parent. I experienced such a loss many years ago at the hands of Falsa.", "Well, if you've always watched over us, then why didn't you protect Calypsa?". I was furious now. "Micka and I never saw eye to eye. She loathed me the moment we met. She had always had a thing for your father, but we were destined to be, so there was nothing she could do.", "What does that have to do with letting her beat Calypsa?". Alex considered my question, "She is Micka's daughter. There was nothing I could do to stop her. But believe me when I tell you, I did speak with her.". I knew Micka was impossible to deal with, having dealt with her myself. I realized I was being entirely rude to Alex, who came and told me the truth, even though it was hard to hear. "Sorry. I was just…", "No need to explain. I know what it is you've lost.". I felt my eyes burn again, and I found myself in Alex's arms, crying all over again. Sheena had been the best thing in my life. She had taught me so much, and given me much more. Although Sheena was not my mother through blood, she was still more of a parent to me than my actual father had ever been. All he did was ask me to kill my sister. I chose not to listen, and now, I've lost Sheena.

It had been a long while that I had been sitting with Alex. She aided me back to the castle. When my mother saw who was helping me inside, she looked frightened. But then relaxed, as Alex approached her and embraced her. My mother started to cry again. Later that evening, me, my mother, and Alex, were all sitting in our dining area. They had been reminiscing about the war twenty years ago, and when my mother first met Sheena, "…and even though we were going into the Dark Wood, which at that time had way more life in it, your mother felt comfortable knowing Sheena was in charge while she was gone. Your mother had a thing for her because she sensed her strength.". The little creature known as Casian was sitting on my lap, giving small glances at Alex. It had finally leaped off my lap and onto her chest. "Oh, my dear, Casian, I have missed you so much. Did you want to come with me?". Casian licked Alex's face in reply. Seeing Casian happy to see Alex made me trust her more. After all, I had almost died saving the creature. "Mom, Alex told me about Desian.". My mother froze at the mention of Desian. She slowly looked towards Alex, "There was no point in hiding that any longer. She has the right to know how she was made.", Alex said, calmly continuing to play with Casian, who was nibbling on her finger. "Desian was the only thing that made me feel weak. Nothing else in my life ever made me feel that way. You can understand why I don't like to talk about it.", "But how can you stand it? Aren't I a constant reminder?", I asked incredulously. I failed to see how not talking about it could help her forget that nightmare. "Because you aren't the child of someone I hate, you are the child of someone I love. It may not have been the best way to have a child, but I'm glad it was with Bastian.". I noticed Alex didn't seem bothered by the fact that her husband had a child with another woman. Then I thought of Ko-e and Calypsa, "How about my sisters? How were they made?". Both my mother, and Alex went into explanation of how Falsa took my father captive, and how Micka and my father were together. "Micka? My father actually chose to be with Micka?", "She was different back then. She wasn't as obsessed. She had a much clearer opinion on things back then. To this day, I can't imagine what changed her.", my mother said. To me, Micka had never liked my mother, and from what Alex said, she never liked her either. It seems to me like Micka was always who she is now. There were still questions I felt needed answering, but Alex stood up, "I should get going. My son and husband are going to begin to worry.", "Why doesn't Bastian come here?", my mother asked. "He is quite busy, Alisa. Very busy indeed. He's got his other planets to worry about.".

I pondered on what those other planets were like and if they were extremely different from us. "Amana, would you mind walking with me to the garden?". I found it strange that she wanted my company, but I decided to oblige.

We got down into the garden, and Alex faced me, "Amana, you know that you are not normal. You are a goddess. You are one of Sebastian's children, which makes you a lot stronger than most Plinthinians.". I nodded. I obviously had figured that out by now and didn't understand where she was going with this. "My point to all this, is that you are going to need the proper weapons to win this war.", "And you're willing to give me these weapons? Why me?", "Because me and your father know that you will win, and that when you do, you will need a place to operate. I would like you to come with me.". I felt uneasy. "What about my mother?", I asked. I knew she was completely distraught over losing Sheena and I didn't want to abandon her. "She will be fine. Alisa is strong and will be fine without you for a bit.", "But where is it you want to take me?". Alex smiled and placed her hand on my shoulder, which gave a jolt throughout my whole body. "We are going to Alexandria. It needs a new ruler, and I want that to be you.".

SCION: Amana had departed with a gorgeous woman. Where she had departed to, even Alisa didn't know apparently. At first, she was outraged that this woman named Alex would take her daughter and not tell her. But then later she decided there must be a good reason. I was still thinking about what had happened with Calypsa. I couldn't get that image of her covered in blood out of my head, nor get the taste of blood out of my mouth, no matter how many times I washed it. I was feeling the worst of it. Amana wasn't paying me much attention while she was preparing against Calypsa, but Ko-e wasn't here either. And while women throughout the village were going out of their way to talk to me, I didn't feel like I could give any of them the time. I wondered where my cousin had gotten to and if she was okay. Then I started to think of my mother and realized that all the anger I had for her, I didn't want to end up like Amana. Holding onto a lifeless body that I had the chance to hold before it was lifeless. I made my way towards the castle to let Queen Alisa know that I was going to Dasha. When I came into the castle, blood was still being wiped off the walls. The former king and queen, Derek and Shay, were standing there with Alisa. "I'm sure Alex will bring her back. I think she is giving her goddess training. It makes sense.", Derek was saying to Alisa, who had her face in her hands. "Queen Alisa…", I said, hoping I didn't sound too demanding, "…I am going to go to Dasha to see my mother. I know that Micka is locked away at the moment and…". Queen Alisa held up a hand, "No.". I thought I knew why she was saying no, "Queen Alisa, please, I have to…", "YOU IDIOT BOY! WHAT DO YOU THINK WILL HAPPEN IF YOU GO TO DASHA?! YOU DON'T THINK CALYPSA WILL IMMEDIATELY COME FOR YOU?!". Alisa had been crying. Her face was almost blood red, and her eyes were puffy and wet. "Now, Alisa, he only wants to make sure his mother is okay. I don't think keeping him here is completely necessary.", said Derek. "Father, the girl has an obsession with him. You should know what a goddess' obsession is like.". Derek considered, then faced me, "Perhaps it might be best after all if you waited.", "How is it you can stop me from going to see my mother? I have rights!", I yelled. "Fine. Go and die, then. It will be one less headache for me.". Alisa stood up and walked out of the room.

Later that day, I gave more thought to what Alisa said, and realized she had a point. Still tasting the blood in my mouth from Calypsa's kiss, I made my way to Alisa's chamber. When I got close, I could hear her speaking, "…please, Sebastian! Just let me have Sheena back! You knew this would happen! You knew Calypsa would kill her! You owe me you bastard!". I didn't want to intrude on her extremely offensive prayer, but before I could turn and walk away, she saw me, "Scion, come here.". Alisa looked very beautiful for her age. She was wearing a very beautiful sleeping dress and seemed to be feeling somewhat better. At least her eyes weren't wet. "Scion, you should go to your mother. It was selfish of me to try and keep you here.", "Well, I know you were only trying to protect me, so…", "No, it's more than that, Scion. Amana cares about you. So does Ko-e, and I would feel no better than Micka if something happened to you.". Alisa walked towards her cabinet and opened it up. Inside was a very gorgeous sword. Alisa took it out and handed it to me. "This was Sheena's. I gave it to her the day she became leader of my forces.". Tears were forming in Alisa's eyes again, "I want you to have this sword, Scion. You will be protected from Calypsa.", "I don't get it. Why didn't Sheena have this sword when we were fighting?", I asked, thinking she could still be here right now. "Because, Sheena had put it away years ago. She wanted Amana to have it…", Alisa found her bed, and started to cry with her face in her hands, "Scion, you must listen to me. I know it isn't going to be easy, but believe me, Sebastian was right about you. You have a huge part to play here, and perhaps, it was always so. Calypsa loves you and doesn't know how to act on those feelings for you. Especially now that you want nothing from her. But in the end, it will be you, and possibly Amana, who destroys her.", "Where do you think that woman took Amana? And who was that woman?". I knew I was taking a gamble, but at the moment, Alisa seemed talkative. "She is Alex, wife of Sebastian.".

I kept running things through my head. So, Sebastian has a wife, a son, and three illegitimate daughters. Although Ko-e was the oldest, technically Calypsa was the oldest because she was first created. But through some strange magic, Ko-e was born first. So, this meant that Amana was the youngest. But, Alex took Amana with her wherever she took her. I kept trying to think where that would be, before it finally dawned on me, that it was Alexandria. Funny, too, for a genius to take so long to figure that out, but the other part I had to figure out was that Alex was short for Alexandria. I knew this had a significant meaning. In other words, none of the other goddesses had that name. So, this meant that she was always destined to be with Sebastian. Or at least that's how I saw it. I started to really miss Ko-e. I had left Kindy three days ago, and had a peaceful parting. Kindy was still recovering from Calypsa's assault but would soon be ready for a hard retaliation. Alisa, before I left, had taken over Amana's project. She had created what she called a hand-cannon. It was a very powerful weapon and could kill from a great distance. I, of course, had helped in its creation. Alisa didn't like me very much at first, I was able to tell. But after Sheena was killed, and Amana left with Alex, either she was really lonely, or she started to appreciate my genius. Micka was locked up from what I knew, and what I feared most of all, was that somehow, she'd escaped. Then I realized that Calypsa would free her mother. Truthfully, I was headed to my death.

Two days later, I ran into a highly unexpected individual. It was a long time ago in Dasha, when I first started school. Not everyone was cut out for school, and Micka in her queenly way, decided that if you didn't want to go to school, you had no place in Dasha. She exiled a certain number of young men and women, but was forced to take some of them back when their families started to complain. This led to a rebellion. And of course, Micka reveled in it. She killed those that spoke out the most and quickly eliminated her problem. One of those exiled was a boy named Hoss. Hoss was just a big bully. My first day of school, Hoss and some of his friends attacked me, after I called Hoss a pig in cotton. Of course, the whole thing started because of Calypsa. Before I knew her, she was the dream of every boy in Dasha. Hoss would stare extremely hard and talk about what he'd do if he could. I was always insulted by Hoss. So when I called him a pig in cotton, he didn't take to that well. Especially because I shouted it in front of Calypsa. Since then, I had only heard certain things about Hoss. But now, he was right in front of me and looking quite menacing. He had a nasty scar on his face and looked like he'd been clawed by something. Looking closer at the claw marks, I realized I'd seen them before. "Well, this is unexpected. Scion Tin, didn't expect you to just be riding through the woods. Not at this time anyway.". Hoss reached into his sack and pulled out a paper. He brandished it in front of me and I saw my face and Amana's. "You do realize this is obsolete right?", "There you go with those made up words again.", Hoss and his cronies laughed. There were four of them and one of me. I had the sword that Alisa had given me, and Hoss noticed. "And what's this you got here?", he said, reaching for it. I pulled my horse back, "Hoss, you idiot! Don't touch that!". Hoss looked like I had just slapped his mother and took great offense to my refusal of letting him grab the sword. He took a rock off the ground and threw it at me. I jumped off my horse to dodge and Hoss' cronies surrounded me. "Now, I said let me see that.", said Hoss, walking towards me. I took the sword out of its sheath and it glowed crimson. As I started to wonder why it was doing that, Calypsa landed right behind me. I fell on the ground, and Hoss and his friends laughed. "Did you guys know the princess could fly?", said one of the cronies. Calypsa didn't look angry this time. She looked almost normal. "Hoss, right? I have a proposition for you.", "A proper what?", said Hoss, who was watching the princess with perverted interest. "Let me dumb this down. I am giving you a job.". Hoss' expression became one of understanding. "And what is this job?". Calypsa picked me up from the ground, and once again, went in to kiss me. This time, I didn't taste blood, but rather, it tasted good. I allowed her to continue to kiss me. When she broke away from me, she said, "Kill yourselves.". One of Hoss' cronies took his dagger and put it through his own neck. The other cronies began to follow suit, leaving Hoss standing by himself, frightened. "What's the matter, Hoss? You don't seem so keen for the job.", "Please, I just got better.", Hoss pleaded. "Calypsa! Stop this! Why did you even do that? What was the point?", "I can protect you, Scion. That is the point.", "I don't need your protection!", I yelled, pointing the sword towards her. "You think that sword will protect you from Amana? Or even Ko-e?", "They don't have a problem with me, they have a problem with you!". Calypsa laughed that same cold laugh from when she murdered Sheena. "Scion, you are mine. I decided already. I will never let either of my sisters have you. They will burn before they have you. Now, stop this, come with me, or I kill Hoss.". I didn't care for Hoss, but I didn't want him murdered either. "I'll come, but you have to let Hoss live, Calypsa.". She considered for a minute, then, Hoss took his blade out and pointed it towards his stomach. Small blood trickles were starting to leak. "CALYPSA!", I shouted. Hoss dropped his blade and started to cry. "I was only teasing. Come now, Scion. We'll go to my kingdom.", "Back to Dasha?", I asked, getting the feeling that isn't where she was referring. "No…my kingdom, in the Dark Wood.".

CORSA: Dony and I had been hiding out at his house. My parents and sister had been taken, and Ko-e was nowhere to be found. At first, I was angry that she didn't show up to help my parents. I was angry when I heard that she came but left without any word. I was so angry. Then these other soldiers showed up. I had no idea who they were. The armor they wore was golden and silver. The man who led them was a stranger to me, but I heard someone call him Caprius. I remembered that was the name of Falsa's son. And of course, Ko-e had told us that he was her brother. He descended on Dasha so frighteningly, that Queen Micka was locked away in her own kingdom. Dony and I were hiding out for a good long time. A month had gone by. When I finally felt we could hide no longer, I knew it was time for us to find out what happened. "Dony, I think it's time to leave. I need to know where my parents are.", "Corsa, I have someone you may want to speak with.". As I pondered on who, this person was sitting downstairs, "MILEEDA!". I ran to my sister and embraced her. She was different. Her skin was light blue, and she was somehow stronger. "I've been hiding out with Ko-e.", "So, what is she doing about our parents? Where are they?". I could see the answer in Mileeda's eyes. "It's too horrible to speak of.". I watched as my sister sat down upon the couch and wept. "Mileeda, just tell me, I can handle it.", "When…Ko-e…rescued me, we went to see if anyone else had been experimented on. Our parents were not… test subjects, but rather was executed at the hands of one.". I felt my face burn. "It's Ko-e's fault! If she had never come into our lives…", "Then we would have been raped and left for dead in the woods.". I considered what Mileeda said. I knew she was right. If Ko-e wouldn't have been there, we'd be dead. We owed her our lives. I couldn't hold this grudge against her. "But, Mileeda, what's going on now? What about these other soldiers?". Mileeda explained that they were from Alexandria and that they were taking orders from Alexa, who was Caprius' wife. She had left for Nasher and now was occupied there. "Where is Ko-e now?", "She is rescuing Scion, who has been taken captive by Calypsa.". It all seemed so strange that this was happening. "Why did you come back here?", I asked, starting to get the feeling my sister didn't come back for me. "I've come to kill Queen Micka and avenge our parents.".

Over the course of the next three days, I learned my sister was as powerful as Ko-e. She was empowered by the energy of Heaven. I had no idea what that meant. Micka did this to her, thinking it would harm her, but it made her an enemy who was strong enough to fight her. We walked the kingdom freely, because all the Dashin soldiers were afraid of the Alexandrian soldiers. But getting into the castle to get to Micka's cell was a lot harder. The Alexandrian guards were stationed at every entrance of the castle, and this made it impossible to try and do anything related to getting inside. They were told to guard Micka until Alexa returned. "Maybe we should just go help Ko-e instead? I'm just saying, doesn't that kind of go with what we are trying to do?", Dony asked Mileeda one day, as we had just finished another reconnaissance mission. "Micka is the architect behind this whole thing. She has to pay, and I want to make her.". Mileeda didn't sound like her old self. I could tell she was battle worn. As the days had passed us by, she was revealing more and more of her new transformation. She was smarter. She was always vigilant, and from what I could see, she wasn't sleeping. Strange of all was her new blue skin. Sometimes she would look normal. But other times, she would transform into her blue form. While I could tell we were both hurting over our parents, Mileeda wanted blood. I just wanted to live. I started to think about what my sister was getting us into.

One day, I heard a bit of a commotion, and decided stupidly to follow the noise. "…Tisiphone says she's here to speak with Micka. Should I let her through?", "Queen Alexa said nobody is to come through without her consent.", "That's the thing, though, she's got it.". I saw a woman standing at the front of the stairs. She had beautiful black hair and was wearing a look of utmost anger. I knew a path into the dungeons that I was quite sure nobody knew of. The only reason I hadn't mentioned it to my sister was out of fear. But I knew to take it now. I was curious what this, Tisiphone, was doing. I remembered that she was the Queen of Nasher and mother to Nigel. I went to the med area, where there was a run off that if you follow long enough, leads to a cracked wall that can fit one person. I climbed through the crack and that's when I found Micka's cell. On the other side of the door, you could hear Micka speaking with someone, but I couldn't make out the words at first. "We have to wait. We can't rush this. If I come at Alisa now, while she is vulnerable, she stands a good chance to win. I've seen her overcome the odds before.", "But she can't win, without Sebastian…", "I agree, but Calypsa has gone rogue…", Micka stopped talking and listened. The guards were making their way toward Micka's cell. "OPEN THE DOOR!", one of the guards yelled. "Well, Tisiphone, I was wondering when you were going to show up. I know your husband is too much of a coward to assist you in anyway.", "Shut up.", Tisiphone responded. Micka just smiled and continued glaring at Tisiphone. "All those years ago, you murdered my father, and now look at you. Locked away in your own kingdom. Tell me, how does it feel?", "Oh, I won't be here much longer.", "What is all this you've written?". Micka looked at her walls, which I noticed were covered in circles. "Oh, you wouldn't understand. Only the gods can understand this. Do you remember when I first became your queen? You were so excited. And then, Pietro happened.". Tisiphone was angry when she walked in, but now her face was so screwed up with rage, that all the pretty features in her face were gone. "Don't you dare mention him…", she said with a shakiness in her voice. "Why not? He was a handsome gentleman. Your father approved of him. But remind me again who killed him. Oh yes…I remember, it was your so-called god.". At this point, Tisiphone tried to storm into the cell, but the Alexandrian soldiers didn't let her pass. "You are still the vilest person alive! I knew we should have killed you!", "Well, then you would have been no better than me.". Tisiphone stopped struggling against the guards and stormed out of the cell. I watched as Micka started to laugh and returned to doing whatever she was doing.

After I made it back through the med bay, I wanted to catch Queen Tisiphone. I didn't know why, but I felt compelled to speak with her. I continued through the city, and it was still dark out. Most of the city was quiet. The usual night urchins were in hiding due to the Alexandrian soldiers hanging around. I found myself at the royal stables and was lucky enough to see Queen Tisiphone getting ready to depart. "WAIT!", I shouted. The guards noticed me and quickly blocked my path. "Please I must speak with the queen before she leaves!". Tisiphone waved her hand and the guards let me pass. "What is it you want to speak to me about?". I quickly explained about my sister and what she wanted to do. "Hmm…well if I had to hazard a guess, the reason you are telling me this is because you are afraid for your sister.". I nodded. "Well you should let her get on with it. Micka doesn't deserve to live. She killed my first love, then my father.", Queen Tisiphone said, still prepping her carriage, and fiddling with a bag in frustration. "I understand. She killed my parents, but I can't let my sister do this. It will change her.". Tisiphone looked down on me and sighed, "It sounds like she already has. What she has been through would make anybody a murderer. But now, I'd like to speak with her. She may have information concerning Ko-e.".

Tisiphone and I made our way towards Dony's home. I was completely worried now. Something about the things Micka was saying prior to Tisiphone showing up at her cell. This must have shown because Tisiphone was watching me with worry. "What's the matter, child?", "Well, Micka was talking to someone in her cell.", "There was nobody there.", "I know that, but she was talking to someone and someone was answering her.". Tisiphone tried to think about it for a while. Just then, Dony came rushing towards us. "Corsa! You have to stop her!", "What are you talking about? What's happened?", Tisiphone responded. "It's Mileeda. She's gone after Queen Micka. I tried to stop her, but she knocked me out.". I looked at Queen Tisiphone with a 'see I told you' look. We both rushed back towards the dungeons and saw that the door had been opened. We rushed in and found my sister incapacitating the guards. "MILEEDA!", I shouted, looking on her in horror. I realized she hadn't killed them, just knocked them out. She continued to Micka's cell. Once again, I could hear Micka discussing something with a disembodied voice. "…She comes, she comes…", "I'm fully aware. Do not worry, she will free me.". Suddenly, you could hear a door being torn open. "Hello, Mileeda. I know why you're here. But you are wasting your time.", "I don't think so.". Tisiphone and I came down just in time to see Mileeda snap Micka's neck in her hands. "Mileeda, what have you done?", I asked her. I couldn't believe that she killed our queen. But then, I saw something that scared me to death. Micka blinked her eyes and smiled. Mileeda dropped her and Micka stood up and brushed herself off, "Well, that was dramatic, right?", "How?", Tisiphone sputtered out. "Well, for one, I'll let you all in on a secret. I am a goddess. And I believe that my time here is done.". Micka suddenly disappeared on the spot. As she faded, I noticed a black ring glowing on her fingers. "DAMN IT!", Tisiphone exclaimed, kicking the broken door. Mileeda just knelt on one knee and shook her head, "Ko-e isn't going to like this.", "Where is she?", Tisiphone asked. "She is in the Dark Wood. That's where Calypsa took Scion.". We decided that we would go there.

As I was gearing up for the trip, Mileeda approached me. "I don't want you to come, Corsa.". I stared at her in disbelief. "What the hell are you talking about? Of course I'm com…". Mileeda cut me off, "Corsa, last night was very frightening for me. I don't want to lose you. Please, I need you to just stay out of this.". I didn't know what to say. I was looking over my stuff and thinking about our parents and what they would want. "Mileeda, I have every right just like you to try and avenge our parents!". Mileeda had tears in her eyes now, "This isn't just about vengeance. This is about saving our world. Something that you don't need to do from the battlefield.". I looked at my sister. She was different. The old Mileeda wouldn't want anything to do with this fight. But the new Mileeda was a product of the crimes that had been committed against her. She was determined, and I knew she would force me to stay here. I quickly embraced her. I didn't want to let her go. I didn't know when I'd be seeing her again. I felt my tears on the fabric on her shoulder. "Do not cry, Corsa, I promise we will see each other again. But for now, I must do what I can to help Ko-e. You can help by staying here and being safe.". Tisiphone entered the room, "I'm ready to depart. My son will be meeting you on the edge of the forest. From there, he will accompany you into the Dark Wood. It is very important that we find Ko-e and Scion. I think Scion has a lot to do with this situation.". As Tisiphone and Mileeda left from the stables, Tisiphone pulled me to the side, and told me something, "Listen, I don't think it will be safe here. You need to find some wild country. Stay hidden for a time. Dasha will soon be ground zero.". While I didn't fully understand, I gathered enough not to stay in Dasha. After my sister departed, Dony and I started to prepare to leave as well. "Are you sure about this, Corsa? I mean, why even go through all this? Micka is gone now, right?", "But she will be back, Dony. She is the queen.". Dony didn't argue after this and just continued packing.

AMANA: After everything that had happened. The thing I feared the most was losing my mother. She was all I really had left now.

Alex reminded me that isn't really the case. "Before I can train you physically, I must train you mentally. It is important that you think like a goddess.", "And how does a goddess think?", I asked half sarcastically. Alex could tell I wasn't being serious and mentally smacked me. "OW! Why did you do that?!". Alex gave me a stern look, "THIS IS NOT THE TIME TO PLAY GAMES! DO YOU KNOW WHAT IS GOING ON DOWN THERE?!". We had been in Alexandria for a week. In all that time, all Alex had done was mentally beat me and make me feel worthless. I was starting to think that she wasn't actually teaching me anything, but was just abusing her power over me. "How does this help me, Alex?", I asked one day, after taking a rather brutal mental beating. It had left me with a pounding headache and a very sore body. "This is what you will be facing when you face Calypsa for the final time. Not to mention when you face her mother, which you will.". What the hell was that supposed to mean? There were times when Alex and I would just sit there and not say anything. Alex called this, getting in touch with the universe. I was starting to feel like there was nothing really happening for me.

Alexandria was a beautiful place. The castle looked like it was built by a god, and everywhere you looked, you could see nothing but green and purple beauty. Alex told me that Alexandria can hold over two-million people. I was surprised by this, because Alexandria was just a big floating rock. I would often just walk in the royal garden and look around. I was surprised to see that kind flowers grew here. I pondered on how Ko-e could grow up here and still be unhappy. This place was Heaven. Literally Heaven. Not just that, but the sky looked different from here. From this place, you could actually see the other planets created by Sebastian. Another thing about Alex was that she didn't speak much about my father. I could tell her main focus was to teach me. But I couldn't understand the part of me that didn't care for what she was teaching me. Even though she kept telling me to learn the way of the goddess, I continued to overlook her teachings and make my own way around. The servants were very kind and helpful. Because I was Ko-e's sister, I was given extreme special treatment. The food was like nothing I'd ever had. The wildlife was similar to the wild life on Plinth. Casian was the only one of her kind, and apparently was a gift from one of the other planets. Casian has been around since the beginning of Plinth and was my father's most loyal pet. I reveled in the splendor of Alexandria and for some time had forgotten about what was happening below me.

One day, as I was taking one of my walks, a servant named Losa, caught up with me. "Excuse me, Amana, do you mind if we have a word?". The truth was I did mind. I had been avoiding Alex, on account of I was tired of the hardcore training, and everyone else seemed to want to kiss my ass. "Sure, what is it?", I answered grudgingly. "Well, I've just seen Ms. Alex looking for you. Is there a reason you're hiding from her?". Losa wasn't exactly somebody I saw myself confiding in, but I could tell she was close with Ko-e. From what I had gathered, she was her teacher. "I'm just getting some air.", "Well, I do hope that's all it is. Because from what I heard, you are our only hope in this conflict. You have to end all this.". I was pissed. "Where exactly did you hear this?", I asked through gritted teeth. "It's a prophecy. Would you like to see what I'm talking about?". I was curious to understand her meaning, so I followed her to a crevice within the side of the castle. In this small crevice were books. Losa seemed quite familiar with the books, so I assumed they were her's. "This is what I was referring to.", Losa said, handing me a very old and dusty book. The book had no title but seemed to have a strange energy coming from it. As I began to open the book, Parnim had appeared, and quickly snatched the book from me. "Parnim, what are you doing?!", exclaimed Losa. "YOU of all people know what this book is meant for, Losa. We cannot show this to her.", "What is that book, Parnim?", I asked, trying to contain myself. "This is an ancient book written by an unknown man many years ago. What's written in this book are certain events that will shape this world. You can't know what's in it, because you're in this book.". Now I wanted to know more than ever. Unfortunately, Alex found me, and forced me to head to the fields.

As we trained today, Alex had me doing psychic blasts(breaking things with my mind). I couldn't stop thinking about that book. It was messing with my concentration and I had accidentally blown up a pitcher being carried by one of the servants. "Amana, what is on your mind?". I tried to think of an answer right there on the spot, but couldn't. Alex looked highly annoyed, "Amana, I'm starting to get the idea that you don't care about this training.", "I do, it's just...", I trailed off, because I knew what I was going to say. "What is it?", Alex asked impatiently. "There is a book that...". Alex cut me off right away, "This book you're talking about, is the reason this war is happening. You needn't worry about that book.", "But it might tell me something that will help! Some way I might not have to kill Calypsa!". Alex looked at me with pity. "So, the truth comes out. You're not taking this seriously, because you don't want to have to kill your sister.". I knew every part of me should hate Calypsa. She tortured Scion after she had me rescue him. She set up Mileeda and her family. She almost killed me. She attacked my kingdom and successfully killed my stepmother. So, yes, I had every reason to want her dead. But there was another side of me that recalled all our good memories. All the work we had put into making Plinth more relaxing. All those times we tried running away together.

That night, I had a strange dream. I was five years old again, and Calypsa and I were at The Willet, playing in the water. I noticed something strange, though. There was a grownup Calypsa watching us. She wasn't making any moves towards us. She was just watching. She seemed unaware that I was aware of her presence. When Calypsa ran off, I followed her, and the adult Calypsa followed as well. "Amana, we are real sisters, aren't we?", the child-Calypsa asked. I was about to answer, when there was somebody else there. A man. I realized it must be Sebastian, but he looked different. He was watching Calypsa splash around. "I see you, Amana.", he said, turning to me. I felt a fear go all the way down my spine. I woke up, sweating, with Alex holding me in her arms. Some of the servants were standing around, and Losa walked up to me and Alex, "What happened? You were screaming murder.", "I was?", I panted out, still breathing hard. Alex had a stony face. She looked like she just witnessed a murder. "Do you know anything about that name you were screaming?". I didn't think I was screaming a name. I shook my head. Alex got up and walked out of the room. I looked at Losa, "Who's name was I screaming?", "Desian.".

CHAPTER 10

From The Future To The Present

SCION: I didn't know if I should consider myself a prisoner or if I should just take the offer Calypsa had given me. The Dark Wood was more of a trying place than frightening. I watched, as people who seemed to materialize from nowhere, built buildings, and planted fruits and vegetables. Calypsa was quite proud of herself, and for the first time in a long time, she seemed to be her old self. "Where did you find all these people, Calypsa?", I asked her one day, thinking that perhaps she had taken them from somewhere. "Most of them were bandits. I figured they would jump at the opportunity to have a new kingdom.". I couldn't believe how that sounded, so I had to ask, "And what is the purpose of this?". Calypsa gave me a look, and then laughed, "Well, I'm free now, aren't I? I'm no longer living under my mother's finger. She is locked away in her own kingdom, and I am building something nice here. It's why I wanted you to come with me, Scion. Amongst other things, of course.", she said, giving me a look of admiration. "Those days are over for us, Calypsa. You saw to that.". She gave me a look of amusement. "I've already told you, you're mine. I don't know why you can't see that.". Calypsa grabbed me and placed her lips on mine. I embraced her. She led me to her quarters, where we began kissing on her bed. As I wrapped my arm under her backside, it suddenly dawned on me, "I can't do this. I'm sorry.". She jumped off the bed looking slightly hurt. "Is this because of your feelings for Ko-e? Is that what this is?". I looked down. In my mind, I saw Ko-e's face and the bewildered look it wore at my betrayal. "Okay, I see. Scion, you will love me again. Because if you don't…", she made a gesture, and Hoss came into the room. "Has he been there this whole time?", I asked. "Yes, I've kept him here as a little incentive.". Once again, she made him take a knife and put it in his gut until he began to bleed. "Calypsa, please, just stop this!", "No, Scion, you stop it. Stop playing these stupid 'I want to be a hero' games. You aren't a hero, Scion. You hate this man. He tortured you when you were younger. Why do you want to save him?". I couldn't think of an answer right away. The only thing I could come up with was, "Because life is sacred, and it isn't our place to judge people like that.". Calypsa stared at me for a minute, then took the blade away from Hoss' gut herself. She then placed it up to his throat. Hoss was crying like a baby. "Okay, enough games. Either you make love to me right now, or Hoss dies here and now.". I didn't see any other way. "Okay, just stop. I'll do whatever you want.".

I never felt so dirty in my life. I snuck away from Calypsa, who was still laying naked in the bed, and I made my way towards the edge of the woods. The village that Calypsa was building took up only a quarter of the woods, so it wasn't very big. As I found my way to the entrance, I was grabbed and pulled into a giant hole in a tree. "Scion, are you okay? I've been trying to get to you for days.". It was Ko-e. I was so overjoyed to see her that I didn't realize that I had begun to cry. It dawned on me later how terrified I was. Calypsa wasn't just some woman. She was a goddess, with a vendetta that heavily involved me. Alisa was right, I shouldn't have left Kindy. I was so keen on being involved before, but now I finally understood the stakes. I was sure that Calypsa would get bored with using Hoss to force me to do whatever she wanted. Soon it would be me, or someone more important to me. I kept trying to think how I could get away from her.

After I explained everything to Ko-e, she reacted pretty much how I imagined, "She's been taking advantage of you? That's it, I'm going to kill her.", "Ko-e, you aren't a killer. But Amana is. Amana can kill her. She's in Alexandria with Alex.", "ALEX?! MY FATHER'S WIFE?! We must depart for Alexandria at once!", "Why? Is Amana in some kind of danger?", "No, but there is obviously more going on. Why would Alex come here with everything that's going on in the heavens?". I didn't know what was going on in the heavens, but from the way Ko-e said it, I gathered it was more intense than what we were dealing with. "What's happening there?", "Scion, the other planets are at war with each other. My father and brother are trying their best to end the conflict. Alex has been with them. But if she has come here, that means that something more serious is taking place.", "And you don't think this war is the main reason she might be here?", "Amana and I can deal with this, but Alex is above these kinds of petty things. I don't understand why she is here.". Before Ko-e and I could make a move, Calypsa was standing on the outside of the tree, "Scion, I told you, you cannot escape me.". She reached in and Ko-e grabbed her. The two began to fight. Eventually, Calypsa over-powered her and looked in my direction. I got up to run but felt my body freeze as I turned away. Calypsa was getting stronger. "Tsk… now what should I do with you, Scion? Oh, I know exactly what to do.". She started removing my clothes. Ko-e opened her eyes but was unable to move as well. "Oh, poor Ko-e. Didn't think this through, did you?", Calypsa asked, holding up a strange vial with what looked like golden liquid. "It is what it looks like. Gold in pure form. Ko-e won't be able to move for the next two hours. Which gives you and me plenty of time, Scion. My hormones have become more ferocious since you've been gone. Ko-e let out a silent scream and struggled on the ground but couldn't move. "DON'T YOU TOUCH HIM!", she managed to yell out. But, Calypsa was already stroking me.

Calypsa tortured me and Ko-e over the next few days. She would often switch between raping me and deciding if she wanted to kill Ko-e, or Hoss in front of me. When Hoss first saw Ko-e, he tried to escape. It dawned on me that Ko-e and Hoss must have encountered each other at one time. Then she got really creative. "Ko-e, since you want Scion so badly, why not have him?". Ko-e was untouched in the art of sex. It pained me to take her innocence the way I was forced to. It became quite depraved over time, with Calypsa joining in and forcing Hoss to watch, and taunting him, "You'll never experience what it is like to be with a goddess. You're fat, ugly, and just down right not worth it. Look at Scion. He is perfect. Perfection in every way.", "Calypsa…please…no more…", Ko-e pleaded with her sister one day. "You are right, aren't you? I have grown bored…of Hoss.". She made me pick up a blade and stab it through Hoss' head. Ko-e began to sob. I felt completely broken. "Now, shall we get back to our game?".

Calypsa was asleep. I had woken up and realized I had control of myself. I quickly and quietly moved away from Calypsa. I found the golden liquid she had been using to keep Ko-e weak. I quietly disposed of it, then turned to wake Ko-e. Ko-e was not sleeping. She was awake, with tears falling from her eyes. I lifted her up, because she was unable to move too much. She saw that I had poured out the golden liquid. "You, fool.", she whispered, "It would have weakened her…", she said softly. I felt like an idiot now. But then thought, what if there is a main source? After all, where did Calypsa get hers? We made our way through the woods. Me carrying Ko-e on my back now. Then, someone unexpected appeared. "Alexa! Where the hell did you come from?". Alexa looked different somewhat, but none the less, held out her hand, "Scion, you need to come with me. Ko-e, you stay.". As confusing as this was, I didn't have any intentions of leaving Ko-e to suffer. "Go with her, Scion.", Ko-e said weakly. "I can't leave you. Not after what she has done to us.", "Alexa knows what she is talking about. I trust her.". I looked at Ko-e again, who gave me a sad smile. "I'm not leaving.", "You don't have a choice.", Alexa said, grabbing me. Somehow, we were in a different location. I looked around and everything was new to my eyes. There was furniture, but I had never seen it's like before. There was a strange item that gave out moving pictures. I was freaked out by the sudden change of scenery but felt relieved when Ko-e was standing right next to me. "Thank goodness we didn't leave you.", I said, throwing my arms around her. Alexa and Ko-e exchanged looks. I noticed Ko-e was dressed differently, wearing similar clothing to what Alexa was wearing. "I'm not the Ko-e you just left.", Ko-e said. I stared at her and looked around. "Where the hell are we?", "Ko-e's home. Thirty-five-hundred years later.".

TIG: In the time that had passed, the young girl who was bitten by Nover, was finally starting to come down. Before, she was deathly sick and craved Plinthinian blood. But now she was transitioning into eating regular food again. Her mother was quite pleased with our med staff and the care we provided for her during her stay. Nigel took them to their home and I felt extremely relieved. Caprius was still sick, but seemed to also be getting better. The cut on the side of his head had turned into a scar and it wasn't glowing anymore. But the best part is, he was able to speak now, "When I get out of here, I am going to tear Micka apart!", "Come on, man, you don't mean that.", I said, trying to keep him calm. "No, screw you, Tig, I almost killed my wife! Have you heard anything from Amana about where Alexa might be? Or even how to fully cure me?", "Well, I'm afraid that I don't know where Amana is, and I'm also very sorry to tell you that Alisa refuses to say.". Caprius looked like he was thinking, then he stood up. "Caprius, you're not fully healed! Please, you need to sit back down.", a nurse was telling Caprius. "I know where she is. I need to go there at once.". Caprius started to walk but fell over. The nurse quickly helped him back in his bed. "Listen, Caprius...", "No, listen to me, Alex has taken her to Alexandria. That means that something really bad is happening. I need to get there and see what Sebastian wants me to do.". Caprius tried to get up, but the nurse held him down, "Now you look, I don't care what is going on, I'm telling you, that you can't go anywhere! So, if you want to go, you need to rest and not move for the next few days. Your condition is still new to us.". Caprius looked like he was going to retort, but thought better against it. "Nurse, what is your name? The way you handled him so well...", "My name is Dalia. But thanks for asking something you should have known, Your Majesty.". Dalia walked away from me, leaving me confused. Perhaps she was referring to the fact that I should know my people, but that seemed unfair, there were far too many to remember.

I tried to think what Dalia may have meant, but then, Tisiphone arrived, with her armor covered in blood. "Where is Nigel? I asked him to meet this girl I sent to the Dark Wood.", "WHAT'S HAPPENED TO YOU?!", I bellowed out. "We were attacked in Kindy! Calypsa has an army of undead, just like...", "DON'T SAY HIS NAME!", I hissed. Saying the name always made me feel like I needed to look over my shoulder. "Look around you, Tig, Desian might as well be back! Calypsa killed...", Tisiphone choked up. I placed my hand on her shoulder, "Who?", I asked, concerned. "Sheena. Sheena is dead. Calypsa killed her.". Tisiphone fell into my arms sobbing. "There now, My Queen. Come on, let's get you cleaned up.". I took her up into our royal chambers and undressed her. I helped her climb into our tub. While she sat there, I washed her off. "She just killed her, Tig. She didn't even show any kind of remorse to Amana. She killed her sister's mother and didn't even care. And you wanted our son to marry that witch!". I said nothing. For years I listened to Tisiphone tell me of the real Micka. Of course, I never listened, because I grew up with Micka and thought I knew her better. "And do you want to know what I've learned about Micka? She is a goddess! She's been keeping that from us!", "Now I know that isn't right! I knew her from the time we were children. Don't you think I would know if she was a goddess?", "Tig, I don't know what her parentage is, but from what I saw, I know she is a goddess.". I thought about it for some time. When we were younger, I remember how she would latch onto me and Bastian. When I confessed that I liked her, she told me she preferred Bastian. It hurt so much, I stopped talking to them both. It wasn't Bastian's fault. I knew that. But I was a bitter youngster. Micka's father was very protective of her. I remember when he used to get angry because Micka would sneak us in. Once, as me and Bastian were running out, he threw a cup, and it hit me in the back of my head, and I barely remember waking up to Micka and Bastian laughing at me. As children, we had fun times. I wish I could go back to those days. Those days were better than what we were living now. Micka being the enemy, and my own best friend's daughter trying to kill everyone. It was times like this I wished Sebastian would come down from his seat in Heaven, and just be around us. Micka was evil. I had to accept that, but so was Calypsa. Both Ko-e and Amana were good from what I knew of them. I miss the days where we were just having fun.

After Tisiphone's bath, I helped her lay down. "You need rest, Ti. I'll go and get you some tea, okay?". She nodded and closed her eyes. I proceeded into the kitchen area. As I was walking, I felt a strange sensation. Suddenly, there was a cloaked figure standing in my path. I shook my head and realized I was really here and this individual was here as well. He pulled his cloak down and it was Bastian. I hugged him without thinking. "Bats! It's so good that you're here! There's so much going on! Calypsa killed Sheena, and Micka is a goddess, according to my wife, and I don't know what to do!". I realized, Bats was just staring at me. "What?", "I'm not Bastian.", the figure said, with a twisted smile. I started to back away and the figure moved towards me, "You can help me... You can help find us.". I didn't know what the hell he was talking about. I started to run. I ran out the door, and then ran into the next room, which somehow was the same room I just left. I bumped into the figure, who looked down on me. But then, they were gone. And in their place stood a very beautiful figure. "Alex?", I questioned. She nodded and helped me off the floor. My face was hurting. "What happened? Who was that?", "Tig, I don't know how to tell you this, but Amana is in trouble, and I need your help.".

ALEX: Tig took the information like I thought he would. He was scared, but brave enough to help. "So, let me get this straight; Desian is possessing Amana, and you don't know how to stop it? But you have a feeling that I can help with this situation? What about the fact that we just found out Micka is a goddess? What about that?". There was a part of me that always knew Micka was different. A part of her never made sense to me. Why did Falsa choose her to be Queen? Even more confusing, was the fact that Micka seemed capable of using godly items that required godly blood to use. Then, as I thought about it some more, I realized, Alisa was capable of the same feat's. She could use godly items, but I knew her parents. They were Plinthinian and held no special powers. "Tig, I honestly don't know what to say to that. Micka isn't my main concern. Desian is, and what he is doing.", "But I thought Bats got rid of him?", "I'm afraid it isn't that simple. Desian couldn't be killed. He is a part of Bastian. But what I'm confused about is how is he able to do this.", "Maybe it has something to do with what happened in that cave twenty years ago.". Tig didn't realize it, but he was right. Desian forced Amana's birth for a reason. Perhaps he knew he would be able to possess her. Then it dawned on me even more. "Desian needs another connection. Something that keeps him tethered here. You don't think Micka would go that far, do you?", "Alex, you are the goddess. You tell me if she would.". Tig was right. As a goddess, it was my place to approach her and ask. "Okay, I will go to her.". All I had to do was think about Micka, and I found myself before her.

She was on the edge of the Dark Wood. She was watching something but sensed my presence. "Alex, finally come down from her perch. Welcome back to hell.", "Micka, I just need to ask you something.", "Why waste time? Let's get this over with!", Micka said, unsheathing a sword from her backside. "Micka, this isn't about you and your daughter.", "Oh, I know what this is about. It's about Desian, and why he's getting stronger.". As much as this took me by surprise, it was nothing compared to what happened next. A force hit me from the side. I looked, and couldn't believe my eyes. "Amana?! What are you doing here?", "She isn't Amana anymore.", Micka said, with a very strange smile. Amana lifted me up with one hand by my neck, and punched me in the face. I flew six feet, and hit a tree. "Amana, wait…", I pleaded, but she was already on top of me, punching me repeatedly. "You thought you could just come down here and tell ME what to do? You were sorely mistaken, Alex. You see, down here, I'm the queen and the goddess.", Micka was saying. Amana stopped punching me. My vessel was too damaged to try and move. "Now, kill her.". Amana lifted my vessel and punched me through the heart.

AMANA: When I came to, I realized I wasn't in Alexandria anymore. I looked around and noticed Micka standing next to me laughing. I was holding something in my hand. It was Alex. She was beaten and from the looks of things, dead. I dropped her, horrified. "Alex?! What happened?!", I said, crawling up to her body, and placing my hands on her face, "Who did this to her?", I asked, trying to keep the tears in. "You did, my dear.", Micka said, with malice in her voice. "I couldn't… I would not have…", something inside of me told me I did do this. I backed away from her body, and Micka walked up to me and placed her hand on my shoulder. "There now, child, relax. You've done nothing wrong. She had no right to come here.", "What are you talking about?". I looked at my hands, covered in Alex's blood. I put my hands in my hair and pulled on it. I felt dizzy and delirious. Micka was just watching me. "What the hell is happening to me?!", I yelled at Micka, who just smiled. "Your true father wishes to have words with you.". There suddenly was a strange glowing hole in front of me. I looked closer at it and it was a strange man. "You've only destroyed her vessel. She isn't dead.", said the strange man, walking to Alex's body and stroking her face. "Such beauty. Yet, she chose my weaker half. Something I'm quite sure Micka here has come to realize, was a mistake.", "Who are you?", I asked him. "I'm the reason you exist Amana. And for that reason alone, you will do what I tell you.", "If you have anything to do with this…", I said, pointing at Alex's body, "…then I will not be listening to anything you say!". The man walked up to me and stood face to face with me. "You say that, as if you have a choice in the matter.". I felt my energy leave me. I wasn't in control anymore, and the man was gone. He was possessing me. I felt him in my bones and was scared to death. I called out for my mother in my head, then I called out for Alex, then I called out to Calypsa. What made me call her, I didn't know, but sure enough, she came out of the woods. "What the hell is going on?". Ko-e was with her and she looked weakened. But still concerned. "My daughter. I see what you have done.". Calypsa looked sick. "Mother, what are you doing here? I thought you were in the dungeon?", "I've escaped to come be with you.", Micka said to Calypsa. Calypsa looked around at the scene. Ko-e limped to Alex's body. "Amana, what have you done?", she asked, holding Alex's body. As I tried to say it wasn't me, the words would not leave my mouth. Something in Calypsa's eyes suggested she wasn't happy to see her mother. She came towards me and stared into my eyes. "You are not my sister. What have you done with her?", "This is better. She is our instrument of punishment now.", said Micka. Calypsa stared at her mother for a minute, then looked back at me. "I don't know what you've done to Amana, but you need to undo it. Now.", "After everything that's happened? You want to save her? Are you insane? We've come too far for this, Calypsa.", Micka said, frustrated. "Who exactly has come too far? I don't remember going anywhere with you.", Calypsa replied, placing her hand over my eyes. I felt a burning sensation, and then the man was visible again, and I had control of my body. "NO!", Micka yelled, but Calypsa grabbed her mother and slapped her. Ko-e was still holding Alex, tears coming from her eyes now. "Now I know you've lost it.", Micka said menacingly. She quickly grabbed her daughter and swung her by her hair and threw her. I quickly joined in, taking out my sword and swinging at Micka madly. Micka deflected me and cut me across my face. I felt the blood burn my eyes. Then, Micka flew into a tree and was knocked out. Both Calypsa and I turned to see Ko-e, with a look of hatred upon her face. She looked at Calypsa, "Don't think this changes things between us.". Calypsa nodded. "Well, it was fun while it lasted. I'll be taking my dear mother. You two, get out of here.". I looked at Calypsa. She gave me an understanding nod, picked up her mother, and departed into the woods. Ko-e grabbed me and said, "Let's go back to Alexandria.". The strange man was nowhere to be seen, but before he disappeared, it looked more like a woman.

KO-E: Amana was still weak, but was capable of moving around. I could see she was more worried about me, but she didn't need to know what Calypsa did to me quite yet. "Amana, you need to eat.", "I'm not hungry.". Amana had been refusing her meals, as well as ignoring the training I tried to pick up after Alex. Of course, I had gone through it already, and understood the purposes of it. Amana hadn't had her goddess experience yet, which is why she was still ignoring the training. I knew it would take Alex some time to make another vessel, so I tried my best, but Amana was too shaky and angry. "What's the point, Ko-e? We can't defeat Desian. I'm not hungry and I don't want to train.". She walked away and disappeared into the garden. There was a part of myself that couldn't really see myself training Amana. Especially since I had been forced to have sex with Scion. While there was a good feeling in there somewhere, it was tainted by the fact that Calypsa had weakened me, and mind-forced Scion. And I couldn't help but wonder where Alexa took him. Losa was glad to see I'd returned, but was very worried about Amana, "She woke up in the middle of the night and fled. We couldn't stop her. We didn't know where she went or what she was trying to accomplish.", "Well, she killed Alex's vessel, but it wasn't her, it was Desian.", "Desian? Where in the world did he come from? I mean, Amana was screaming his name in her sleep…", Losa said, thinking this over. "There isn't time to ponder on that now. We need to find out what Alex knew, and why she came here.". Losa nodded her head. Alex was someone I'd only ever seen in my dreams. She would visit me and spend time with me. I was angry with her for not telling me the truth about my mother. But there was more for me to learn.

Amana had not been seen since our last meal, where she ran into the garden. I grew more and more worried for her. I knew something wasn't right and couldn't just abandon the situation. Alexandria was huge. It wasn't just some castle and garden, it was a gigantic city, towering above Plinth. There were three different villages, all surrounding the castle and the garden. The villagers are different from Plinthinians. The people here were accustomed to peace. They were surrounded by powerful galactic energies that fueled their happiness. There wasn't a single bad soul in Alexandria and maybe that's why I am how I am. As much as I wanted to kill Calypsa, there was something inside of me that suggested that it's not in my nature. It took me a total of five days to visit each village and ask around about Amana. Finally, someone told me that they saw her heading back towards the castle less than three hours ago. I rushed to the castle, where there seemed to be some kind of commotion. "What's going on? Where's Amana?". Parnim came running out of the library, "Ko-e, you have to stop her! She's going for the Book of Truths!". I had never heard of this before. When I went into the library, Amana was staring into a book. She had crafted a ring of fire to stop anyone from getting to her. "Amana, what are you doing?", I asked her. She looked up at me with a strange look in her eye. The fire slowly disappeared, and she walked to me and handed me the book. I looked inside and found myself taken somewhere else.

FALTA: Alexandria was my home for as long as I could remember. Wilson, the kind old man who helped me with my training, had been training goddesses for years. I had to take a long training session into the summer because I lacked the understanding of a goddess. Of course, this is just what I was told. There were other goddesses before me, but they had died. Another thing I had been told. Sebastian, the man I would come to love and honor, was far away from me, but I kept the hope I'd meet him. While taking to the garden one day, there was a strange voice that spoke to me, "Hello, Falta, training got you down?". I looked for where the voice was originating, but couldn't seem to find it. "Excuse me, but, where are you?", "I'm here, but I'm not. Can you help me?", "Um, help you what?". The voice was quiet, but calm, "I need your help to exist. Sebastian put me here. I can't really live unless you help me.", "But if Sebastian put you there, is it your prison?". The voice was silent for some time, then, "No, I am Sebastian. I am a part of him that he discarded, but he needs me. He just doesn't realize how much.". I was becoming convinced. "If you are Sebastian, then does that mean that I am the goddess who will finally meet you?", "Of course, Falta, why do you think I'm contacting you?". I was so excited. "But you can tell no one of this conversation. Do you understand?". I nodded and beamed. "There is a book in the library that can help me. It's called the Book Of Truths. I need you to find it and read what it says. Can you do that for me, Falta?". Without an answer, I rushed over to the library. I looked around, but couldn't seem to find what the voice told me to find. I searched and searched and started to wish I'd gotten a description of what the book looked like. Just as I started to head back to where I heard the voice, that's when I saw it. A strange book, with gold rimming, and no title. I opened it and found myself watching, as a young girl was standing in the library. "Tila, you can't be in here! Not this section! Come on.". The girl, Tila, was being pulled by a very young looking Parnim, and she sported bright purple hair. I wondered who she was, but knew she must be a goddess if she is here being trained. The girl was very somber and gave no hint of her next action. "YOU LIED TO ME! I'M NEVER GOING TO KNOW SEBASTIAN!". Tila ignored the cries of those surrounding her and jumped from Alexandria.

KO-E: I found myself standing in the library again. My mouth was hanging open, and Amana closed it. I didn't know what to say. "Was that woman we just saw, was she…?", "Micka's mother? I believe so.". I fell to my knees. I couldn't believe what I just witnessed. "But the other girl, with the black hair that was called Falta. Whatever happened to her?". Amana gave me a look that suggested that I should know who that woman was. After pondering on it, I knew. "My mother. That was her.", I said in awe. But she didn't seem evil in that…whatever it was. She was a normal girl. But that voice that was speaking to her… "You don't think that my mother knew Micka's mother, do you?", "Ko-e, do the math. Your mother made Micka Queen of Dasha. I can only assume that it was out of some weird way to honor Micka's mother. The real question is, where is Tila?". Me and Amana thought on this. This, Tila, was very important. She was a goddess like ourselves, but was also the mother of Micka, and the grandmother of Calypsa. Tila reminded me of myself. I also ran away from Alexandria when I discovered I was being lied to. "Wait, didn't your mother say that Micka's father was killed twenty years ago?", I asked Amana, who replied, "She also said that Micka's mother died when she was young, and that Micka has no recollection of her. Which means there's a chance that she may be dead.", "Amana, goddesses can't die that easily. The only thing that would make sense, is that she was killed by another goddess or a god.", "I'll go with the goddess option.". Amana said, making certain eye contact with me. "Amana, are you trying to say that Falta killed Tila? That's impossible. There has never been more than one goddess in Alexandria, not counting right now.", I said quickly, before Amana could give a cold answer. "But we don't know that!", said Amana, now pacing, "Parnim, Losa, your brother, Alexa, my mother, everyone has been lying to us! We have no idea what really happened. And in case you're forgetting, your mother, Micka, and Alex were all here on this planet at the same damn time!". I had no answer for this. All three women were goddesses. And it also meant that Tila gave birth to Micka while Falta was the current goddess. "But the voice that was speaking to her, what was that? Or who?", "I know exactly who it was.", said Amana with a slight hint of anger in her tone, "It was our father's other side. Desian. This must be what led to the last war. Falta changed her name to Falsa, after the kingdoms decided to kill her.", "Kill her?", I asked, confused. "Wow, so you didn't know that either. Well, your mother was killed for spreading our father's good word. Desian made her another vessel and she returned as Falsa.". I began to see why Amana was so angry. "They should have told us. They should have told me.", I said, now hearing anger in my tone as well. Well I'm sending word to Calypsa. Micka is with her and maybe she can get some answers for us.". I didn't like the idea of involving the sister who basically raped me, but decided it was the best course of action.

CALYPSA: I had received word from Amana about something very disturbing, even for me. I knew I had to discuss this with my mother. I made my way through my village. Along the way, some of the children who were living here, offered me fruits and sweets. I smiled at them, "Not right now, little ones. But I'll come back.", I said, winking at them. I found my way into my prison, which I had hastily built soon after me and my dear mother arrived. My mother was sitting in her cell, writing in Godlic. "You must be so tired of cells.". Mother looked at me for some time, not saying anything. Finally, "I don't know. I've grown accustomed to them.", "Well, I won't waste time, there is something important I need to ask.". Mother sat up attentively. "What can you tell me about your mother?". Mother looked at me with a smile, "What have you learned?". I told my mother what Amana had sent to me. At first, she didn't seem surprised, but then she had a look of shock. "Falsa told me that my mother was a goddess, and I kept that secret for many years, but what you're telling me…is that you suspect…she killed my mother?". Seeing as how my mother kept this from me, I now had a better understanding. "You are a half breed. Just like Amana. I get it now. You're angry that Sebastian chose Alex over you. That's why you're helping Desian. But surely you know he is lying to you. He isn't going to make you his queen.". Mother laughed and stood up, "Silly girl, you think that's what I want? No, what I want, is just this planet. That's all I want. This is our planet, Calypsa. Nobody has the right to tell us how to live on it.", "You idiot, if Falsa did kill my grandmother, it was under HIS orders!". I found myself yelling at her. Mother sat back down and pondered on this. "Desian will get his, but for now, what we need is to establish that this is our planet.", "Tell me what you are really doing.". My mother turned from me and went back to writing. The writing she was placing on the walls read; (THE WEAK WILL PERISH BUT THE STRONG WILL GAIN HEAVEN).

After I left my mother's cell, I headed back to my home, which wasn't a castle, but it was good enough. Hoss' body was starting to smell, and I still had uses for it. I poured the green and red concoction I came up with once I had escaped Dasha. It was designed to bring back the dead. The people here weren't bandits like I had told Scion, but were the dead that I found in the woods. Sebastian killed all of them. Along with Alisa and Alex. I gave them a second chance, and, of course, they are repaying me by turning this run-down forest into a kingdom fit for all of us. Hoss woke up with a frightening scream. "Calm yourself, you've been brought back.". Hoss looked around and realized he was still in my home and tears started to roll from his eyes. "Please let me go! I get it, I'm ugly and I'll never…". I stopped him from completing his sentence, "Listen to me, you are going to find out where Scion is for me. You find Scion and I'll let you go.". Hoss looked around, "But isn't he here?", "No, he escaped some time ago. Now, you had better find him or I'll take back my gift.". Hoss jumped up and ran out of my hut. I knew he was probably going to try and escape, but I would remind him later that he couldn't escape me, no matter how hard he tried. I proceeded to write back to Amana;

Dear Amana,

I know that we aren't really on good terms, but at this point, I fear something more sinister is taking place right under our noses. My dear mother knew of her mother, but not that Falsa had killed her. I believe she is still attempting to contact Desian. I have no new information at this time.

p.s

Tell Ko-e that I'm sorry for what I did. I shouldn't have made Scion do that to her.

I knew it wouldn't mean much, but whatever was clouding my judgment, seemed to be gone. I feel like it may have had something to do with Desian, but I couldn't be too sure. There was a part of me that still wanted to hurt people.

As I made my way through the woods, I ran into Alisa, who was standing against a tree. As I looked at my surroundings, I realized I must be sleeping. "What do you want?", I asked, still not very happy with her. "I was wondering what you were doing is all. I see you've taken over the Dark Wood. The people that you have living here, I know what you've done.". I stared at her, waiting for what I knew she was going to ask, "You could bring back Sheena. Please, Calypsa, you took her from me and Amana, the least you could do is bring her back.", "I can't.", "WHY?!", Alisa asked me pleadingly. "Because, I can't bring back people that have passed on.", "What the hell does that mean?", "It means that Sheena was one of the first I tried to resurrect, and she wouldn't come back.", "Why wouldn't she come back? She was taken too soon.", Alisa said, glaring at me. "Alisa, I'm sorry. I didn't mean to kill her. Something was inside of me making me do all those things. I wish I could bring back Sheena. She was always kind to me. But, Sheena was happy where she was.". Alisa looked like she was thinking for a minute. "Where is Amana? She was here.". I quickly explained everything that had happened. Alisa looked stunned and frightened. "I need to get to my daughter, now! Can you help me?". I wanted to, but knew I couldn't leave these people. "I'm sorry, Alisa, but I must help these people heal from what Desian did to them.", "I see... Well, then, that's fine. I'm glad that you aren't like your mother.", "Who says I'm not. I might see clearly, but there will always be a part of me that is like my mother.". Alisa nodded, and I awoke.

SCION: The food was amazing, the architecture was amazing, the people were amazing, the inventions were amazing. Everything about this time that Alexa had brought me to was incredible. I was losing track of the time and going anywhere and everywhere. The kingdoms had been taken apart and turned into major cities. The city we were in now was Edge City. Edge was separated into two parts, north and south, both which were separate cities. There was a civil war one-hundred years ago that led to the separation of the north and south. Each had their own parliament and was set up with their own guard force, and an army, if you can believe it. The guard force focused on the criminal activity within the city, whereas the army focused on major incursions. Most of the Edgian soldiers were off in other lands fighting. War hadn't been seen in the city since the civil war, but there were gang battles, which sometimes ended with innocent casualties. Most men and women had jobs that paid as much as I was making back in Dasha. There were lesser jobs, though, that paid less. A gentleman that reminded me of Hoss, made me a sandwich known as a burger. The first time Alexa showed me this, I questioned how anyone can eat something like that. But once I tried it, I was hooked. The other foods were chicken, salads, beef, and pork.

You could cook them in many ways. Then there was the clothing. There was design to it. Artwork had been added and sometimes even characters. Television was one of those incredible inventions. We had something similar, of course. The computer. But, in this time, the television and the computer were two different things. My invention, the computer, had become something else entirely. But there was only one person who had the ultimate access. Amana. Who, at this time, was in Alexandria and had a special army unit called P.E.D. Ko-e was once in it but left, due to differences with Amana. I hadn't seen Amana at all. Alexa said I don't want to see her. But I missed her. And most of all, I missed Ko-e. The Ko-e at this time has no interest in me and acts like I'm a criminal. When I asked her why she even saved me, then? She had no answer and left me with none.

While waking up one morning, there was a commotion outside. A whole army unit was standing out there ready to come in. I jumped from bed. Alexa had already told me we aren't supposed to be here. I ran out of my room and bumped into Alexa, who grabbed me and directed me to a closet that was designed by Ko-e to throw Amana off. From inside the closet, I could see Ko-e going to the door. "Amana, this is getting old. Are you really here again?". Amana stepped in with five others, who spread out and went into different locations in the house. "Ko-e, once again, there was an energy signal that suggested a time displacement.", "This early in the morning? Amana, I just woke up.". Amana walked up to Ko-e and stood face to face with her. "So, you really are just going to lie to my face, aren't you? Well there have been witnesses. Witnesses that say somebody resembling Scion Tin, is walking around the city. So, what do you have to say to that?", "A descendant perhaps?", Ko-e said, in a not worried tone. "A descendant...", Amana repeated, "We both know that Scion and Alexa disappeared years ago. Now, people are saying that they've seen them, walking around.", "How do these people even know that they are from the past, Amana, really?". Amana walked around Ko-e and came straight to the closet door. She opened it and I thought she could see us, but she checked, and didn't see us, even though she was looking right at Alexa. I noticed that she had a scar on the side of her face and I wondered where she had gotten it. She closed the door and spoke to Ko-e, "Well, I don't know how you're doing it, but when I find out, I'm taking you in.", "Why not just have me killed like Calypsa? That would make things easy on you.". Amana glared, and then turned, and left. "I didn't know Amana had Calypsa killed!", I exclaimed, climbing out of the closet. "It's a long story, Scion. It's better if I don't say anything.", "No, that's not good enough. I need to know what happened.", "Okay, well, sometime after you two disappeared, things got heated. From there, Amana knew what she had to do. She didn't have the strength, so she asked someone else to handle it, plain and simple.". I glared at Ko-e, who glared back. "Scion, look, I get it, but I'm a lot older than the Ko-e you know. I have no romantic interest. I'm only looking to right the wrongs done by Amana.", "But what wrongs?", I said. Alexa looked at me with sad eyes, "Amana killed my husband. She killed the one man I loved. If it wasn't for her, he'd be here today. Ko-e begged Amana not to do it, but she refused to listen. Amana is on a trip, and she must be stopped, before she hurts somebody else.", "Not to mention she had our sister killed.", said Ko-e, with an irritated tone. "But I thought you hated her?", "Time brought me perspective. I know that Calypsa was cruel, but she was our sister. She saved my life more times than she hurt me. I can't be angry with her.". Now I was even more confused by Ko-e. First, she brings me here, then refuses to speak with me. Then she acts like I'm some kind of criminal, then now she throws me off with her confessed love for Calypsa. "DID YOU FORGET WHAT SHE DID TO US?!", I yelled, hoping something might trigger in her. "Scion, that was decades and decades ago. You really think after everything that happened within that time till now, I would still hold a grudge about that?". Now that actually made sense, and for the first time since my arrival, I felt out of place. "Look, what Ko-e is trying to say, is that she didn't bring us here.", Alexa said, along with a pitying look. "When Alexa first arrived, I wondered what the hell was going on. She showed up on my doorstep. It dawned on me right away why we never saw her again. This led to Caprius turning Plinth upside down. It led to his death.". Ko-e turned away. "You see, Scion, when I disappeared, somebody in this time brought me here. They brought me specifically. But according to Ko-e, this isn't what originally happened. Amana is aware of this and that is why she is searching for us. This person who brought me here is messing with a power so dangerous, it could implode everything Sebastian ever created.". It was dawning on me now. The sense in it. "Time… If this continues, time itself is at risk. Why keep us here? Why not return us? And why bring me here?". I somehow knew before she said it, "BECAUSE IT'S YOU, SCION! YOU'RE THE TIME DISRUPTOR!".

ALISA: Everything seemed to be tumbling around me. Desian did something to my daughter. I had stood by and mourned long enough. After my conversation with Calypsa, I was more convinced than ever that Alex knew this. This is why she came to Amana that night. She wanted to prevent whatever Desian is doing. But I wasn't going to let it happen. I started for the stables. Men who had lost loved ones that day Calypsa attacked, were eager to strike back at Dasha. I, of course, knew it would be a waste of time. Calypsa was in the Dark Wood, Micka was her own daughter's prisoner, and Dasha was occupied by the Alexandrian army, and the Dashin soldiers weren't doing anything about it because their royalty wasn't around. I didn't know who would command the forces of Alexandria with Alexa missing, and Caprius being held in Nasher for his health. Then I remembered, Ko-e. Who at that moment was arriving along with Amana. I rushed to her and threw my arms around her. But she seemed cold. I let her go and placed my hands on her face, "I've missed you so much. I heard about what happened and…", before I could finish my sentence she pushed my hands away. "When were you going to tell me the truth about your mother?". I looked at her confused, not knowing what she was talking about. "Amana, there is nothing to say about my mother. You know her. She was the queen.". Amana gave me a confused look, and then realization spread across her face. She embraced me in a hug and didn't let go for a while. "What is going on? What are you talking about?". Ko-e was looking at me with pity as well. I began to feel little. "Mom, you can enter into people's dreams and you never thought about that, did you? Or about the fact that you can wield godly weapons. Like that teleporter ring you took from Micka twenty years ago.". I was confused as to how they had these details. "I need you two to tell me whatever it is you're not.". Amana placed her hands on my shoulders, "Mom, you're a goddess.".

I had been extremely busy since Amana and Ko-e's arrival. I had been keeping busy on purpose. Mainly because I refused to accept what they told me. I knew who my parents were. I loved them. They are Derek and Shay Tia. They were the King and Queen of Kindy and I was their pride and joy. They raised me to be tough. They lied to me for a large majority of my life to make me into what I am today. The best queen Plinth has ever known. Kindy is a peaceful happy kingdom, and thanks to Micka, it is now on edge. People wanting blood or just plain looking out for another attack. Ready to flee, or fight, or die. I didn't like seeing my people like this. Amana, being my daughter, held similar feelings, and was growing tired of my avoidance. She cornered me in the morning when I awoke. "Good morning, Mother. Ready for the truth this morning?", "Amana, please, I don't want to talk about this.", "Well I brought some people here to help me. My mother stepped into the room, along with my father. "Please, I don't want to hear this. I don't care.", "Alisa, we need to tell this to you. Because if we don't, we will continue to be living somewhat of a lie.". I looked at my mother and father and tears came to my eyes, "Okay, fine, what is this story?", "There was a young girl many years ago. Her name was Tila. She came here, scared and alone. She had two children. One had vibrant purple hair, and the other bright red. She said she couldn't take care of both and chose to give you to us.

Over time I grew to love you.", my mother said, also tearing up, "You were the most vibrant girl in the world. But that's when Wilson came to us. He told us your mother had been killed. And that your sister and father were in Nasher. He told us that you would be destined for terrible things. I didn't believe it, until we met Sebastian. It was then that I knew that Wilson was right.". I remembered how Wilson stayed with me. I remembered all the training that he gave me. He even told me that the training he was giving me was the same way he'd trained goddesses. I always knew Wilson was smart, and hardly brought into him training goddesses. But now, it was making sense why he would train me. It wasn't because I was a princess, it was because I am a goddess. "But, if what you're telling me is true, then that means, Micka is my sister. Is that what you want me to believe? My sister is the most vilest woman on Plinth?", "Not just your sister, your twin sister.", Amana said. I didn't know how to respond to this. I remember when I first met Micka. I was saving her life. While my father was lying there, dead. At the time, I had no idea he was my father. Now I just looked at the whole thing as foolish. "Micka and I are twins?". I hardly saw a resemblance. I didn't see how we could be related. I looked like my mother, Queen Shay. Then something else started to dawn on me. "Was my father…?", "The Prince of Kindy? Yes. He met your mother while traveling, and the two fell into such a deep love, he renounced his royalty, and went to live in Nasher. He sent your mother to deliver you unto us, because he couldn't bear to face us, and we have raised you. So, yes, we are your family. We are your grandparents.", "But that means you're Micka's as well!", I yelled, looking at them in horror, "Why haven't you told her?", "I wanted to! Twenty years ago, when she first came here. I knew it was her. The purple hair, the beautiful face. She was the spitting image of the woman that came here and took away my son. I know it was wrong, but I blamed her some. We locked her away, your father and I. We didn't know if we should tell her the truth or not. I also knew she was lying to me about why she was here. It pained me that the first meeting of my granddaughter turned into a nasty altercation that ended in Wilson's death.".". I remembered that. Me, Sebastian, and Caprius, returning here, to find that Micka had killed Wilson. It was all coming together. Falsa knew Tila. She probably killed her. Then she gave Micka, Tila's daughter, the commoner, the throne. She did this because Micka is a goddess. And she knew it. She knew I was a goddess. She knew we were sisters the whole time. She may even have pitted us against each other by sending her here to kill Wilson. Falsa turned my sister into her. "I want to be alone. Please.". Everyone turned to leave, except my mother, who I now had to accept was actually my grandmother. "At the time, Alisa, it just didn't seem right to tell Micka we are her family.", "She has been alone all this time. Thinking she had no one. You allowed her to abuse YOUR great-granddaughter. How could you? This is worse than the lie you told me for so many years. I grew to understand that one. But this one…". Shay had tears dropping off her face, "If you were to lose Amana forever to Scion, would you not hate the boy?", "Oh, yes, Scion I would hate. His child, I would never.". Shay stormed out of the room, leaving me to ponder if Micka knew we were twins. I needed to know. I closed my eyes and put myself into a deep sleep.

Micka was sitting in her cell. She sensed me and looked in my direction. "Alisa. What do you want from me?", "Did Falsa tell you?", "Did she tell me what?". I was nervous. All the times I'd been in Micka's vicinity, I'd never felt this nervous. "About…about Tila.". Micka looked more confused than I did. "Alisa, what the hell are you telling me? Out with it!", "We are twins.". Micka looked like she was about to say something, then laughed. She continued to laugh for long minutes. "Are you done?", I asked impatiently. "No. Far from it.", she said, finally calming down. "You expect me to believe that? We are twins? The man, who you so casually stepped over, that day we first met, was your father?", I nodded. "And my mother, Tila, a well-oiled bonafide goddess, just like Alex and Falta, was also your mother?". I nodded again. "And all this time you've been in Kindy, being raised by two people who aren't even your parents?", "Well, about our father…". I quickly explained the story. Micka grew stone silent. "No.", "Micka…", "NO! I am not listening to this! My father was the Prince of Kindy? I'm supposed to just believe that? Kindy never had a prince!", "It did. They just, sort of wrote him out since he abandoned his position.". Micka was growing angrier, and I was having regrets coming to her. "Alisa, if we are truly sisters, then take my hand.". I didn't know what she expected from this, and I knew better than to trust her, but something inside me at the moment said I should do it. I reached out, and at that moment, I felt a warm feeling sweeping through me. I felt our connection. I realized it was always there, but I just never considered it. Micka smiled and released my hand. "So, it's true. We really are twins. So now what? Do we hug? Share stories about how different our lives were growing up? What do you expect now, Alisa?", "To find our mother.", "She is dead. Falsa killed her.", "No, that's just what the girls think. I know she is alive. Didn't you feel it right now?". Micka closed her eyes and touched the Godlic writing. She held out her hand for me to grab her. When we touched, I could suddenly read the writing. "Micka, what does that even mean the strong will gain Heaven?", "It's something written before our time. Before anyone's time. Have you heard of the Book Of Truths? I believe our daughters have come into contact with it.". I hadn't heard of it, and Amana and Ko-e didn't say anything. I tried to put the pieces together that Micka was giving me, but they were only confusing me more, "Micka, I'm going to come here and take you out of this cell, but I want to know one thing. Will you look for Mother with me?". Micka looked at me for the first time in a long time, with the look of a girl who was lost. I could tell all the hatred she had built for me was subsiding with the knowledge that we are sisters. She slowly nodded her head.

When I awoke, it was the middle of the night, and I knew I had to leave. With everything going on, finding Tila was important. I made my way to the stables and took one of the thunder horses. These were rarely used because they made a lot of noise. As soon as I started it, Amana came out of the stable, where her horse, Mod, was kept. "So, I was right to assume, then.". I felt foolish being caught by my own daughter. "Mother, I know what you are going to do, and you need to remember that Micka is the one who is declaring war on the planet. Because of her, Sheena is dead, and countless others.", "I KNOW THAT!", I yelled, feeling irritated that she had the nerve to remind me of this. I reminded her, "YOU ARE THE ONE WHO TOLD ME THE TRUTH!". She looked guilty. "I thought you knew and that you were keeping it from me. When Grandma told me the truth, I knew that I was right.", "Right about what?", "Desian and the long game.". I wasn't understanding what she was talking about. "Desian's long game? What do you mean?", "Desian, many years ago, was sealed into the planet. He made a wound where he could seep into this world. He then waited till a good enough time to tempt fate. He saw your mother and introduced her to the Book Of Truths. But, she didn't aid him. The next goddess, Falta, was dumb enough to listen. That led to the events of twenty years ago. But, Desian wasn't trying to accomplish his goal then, he was just distracting and setting more things into motion.". As Amana said this, a hooded figure revealed themselves to be Alex. She looked the same and didn't look dead at all. "It's a new vessel, Amana.", she said, before Amana said anything. "There is something I need to tell the both of you. I should have when I learned of it. The truth is, Desian planted his soul inside of Ko-e years ago. He has been hiding inside of her, until Ko-e came into contact with Calypsa. Then, Calypsa took on some of his essence. This is the explanation for her strange behavior as well as yours, Amana. Inside of you girls, exist Desian's essence. But even worse is, I've recently learned something else. There is a woman alive who is a goddess. A woman somewhere hidden on this planet.", "Yes, Alex, it is my mother.", I said. Alex stared at me. "I knew it.", Alex said excitedly, "I always had a strange feeling you were more than just a princess.", "The woman you're speaking of is also Micka's mother.". Alex's smile faded. "She and you are sisters? Hmm, I was afraid of something like this years ago, but it seemed impossible.

The Trinity.". I had never heard the words, but Amana was staring at Alex with complete fear. "I heard those words in the Book Of Truths. When it showed me Tila, it mentioned she was part of the Trinity. What is that exactly?", "Me, Alisa, and Micka. We are the Trinity. We are the three goddesses that weren't supposed to be. We have a power that we share, if we come together. It could destroy the world. Me and Sebastian thought that it was you three girls. Ko-e, Calypsa, and Amana, but now I know the truth.", Alex finished, rubbing her temple. "But why would it be us? What is different about us?", "We don't have Desian inside of our souls. We are untainted. We can become one.". I still didn't know what the hell that meant. "When you say become one…", "It is exactly like it sounds.". Something told me I didn't like the sound of that.

NIGEL: Mileeda was easy to spot. She was blue. I hadn't seen anything like it before and reminded myself this truly was the end times. "You must be, Mileeda. My mother…", she put her hand up, gesturing to me to be quiet. "Ko-e isn't in the Dark Wood anymore. She has gone to Kindy with Amana.", "Then what are you doing out here?", "I'm going to kill Queen Micka. Calypsa has locked her mother away and I'm going to use this opportunity to do what I failed to do last time.". I considered what she was saying. It was no secret to me that Micka had killed my grandfather. Mother had told me the story several times, but like father, I knew that trying to get vengeance meant going to war. "Mileeda, perhaps we should depart. I mean, if Calypsa has her locked away, it seems like a lot of trouble.", "I'm going to kill her, too.". I knew I had to do the princely thing and drag her away. As soon as I touched her, she grabbed my hand and squeezed it. "Ouch! What the hell?!", "I TOLD YOU, I'M NOT LEAVING!". Rubbing my hand, I backed away, "Why do you need to kill them so badly?", "They murdered my parents. They are going to pay for that.", "Micka killed my grandfather, you don't see me storming in there.", "Did you ever know your grandfather?". She had me there. "No. I didn't. I guess I see your pain, but I'm telling you, this is foolish.". Mileeda turned to look at me, then fell into my arms, sobbing, "THEY DIDN'T DESERVE IT! THEY WERE ALWAYS GOOD PEOPLE!", "Most don't deserve to die, my friend, but sometimes, bad things happen to those who have good hearts.", "I know I shouldn't be here, but I don't know what else to do. I can't face my sister, I don't know what's happening with Ko-e, and I'm just trying to chase what seems right.". Mileeda put her face in her hands. I knew how to comfort an upset woman. I placed my hands on her shoulders and looked her in her eyes, "Put all your anger into me.". Before I could do anything, Mileeda was kissing me.

By the time we had woken up, Mileeda was gearing to leave. The blue tinge in her skin was replaced by normal pale white skin. "Where are you riding?", "I don't know. Ko-e said Scion is with Alexa and I don't know where they are, but I think I should look for them.". I was asked to look for Ko-e a while back, but of course, her brother had infected a soldier with some disease. I quickly explained this to Mileeda who pondered on it. "I haven't been this way for long, but it has somehow made me smarter. Something tells me that Scion and Alexa are beyond our reach at this point.", she said with a scowl. "Why don't we just go to Nasher and see what my father says?", I suggested. Before Mileeda could answer, Calypsa came out of the woods. She looked from me to Mileeda, then smiled. "Welcome! Please, join me.". She turned back around and went into the woods. Mileeda and I gave each other uncertain looks, but followed.

Calypsa led us to a clearing that had a somewhat large village in the center. In the back was a house that looked like it was being renovated. The people in the village were working hard. They seemed too busy to stop and pay attention to us. The children were all playing, and some grabbed Calypsa's hand as she walked by. I noticed she playfully obliged them. This Calypsa wasn't anything like the one I had been hearing about. She was supposedly evil and a murderer. I looked towards Mileeda, who looked like she was waiting to strike. Finally, we entered into the home being remodeled. It was very fancy. From the looks of things, the PE was being run through here to support the rest of the village. "Calypsa, this is amazing.", I said. Mileeda shot me a dirty look. "Thank you, Nigel. Mileeda, what do you think?". Mileeda looked mutinous. "I can see what you think. I'm sorry about your parents. It wasn't me that condemned them.", "Are you going to try and say it was all your mother?". Calypsa went into explanation about Desian, and how he was possessing her and Amana. She also explained that she was working with her sisters to try and save the planet. Once again, I felt confused. "Desian is the guy my dad is afraid of. How is he possessing you and Amana?", "Through Ko-e. It is a really long story, but just trust me that I will make sure my mother pays for the things she has done. I'll take you to her, but you can't hurt her.". Mileeda glared at Calypsa, then nodded. Calypsa led us to her mother's cell in a small but effective prison. At the end of the hall, I assumed Micka was there, because there were two women outside her cell. One I immediately recognized as Alisa and the other was so beautiful I lost all train of thought. "Alisa, Alex? What the hell are you two doing?". As Calypsa asked this question, Micka was stepping out of her cell. "NO! WHY?!", Calypsa shouted, running towards them, but before she could do anything, all three disappeared on the spot. "I WILL NOT LET HER GET AWAY AGAIN!", Mileeda exclaimed and ran out of the prison. Calypsa just sat there with a confused look on her face. I chased Mileeda out of the prison, "WAIT! Mileeda, that was Amana's mother. She hates Micka, she must have a reason.", "I don't care what the reason is! I'm going to find all three…", before she could finish her sentence, Calypsa tapped her on the head with a strange glowing sword. "That should take care of her for a while. Follow me. I'm going to contact Amana.". We went back to the house, Calypsa, carrying Mileeda on her shoulder. When we arrived, Calypsa placed Mileeda on her bed, then went to her desk and scribbled a letter. She sent it off and we waited. Finally, a reply arrived, and Calypsa quickly read through it. "So, apparently, Alisa is my aunt.". Feeling I didn't know what she could mean, I asked, "Your aunt?", "My mother and Alisa are twins, and now are on a quest to find their own mother.", "So, what does that mean?", "It means that Micka is out of our hands. We need to focus on the more current threat of Desian. And we need to find Scion.", "What's the significance of finding him?". I couldn't see what we needed him for. He was the guy that created the computer, but what could he do about Desian? "Scion has a major part in this. I still haven't figured it out yet, but it will come to me.".

SCION: I spent a large amount of time now trying to figure out how I could do something like this, and what my motives would even be. But not only that, how was I still alive? Shouldn't I be dead? I knew Ko-e knew the answer, but for some reason, didn't want to tell me. Amana didn't come back, but I was also trying to figure out where these other time displacements were taking place. I had ventured into Edge city to look for any signs. I had constructed a makeshift modulator that would read the readings the time displacement left behind. Often, I would find faint traces and follow them to dead ends. Other times, I would find a more interesting situation. Energy signals large enough for the individual to be right there on the spot. But when I'd get there, it was empty, and nothing seemed out of place.

Eventually, I decided it was too risky to sneak out of the house anymore. I noticed P.E.D soldiers almost everywhere I went. Most were in obvious incognito outfits. But the others were in uniform. I remembered Ko-e had told me that P.E.D was a secret military force, and that they had the tech to erase memories. She said this whole town was ripe for what she called 'brain fixtures', the rearranging of one's memories. Amana could literally craft new memories into someone's cerebral and make them forget whatever traumatizing event took place. "How many of those events have you had?", I asked Ko-e one day, as we were sitting for dinner. "Well, not many. There were a few close calls. But for the most part, me and Amana were together, then.", Ko-e said, with a reminiscent face. "You still haven't fully told me why you two aren't on talking terms.". Ko-e looked at Alexa, who was biting into a fried chicken thigh. "Dom luk af me.", Alexa said, with a mouth full of food. "Scion, I just don't think I'm ready to tell that to you yet.". I was starting to get the feeling it was more than what she had said before. "Look, you said Amana killed Caprius, and that's why you were upset with her. But that was way before. And you were still with P.E.D for all that time. So, what really happened?". Ko-e looked at me sadly and then bowed her head, "Scion, you remember when I told you that you're the one messing with time?", "Of course I do! I've been trying to understand it.", "Scion, your mind isn't ready to comprehend why you would do something like this. And I'm not ready to tell you. It's better if we just focus on stopping you.", "And how am I supposed to stop myself.", "It's already being done.", Alexa said, watching me curiously. It slowly started to dawn on me. "You brought me here, because you want my current version to disappear. If I exist on this plane long enough, I'll cease to exist in this future.". Ko-e nodded. "More than that, you'll be able to start over here. None of the past will affect you.". I saw a flaw in this logic. "But how was I able to make it to where I am? The journey that brought me to this future.", "Scion, that wasn't a good journey. Why do you think you were plucked from that time? Because events that took place, then, led to decisions you are making now. It's the main reason that I know what I'm talking about.", "No, Ko-e, even I can see that if you keep me from doing whatever I did, then, it will affect the future worse than how I'm affecting it now.". Alexa looked like she had seen a ghost. Ko-e looked angry. "Ko-e, could that be right?", Alexa asked fearfully. I could tell this was going to be tough. "Ko-e, listen to me, whatever it is you're afraid to share, I think that Amana might be right. You can't let me and Alexa stay here.", "Alexa is fine. She disappeared. You on the other hand, you help us defeat the Unknown. Then you went on to find certain things. Certain things that gave you eternal life.". I froze. I had thought about it, but then again, knew it was impossible. But if what Ko-e is telling me is true… "Are you telling me I found the Tree Of Curses?". Alexa dropped her jaw, "But that doesn't exist. It's made up!", "No, it isn't Alexa. And only Scion at the time could understand that what most considered a story of caution, actually was a map.".

The story of the Tree of Curses goes way back before the Sebastian/Desian war. It was in a time where the god was considered a threat. The goddess of the age is rumored to have turned into a tree. The tree had certain points on it that held significant meaning to the god's return. On the lowest branch was his ability to care. On the middle branch was his strength and the top branch was his wisdom. It's said that whoever can spot the Tree Of Curses will be given a gift. A gift so powerful it would make the discoverer the most powerful man or woman on Plinth. But this was a story. The whole story is that the goddess will consume your soul and you will forever be stuck in the tree with the goddess. Most thought of this story as a warning not to search for such a tree, for fear of what happens when you find it. But others twisted the tale, using it as a fear factor against their children. But I saw it as something entirely different. I saw it as my answer to everything. The branches weren't just significant towards Sebastian, but also to those seeking the tree. The drawing of the Tree Of Curses to the untrained eye looked like a regular tree. But I saw that the branches were lines. Lines that led through certain lands on Plinth. It was at this time that I discovered that the branches would lead me to the tree. But I thought, what if I'm wrong? It would end up being a fruitless quest. I decided to bury it and to stop thinking about it. The likely hood that I would find the Tree Of Curses was so low, that it was like Micka giving me the best sex of my life.

As I continued to ponder over the course of the next week, I found myself walking around the city again. I noticed a small girl, who had such shiny black hair, she caught my attention. She waved and directed me to follow her. She led me to a strange chapel. As I walked inside, the girl seemed to disappear, and I was staring down rows and rows of seats. Leading up to the stage was a vibrant purple rug that seemed to glow. On the stage above the pulpit, was an image I had to assume was of Sebastian. He was wearing a white gown and stretching out his arms as if walking towards something. A man in a similar white gown was sitting at the front. Before I could turn and walk out, the man spotted me, "What brought you here, my son?". I moved towards the man, feeling unsure. "Did you notice a small girl? I could have sworn she came this way.". The man looked like he was thinking about something, and then, patted the seat, gesturing for me to sit next to him. As I sat down, the man stared up at the image of Sebastian, "When I was a young boy, I didn't believe in Sebastian. I ran with a tough crowd, and did a lot of things I'm not proud of. Do you want to know what finally stopped me?". I nodded, confused as to why this man was telling me all this. "Well, one day, as I was going to hit a lick at this local store I always used to hit, a young girl grabbed my hand and asked me for directions. Before I knew what I was doing, I had shot that little girl.". I looked at the man in horror. Before I could tell him what a disgusting creature he was, he continued, "The girl wasn't dead, and I rushed her to the nearest doctor. I told them exactly what I did, and of course, they called the Guard Force, and they came and took me in. I spent twenty-five years paying for that crime. And all I could think about after that, was how I would never hit another lick again, if that little girl lives. I never prayed to Sebastian, but that day I screamed at him. When I heard that the little girl lived, that's when I took on this new life. I never did another wrong thing in my life. What brought you here, young man, was the glory of Sebastian.". I knew this old man had no idea what he was talking about. "What if I told you, I know one of Sebastian's daughters?", the man looked at me and smiled, "Ko-e. She comes here often.". I was surprised by this information. "Sebastian doesn't always show us exactly what we need to see, boy, he gives us lessons that teach us these things. Experiences. That little girl you followed in here, she wanted you to come here. There is something here perhaps that will help you.", "Where do I look, then?". The old man pointed in the direction of a door. I stood up and looked at the man again. He nodded for me to go that way. I did. As I walked inside of the room, I noticed it was a huge grave site. Inside was a tombstone labeled; HERE LIES COPHONE. A BRIGHT LIGHT TAKEN TOO SOON. As I looked it over and over, I couldn't help but notice the style of writing. Since I had been here, I noticed writing was different. It was nothing like three-thousand years ago, but the writing on this tombstone dated almost till back then. At least it wasn't like the writing of this day and age. The old man entered the room. "Who was this 'Cophone'? How old is this grave?", "It was way before my time, and as for her identity, she was one of Sebastian's grandchildren.", "But he never had…", I found myself trailing off. It had been three-thousand years. I imagined Amana and Ko-e had no children. Calypsa was dead, so there was no worrying about her. I remembered Sebastian had a son, but couldn't see why his child would be here. I gave the old man a confusing stare. "Perhaps, you should speak with Ko-e.".

I started back to Ko-e's house from the church, but heard a familiar voice from behind me, "Okay, Scion, enough is enough.". It was Amana. She didn't have her army with her. "Who was Cophone?", "That isn't for you to know, Scion. As a matter of fact, I warned Ko-e against giving you that exact info.", "When did you warn her of this?", "Well, we had a private meeting in which I got her to secretly confess she is harboring you and Alexa. Your past versions.", "So, Alexa has a future version as well?", "Yes, she is right here.". I turned to face a blue-haired woman, with an old wrinkle under her eyes. It was an aged Alexa. "But how can she be here? And old?", "Well, it's a long story, but you need to know something, Scion. You can't know Cophone. You need to go back to your time and forget the things you've seen here. You can come with us now, or we can take you.". I saw behind Amana, the little girl I followed into the church. She was shaking her head no. "I can't go, Amana. I'm sorry.", "Do you think I'm giving you a choice, Scion? Dealing with the future you is bad enough.", "I plan to prevent myself.", "You can't and trust me, you won't. You aren't going to stop, Scion. Because you believe you are right.", "Does Cophone have anything to do with this?". I saw the answer in Amana's eyes. "Amana, who is she?". Amana took out a hand-cannon, and pointed it in my face, "Alexa is going to cuff you and you are coming with us, Scion.". The little girl started to cry, and I quickly ran away. "Shit! I need units six and nine to move in, he's headed your way.". I heard Amana sending somebody else after me. I had been around Edge long enough to know some good hiding places. As I was running, I found myself running into the younger Alexa. Ko-e had opened some kind of portal. "Scion, I'm sorry.", Ko-e said with tears in her eyes. She came up to me and put her hands on my chest. "Cophone, I didn't want you to know about her.", "How did you even know where I was?", "Cotton called me. The priest at the church.". I looked into Ko-e's wet eyes, and saw something I hadn't seen since I got here. "You do still love me, don't you?", "Yes. After all, you are the father of my children.". I dropped my jaw, "Children? As in more than one?". Ko-e continued, "We have a son, he was our first born. But we had a daughter as well.", "Had?". Ko-e's eyes started glowing with tears, "Cophone, was our daughter, and because of Amana, she is lost to us!", "This is why I'm messing with time? I'm trying to save our daughter?". As Ko-e nodded, the little girl appeared behind her, smiling. I realized she was my daughter's ghost.

AMANA: The days since my mother had departed to find her and Micka's mother seemed to be long gone. Me and Ko-e were in Kindy trying to ramp up protections from Desian. "If he is going to possess one of us, then what is the point of these protections?", Ko-e was asking me one day, as I had another cannon fitted onto a gate that I had built. "Ko-e, if he possesses one of us, it won't be a big deal. We will be ready for him.". Although Desian was the evil estranged side of my father's personality, he seemed more like an evil uncle. We didn't know when he would strike or even if he really could.

Part of me knew he was weaker, but another part of me knew that he's tricky. I still hadn't asked Ko-e what happened between her and Calypsa, but she didn't seem too keen on talking about it. As I made my way around the kingdom, people started to hail me as the new queen in my mother's absence. I, of course, corrected them, and informed them my mother would be back. In truth, I wasn't sure of this. Finding out your worst enemy shared a womb with you at the same time can be a life changing thing. Especially finding out you are a goddess. I wished I could be with my mother. I mentioned this one day in front of Ko-e, who said nothing and left me alone. Ko-e was becoming more sordid as the days passed. She didn't want to be around anyone, including me, and seemed highly distant. I realized she missed Scion, and wanted to be wherever he was, which we still had no idea where he and Alexa disappeared to.

One day, Ko-e came to me, "I'm going to Nasher to be with my brother, is there anything you need from me?", she said coldly. "Well, not really, but are you sure you have to go?". Ko-e gave me a look of sadness, "Amana, there is so much I don't understand anymore. I once hailed my mother as a hero, now I know her only as an evil woman. Selfish. And she almost killed everyone. My brother was no better, and I haven't seen him since I learned the full truth.". Now I understood what she was feeling. "Go if you must, but, Ko-e... ", "Yes?". I pulled her into a hard-pressed hug. I loved her. I didn't know her for as long as I've known Calypsa, but I loved her. Ko-e wrapped her arms around me as well. "Don't worry, Sister, we will see each other soon.". Ko-e left, taking another look at me before she disappeared. And as she disappeared, a bright light enveloped the whole room, and suddenly out of what seemed to be a hole in the fabric of the air, Scion ran out. I could see something following him, but the hole closed before whatever it was could get through. "Amana! When am I?!". I had no idea what he was talking about. "Scion, where have you been? We've all been worried about you! Ko-e just left. You may still be able to catch her.". Scion stood up and grabbed my arms. "Amana, you need to listen to me, but we can't talk out here, lets go to the castle.". I led Scion to the castle, and we went into the room where my mother usually hosts these kinds of private meetings. Scion looked different. He wasn't wearing his usual confidant look. He was unnerved. "Scion, where did you come from, and what was that thing you exited out of?", "It's called a wormhole and they coincide with time travel.", "Time…travel?", I repeated, thinking that can't possibly sound how it sounds. "Amana, I've been three-thousand years into the future, and I've met you and Ko-e there. I've also met Alexa, who by the way, is still there, and she isn't coming back.", "What about Caprius?", "That's her problem, but what we need to discuss is my daughter, and how you are going to kill her.".

CHAPTER 11

The Undying Cophone

SCION: I pretty much saw Cophone everywhere I went. She seemed to be haunting me. As for Ko-e, she had become more open with me since telling me the truth. I was curious about our son, but Ko-e said I knew too much already. As I tried to put Cophone out of my mind, so that I wouldn't screw with time, I kept finding it almost impossible. But the one thing Ko-e still hadn't told me, was how Amana killed Cophone. "Well, to tell you that story, it will take time. I'm afraid we don't have that time, Scion. Amana is coming for you here. I've decided to let you go. It's time you went back to your own time.". I looked at Alexa, who was all settled to stay. "But what about Alexa?", "Don't worry about her. Believe it or not, that woman you met wasn't Alexa. Alexa died years ago. That woman was…", before Ko-e could finish her sentence, there was banging on the door. Ko-e opened it, and Amana, and her two personal goons stepped in, along with the strange older woman who resembled Alexa. "Ready to go, Scion?", Amana asked, with her arms folded on her chest. I looked to

Ko-e, who gave me a reassuring nod. I left with Amana and she led me to a vehicle with wheels that were made of rubber. I'd seen the vehicle before because it seemed all of Edge had one. It was called a flar.

"Amana, I need to know about Cophone.". Amana sighed, but took a deep breath, "Well, I wasn't trying to kill my niece. I was trying to help her. But it was an impossible situation, Scion. It's the reason that I did what I had to do. It wasn't easy for me. I loved her.", "What did you have to do? What was the problem?", "Cophone was a very powerful goddess. But she couldn't control her power. She was on the verge of exploding with all the energy she had built up inside of her. She was basically a nuclear reactor walking around in Plinthinian skin. I tried everything imaginable that would save her, but in the end, she went critical, and I had to make a choice. I sent her into Space so that she could die in peace.". As Amana finished, I felt tears coming from my eyes. "But what caused her to be that way?". Amana, once again, sighed, "It may have been my fault. When I realized the power she had, I roped her into joining P.E.D. I told her that she had a responsibility with her powers. I didn't realize it, until it was too late, but the more she used her power, the more her power consumed her. I lead my niece to her death.". Amana put her face in her hands, and I noticed, she truly was sad. But there was a part of me that was too angry to care. Before I could say anything, a force hit the side of the flar. The flar rolled and hit a wall. "IS EVERYONE OKAY?!", one of Amana's goons asked. As I was removing the safety strap, my door opened, and someone pulled me out. I didn't recognize this person. "Come on, we gotta get moving!". I followed, not knowing where I was being led. Finally, the person threw something in the air and I recognized what it was doing. It was altering the air particles and making us invisible. It was an updated version of Amana's void disruptor. The person looked at me and stared at me in shock, "I've never seen you look so confused before...", "I'm sorry, who the hell are you?", "All in good time, but for now, there is somebody who wants to meet you.". I saw the younger woman who was with Amana, rushing into the alley. She threw something, and the air particles started to return to normal, rendering us visible. But before we turned completely visible, something took us. I found myself flying up and up, all the way out of the atmosphere, and into what looked like some kind of vessel.

I was freezing cold and had no idea where the hell I was. The person who had taken me out of the flar, grabbed my arm, and led me down a strange looking hallway. Everything was black, and everything had a glowing hole on the side. I soon realized these glowing holes were windows. I looked out, and all I saw was blackness. There were bright bulbs that seemed to glow intensely, and I realized they were stars. Then I realized I wasn't on Plinth anymore. I was taken into a room that resembled a throne room. Sitting on the throne was a highly recognizable individual. "So, you finally made it. Or, I finally made it.". The man stood up and walked around me in a circle. "I don't remember being so…what's the word I'm looking for? Oh yes, confused.", "That's what I said!", the other man said. This man was my future version. "I don't understand, how am I so young?", "That was a long time ago, my friend. I can't let them send you back without you knowing the full truth. Follow me.". I followed myself out of the room and back into the strange hallway. "What is this place?", I asked. "It's my home. And yes, a gigantic spaceship. I can travel all over the galaxy with this. Hell, even visit other galaxies. I designed this myself. Have you ever heard of the Milky Way? It's filled with planets that don't really have a lot of life, but there was one.". As I watched myself reminisce about something I hadn't seen yet, he led me to a room that was decorated purple and pink. In the center of the room was a coffin connected to some machines. As I looked at the coffin, I saw you could see through the top. It was Cophone, but she wasn't a little girl. "How old was she when she died?" I asked, confused, because suddenly her younger ghost appeared. "She was sixteen when Amana attempted to let her blow up in Space. I was able to stop the blast and, ever since, have kept her alive in the containment-box.". I stared at her and she was truly my daughter. She was the spitting image of Ko-e, but had my eyes and nose. She was extremely beautiful. "So, what you're saying is there is a chance to save her?", "Well, yes, and also, no.", "That doesn't make sense.", I said, frustrated, "Why are you tampering with time? You know what it's going to do, don't you?", "Of course, I know what happens. It will change history. But what you need to understand, as a father, a parent, you would do anything to save your child. Even commit evil atrocities. Amana is far from innocent in any of these matters. I've known her for three-thousand years, and in all that time I've known her, Amana has always looked after one single thing.", "And that is?". Future me ran his fingers through his hair and looked me in my eyes, "Ko-e brought you here, to show you the truth. The truth about Amana. She's pregnant. She gave up on trying to save Cophone, and didn't even ask me for help with saving my own daughter's life. Don't you see what I'm telling you?". I considered it, then it dawned on me, "Ko-e brought me here right after Amana sent our daughter into Space. She wanted me to stay the course I'm on right now. She wants to save our daughter's life, but not mess with time. She brought me here to help. But what I don't get, is what kind of help could I provide?", "You can go back, and when you get here, you can stop Amana. Stop her from ever being a part of our daughter's life. Cophone would never had joined P.E.D if it wasn't for her.". I considered what he was saying, but something didn't seem right. I knew myself pretty well, and what seemed off to me, is that my son was nowhere near. I know that man that pulled me from the flar looked nothing like me at all. "Where is our son?". Future me raised his eyebrows. "We don't talk to our son. He does his own thing. Sometimes he gets in our way, but other than that, he's on his own.". I was confused by this. "Is he a criminal?", "Criminal in these parts isn't really a thing. When you're this high up in the game, things are different. People get killed and die every day out here. The truth is, we rule Space.", "But what about Sebastian? Or his son?".

My other self, let out a laugh so unlike me, that I was beginning to think that being here wasn't the best thing for me. In truth, I was upset that Amana didn't do everything in her power to try and save Cophone, but at the same time, something seemed off. "So, you want me to keep Amana away from my daughter?", "Not just Amana, but Lona as well.". My mother? "What does Mother have to do with this? Didn't she die thousands of years ago?", "Oh, poor Scion, you don't even know. Of course, you don't, I forgot how you found out...". Now I was feeling foolish, "Found out what?", "Alexa's daughter, Lona. She is named after your mother. She is the second strongest power here in Space, and she wants to use Cophone.", "Use her for what? She can't do much from this box.". Once again, my other self let out an estranged laugh. "Let me help you understand, Lona wants to destroy Plinth. She wants to blow it to kingdom come. USING our daughter, as the bomb.".

I felt disgusted. Why would somebody want to kill a lot of people like that? Desian made sense. He was angry, and the creator. But Lona was the daughter of Alexa and Caprius, and she was angry with Amana for killing her father. Which now I still was very confused about. I realized quickly that I had a lot of men and women on the ship. There were the cooks, the engineers, the hands, the soldiers, and some small children. Space was incredible. Sebastian had created all of this. I now marveled at his creations. Slowly I was beginning to understand why I was living in Space. Space was filled with all sorts of destinations. Visiting other planets was the best thing that had ever happened to me. I didn't pay much attention to the business that I had going on. I mostly just explored and made sure I was back on the ship before it departed. When on the ship, I spent time trying to unravel the mystery of the whole situation. Some time ago, Caprius did something that caused Amana to make the ultimate choice and kill him. Soon after that, Lona swore vengeance. Then I tried to understand my role. I was messing with time to try and save my daughter. Now, at the same time, the child that IS living, my son, doesn't want to talk to me. Now, while that is going on, Amana is trying to stop me, but lacks the resources. I'm way more tech-savvy than she is. This surprised me because I still remember when we first met. Calypsa was already dead, and Lona, my cousin, wants to destroy Plinth to spite Amana. The questions kept coming. As I tried to figure out what I was going to do about everything, I ended up back on Plinth. "Why are you bringing me back?", I asked. "Well, I've told you and showed you everything you need to know. So, let Amana send you back now. Good luck.". I watched myself get beamed back up onto the ship. I couldn't see it because it was in Space and passed the thermosphere. Before I could think of going anywhere, P.E.D vehicles surrounded me. Amana stepped out, along with ten other people jumping out of the flars, surrounding me, and pointing their hand-cannons. "Scion, come with me now...", "IT'S FINE! IT'S FINE! I'm going already.".

When we reached a certain port, I was pulled out of the flar and put into some kind of pod. I felt the pod being lifted and when it landed, I found myself on what I could only describe as a floating city. It was an entire military base. Down in the center part, you could see some kind of statue. It looked like a commemoration to something. But unmistakably you could make out the letters P.E.D. As I looked around, I saw a very familiar statue. It was Sebastian. But it was more of a decoration than an honorary thing. I was being pushed along, and finally was brought to a strange room. From inside this building, out the window, you could make out the silhouette of a castle. It seemed run down and wasn't in use anymore. "Well, here we are, Scion. The only time-machine located on Plinth. I remember our discussion about time travel. It was strange at the time, but I've seen stranger. Get in.". I didn't remember having that conversation. As I was stepping in, an alarm triggered. "Hurry and get this thing started before it gets here, NOW!", Amana yelled. I wanted to ask what she was talking about, but instead, I was in a blurry room. I couldn't see exactly where I was, but I could hear a strange moaning sound, and I could see a black hand reaching for me. I found that I could run, so I did. I looked behind me to see what was chasing me and it was a disgusting creature that was headed towards me. I didn't know what it intended upon catching me, but I didn't want that to happen. I ran as fast as I could, and the creature was gaining on me. I fell over and then all of a sudden, I found myself falling through a hole, and I ran straight into Amana.

AMANA: Scion breathlessly explained the future to me. Some parts, I couldn't believe, other parts seemed to make sense. The part that upset me, was that I wouldn't try to help my niece more than I did. Scion even told me that I remembered this conversation. "Look, Scion, I would never allow anything like that to happen to your daughter. You have to believe that.". Scion shook his head, "You don't get it. Now I get why I didn't get it.". I was very confused. Once again, Scion went into explanation about himself in the future, Lona, who is the daughter of Alexa and Caprius, and he informed me that I was carrying. "But who was the father?", "Amana, when I saw you, you weren't exactly showing yet. But that scar was there.". Scion said, pointing at the scar on my face. "Micka…", I said under my breath. "Micka did that? To you? How?". I went into explanation of everything that's happened since he disappeared. I told him how my mother and Micka are twin sisters. I told him how they are on a journey to find their mother, who we believe may be alive. I then informed him that Ko-e, Calypsa, and I were now together and finding a way to fight Desian, who was behind everything from the start. Realization dawned on his face. "Amana, you need to listen to me, I believe, Desian is hardly the issue. It's Lona we need to be worried about.", "Why should I be worried about something that isn't coming until three-thousand years later?", "How do you think I got there and back?". I considered what he was saying. It checked out. "So now I have to be worried about a time traveling goddess as well? Is that what was chasing you back there?". Scion shook his head. "I don't know what that was, but I'm afraid for us. All this time travel is going to affect something, I'm sure of it.". Scion had been through a lot, that I could tell. "Scion, why don't you go back to Dasha? You can go see your mother.". Scion thought for a minute, but then nodded and turned to leave. Leaving me with my own thoughts.

Having Scion back was great, but knowing that Alexa was still in the future and she wasn't coming back bothered me. I was able to see what was going on. Ko-e figured that if she brought the past Alexa to her time before she had Lona, then Lona will never be born, and we won't have to fear anything. It seemed like a sound plan, but I wholeheartedly agreed with Scion, that messing with time like this would have some effect. I tried praying to my father, to see if he had any guidance, but he wasn't answering. I then prayed to Alex, even though I knew she was somewhere with my mom and Micka. Alex responded by bringing me into a dream state, so she could speak with me. I quickly told her everything Scion had told me. "Amana, you need to know what we know, and that is that we are aware of your future version. We know that you are in charge of a secret military force, and we know about your daughter.". I opened my mouth and closed it again. "How can you know?", I asked in a whisper. "Your mother has been there as well. Alexa, too, has been there and back and told us of you. We didn't know all that time travel stuff, and we didn't know about Cophone.", "I didn't know I had a daughter. Scion said I hardly showed.". Alex had a look of understanding, "Your mom traveled further than Scion, then. She went into a time where your daughter was already an adult.", "How is my mother, and…Micka?". Alex smiled, "The two of them are very strange now. But we are in a part of Plinth that's been unexplored. We are fighting creatures we've never seen before, and what's worse, we think that somebody is sending these things after us.", "No idea who?", "We didn't know anyone lived this far. I've always assumed that this was barren land.". I tried to think what she might be talking about, but found myself waking up. "Ms. Amana, you need to come and see this please.". I climbed out of my bed to find something more worrisome. It was

Casian, but she was on edge and wasn't letting anyone near her. "What's wrong, girl?", I asked, holding my hands out for the creature to climb on. She did and immediately started whimpering into my chest. She was shivering and was obviously afraid of something. Seeing as how Kindy had seen enough attacks, I decided to find out what it was. I walked in the direction Casian was facing, and I felt the hairs on my arms and neck rise. I knew right away, something was hiding in the darkness. As I proceeded, I pulled out my sword not knowing what to expect. I saw a black figure moving in the shadows. It was a grotesque creature that seemed to be made of scales and slime. It looked sort of like a giant snake. I raised my sword and the creature lunged at me. Casian fell to the ground and was too frightened to move. I dived at the snake and tried to plunge my sword in its hide, but it managed to maneuver around me. It was circling me. Surrounding me, and I could tell it was planning on squeezing me to death. But just like when Scion had arrived, Alexa came running at the creature and shot it with what appeared to be a hand-cannon. This one looked significantly different from the one's I started, and my mother and Scion finished. "Alexa? I thought you weren't coming back?", "There is a slight change I'm going to make. I've come to get Caprius.". The snake took another jab at me, and Alexa shot it five more times. The snake finally died. "What the hell is this?", "A time serpent. It followed Scion. But there may be more of them. Look, I have to head to Nasher. But I just wanted to tell you, forget whatever Scion told you. Cophone was going to die either way, so you did what you had to.", "She isn't dead, Scion told me she is being kept alive.". Alexa looked shocked at this. "I've got to tell Ko-e. But I'll see you soon. Before I go back.". Alexa gave me a quick hug and ran off towards our stables. I looked at the carcass of the giant snake and retched. Casian leaped onto my shoulder and licked my face.

ALISA: It had been a month since we traveled into this foreign land. The ground was barren. No life at all it seemed, and the water was sparse. I wasn't taking the time to name the few ponds we found because I was more concerned with why our mother would flee here. It didn't make sense. Nobody in their right mind would come here. As the nights passed, the three of us tried getting rest, but found it impossible with all the random attacks. I felt like we were back in the Dark Wood twenty years ago. I kept thinking about Amana, and how I just left her, knowing Desian could possess her at any time. Ko-e was still with her, or at least that's what I told myself to make myself feel better. Micka was being strangely protective of me. During each attack, Micka dashed in to save me when I was on the verge of losing. "You're a goddess, learn to use that!", she yelled at me one day, while we were fighting creatures that were huge cats from the looks of things. Each new battle was starting to seem less and less random. We waded our way through barren fields and found rest scarcely. One day, we actually found another living individual. It was a boy. He was young, which meant his parents were somewhere nearby or maybe there was a whole village. "Excuse us? We are lost. We don't exactly know where we are going, but maybe you can help us.", I said. The boy looked from me, to Alex, then he lingered on Micka. He pointed at Micka, who raised her eyebrow, "I think he's saying he has seen our mother. Well, where did you see her?", Micka asked. The boy shook his head, "Toosa". We looked at each other, confused. "Toosa? What is a toosa?", I asked. The boy shook his head again and then jumped up and ran from us. Micka gave chase. "Micka, wait, we don't know where he's going!". Micka put her arm out, and the boy froze. Micka gestured with her hand, and the boy turned and faced us. "Micka, he's just a kid, let him go!", "A kid who knows where to find what we're looking for. I don't know about you, but I am sick of traveling in this land and getting nowhere. So, I'm putting in some work. Now, let's try this again, what is a toosa?". The boy shook his head repeatedly, then it dawned on me, "Micka, he doesn't speak our language.". Micka released her grip, and the boy turned and ran, yelling, "TOOSA! TOOSA! TOOSA!", "I don't think that's good…", said Alex, watching the boy with concern. "Look, we follow him, he leads us to his people, we find someone who does speak our language, and then we find Tila. Agreed?", Micka asked. I honestly couldn't see any other way.

We followed the boy, and he indeed led us to a village. It was like walking into the past. There were no PE cords running through the village. No shops or businesses that sell anything. It was just little huts, and dirt, and no plants of any sort. There was a makeshift shack at the end. People were fleeing into their homes, as the young boy ran through the village, still screaming at the top of his lungs, "TOOSA, TOOSA, TOOSA!", "I am so sick of hearing that.", Micka said, gesturing her hand, and I grabbed her, "Micka, we don't know what these people are capable of. We need to wait and see what we are...", I stopped talking. Out of the shack, came a man who looked ancient, but everything in me told me he was powerful, despite his meager look. He came up to us, and stared us up and down. He then paced around us. "So, you three think you are the Trinity? Don't make me laugh. You three are just mistakes. You are abominations of the Toosa.". Once again, we all looked at one another. I was surprised this man spoke our language so well. "Who are you, sir?", I asked. "I am the guardian of this village.", "Well, you guys couldn't keep up with the rest of Plinth or what? I mean, where is the PE?". Even though I knew Micka was trying to make light, I didn't appreciate it. "Sir, can you tell us, what is a toosa?", "Toosa, in the Yindin language, means witch. Your mother is the witch. She is evil, and we have lived in fear of her for many years now.". Although the slur about my mother should have bothered me, I was more interested in these people. "Did you call these people 'Yindin'? I've never heard of them.", "Of course you haven't. Look how far we live from everything.", "How did you learn to speak our tongue?", Alex asked, also intrigued. "My family has been taught for generations. We were preparing for when we could no longer hide.". Alex left from our side and started making her way around the village. "Can you tell us where our mother is?", I asked, trying not to sound like I meant any harm. "Sure, I could tell you where she resides, but I wouldn't recommend going in there. Even for a goddess, the place can be dangerous.". Micka gave me an incredulous look. "How can you know about us? Tell me exactly who you are, or I will burn this village down.". Micka said, threateningly holding out her hand towards the old man, who didn't look remotely afraid. "So, threats? I see… You truly are your mother's daughter, but you, Alisa, you are different. Come, both of you, I will tell you a story you've never heard before.

We followed the man into a nice little hut. Inside wasn't much. Just wood where there was obviously fire, and in the corner, sheets of what looked like animal hide. There were prints all over the walls of the hut. Looking closer, I saw they sort of told a story. As I looked around more, I saw Godlic writing on the walls as well. "So, you two want the truth of yourselves? Well, the truth is, your mother learned she would never have what all you goddesses are promised when you come here. The love of a god. Have you ever questioned why goddesses would come here seeking that? Why were they sent here in the first place? Or where they actually come from?". I realized I thought of that when I first met Alex, but didn't really get the chance to ask her. Alex was always different. She always had a haughty way about her that kind of made you sick at times. She knew about where she was from, but for some reason never spoke of it. "Is the goddess' planet one of Sebastian's creations?". The old man looked tense at this question. "How old do you think this planet is?", "Well isn't it only three-thousand years old?". The man let out a laugh that suggested I was horribly wrong. Micka and I looked at one another. "Well, then, how old is this planet?", "How about forty-thousand years old?". I couldn't believe that. "It took forty-thousand years to discover PE? Yeah right. Wouldn't they have discovered this a long time ago. And how come there aren't any remnants of that time?", Micka asked in a sarcastic tone. The man stared hard into Micka's eyes. I on the other hand saw things in a different manner. If the planet really was that age, it made sense. "When did Plinthinians first show up on the planet?". Once again, the man let out a sigh and pointed to the pictures on the walls, "Many, many years ago, there was a race of beings called the Praximites. They came here and found that this planet was barren. They used this planet as a harvesting planet. They came here to grow crops. They placed a barrier around the planet to hide it from the other ones. This way, no one would discover their secret. The Praximites realized they couldn't harvest all over the planet. They needed more hands. So, they created a bio-organic organism that could help keep the planet up to date. They called these beings, Plinths. The Plinths tilled the land, planted, and eventually turned this planet into a paradise. They started to feel like the Praximites weren't needed anymore, and so, the Plinths revolted against them. The Praximites were a peaceful race and weren't ready for what the Plinths did to them. The Praximites were forced to go into hiding, while the Plinths, built cities using your so called glorified, PE. There was power everywhere, and vehicles for faster travel, and the people decided to name the planet after themselves, thus, Plinth was born, and the people became, Plinthinians. Now, at this point, the Praximites felt robbed. The Plinthinians had taken their technology, their weapons, and their pride. The Praximites knew they would have to fight. But the Plinths had become too powerful, and in a last-ditch effort, had wiped the rest of the Praximites from the planet. Or so they thought. There was one Praximite who remained, and he decided to destroy everything. He took it upon himself to cause the sun to throw energy at the planet. It was such a massive amount that it completely destroyed all the Praximite technology, and the Plinths were forced to start over. For the next. thirty-five-thousand years, Plinths built castles, and chose royalty, and fought amongst one another over land they once agreed was all Plinthinian. The one Praximite came down here and tried to live amongst the Plinths. He tried to rally them together like they used to be, but they killed him. Now, that same Praximite…". I held up my hand, "Are you saying Sebastian, was this lone Praximite?". The old man nodded his head. "My people, the Yindin, are the last remaining

Praximites. We live on this fringe and call ourselves Yindin(people without a home). Our home is out there, this planet isn't ours, but we can't return, because to try would mean waging a war we already lost. We no longer have our weapons or our ability to fight. The Plinths truly have taken everything from us.", "But this doesn't make sense! Sebastian isn't just some alien! He's a god!", Micka shouted. "I'm sure one as young as yourself would believe he is a deity, but the truth about your 'Sebastian' is that he was a genius, who learned secrets of the universe he shouldn't have learned. Our people were meant to guard over the planets, but he saw himself as the only one who was powerful enough. You see, he was also the one who created the Plinths. He felt responsible for his own people's destruction.". It was starting to make sense to me. Sebastian being a god always felt out of place for me. "But this doesn't explain our abilities. Why do our daughters have strengths like they do?". Once again, the old man chuckled, "It is the pure Praximite blood. You see, we Praximites were once very strong. The remainders you see in this village are sadly shells of what our race once was.".

After listening to the old man's story, he revealed his name was Coxtil. He told us more of his people, the Praximites. He explained that they were created to take care of the other planets. The planets we believed Sebastian created. We were fools. But we can't possibly be that foolish. In all terms, the Praximites sounded like a race of gods. They had technology we couldn't even dream of. Even what we are discovering now was just a reinvention of what they had thousands of years ago. It even made sense why Sebastian went out of his way to protect this planet. I needed to find Alex, who could explain better what Heaven is. When I found Alex, she was speaking with the Yindin people in fluid Yindin. "How did you learn their language?", I asked, astonished. "Well, it's quite easy once you really sit down and talk. Their stories are really fascinating.", "I agree. Especially the one about Sebastian not really being a god.", Micka said, approaching us. The people scattered at her arrival. They obviously saw our mother in her. "What do you mean? Oh? You mean Sebastian's people? Yes, this is the last of his race.". I stared at Micka, who returned my surprised look. "What? You assumed I didn't know? I've always known the truth about the real age of the planet. We just don't talk about those days.". When the day was over, we returned to the hut where Coxtil told us we could sleep. "You know, for a man who claims he hates our mother and our people, he sure is kind.", said Micka, as Alex was drifting off, mumbling Sebastian's name.

I laid awake, wishing I had a full understanding. I was finding it difficult to sleep. I stood, and left from the hut. My mind wandered to Amana. Poor Amana thought she was a goddess, but it turns out she is half Praximite. Some part of me wondered what I was. My mother was from the same planet Alex was from, which Coxtil never got around to explaining, and Alex refused to speak of. I kept wondering what our planet must have been like, then I heard noises. I left the vicinity of the hut and followed the sound. It was like a low buzzing. As I felt the vibrations of the noise, symbolizing it was getting louder, I realized that it was being directed at me. As I found myself leaving the village and traveling further into the unexplored territory, I found what I was looking for. A woman was blowing into an object. She had vibrant purple hair, and was wearing a green robe. Upon my arrival, the woman stopped playing and looked in my direction, "Well, it's about time. I was wondering when you'd get here.". She stepped down off the rock she had been on, and started to walk towards me. I saw my resemblance in her right away. While I did indeed inherit my grandmother's hair color, I also inherited my mother's beauty. Much like Micka, we both shared in our mother's facial features. Funny, all the time I knew Micka, I never considered how much alike we looked. The woman placed her hand on my face. She wasn't old looking at all. "Tell me, Alisa, how have your grandpare...", I found myself yelling at the top of my lungs, "HOW DARE YOU?! YOU ABANDONED US! YOU HORRIBLE WOMAN! I CAN NEVER FORGIVE YOU!". I stopped to catch my breath, and Tila just smiled at me. "I don't blame you for being angry. There are a lot of things you don't know.", "Well those people down there say you are evil.". Tila looked at the village in the distance. "I haven't always been kind to them, no. But they aren't so innocent. Don't let them fool you. The Praximites are forever planning vengeance.", "How? That's the last of them isn't it?", I found myself asking. "No, it isn't. The last of them is up there.", Tila said, pointing up. "Sebastian?", I asked, and Tila shook her head. "When I first came here, it was to learn the truth about myself. When I first learned of the Praximites, I thought they were my people. Later I learned I'm something totally different. I stayed in this land, because I knew Falsa would try and kill me. I didn't want to go to war, so I came here. As for me being evil, I've only ever scared them off. It's better to be alone out here.", "And what of me and Micka?", I asked, my blood beginning to boil again. "You two were perfectly safe. You didn't need me.", "MY FATHER GAVE UP HIS THRONE FOR YOU!", I found myself yelling again. "A father you didn't even know.". I was lost at this. "Listen to me, I left Micka with her father, and you with your grandparents. I did this because I needed to learn. Not just for me, but for you two as well. The only reason I didn't return is, well, I learned that Sebastian was with you two.". Mother blushed somewhat, and I knew why. "I knew he would choose Alex, because she was his destiny, but I couldn't be there. Not when Desian showed up. Desian convinced me to read the Book Of Truths. I could sense his evil. Him and Sebastian go way back. Even further than you know.".

My mother told me the tale of the true beginning. The Praximites came here to harvest for themselves. Their job...was to watch over the other planets. They were created by a being of much greater power. Sebastian was more like the right hand to this greater power. Sebastian was a genius, with the ability to give life. He gave life to the Plinths, and they slowly began to rebel against the Praximites. Eventually, the Plinths overthrew the Praximites and took over the whole planet. The Praximites were forced into hiding from the Plinths, and this is when Bastian stepped in. He knew the only chance he had was to start over, but he knew it meant killing his Praximites, or at least the ones that were left. After restarting the civilization, Bastian watched the planet progress for thousands of years. Four-thousand years later, the Plinths were killing each other. Sebastian saw that once again, he would have to take action. He took a different approach. After all the years that had passed, he knew that the people would see him as a god, and this wasn't in his favor. The people feared him and murdered him. Now, from this happening, a new tradition began. A planet outside of this galaxy called Peroxa, is the home place to all goddesses. Peroxa was a planet, where long ago, it was the sister planet to Praxima. But Peroxa fell out of orbit. The energy surrounding the planet is what kept the planet intact, and in its own orbit. Over time, it became a place that also was hidden from the other planets, surrounded by an electrical storm so vast, that any ship that tries to pass through is destroyed immediately. But the Peroxians figured out how to get past the storm. The Peroxians are a race of females. Their whole planet was made up of women, who had lost all the Peroxian men during their fall out of the galaxy. The women knew they wouldn't be able to live and thrive without men, and this is where Bastian struck a bargain with them. The Peroxians would be given the technology to survive without men, but they can only continue to breed women, and they must be taught in the ancient ways of Praxima and Peroxa. And everytime he calls for one to be sent to Plinth, they must abide by this rule. So Peroxian is what I'm mixed with. But the Peroxian blood mixed with the Praxima blood creates a fusion that is so strong, and even endows abilities. This answered why we were different from Plinthinians. It also explained why our daughters were a lot stronger. Sebastian's pure god blood, mixed with Peroxian blood, was increasing their strength. It also answered why Alex was much more than us. She was pure Peroxian. She knew what she was, but never spoke of it. "Why doesn't Alex ever speak of Peroxa?" I asked my mother, finally starting to understand her plight. "Well to be honest, Alex isn't what she thinks. I don't remember much about Peroxa myself and I would find it strange if Alex did.", "But what about...?", I cut my question off because I heard a noise. It was Coxtil. He was holding a strange blade and it was covered in blood.

MICKA: I woke up and realized that Alisa was gone. I got up and looked towards Alex, who was still sleeping. I walked out of the hut and looked up and down the village. People were coming out of their homes. The men looked like they were going hunting. I saw the same little boy from earlier, helping a little girl get water from a well. I hadn't noticed that well and wondered exactly where the water was flowing from. I saw Coxtil looking over the village and decided to speak with him. I still had questions that I felt weren't properly answered. There was so much that Falsa never got around to telling me, but she told me what I felt were the most important parts. My mother was a woman named Tila. She was a goddess, which makes me different. But from there, I don't understand why she chose not to tell me about Alisa. Why keep us in the dark about our relationship? I kept running that in my head. I still didn't understand why mother would come here, and I was still confused as to how the Praximites died, but the Yindin was the last of them. "I can see you have questions, child, come.", Coxtil directed me to follow him. As we went into the larger hut, I looked closer at the writings in this one. "So, this language I call Godlic, is really Praximite?", "Oh, no, that is indeed Godlic. The only ones able to understand the writing have Praximite blood. And while I know you can read what it says, I'm curious to know why you haven't acted yet?". He wasn't wrong. I knew the writing said something along the lines of 'The weak shall perish, but the strong will inherit Heaven'. As I pondered, certain details started to come to mind. Like who the weak actually were, and who the strong was considered to be. I used to think that this meant that the goddesses would rule, but now I was slowly starting to realize I was misinterpreting the story. I quickly set to defend myself, but before I could do anything, Coxtil had taken out a blade and sliced my abdomen. I fell to the floor. I tried to get up but couldn't move. "Don't worry, you won't die here. Not until I've collected your sister's blood as well.". I looked up at the wrinkled old man, "I don't understand… Why?", "You don't need to.". I felt a sharp kick to my face.

ALEX: I knew something was wrong right away. Both Micka, and Alisa were gone before I awoke. I could have sworn my senses picked something up. As I left the hut, I looked around the village, and Alisa and Micka were nowhere to be seen. Coxtil was leaving the larger hut further down from the one we were sleeping in. I noticed a knife in his hand, covered with blood. I ran to the hut and found Micka, trying to hold her stomach, while blood poured out. I rushed to her side and took out some of the med-paste that Amana had given me. I then put her back against the wall of the hut. "Alex…he's going after Alisa…", Micka managed to tell me. I left her there, knowing she'd heal, and quickly pursued Coxtil.

As I went deeper into the Yindin territory, I was surprised to find a lot of old structures. Most was just rubble on the ground, but there were also large boulders that you could tell was apart of a building of some sort. I listened for if anyone was nearby, then I heard a yell, and I rushed forward. "…I shall take blood from all three of you! Trinity must NOT RETURN!", Coxtil was saying. As I neared, I saw that Alisa was wrestling with him for the blade. I waved my hand, and Coxtil flew some feet. "Are you okay, Alisa?". Alisa nodded her head towards the woman behind her. "Tila…". Tila approached me, "Alexandria…my final child.", Tila said, embracing me into a hug. "We must flee this village if you girls are to be safe.", "I don't understand, what do you mean?", I asked confused. "How much do you remember of our home?", "I…well I remember…", it was at this time that I realized, nothing I did would have jogged my memory. Tila just referred to me as her child. But that's impossible. I had indeed been in the heavens recently, and knew that Peroxa was safeguarded by the electrical storm. "What are you telling me?", I asked, waiting to see what she was going to tell me. "We are not safe here, because it was destined that the three of you would show up here. The three of you don't realize this, but there is something special about you. I saw it in the book. It's the reason I ran away from Alexandria. All three of you are my daughters.". Alisa was distracted by our mother's story, giving Coxtil the chance to slash at her leg. He then turned to run off, but was cut off by Micka, who showed up, looking extremely angry and in pain, "YOU ARE GOING TO PAY FOR THIS!", she said, in her most menacing tone. Coxtil looked around, then took something from his pocket, threw it on the ground, and we were covered in dust. When the dust settled, it was just the four of us. Micka noticed our mother for the first time, and I wanted to tell her we are sisters, but decided to wait and see what else Tila had to say.

As we made our way to Tila's hideout, she spoke to us. All the hate that Alisa and I had for Micka was completely gone, as we were running alongside our mother, like three young school girls. Tila spoke in a soft voice. She regaled us with her story of how she came here, and what really happened with Falta. "…so, you see, she was only doing what she thought was the right thing. I didn't blame her, but the truth is, she was on my side. When I asked if she would look after the two of you, I never thought she'd be so far gone as to attack you, Alisa, but I think she saw a better connection with Micka. After all, you grew up in a castle and was raised on better morals. Micka grew up in a small village where she had no idea of her connections to Kindin royalty. I believe Falta knew she could use that to her advantage. It's also most likely the reason she never told the three of you that you were sisters. She counted on your grandparents never revealing it. And once she had turned you over to her side, Micka, she knew she didn't have to worry.". Micka was very silent. She took in our mother's words with great consideration. Alisa was also pondering on our mother's words, "Alex, you are awfully quiet.".

I looked up, and noticed Tila smiling at me. "Well, I don't know what I'm supposed to say. I can't believe this. How am I supposed to feel? This was supposed to be Alisa and Micka's journey.", "Not true, it is very much yours as well. I don't think you girls realize how special you really are.". Tila had led us to a strange structure. It was shaped like a giant square, but there was an entrance into it. The ability to build something like this required technology that did not exist on Plinth today. As I felt the walls, Tila placed her hand on the door. When she removed her hand, I noticed the small prick where her hand was. "It's a blood door! This is amazing! I've never seen anything like this here. What other feats did the Praximites manage?". Tila smiled as we crossed the threshold. "Well the next great thing they accomplished was saving their race. And they did it, in a way that you wouldn't believe was achievable today.". Alisa was looking around at the abandoned equipment. She started to study something she saw on the ground. Micka looked terrified. "There is something here. I can feel it. It's calling me.". Micka put her hands to her head and fell to her knees. Tila went to her, and placed her head on her shoulder, "It's okay, Micka, don't be frightened, it isn't going to hurt you.". Alisa rounded on Tila, "It wants to do far worse. Is this thing correct?", Alisa asked, pointing at what looked like some kind of diagram, with an experiment on it. It depicted two men and three women. The men were somehow merging together, and the women were doing the same. Written above the men was the name, SEBASTIAN, and above the women, TRINITY. Suddenly, I knew what this place was. "This is where Sebastian was created. The true story of Sebastian and Desian.", I said, looking at the ancient technology, realizing it was the same that we had in Heaven. Alisa looked like she had seen a ghost, "Mother, what does this mean? And what is the true story of Sebastian and Desian? I don't understand.", "Many do not, Alisa. The story was changed and altered many times. The truth is, Sebastian was a great scientist, because the Praximites learned to make multiple beings out of one. Technology they shared with they're sister planet, Peroxa.".

The story was one I'd only heard whispers of. Until Tila shared this story, I believed I had all the answers, or at least most of them. But now I was learning how much I truly did not know, even about myself. The Trinity wasn't a thing, or some event that would take place, it was a person. Or rather, three persons. Three women made up the being that is Trinity. Just like Sebastian, she is an ultimate being. Someone with the power to create or destroy. Women are considered superior, but lack a certain something to help them control themselves. So, this is why Trinity was made of three women. Peroxa and Praxima were the first two planets that held life. Life had spread from these two places. The advancements of both races were incredible, but they had a guiding hand. There was a being who had gave them life, and he gave them the position to watch over the other planets. But both planets were faced with impossible situations. Praxima was barren, and food could not grow there. Which is the reason they came to Plinth to use it as a source for they're crops. Peroxa was falling out of its orbit, which in the end, all the men banded together to try and stop it. They crafted a machine called a larken. It was designed to push the planet back into its orbit. All the Peroxian men went to protect the women and what they considered the strength of their race. But the planet destroyed the larken and all of the men, leaving the women to be the only sex left on the planet. While this happened, the Praximites were fighting Sebastian's creation, the Plinths. Both races sadly lost, but the fractured remainders fought to keep going. The Peroxians and the Praximites in a last effort to save their race, came together secretly upon the planet Plinth. They made sure to keep far away from the Plinthinians that were taking the planet for themselves. They built this place we were in at the moment thirty-nine-thousand years ago. It was one of many labs apparently. But here, they succeeded in what they were attempting. To make multiple godly beings from one. Just like how I was named Alexandria, and the place Sebastian made for himself here had the same name, I never had added this into the meaning of Alexandria being somebody Sebastian once knew.

Moreover, Micka and Alisa are also people he knew. Desian and Sebastian. These were the results. Results powerful enough that this planet could be ours, since ours were either too barren to live on or too dangerously surrounded.

The result of the experiment was that Sebastian and Desian, even though they were separated, could still psychically feel the other's feelings. These beings were immensely powerful. They held the ability to shake the planet until it was nothing. They were put back together. In this form, they were omega-level powerful. They quickly flaunted their ability over the Plinths, forcing them back into the slavery they had fought hard to escape. For two-thousand years, Sebastian and Trinity ruled over the planet, but the other planets that life was slow to come to, had discovered the abandoned technology of both Praxima and Peroxa. They reverse engineered it, and soon were capable of Space travel. Sebastian saw the danger in this and knew the planet had to be protected. There was one way to ensure the planet remained hidden forever, but it required a large sacrifice. Sebastian and Trinity had fallen in love, and could hardly be found apart. When the threat of the other planets started to loom in the distance, Sebastian convinced Trinity to power down to her other selves. That doing so will create an energy barrier so powerful, nothing could penetrate here, ever. Trinity did it, out of the love for her man, and her spirits were sent elsewhere. Where they would wait until the time to rise would come again. As for Sebastian, he had to give up his fruitless quest of searching for a way to save his people and allow the Plinths, his creation, to flourish. For many years, Sebastian watched from his perch in Alexandria, but felt he could no longer just watch, as his creations started to fight amongst each other. This part of the story, I knew. It was when Sebastian accidently created Desian. But now I fully understood that Desian was always a part of Sebastian. Sebastian must have used too much of his power, exerting himself and forcing him to power down, and release his other half. It all made sense now more than ever. Even how Desian felt made sense. I'd be angry too if I retained all of that memory. I mean seriously. Desian once mentioned something about creating Alisa, but I assumed he meant as a Plinthinian. Now I knew that he was referring to Trinity. Even why me, Micka, and Alisa all felt a strong passion for Sebastian. Because we were all with him, when we were together, as one, as Trinity. The thought of becoming Trinity, scared me more than anything ever has, while at the same time, I kept stealing glances towards my sisters, wondering what they were thinking.

MICKA: The idea was preposterous, yet I could literally feel the truth in the matter. While there might be some holes in Tila's story, she wasn't wrong about Trinity. I glanced at Alex and Alisa. Alex was looking frightened, which surprised me, since she had been living in Heaven all this time. Alisa was looking curiously around, while Tila was watching all of us. I looked around the structure and saw other diagrams depicting the same process of diffusion. One diagram explained a difference to what my mother had just told us. According to this diagram, Trinity was Trinity before Alisa, Alex, and me even existed. I realized at this time that Alex was related to me and Alisa somehow. We were blood bonded. I didn't know if they could feel it the same way I could. "Yes, Micka, come to me, it's time.", a voice spoke in my mind. I looked around for what might be causing this voice, but everything just seemed ancient and outdated. I looked towards my sisters, who were still just as confused as when we entered. "Micka, it's time for us to become ONE once more!". Once again, I heard the voice, and this time, looked to see if I was the only one. Apparently so. Alisa was looking at some kind of control board, while Alex was still struck with fright. "Alex, why are you so fearful?", Tila had asked. "I know what this place is. It's hazily coming back to me. This isn't to combine people, it was to contain their strength.", Alex said, finally moving towards Alisa, and examining the same board. I was still trying to figure out where this voice was coming from. I heard what sounded like liquid and noticed something that

I know wasn't there before. There was a pink lake behind all the ancient machinery. As I approached it… "YES, MICKA! COME!". I couldn't stop myself from jumping in. "MICKA!", both Alex and Alisa shouted, rushing towards me.

Inside of the lake, I could feel energy all around me. More energy than when I first drank the revealer fluid. I could hear the voice, but now it sounded like it was coming from all around me. I saw bubbles rising all around and felt the presence of someone else. I realized Alisa had jumped in after me. Alex had followed, and both women were reaching for me. As I reached out to grab them I didn't feel like me anymore. I watched as the lake started to dry up and I was overwhelmed with memories that I was barely starting to recall. My very last thought was of Sebastian.

TILA: I watched as my daughters had all jumped into the lake. I had no idea what it was going to do to them. I began to worry that bringing them here was a mistake, but then the lake started to dry up, and there was a naked woman lying in the center. I made my way down into the ravine, and saw that the woman needed help. As I reached for her, I felt a sharp jolt from my hand, and up to my shoulder. I reached my arm back. The woman stood, and I saw that she was the spitting image of Micka and Alisa. Her hair was a strange combination of purple and pink. She looked me over for a few seconds before speaking in a language I couldn't understand, "hjojh?", she said. "Um, I'm sorry, but I don't know what you're saying.". She thought for a minute, then reached and touched my head. I saw my granddaughter, Calypsa, in the Dark Woods, and I saw Amana as well. "hjoinhk.". Although I didn't know what she said, I knew what she meant. She was telling me that they are both my grandchildren and that I need to go to them. I nodded, and as I did so, she looked up at the machinery. She held her hand out for me to grab it, then floated to the surface. She was magnificent to behold, and I couldn't believe she was my blood. She pointed at a machine that seemed to be in almost whole form. "hjoinkiglnhome.", "You mean this thing will take you home?", I asked. Trinity nodded and snapped her fingers, and clothes appeared on her body. She then held her arms out in a hugging motion. I came towards her and she hugged me. She broke apart from me and looked into my face and smiled. She then stepped into the machine, which immediately cut on. There was a blinding flash of light, and she was gone.

CHAPTER 12

Enter Trinity

AMANA: It had been three months since my mother left, and Scion and Alexa had returned. So much had happened in-between these months. Scion had arrived back in Dasha to discover it was now in a state of disarray. With Micka and Calypsa out of the castle, a man named Tommer, had taken over the throne. Dasha had become as lawless as it was before. Alexa had traveled to Nasher and reunited with both Ko-e and Caprius, who had ordered the Alexandrian soldiers to return to Alexandria. I had spent a large amount of time trying to fix whatever had happened between Calypsa and Ko-e. Both still refused to speak of it and at the same time, both were taking great strides in denying the other was their sister. Besides this, Calypsa was on the road to being happy. Nigel and Mileeda were present in her kingdom in the Dark Wood, and were helping her make it into a legitimate kingdom. She had finally called her kingdom, Callista.

I was hanging around the castle these days, planning and prepping from behind the safety of its walls. Casian was always with me. She would often play assistant to me, and hand me small objects that fit into her mouth. I was quite surprised with the smarts on her, but had to remind myself she is older than even my grandmother. Each day that passed by, I became more worried about my mom. She was with Micka after all, who even though I knew they were sisters and everything, didn't make me trust her. Alex was with them, too, and Alex was powerful, and my father's wife, so I figured she should be good. Then I remembered Desian and Micka made me kill Alex's vessel. I decided that I had been in the castle for too long and it was now time to step out.

Before I had even left the castle, I was shocked to see Ko-e and Alexa making their way towards me. Alexa was still wearing the strange clothes she got in the future. "Amana! We need to talk, now!", Alexa shouted. I turned back around and headed back into the castle. We retreated into my meeting chambers. Casian had jumped from my shoulder to greet Ko-e. "Amana, we have gotten the news that Tila has been spotted heading for Kindy.", "Really? I mean, that's good right?", I asked, not seeing the issue right away. "Amana, she is traveling by herself. It appears she has either left Alisa, Micka, and Alex behind, or she has done something to them.", said Alexa. "Listen, Tila doesn't strike me as somebody that would hurt her daughters. There must be some explanation. And how is it that you've heard this and didn't attempt to intercept her?". Ko-e replied, "Well, it's because we tried to, but something was blocking us from getting to her. Some otherworldly force is protecting her.". As I tried to figure out what that was, a guard had knocked on the chamber door. "Ms. Amana, sorry to bother you, but there is a lady who claims she has news of your mother. Should I allow her in?". I nodded. The man left to go fetch the woman. "Well, we shall learn the truth, because I believe she is here.".

TILA: I had never met my grandchildren, never even seen what they looked like, until Trinity showed me. Getting to them was more complicated than I cared for. Calypsa was in the Dark Wood, and Amana was in Kindy. Both places held terrible memories for me.

In the Dark Wood, Desian resided, while in Kindy, Queen Shay most likely would have me killed. I feared what the results would be. The journey was hard and nearly long. Along the way, a clutch of men had stumbled upon me resting, and soon, tried to attack me. I watched, as one by one, each went mad and attacked the man next to him, allowing me to get away. Trinity was watching. As I proceeded, there was a carriage two days later. Out of the carriage came a face I'll never forget. "Falta!", I shouted, not realizing that this was her daughter. The girl stared at me for a while, before finally uttering the name, "Tila…". But before I could say anything, her and the other woman she was with, were swept up into some kind of storm. A bit worried about their wellbeing, I proceeded towards Kindy.

When I finally reached Kindy, soldiers surrounded me, "STATE THE NATURE OF YOUR BUSINESS!", one of the men yelled at me. "I am here to see Amana, with news of her mother.". The guards all looked at one another, then one whispered into another's ear, and that man ran off in the direction of the castle. "You will wait here until Princess Amana deems it okay for you to enter Kindy.". I nodded, thinking of Queen Shay, and not my granddaughter. I waited for what felt like thirty minutes, then, finally, the soldier returned, and led me to the castle. Once inside, Ko-e and Alexa had beaten me here, and were looking at me as if I was going to pounce on them. "Sorry about before, I didn't know that would happen.", I said, trying to soothe things. Alexa had her hand on the hilt of her sword. Amana was just staring me down, trying to figure out what I might be up to. "There she is, Amana. This is the woman that attacked us.", "No! I didn't attack you! I believe Trinity was just moving you out my way!", I said, starting to panic. Shay had come from around the corner with her husband, Derek, and upon seeing me, seized up and let out a small moan. "NOW, HOLD IT!", Amana yelled, putting her hand in the air. "We do not know why Tila is here, and we don't know the full situation, so until we learn, I don't want anyone doing anything hasty.".

I quickly found that I favored Amana. She was very much more diplomatic than the others, but she had been raised by a diplomat after all, so it made sense. Once we had made our way into the meeting chambers, everyone turned to me. "So, are you going to tell us or keep us in suspense?", asked Alexa. She was a very rude woman, I thought. "Well, I don't really know where to begin. Have you all heard of Trinity?", "Ko-e and I have, so what about it?". Amana was sitting on the edge of her seat, and I could tell she was gearing up for bad news. "You mustn't worry, Amana, your mother is fine. She has ascended into Heaven.". At these words, both Shay and Alexa stood up. "WHAT DOES THAT MEAN?!", Alexa shouted angrily. "Alexa, calm down! I think I know what she is talking about. Alex was right, wasn't she? They became one?". Alexa stared at me as I nodded. Amana stood up and put her face in her hands, "And when they became one, what happened exactly?". I told the whole story. "So, she couldn't speak to you in a dialect that you understood?", Ko-e asked. "Well no, but she touched me and told me to find her daughters.", "So now that they are one, we only have one mother is what you are saying.", Amana said, now rolling what I recognized as a kind cigar. "So, what has happened to my granddaughter?", Shay asked, glaring at me. "She has returned to her true form.", "So, she is dead? That is what you're saying? She is gone and only this…Trinity is all that's left of her or Micka?", "My daughters never truly existed. They were three parts of a whole being. Trinity is as powerful as Bastian and Desian when they are one. Don't you understand? Alisa, Micka, and Alex were just vessels. I was just a vessel to carry them.", "But that doesn't explain Alex! Who are her parents?! Where did she come from?", asked Alexa. "The truth is, she, too, is my daughter.", I answered, and I saw the shock on their faces. "And before Alex fused with her sisters, she knew. I told her.", "So, Alex, too, was our grandchild?", asked Shay, and I nodded. I could see every face confused. "Just tell me if I need to mourn my granddaughters or not.", Derek said, finally speaking. "I'm sorry, but I just don't know. I'm asking myself the same questions.".

KO-E: Alexa and I remained in Kindy over the next few weeks. The tension between the former queen, Shay, and Tila were mounting. Of course, Amana and I knew why, and we shared this with Alexa. "So, Kindy had a prince? I can't believe this. So that's how Micka lived. Her father was the one who would deliver the kind seeds to Alexandria. Now it makes more sense.", Alexa had said once Amana and I had shared this secret, "And the reason Shay is upset is because Tila was the one who took her son away. But she can't be blamed for that. All she did was fall in love.". On this, I agreed with Alexa. Calypsa had been made aware of her mother's situation and had just as many questions as we did;

> Dear Amana and Ko-e,
>
> I am very confused by what I am reading. So, you're saying that our mothers are now some ultra being and have left us here? Will I ever see my mother again? And what of Alex or even Alisa? I don't understand. Please come to Callista so that we can properly discuss these events.

Amana was making ready to depart. I was watching her pack. "You're going to see Calypsa?", "Yes, of course I am.", "I'm just quite shocked with how quickly you've forgiven her for nearly killing you. And murdering Sheena.", I said. Amana turned to face me, "Ko-e, that was months ago. I'm over that. Besides, she wasn't in her right mind, that was Desian controlling her.", "So, she says.", "What did she do to you?", Amana asked me impatiently. I grew silent. "So, you still won't share with me? Did she do something to Scion?". I continued to ignore her. I turned to leave. "She asked if we could both come, Ko-e.". I knew she wanted both of us there, but I wasn't sure I was ready to face her. I felt like she had tainted something good that I had with Scion, and I was afraid of even facing him. I hadn't seen him since Alexa showed up and took him away. And Amana had already told me that he was back in Dasha. "Look, you don't have to tell me if you don't want to, but sooner or later the truth will come out.", Amana said, leaving me standing by myself. I proceeded to follow her at a slow pace. That's when we heard the yelling, "MY SON IS DEAD! AND I DIDN'T EVEN GET TO SAY GOODBYE!", "AND HOW AM I AT FAULT FOR THAT?!". Amana and I rushed toward the sounds and found Derek, trying to block an angry Shay, and Alexa trying to block an even angrier Tila. "What is going on?", Amana asked, walking right into the scene. "Your fake mother here is upset about what's happened to MY DAUGHTERS!", Tila said, putting emphasis on the last two words. "I RAISED HER! AND I WAS BARELY GETTING TO KNOW ALEX AND MICKA!", Shay was yelling. Amana was looking between her grandparents and suddenly took out a strange weapon and aimed it in the air and let off a huge blast sound. "I've heard enough. First off, Grandma Shay, you lied to my mother about who her real mother was out of anger. You didn't tell her about Micka, because you wanted to forget. This behavior is unacceptable. As for you, Tila, we've never known you, but how are you any better? You show up here and tell me my mother is gone and is never coming back.". Tila looked at Amana impatiently, "IS THIS WHAT YOU THINK I WANTED?! I DIDN'T KNOW SHE WOULD LEAVE!", "You knew something like this would happen. Don't try to lie to me. You're my blood, but I don't exactly trust you yet, just like I've lost trust in the both of you alike.". Amana said, looking at Shay and Tila, who both looked like they had been hit in the gut. "Amana…", Shay started to say, but Amana cut her off. "I'm now the Queen of Kindy. So, this is what I want to happen. I want Alexa to rule, while me and Ko-e are visiting Calypsa.". I wasn't happy about how Amana was throwing me into her trip, but decided against arguing. She was right, I would have to face her sooner or later. I was wondering how Scion was coping, considering everything that was going on in Dasha.

SCION: "Scion, we are going to be late, we have to hurry!", my mother was shaking me awake. After my return to Dasha, a man named Tommer had taken over Dasha Castle. He was a ruthless son-of-a-bitch that had already started killing families that didn't agree with his agenda. When I first got here, I saw that the computer shop where I worked had been closed and boarded up. The financial state of Dasha was suffering because of it. Some men who recognized me, arrested me, and took me to Tommer directly. "So, this is the vaunted Scion. The one our princess chose to debase herself with.", Tommer said, looking me over, sitting on what was once Micka's throne. I stayed quiet. There was no telling what this Tommer had in mind, and what was worse, was that he had chopped off the heads of the men and women who had wronged him, and mounted them right next to the Falsa statue. "Nothing to say, sir? Where have you been this whole time?", "You wouldn't believe me.". Tommer looked at me straight in the face, and I saw the roughness in his eyes. "Listen to me, you don't want to reveal where you were? Fine. But you will tell me where Calypsa is. I know you have an idea of that at least, considering your relationship.". I didn't know what to say at first, so I settled on a huge truth, "I'm not with her anymore and I don't know where she is.". Once again, Tommer stared at me like he was staring through my soul. Then he grabbed me by the back of my neck, "Allow me to show you something.", he said, leading me out of the throne room and down into the lower part of the castle. We stopped in front of a door that had a strange symbol on it. "This is Queen Micka's personal vault, do you know how to get in here?". I shook my head. Tommer slapped me against my head, "Try and think, you are the smartest man in Dasha after all.". Looking at the door, I could see that some kind of key was required, but there weren't any keyholes, just this symbol that seemed sharp enough... "I think it requires blood.". Tommer looked at the door again and then back at me. "I will learn how to open this door, Scion, even if I must blow it out of the way. Take Scion to his home.". The guards grabbed me and escorted me out of the strange room and led me into the village. My house had signs on it that said no one could enter. The men ripped the sign off the door and let me go inside. My mother was already inside of the house and rushed to hug me as soon as I entered. The men left, closing the door behind them. "Scion, I'm so glad you're back! I was worried about you.".

My mom told me everything that had happened to her since I had been gone. She had met Alexa and was happy to know that she was a queen, but wasn't happy about who her husband was. She had explained how Tommer took Dasha. After the Alexandrian soldiers departed, people started to realize nobody was on the throne. There was blood and chaos in the streets, then, out of nowhere, Tommer appeared. He ruthlessly took over everything, including the army. Now everyone is trying to stay on his good side. He has created a curfew and has said that anyone who breaks it will be punished severely. One person had already tested this, and that man is no longer with us. It had been the drunk my mother was with. My mother had been on her own, and was afraid she had lost everyone, and was overjoyed when I entered my home. I, in turn, told my mom some of the things that had happened to me, leaving out a large majority. Specifically, what happened in the woods with Calypsa, and what happened in the future.

Today we had to report to the strange room where Micka's vault is. Apparently, Tommer believed that I could open it and intended on having me handle it. He had sent someone to my house the day before with precise instructions on when to arrive and what to be wearing. He advised, come or else. So, my mother took it very seriously. Why he wanted her there was obvious. He needed me to open the vault. My mother was my incentive. "Ah, Scion, good to see you, my friend.", said Tommer, as he greeted me once we had arrived. "And, Mrs. Tin, good to see you as well. Now, let us begin. As you can see, we've had this powder delivered all the way from Kindy. An invention of Amana's apparently. I want you to find the weak spot in this door.". At the mention of Amana's name, I was wondering what was keeping them from coming here. Ko-e hadn't even tried to come. I was beginning to think they had forgotten about me.

The first day of attempting to get into the vault was a massive failure. Tommer wasn't hovering around but would check on my progress. After the first day, Tommer had a guard escort my mother home, while he kept me behind to talk, "I'm sure I don't have to tell you, boy, that there is a time frame for you to get this door open. I want it done two days from now or else I will do things to your mother that will make you wish you succeeded today.". With that, Tommer let me go. It was at that moment that I knew I wanted him gone. That night, I was remembering my future-self, and wondering why I didn't tell me about Tommer. As I was sleeping, I found myself in a strange space. I was standing before the vault door, and Tommer was standing over me, but there was a strange glowing figure in the corner. They gave off a strange pink light that I couldn't quite piece together. Then it started to make a high-pitch sound, and I was grabbing my skull. It felt like it would rip apart. As I continued to hold my skull, the pitch started to die down, and next I heard, "Scion, it is me.". I looked up, and Micka was standing before me. "WHERE ARE YOU?! AN ASSHOLE HAS TAKEN YOUR KINGDOM AND HE…!". Micka held her hand up, "Scion, you can easily remove him from the throne. It isn't that difficult. After all, technically, you are the king. Why do you think he is so afraid of you?". I looked at her, confused by why she would be talking to me in this way. The last I saw of Micka, I was quite sure that she hated me. "Micka, what is going on?". I watched, as Micka faded, and turned again into that pink light. She was then replaced by Alisa, "Does this form make it easier for you to understand, Scion?". I blinked my eyes, "What the hell is happening?". Alisa looked confused, like she didn't know what to say. "hojoukhkl", "What?", I said, for it sounded like she was speaking in a different language. Then she turned into the pink light again, and this time, there was a woman standing there, with strange hair, and a face so pretty, that any man would worship this woman. I felt the urge to kneel but was too frightened at the moment. The pain in my head returned and I couldn't directly look at her. "hokjuin. I'm sorry, Scion, I didn't think this would happen.".

I awoke with my entire body in pain. I was screaming so loud, my mother rushed in and tried to calm me, but the pain was intense. I ran out of my bed and jumped into my shower. The water felt soothing, but the pain was still there. I heard my mother scream and I rushed out to see what was happening. That's when I saw the pink light again, but it was filling my whole house. The pain was eating me from the inside. Then I saw a woman. She looked like Alisa or Micka but seemed to have very strange colored hair. It was a mix of purple and pink. As I started to gain my vision back, I noticed my mother was sprawled across the floor. I ran to check on her and there was a pulse, but she was out like a light. "Scion, it appears I must speak with you this way. I can't properly control my vessel yet, and I think I might have damaged you.". I had no idea who this woman was, but then I recalled Amana telling me that her mother, Micka, and Alex have gone on some journey to find their mother. I hadn't heard anything since I had left Kindy, so there was no telling if Amana was aware of this woman. "Who are you?", I finally managed to say, the urge to bow before her still pounding in my head. I finally did. "I am Trinity. But we have met before, Scion, just not like this.". She grabbed my head while I was still kneeling and showed me what she was. I sat back, unable to grasp it. "Do not fear, Scion, for I have come to help you reclaim my kingdom.", "Your kingdom? But...?". I saw what she was. She was all of them. Micka, Alisa, Alex, even the other goddesses. Trinity was all of it. "But what's happened to...?", "We are all here, Scion. We are one. We are beyond the kingdoms of Plinth. Now we need you and my daughters to take care of the planet. It is your duty. Sebastian, my husband, has deemed it, many millennia ago.", "What does that even mean?", I asked, confused by everything that she was saying to me. I felt myself starting to go back into the kneeling position, when there was a bang on my door. I felt like I was waking up and looking around, Trinity was gone. My mother was in a corner and from what I could tell, something was terribly wrong with her.

The banging on my door continued and I knew it had to be Tommer, coming to force me to try and get Micka's vault open. I put my mother upstairs in my bed, then rushed to open the door. But to my surprise, Corsa was standing in my doorway. She pushed her way in and stared at me, and I noticed huge tears in her eyes, "You have to help me, Scion. They took Dony, they have him. Please?". I looked at her. She was completely broken. "Where is your sister?", "She went to find Ko-e and I haven't heard from her since. Now this Tommer guy is saying he is the king. Scion, what is going on? And please! Help me get Dony!". I knew she had lost everyone. "It isn't safe here. Tommer's men will be coming here for me, Corsa. They want me to open Micka's vault and I can't. Nothing we try works. I'm afraid you'll be seeing my head in front of Falsa's statue. Wait a minute...", an idea had just popped in my mind. God blood was probably needed to open that door. I noticed when I was living with Ko-e in the future, she had doors like this. "Corsa, I might know a way we could save Dony, if the bloke isn't dead already.". Corsa gave a small whimper, "He isn't. They are keeping him in the dungeon.", "Perfect, that is near the vault. I have the formation of a plan, but it will require a bit of sacrifice on your end.", "What do I have to do?", Corsa asked, readying herself. "Well, the king wants to know where Calypsa is, and I know where she is. But what I'll need you to do, is tell the king you can lead him there. I'll do the rest. And mention to him that I was there, but wait to mention it till after.". Corsa looked at me confused, "After what?", "Are you familiar with, grave robbing?".

CORSA: I always knew Scion was insane, but at this point, what more could I lose? There was a curfew now and being out late was dangerous, but Scion had a way of masking us. He had an invention from Princess Amana called a void disruptor. It made us invisible and nobody could see us. "I don't get it, Scion, why don't you just use this and hide from Tommer? Or maybe we just easily sneak in and save Dony?", "If it were that simple, Corsa, we would, but it isn't. Tommer is expecting me to pull some smart moves. And while he doesn't know about the disruptor, there are too many guards to try and sneak in, even if we are invisible.", "Well what does digging up Falsa do?", "We just need some part of her flesh to touch the door.". I stopped. "Wait, you're actually going to open the vault for him?". Scion turned and faced me impatiently. "Didn't I tell you that you were going to lead him from the castle? I'm opening the vault for me.". Now I was more confused. "And how does this save Dony?", "Well, Tommer probably knows that Calypsa is powerful. He's going to take a good amount of men with him to try and overpower her. Meaning we will have an easier time saving Dony. Besides, I stopped at the computer shop and gathered some parts and made a little something that might help.", Scion said, patting the ridiculous contraption he'd been fiddling with all day instead of rescuing Dony.

Dony and I had taken Tisiphone's advice and had departed for greener pastures. At first it was easy, but then we started to run low on supplies and this made me irritable, "I thought you would take care of me?", I snapped at Dony. "Corsa, I am trying the best I can, but since we can't go back into Dasha, I think we should head for another kingdom. What about Kindy?", "No. We need to stay far away from everything like my sister said. We just need to find food out here. Something any real man would be able to accomplish.". Dony had moved irritably around, trying to find some kind of food source. There were animals all around, but Dony wasn't very good at hunting. I did most of it, for my father had taught me and Mileeda how to hunt. I was starting to get really fed up with Dony. He felt useless in this whole situation. As the months started to go by, with no word from my sister or anyone, I knew that we had better find some kind of shelter soon. We had been staying where Mileeda and

I had been staying during our enlightenment journey, which was finding soft patches of ground to sleep on. Looking back at that now, I wished that we had never gotten involved with Sebastian's family.

"I'VE HAD IT! YOU WANT ME TO BE A REAL MAN?!", Dony yelled at me one day, as I had been badgering him again about his pathetic hunting habits. "That would be so relaxing.", "Well then fine! I'll show you what a real man does. I'm going home!". Dony had stormed off in the direction of Dasha. I had wanted to stop him, but I was so angry. Later, I regretted letting him go and was becoming frightened. I decided to go to Dasha. As I made my way in, there were men who looked at me and watched me as I crossed the gate threshold. I started to move about the village and noticed that there were signs all around talking of a new king named Tommer. I knew who Tommer Din was. He was the father of Hoss Din, the man that had tried to take advantage of me and Mileeda months ago. I started seeing other signs about new laws and regulations and a very prominent one talking about a curfew. I became increasingly worried about Dony and how he had stormed off. It was late in the evening, and if he had arrived when this curfew was in effect, he could be in some kind of trouble. I rushed to his house, hoping to find him, but there was nobody home. I then rushed to his job, thinking maybe they took him back, but they immediately told me that he had been arrested. "If you like, I could take care of you till Dony comes back.", said a particularly greasy man. I quickly left that place and rushed to the dungeon, which I noticed was heavily guarded by soldiers. I started to panic and wondered how I was going to get to him.

Not too long later, I realized Scion's house had been closed off, but I noticed his mother was entering and exiting. I had watched Scion's house for a few hours and then departed to the dungeon again to see if I could somehow get to Dony. I saw that both the guards who were standing by the door seemed to be arguing about something, so I snuck around to the crack that I knew about and snuck inside.

The guards that were watching the cells were moving around and leaving some cells unattended for some time. I started slowly looking for Dony. I found him five minutes later, sobbing in his cell. "Dony, it's me.". Dony looked up and put his face in the cell bars, "Corsa! You must leave. If they find you here…". I cut him off, "Don't worry, they won't. What happened?". Dony took a deep breath, "As soon as I came into Dasha, it was late, and a guard told me that I had to go home, but once I started walking home, another guard arrested me and threw me in here. Now they are saying that the king is going to place my head on a pike for breaking the curfew. I thought it was a joke, but it's turned out to be true. Everyone who has been brought in here for breaking curfew has been decapitated! Yesterday, Brins was in here with me, now he's…", Dony stopped talking. "Did they say when this is going to happen?", I asked, becoming increasingly worried. "They said tomorrow night. Corsa, I don't see a way out of this.", "I'LL ASK SCION!", I yelled, forgetting myself. The guards were coming back, due to my yelling. "I'll come back, Dony, I won't let you die, I won't lose you, too.".

From there, I found myself banging on Scion's door. I was relieved when Scion opened it. I knew he would be able to help me rescue Dony. But now, at this point, I was questioning whether we are about to end up decapitated, as we continued to work our way through the kingdom under the cloak of the disruptor. Finally, we made it into the royal death garden, where we quickly found Falsa's grave and started to dig. After reaching her coffin, Scion carefully aimed his strange contraption at the coffin and I watched, amazed, as a beam of light came from out of it. It was a single beam of light and it was burning into the coffin. "Scion, that is amazing! How did you make this?", "Well, between you and me, I've seen the future.". I decided that I wasn't going to ask what that meant entirely and just waited until he was done. Scion had burned a hole into it and jumped into the hole. He stuck his hand into the coffin and ripped out what looked like skin. I vomited. "Are we done here?", I asked, feeling like I would vomit again. "Yes. I believe we are.".

In the morning, Scion made the plan clear. It was frightening, but I saw that it was possible. I knew my sister would kill Scion if she knew what he was asking me to do, but he seemed to trust that this plan would work, and I didn't want Dony to die, so I went along with it. Scion had been collected in the morning to go and try and open Micka's vault, while I hid in his home and waited. Scion's mother wasn't well, and Scion wasn't telling me what had happened. I was feeding her, when she grabbed my arm, "Scion, where is he? Please, don't let something happen to my son, he is all I have.". I stared at her and realized she couldn't see me. "Mam, what has happened to you?", I asked, shocked that someone could be so damaged. I remembered Scion's mom barely, but I knew she wasn't sick. "I saw her. What she looks like, really looks like.". I was confused, "Um, saw who?", I asked. "TRINITY! I saw her! She isn't Plinthinian! I don't know what she is, but she has terrible plans for my son. Please don't let her hurt my son!". I stood up. I had never heard of this, Trinity, and was confused by everything she was saying. I knew Scion would know, but I didn't have the time to ask now. "Listen, I have to go to King Tommer and execute the first part of Scion's plan, but I promise I will come back.". Scion's mother stared off into the distance. Her eyes had been glossed over and she didn't seem all the way here. She nodded and then proceeded to lie back down. As soon as I stepped out the door, I knew something was amiss. There seemed to be some kind of commotion taking place. I watched as some man had been taken out of the dungeon and paraded through the village like some kind of animal. "HERE IS THE FIRST MAN TO SPEAK OUT AGAINST OUR NEW KING!", a guard yelled. As I took a closer look, I realized it was Hoss. Hoss was being led through the village and wasn't showing any sign of fear. I decided to proceed to the castle. As I approached, a guard grabbed me roughly, "What do we got here? A pretty little thing.", he said, trying to direct me in a different direction. I knew what he was going to do, so I thought quickly, "YOU HAD BETTER RELEASE ME! I'VE COME TO TAKE KING TOMMER TO CALYPSA!". My yelling had reached into the halls and the guard quickly released me as more men came rushing out. "Did you say Calypsa? As in the princess?". The man that had been tussling me before slipped out of view. "Follow me please.", commanded a very short man with broad shoulders. He led me to the throne room. "Thank you, Trus, that will be all.". Trus bowed and walked out of the room. "Well, you don't look too important. How is it you know where Calypsa is?", Tommer asked me, with a bored tone to his voice.", "Your Majesty, if I might ask, you seem troubled, why?", I asked, hoping I hadn't overstepped. "Well, the people like me, right? Or am I too strict?". I thought it was worth a shot, "Maybe you shouldn't decapitate people just for being out late?". Tommer looked at me and then let out a haughty laugh. "I have a question for you, daughter of Taxin.", I felt myself blush heavily, "Your family was executed for harboring a fugitive, yet you stand before me, how?", "I wasn't present when my family was arrested.", "And the boy that is in my dungeon now, he is important to you?". I nodded. "Hmm, well we do have a predicament, don't we? But I have a solution you might find agreeable.". I gulped, wondering what the hell he could be talking about. "I am in need of a new wife. And well, you are a very beautiful girl, and a king should have a beautiful wife, don't you agree?". I was now totally scared out of my mind. I wanted to activate the disruptor and get out of here. "Sir, Dony is my mate.", "Yes, and I think if you want him ALIVE, you will agree to my proposal.". It was obvious he didn't know about me and Scion working together, and now I had more reason to want him gone. "Sir, I have only come to lead you to Calypsa. You free Dony, and I take you. You kill him, and force me to marry you, you'll never get Calypsa.". He stood up and grabbed me, "WHAT DO I CARE ABOUT SOME BITCH-PRINCESS WHO ABANDONED HER KINGDOM?!". I was scared, "Please...just let us go...", I pleaded. "New arrangement. You will take me to Calypsa, but you will do it as my queen. If you continue this refusal, I shall do worse then kill your mate. So, what will it be?". This isn't what Scion said would happen, and I wasn't going to marry Tommer, so I kicked him where it hurt. He released me, and as he tried to grab me, I took the disruptor out and activated it. "WHAT?!", he exclaimed, looking in all directions for me. His men entered the chamber, "FIND HER! AND KILL THE CURFEW BREAKER!". I rushed to the dungeon, doing my best not to touch anyone and alert them to me. As I reached the dungeon, Dony and Scion were already stepping out. I ran to them and placed them under the cloak. We then hid in a cell while the men ran in to collect Dony. "HE'S ESCAPED!", one man yelled, and made their way out. At this point, Scion guided us to his house, where he told us to wait.

SCION: As soon as I touched the flesh upon the door, it opened. As I went inside, there were all kinds of strange contraptions. I noticed right away there was a strange red liquid in a vat. I looked around for something that Tommer would be able to use, but it all looked like random junk. Then I saw something really interesting. It was the ring that Micka wore. It showed what looked like the sky. As I took it and put it on my small finger, I felt a really strange energy flow through me. I wished to be outside of Dasha. Why I thought that, I didn't know. But when I looked around, I wasn't in the vault anymore. I was outside of Dasha. Standing in a field right near the homes on the outside of the village. I looked at the ring and knew that I had the power over Tommer I needed. I decided to hurriedly tell Calypsa about Tommer. I thought about where she was, and next thing I knew, I was back in the Dark Wood. Or what was left of it. All around were houses and people with smiles on their faces. They looked around and saw me and some ran towards what looked like an extremely luxurious house. From inside the house came a familiar face. "Nigel?", I asked, surprised to find the Prince of Nasher here. "Oh, Scion, right? It's good to see you again, mate. If you're looking for Calypsa, she is inside saying bye to Mileeda.", "Mileeda is here as well?", "Yes, we are departing for Nasher. I fear I have been away for too long.". As strange as I found it that Mileeda was saying bye to Calypsa, or even what has become of Calypsa's kingdom, I made my way inside the house. Inside was even more luxurious. There was a lovely cream color on the walls, and even some artwork from the looks of things. Calypsa had been busy. When Mileeda was coming out of a room, I was shocked to see that her skin color was blue. "Mileeda, what's happened to you?", "Hello to you, too, Scion, and I'm fine, thanks for asking.". I quickly told her about her sister and Dony. "I have to go back with you!", "Well, Nigel says that you are going with him to Nasher.", "Nasher can wait. Nigel, my love, I must speak with you.". Now I was even more confused. Then, Calypsa came out of the same room Mileeda had come from. "Scion, you're here… I wasn't expecting to see you. What are you doing here?". I told Calypsa everything. The future, Tommer, my mother, and Trinity. "You've seen Trinity? I don't understand. My sisters are coming now to tell me more about her, but you've seen her?", "She is…hard to explain. But she says that I'm to be King of Dasha and that she wants me to overthrow Tommer.", "Then what are you here for?". I thought about that. Then I found myself back in Dasha. I thought about the dungeons and that's when I appeared in the dungeons, right outside Dony's cell. "Scion, what's going on?", "I'm getting you out of here.", "HEY!", a guard was running towards me. I aimed my gauntlet at him and blasted a quick burst of half power. The man flew and hit the wall. There were others. "Are you good with a blade, Dony?". Dony looked like the answer was no, but took the blade anyway. There were more men starting to come, and we charged through them, Dony handling the blade surprisingly well. By the time we had made it to the exit, Corsa was there to greet us, which meant my plan didn't go accordingly, but it worked at least.

I had brought Corsa and Dony to my house. My mother was still sleeping. Corsa followed me into my room and slapped me, "DO YOU KNOW WHAT ALMOST HAPPENED TO ME?!", "Corsa, calm yourself, you had the disruptor, you were safe.", "What has happened to your mother? Who is Trinity?". I looked at Corsa, who seemed almost unable to contain herself. "Listen, this isn't the time, we have to do something about Tommer. He will be coming here, and soon with the ruckus we caused. So, plan, please.". Corsa looked lost. Dony came into the room, "There are men outside, Scion.". Now I was in the dish, I had to figure out what to do. "TRINTIY! SHE IS COMING!", my mother shouted. As she shouted this, the bright light enveloped my house, and suddenly, the woman who had appeared to me before, was standing in the room. She looked out the window, then, to Corsa and Dony, "There is no need to fear, but you must kill Tommer, before he meets with Tig.", "Why?", I asked. The light glowed again, and Trinity was gone. "Thanks for the HELP!", I yelled, becoming fed up. "Scion, who was that?". Before I could answer, my door swung open, and in my doorway was Tommer. "So, you are not only hiding from me, but hiding my future-wife as well.", he said, looking at Corsa. But just like that, there was a yell from behind Tommer, and Nigel and Mileeda had gotten here, "I AM PRINCE NIGEL OF NASHER, AND I DO NOT RECOGNIZE YOUR AUTHORITY HERE!", Nigel yelled at Tommer. Mileeda was holding one of Tommer's men's head in her bare hands, "I will snap his neck if my sister doesn't walk out right now!", she demanded. Tommer smiled. "So, the other sister lives as well.", "And the other sister is very impatient. Now let my sister go or all your men die!". Tommer looked at Corsa, and waved for her to come. She started towards the door and I grabbed Dony to stop him from going with her. As Corsa walked past Tommer, he grabbed her ass and laughed. Corsa turned and slapped him. As Mileeda was rushing forward, Tommer had grabbed Corsa's neck. I shot him in the back with my gauntlet and he released her, and Mileeda grabbed her sister, and led her away. "So, what now?", Dony asked me. "We fight.", I replied, going straight for Tommer. As Tommer and I fought, Dony and Nigel were fighting his men. From almost out of nowhere, Hoss came up, and was taking down as many of the men as possible. I had Tommer by the head, with my gauntlet against his forehead, "Give up.", I said, looking him in his eyes. "I should have killed you sooner, Scion. You have bested me, but I'll tell you now, you may as well kill me, because I am going to kill you and everyone you love.", "WAIT!", someone had yelled from outside. It was Hoss. He walked up to his father, "See, I told you. Scion was coming, and I told you he would take the throne. Scion, let him live, he doesn't have anything.". I thought about it, and decided to indulge Hoss. After all, he is his father. "You are to leave, and never come back here, ever again. And if you do, you die.". Tommer looked at me, then he stood up, brushed himself off and then made his way towards the door. Then, Mileeda blocked his path, "You were going to force my sister to marry you?", Mileeda said, stepping forward menacingly. "Mileeda, he's lost, he is going to leave.", "No, he isn't.". Mileeda grabbed Tommer, who was surprised by Mileeda's strength. "MILEEDA! LET HIM GO!", "I DON'T ANSWER TO YOU, SCION!", she yelled, and then she threw Tommer by his head and continued to glare at me. "LEAVE.", she said firmly. "This isn't over.", Tommer said, and he ran off.

TOMMER: I couldn't believe it. Scion had succeeded. I thought I had Dasha in the palm of my hands, and yet, a stupid nobody took the throne from me. Scion wasn't exactly nobody. He was sleeping with the princess. He probably was able to open the vault the entire time. As I pondered on this, I realized something had been following me. I turned, but nobody was there. I decided it was my imagination. The girl who had threatened me, Mileeda, was strong. I was pondering on how I could gain strength of that caliber, when once again, I felt I was being followed. I decided to break into a run. I ran until I found myself in a strange clearing in the middle of a wood. I had no idea how I had gotten here, but I quickly noticed a very beautiful woman, wearing what I could only describe as armor. She had faded, green-curly hair, and even though she was pretty, she had a very smug face. "Tommer, right? I was told to find you.", "By whom?", I asked gruffly. "Well that is a need to know basis, but you do want to be a king?". I stared at the girl. She was confident, not afraid. "Why are you out here by yourself?", "Don't get any ideas, buddy. Falsa was my grandmother. Her blood runs in my veins. So be careful with what you choose to do next.". I was confused. "What exactly do you want from me?". The girl walked up to me and that's when I saw it. In her eyes, you could see she was battle worn. More so than myself. She wasn't a woman to test or mess with. "My master needs you. My master is more powerful than Sebastian. So, it would behoove you to join me. Trust me, it only benefits you.", "And what exactly does your master want from me?", "How about we walk and talk, and I'll fill you in?".

CHAPTER 13

Amana's Greatest Enemy

AMANA: Ko-e and I had been traveling for a few days when we got our first glimpse at Trinity. The both of us had stopped to rest, and once again, I was badgering her to find out what had happened between her and Calypsa, "I'm your sister, too, and I feel I deserve the right to know.", I was telling Ko-e, as she gradually continued to ignore me. "Well, I feel that it is my personal business and you don't need to know everything.", "Ko-e…", "Please just drop it, Amana.". I decided to leave her alone. "Well what do you think about this whole 'Desian' situation? Do you think he is coming back?". Ko-e looked as if she was thinking hard on this, "Amana, if I may be honest, Desian is a part of our father. I'll say this, I don't think Desian is the one who has been possessing you and Calypsa.". At this point, I was confused. "But then, who else would have this kind of power?", "I don't know, Amana. There aren't many that powerful who could do something like that. Not anyone that I know of. The Unknown…". I laid up that night, thinking about what Ko-e said. The Unknown was a perfect name for this entity. But I knew that father would know, or even, I felt silly thinking it, but Trinity would know.

I was awoken by a scream. I looked to see Ko-e grabbing her head and screaming insanely. "Ko-e, what is the matter with you? Get a hold of yourself!". Ko-e looked at me and placed her hands on my face. "Amana. I saw her. I saw what's become of your mother! She is…", Ko-e stopped talking and looked behind me. I turned, and there was a woman standing before us. "Scion has disobeyed me and will soon see the error of his ways. But you, will heed what I say.". Both Ko-e and I looked at one another. "Are you, Trinity?", I asked, trying to be brave, but everything in me felt afraid. "I am your mother, Amana. I am your creator, Ko-e. I made Falta in my image. I created the goddesses, so that one day, I may return.". I was shocked at this information. "Does that mean Tila as well? What is she to you, then?", "Tila was the vessel that carried two of my most important parts.", "My mother and Micka? But, Micka was evil.", "Micka was who she was, but don't confuse her with this term you use…evil.". Ko-e and I were confused. I could tell Ko-e was confused, because she wore the same look on her face that I had. "So, what has happened to my mom? Alisa.". Trinity looked confused by this question. "I am your mother, Amana.", "My mother is Alisa Tia, and you are something completely different from her.". Trinity walked up to me and then slapped me. I fell to the ground, and Ko-e stood up, and Trinity just pointed her finger at her, and Ko-e was frozen and unable to move. "HOW DARE YOU?! I AM YOUR MOTHER, AND YOU WILL RESPECT ME!", Trinity yelled. I felt her voice literally touching my brain. "But…", I started to say, but Trinity stopped me. "I know this is confusing, but what you must understand, is that as one whole being, we chose to be with your father, even though we were separate.", "That's not what I was told. Alex told me herself…". Trinity faded and was replaced by a blinding light. When the light faded, Alex was standing before us. I rushed and hugged her, and so did Ko-e. "I'm sorry, Amana, Ko-e, it is still hard to control our emotions. We are still trying to remember what it is like to be this way.", "So, you can come and go as you please?", Ko-e asked. "No, I've chosen this vessel because you are familiar with it.", "I want to see my mother.", I said. "Your mother won't come right now, Amana. I don't know how to explain this to you. She is helping Scion and is now in pursuit of the one known as Tommer.", "Then how are you here?", "That is the power of Trinity. I can be in multiple places.". I was stunned. "But why would my mother go to help in Dasha? Why not come to Kindy?". Alex looked confused by this question. "Amana, let's just say that since our return to our true form, there are some things best left not talked about.". What that meant, I didn't know. "Listen, you girls must not let Tig and Tommer work together. They will try to combine Nasher and Dasha.", "Why would Tig do that? He has always been an ally of Kindy.", "Tig is no longer himself.", "What does that mean? What's happened to Tig?", "You will see soon enough. But just remember, I love you both. And Amana… I am your mother.". With that, Alex disappeared, leaving me and Ko-e even more confused.

"Something is happening in Nasher.", I was saying to Calypsa, once we had arrived in Callista. Callista was more beautiful than I imagined. Calypsa had trees knocked down and made more space, while keeping a wide berth of the trees, allowing them to form a circle around Callista. The homes were made of pure wood and stone, not like the cottages everywhere else, which were made of wood and hay. She had even come up with the idea of decorating the homes by painting them different colors, something she allowed her citizens to come up with. The citizens were made up of dead people, who Calypsa had brought back from death, and bandits, who had been without a kingdom for so long, that the welcoming of Callista was a dream come true. Calypsa's citizens had appointed her the honorary Queen For Life Of Callista. More people had started to hear about the kingdom in the woods and were journeying here. There were even Kindy citizens, who after all the attacks Kindy had endured, found peace in the woods. I knew I should be insulted, but seeing Calypsa happy like this was so good, that I didn't want to ruin it. "Nigel was just here, but he departed a day ago. Some foolish thing is happening in Dasha. I sent him and Mileeda there quickly. I have built some interesting devices.". Calypsa led Ko-e and I to a strange lab that didn't look like it belonged in the village. She showed us a machine that looked like some kind of gate. It reminded me of when Scion came through that portal and said he was three-thousand years in the future. "I call it a teleporter. It can take you places instantly. Mileeda helped me design it.". Ko-e raised an eyebrow. "Really? That is surprising.". Calypsa stared at Ko-e for some time before saying, "Ko-e, why don't we talk privately? Amana, you should familiarize yourself with Callista.". The two walked off, Ko-e grudgingly, and I decided to give them their peace. I wanted so badly for them to make up so that we could all be happy. I decided to give the kingdom a walk around. I stepped outside and was amazed with all the stuff I didn't notice on my way in. There were fountains with intricate carvings of fish, and in some even, a strange reptile creature I had never seen before. Towards the outside of the village, there was a garden that had been set up. There were green, blue, purple, and white flowers all over the garden. There was a small statue of Calypsa in the center. I admired the statue because it really was a nice piece of work. I started to realize that the reason Calypsa was flourishing, was most likely because her mother is no longer a factor.

As I continued to walk around the village, I decided to cut into the trees and walk around and see what the perimeter looked like. As I was making my way around, I came across a strange woman with faded green hair. "Who are you?", I felt compelled to ask, seeing as how it was really strange she would just be here. She didn't look like she belonged in the slightest. She had what I could only call armor, and it was strange armor at that. It was black, and looked like something out of this time. "I know who you are. Amana.", she said, taking her blade out of its sheath. "Oh my, are you, Lona?". I knew she was the girl that Scion had warned me about. She was the spitting image of her parents. "Well, this is unexpected. You weren't supposed to know who I am, but I guess it makes it more fun.". I took my blade out as well. "Listen, I don't know why you're here, in this time, but you need to go back to yours.", "Oh, I'm here to kill you, Amana. I'm going to kill you here, so I can return to my time, without you in it.". Lona rushed at me, and I dodged her, and moved to the side. Lona turned quickly and slashed her blade at me and I deflected with my own. "Why do you want to kill me?", "I have a lot of reasons, but the most important one is because I hate you.". She lunged at me again, and this time, I took out my hand-cannon and blasted her square in the chest. It burned upon impact and she quickly tried to brush out the flame. While she was distracted, I ran on her, and started to throw my fists. She took two hits and eventually managed to grab my hands. "I wasn't expecting you to be this skilled already. Perhaps I should have gone further back.", said Lona, as we were clasping each other's hands. Finally, there was a shout in the distance and it distracted me enough for Lona to punch me and run off. I tried looking to where she might have run off to, but I had lost her. So, Scion was right. Lona was a threat that I hadn't been expecting, but now that I knew she was here, it was time to get ready.

KO-E: Calypsa led me to a private room, where she took out two glasses and poured me some fruit nectar. "Listen, about what happened between us, I wasn't myself. And I just want you to get to know me.", Calypsa was saying. I didn't say anything at first, mainly because I was waiting for her to slip-up. I wanted to show Amana the real Calypsa. Then, Calypsa handed me something else. "What is this?", "What I'm giving you is very special. It was something I made when Amana and I first met. It's a symbol of our sisterhood. I thought you should have one, too.". I looked at the flower bracelet she'd handed me, and tears started to form in my eyes. "All I wanted was to meet my sisters, and you hurt me. You hurt me badly.", "Ko-e, I know there is nothing that I can say or do to make you forget this, but I want you to know that I love you. You are my sister and I only want us to move on. Scion has moved on.". I stood up, "AND YOU THINK THAT MEANS WHAT?! YOU TOOK SOMETHING SPECIAL FROM ME!", I yelled, breathing quite heavily. Calypsa had tears in her eyes and had fallen to her knees, "Ko-e, I wish it all never happened! I've lost the man that I loved to you! I know it's my fault, but isn't that punishment enough?!". I thought about the fact that Scion was with Calypsa in the beginning. "I can try to move on, but I don't think I can forget.". Calypsa stood up and looked me in my eyes. Then she held her arms out as if to hug me. I indulged, and a great sweeping feeling had passed me by. I realized I was relieved. As me and Calypsa made our way back out towards the village, there was a man waiting for us on the outside. He had one of the children by the neck while onlookers were yelling and screaming. "What is this?", Calypsa said, as soon as we were in view. The man turned to face us, and I saw a familiar face on a different person. "PRINCESS! I have been searching high and low for you.", the man said, releasing the child. "YOU DARE COME HERE AND DISRESPECT ME?!", Calypsa yelled. "Oh, I don't mean to insult, merely to enlighten. I've come to tell you what your sister is going to do to you.". I had no idea what he was talking about, so I knew he probably meant Amana. "What exactly is my sister planning?", I asked. "Why, she is going to kill dear old Calypsa. Your sister is going to betray you, but if you come with me now, we can prevent that from happening.", "I don't know who you are…", Calypsa started to say. "I am one who knows the future, Princess.", said a woman who was entering the kingdom from the trees. I started to grow worried as to where Amana was. "My master would like you to join us, Calypsa. My master far surpasses your father in strength, and well, we are at war across time. So, will you join us?". I kept looking at the girl, who looked so much like my brother and Alexa, that it finally came to me. "You are related to me.". The woman looked at me. "Hello, Auntie. Wasn't expecting you to be here. But why are you here?". I didn't know the answer to that, but I didn't like this situation either. "Listen, you need to return to your time.", "I'm afraid I can't do that. Not until I've killed Amana.". Now I knew I'd heard enough. Calypsa was the first to attack. She went straight for my niece, who was putting up a good fight. I went for the man, "WHO ARE YOU?!", I asked him. "Something tells me that you care about Scion. Well I can tell you, I'm going to be the one to kill him.". He said the wrong thing. "I will not allow you to talk to me like that, and I will not allow you to hurt Scion!". I grabbed the man's neck and started to squeeze. It was obvious he didn't realize how strong I would be. But before I could snap his neck, he disappeared from my hands. "No, no, no. We won't be having any of that. It is time that I show you the true error of your ways, Auntie.". The girl began to rise into the air. Calypsa followed suit. "You don't realize the mistake you're making. Amana is going to put you down, Calypsa.", the girl was saying, as Calypsa flew straight at her. I looked around and realized the man I had by the neck was catching his breath. I started towards him, but Amana came out of the trees and saw Calypsa in the air fighting my niece. "LONA!", Amana yelled, and the girl turned and saw her and belted at her. Amana pointed her weapon at her and shot off some rounds. One round connected, and it had blown Lona off course, where she landed somewhere in the trees. "Amana, what is going on?". Amana quickly explained about Lona. "So, she is from the future? But I don't understand why she wants to kill you!", "IT DOESN'T MATTER WHY! THIS IS WHAT TRINITY WAS WARNING US ABOUT!", Amana yelled, looking around for any sign of Lona. The man had slipped away during the commotion. "PEOPLE! PLEASE! DON'T PANIC! I WILL ALWAYS PROTECT YOU!", Calypsa was trying to calm down the masses. "I think we should go to Nasher immediately.", Amana suggested. She looked to Calypsa, who was still trying to calm down the villagers. "What just happened right now, will not be happening again, because I am going to investigate this and bring the harbingers to justice!". This was met with tumultuous cheering and shouting. "Whatever you two are going to do, I'm going with you.", "But Callista will be unprotected!", I said, feeling sorry for the villagers. "No, I have protections I can cast to keep them out. To come back here for them will mean death.".

MILEEDA: "So, are we not going to talk about what happened back there?", Nigel had asked for the second time. We were traveling to Nasher, and I had brought my sister with me. Dony had remained behind with Scion to help him establish his place as Dasha's new king. I was still in shock at everything that had happened, and the truth was, I had no idea what had come over me when I was going to kill Tommer. I was angry about what he intended for my sister and from there I lost all train of thought. I didn't answer, because I was afraid it would make Nigel like me less. "At some point you will have to tell me.", "Isn't it obvious? She was going to kill him for me!", Corsa yelled at Nigel. "I understand that, but she wasn't herself.", Nigel said in a worried tone. I continued to remain quiet. "Who cares?! I like my sister like this.", Corsa said admiringly. I still said nothing.

The rest of the ride was a quiet one. Corsa had fallen asleep and Nigel was focused on the horses. Scion had allowed us to take a carriage. While me and Corsa rode on the inside, Nigel rode on the outside. There was a small window that allowed us to speak to one another. "Nigel.", I finally said. "Yes?", "I'm sorry about what happened back there. I don't know why I get so angry.", I said, trying to sound as apologetic as possible, but for some reason, I couldn't be. I didn't care that I almost killed Tommer. He should die. "Mileeda, do you think that the stuff inside of you, is making you more angry?", Nigel asked calmly. How could he be so calm? I kept wondering when he would be rid of me. Corsa made a small whimper and it sounded like she was dreaming about Dony. I wondered what Scion was doing and how being King of Dasha was treating him.

SCION: "Hoss, I will need you to mobilize the men and get them to show me some respect. Dony, I will need you to work with the people and find out what you can about their situations. I need to know what suffering everyone is going through. And you, Trus, I need you to check on my mother from time to time and make sure she is doing okay. BUT DON'T TRY ANY FUNNY STUFF! My mother has someone very powerful watching over her.". It had been two weeks, and all I had done was give orders. I was so exhausted and just wanted to rest. I had finally heard back from Kindy and it was, of course, Alexa writing me;

Dear Cousin,

I've heard about your recent victory and I couldn't be more proud of you. It's about time that Dasha had proper royalty. Aside from that, things have been very quiet, and I haven't heard anything strange. Amana and Ko-e haven't gotten back from Callista yet and I'm still trying to keep Tila and Shay from ripping each other apart. Let me know if you need anything. I'll be here in Kindy.

-Love, Alexa.

With that, it was just a simple matter of business and no war. But a week later, I had gotten word from Calypsa;

Dear Scion,

I don't know if you are aware, but my kingdom was recently attacked by a woman of incredible strength. The woman specifically tried to kill Amana and seemed to have some unknown relationship with us. Is she family? She claims Amana will kill me. What do you know, Scion? Please respond.

-Sincerely, Calypsa.

It was at this point that I became increasingly worried. Tommer was with Lona, and Lona is actually here. I had forgotten about her with everything else happening. But my biggest question is, why was Tommer working with Lona? Lona is from the future and can't possibly know Tommer, unless there is something that I didn't know about in the future. And, Lona has told Calypsa that Amana is going to kill her. That couldn't possibly go over well. I went ahead and went to Callista via my new ring. As I arrived, I saw that Amana and Ko-e were still here, "Ko-e!", I shouted, happy to see her. I embraced her, and she embraced me. "Scion, I've been thinking about you.", she said releasing me. She didn't seem as happy to see me as I was to see her. "Ko-e, what's happened to you?", "Well, Scion, I understand that you've been to the future. I also understand that you saw me there.". I was wondering where she was going with this. "So, what was I like in the future? And why would my niece be trying to kill me and my sister?", "Listen, Ko-e, I know this is all confusing, it was for me as well, but what you need to understand is…". Amana was coming towards me, "Scion, please come inside.". I gave Ko-e a quick look, and she motioned for me to follow Amana. We walked inside of Calypsa's home and went into the room she had led me to before. Calypsa was sitting in there with a strange contraption on her head. Amana was tuning it from the looks of things, and Ko-e just looked irritated. "What is all this?", I asked, curious as to what they were constructing. "You know what I hate, Scion?", Calypsa was asking me, "I hate liars. People who think they can keep stuff from the one's it really matters to share with.". I didn't know what to say because I had no idea what she was referring to. "Calypsa, look…". Calypsa stood up, and the thing that she had been wearing almost fell to the floor, but Amana quickly caught it, "YOU KNOW WHAT I'M TALKING ABOUT! I WASN'T IN THE FUTURE!". Amana looked at me angrily as well and that's when I understood. "You're all angry with me?". I looked at the three sisters, and each one gave me the answer with their looks. "Okay, I understand, but what you have to know is that, Alexa knows this stuff, too, so why are you only angry with me?", "Well, Scion, when you first came back, you mentioned your daughter. The one that Lona wants to use as a bomb. But what you didn't mention, is that I would kill my sister. Or that I had become all powerful or that I was the reason that Lona is here. You said she was trying to destroy Plinth but left out the fact that she was working for someone else from the future.". Now I was confused, because that last part that Amana had mentioned, I didn't even know. I shook my head, and Amana realized right away, "You didn't know she was working for someone?", Amana said, placing her thumb and index finger on her chin. "Amana, I told you everything I know, and yes, I admit I didn't tell you about Calypsa, but only because I don't know what really happened myself.". Calypsa gave Amana a look of worry. "Calypsa, I wouldn't!", Amana said defiantly. "You say that now, Amana, but like Scion just said, we don't know what your reasons will be, but perhaps, Lona does.", "Calypsa, you can't join her!", I yelled. "I'm not thinking of joining her, you idiot, I'm thinking of capturing her and finding out what she knows. She obviously is afraid of us if she is trying to kill us.". Ko-e was watching me closely with wonder on her face. "Scion, how did you manage to appear here?", I showed Ko-e the ring on my finger. "That belonged to my mother.", Calypsa said, recognizing the ring. "Well technically she doesn't exist anymore, so it's mine.", I said, looking at it admiringly. "Yes, but how are you able to use it, Scion? Only people with god blood can use these kinds of items. So how is it that you have the capability?". Ko-e was looking worried now. "Ko-e, I'm still alive in the future. I know, it's okay. Trinity would tell me if something was wrong, right?". Amana looked concerned now, "Actually, Scion, I don't think she would. Trinity is different. She isn't like my mother, or Alex for that matter. She seems to be on a totally different plane than we are. I think that if there were something wrong with you, Scion, she wouldn't care.". I started to worry. "But, I got something special, right? I found the Tree Of Curses!". All three sisters looked at one another. "What did you just say?", said Ko-e, who was now positively frightened. "I haven't found it yet, but I will, and that is how I gain immortality.". Amana walked up and placed her hands on my shoulders, "Scion, you should let me check out your body. I need to see something.".

CORSA: We had arrived in Nasher. I had only been once, when Mileeda and I were very small, and my father had brought us here. I looked around and knew something was off right away. The people seemed to be depressed. I remembered Nasher being a happier place, but now the people all looked like someone had died. We made our way through the village and were headed towards the castle at the end of the village. "Nigel, what's going on?", Mileeda asked, looking around. "I'm not sure, Mileeda. It's not usually like this.". We had stopped, still in the village, and Nigel had gotten down from the carriage to ask around. I stayed inside with Mileeda. "Mileeda, what do you think is happening? You don't think it's trouble, do you?", "Corsa, at this point, I'm always expecting it to be trouble.". There was a group of guards that were headed our way, and Nigel waved them down. "Sir, we have orders to place you and your friends under arrest.", a guard was telling Nigel. "Stay in the carriage.", Mileeda commanded and she stepped out. "Under whose orders?", Nigel asked, becoming infuriated. "I demand to speak to my father or mother.". The guards all looked at one another confused. "Sir, there is...", before the guard could say another word, there were three people walking towards us. One was obviously King Tig, the other was a girl with faded green hair, and next to her was... "No...", I heard myself say under my breath, as Tommer was striding happily alongside King Tig. "What the hell is this? Father, do you know who this man is?". Tig looked through Nigel as if he wasn't really seeing him. "Father, where is my mother?", Nigel asked his father. I noticed that Tig's eyes had bags and he didn't look well. "Where is my mother?", Nigel asked again, starting to become worried. Before Nigel could make another move, Tig punched him, and Nigel fell to the ground. Mileeda tried to attack him, but the girl with the faded hair took out some kind of weapon that looked like a cross between a blade and a saw. She slashed at Mileeda, who, too, went down. I started to panic but remained in the carriage. "Check the vehicle and see if anyone is inside. Take these two to the dungeon.", Tig said with no emotion. He turned to leave. I watched as guards were coming to look in the carriage. I was stuck. But then I had something on me that I remembered would help. I pulled the void disruptor out and activated it. The guards looked inside, and of course, didn't see anyone. "Nobody. Let's take it to the stables.", the leader said, closing the door.

Later, I found myself in a stable. The horses had been detached and I was still hiding under the cloak of the disruptor. I decided to sneak out and walk around invisible until I could find a way to rescue my sister. I had remembered meeting Queen Tisiphone and hoped that she was alright. I didn't understand what had happened to King Tig. I remember him being a jolly kind of guy. He used to boast about Sebastian choosing him to be the King of Nasher. I couldn't understand why a man like him would be working with Tommer. As I moved around in the now darkness, there was chatter coming from out of an alley. I decided to listen, "…all I'm saying is that if this is all true, and Tommer is our new king, what does Tig intend to do?", "I can only imagine his intentions are to subdue us like he did Dasha. But why Tig would allow it, I haven't the faintest clue.". I realized it was two women talking. There was a little girl who was playing with her dolls not too far from the women. "Did you hear about Nigel? He's been taken to the dungeon like his mother. I'm telling you, something isn't right!". I was going to step in when I got distracted. I saw a faint-pink light appear. I went towards the light and found the woman who had appeared inside of Scion's house. "Hello, Corsa. I imagine you need some help.", the woman said, standing proudly. "Yes! My sister has been captured…", I stopped talking when I realized I was still invisible. How was she able to see me? I turned myself visible and the woman didn't at all seem fazed. "I can help you, Corsa, but you must close off your mind.", "What does that mean?", "Just try not to think.". The woman was moving closer to me and I realized she must be Trinity. "What did you do…to Scion's mother?", I asked, hoping to get an answer. "You must not think of that right now, Corsa, you must close your mind if we are to save Mileeda.". I decided to try. At that instant, I was thinking of what had happened and was hoping my sister was still alive. "CORSA! YOU MUST CEASE ALL THOUGHTS!", Trinity yelled at me. I decided to stop thinking and then I felt myself losing control.

I was walking around Nasher, but I wasn't myself. I felt my arms moving at my sides, saw my legs moving, but it wasn't me, it was Trinity, she had possessed me. I figured that if we are saving my sister, then this is perfect, but we were walking straight towards the castle. I tried to steer off, too afraid of going straight there, but Trinity was too powerful and wouldn't allow me to take control. As we made our way through the village, people who were out and about, stopped to stare at me. I was wondering why, when I saw my reflection in a puddle. My eyes weren't my own and did not look normal. Trinity continued to blissfully lead me through the village, towards the castle at the end of the village. As we neared it, there was a group of guards, on patrol it seemed, and they stopped and looked in my direction. "HEY, THAT'S THE GIRL TOMMER SAID TO LOOK FOR!", as a guard shouted this, I saw my hand wave and the man literally exploded before my eyes. The rest of the men were covered in his guts and blood. Freaked out by this, the men started to panic, and Trinity continued to lead me towards the castle. As we got closer, one of the men from the exploding man's group ran past us, alerting the other guards ahead of us. Trinity snapped my finger, and that man lifted into the air and shot off in the other direction. My first thought was, wherever he lands, he isn't getting back up. The other guards were frightened now, but none the less, came at Trinity. Trinity did a sort of dance in my body, eliminating the guards one by one. We made our way up the steps and then we killed some more guards. Finally, we reached the throne room, and

Lona, Tommer, and Tig were all there. Tig was sitting on the throne and immediately sat up when he saw me. "No…", he moaned. Trinity lifted my hand, and Tig tried to make his way towards me, "NO!", he shouted as he lifted his hand. It felt like there was an invisible energy between us. Lona was making her way towards me, "STAY OUT OF THIS!", Tig yelled, as I started to slowly move towards him. "BUT, MASTER…!", Lona was beginning to say, but Tig threw his free hand towards her and she was stuck. Tommer was taking cover. Finally, there was an explosion.

"I swear if they have harmed her in any way…", "They haven't. She is still in one piece. I wonder what happened.". I was coming to and realized I had been placed in a cell. I looked around and saw that Mileeda and Tisiphone were both in here with me. "Nigel and Tig are in the other cell.", "Hello, Corsa.", I heard Nigel say. "How is Tig?", I asked, starting to remember bits and pieces of what happened. "Well, he is back to normal, but he is weak, so he is sleeping. Corsa, what happened?". I quickly explained about Trinity possessing me. It occurred to me while I was explaining that she left me the moment whatever she did to Tig was complete. She just used me. Mileeda looked me over. "And did Tommer touch you?", she asked. "Not that I know of. I was in the castle.", "You still are. Just in the dungeon.", Tisiphone said. "How did you end up here?", I asked her. "Well, Tig brought me here. One morning, he woke up, and he just grabbed me, and led me down here, and locked me up. He said he was protecting me.". I tried to process what I was being told, but now I was more lost than ever, and my chest hurt. We had heard footsteps moving towards us, and then Lona was peering into our cell. "What do you want?", Mileeda asked, angrily standing. "I need to have a conversation with your sister.", "Like hell.", Mileeda said, putting her face on the bars. "Mileeda, it's okay.", I said, getting to my feet. Lona opened the door, and Mileeda tried to attack her. Lona punched her in the cut she had left on her. Mileeda fell to the floor and was too weak to do anything else. Tisiphone went to her and wrapped her arms around her. "I'll be fine.", I said, not really knowing. "Oh, don't worry, I won't kill you. You're too important for that. Follow me.". I followed Lona out of the cell, confused by what she just said. I quickly realized that she was leading me out of the dungeon and back into the castle. "Where are you taking me exactly?", I asked, feeling like Tommer's hand was in this. "Do not worry, Corsa, I'm taking you to the interrogation room to ask you some questions.". I was nervous now and was wishing I was back in the cell with my sister. When we finally arrived at the room, Tommer was inside waiting. "I told you, you are not privy to this.", "And I told you, anything to do with this one, I want to be privy to.", "You will wait outside, or all bets are off, and I kill you.". The two stared one another down for some time before Tommer got up, giving me a perverted look on his way out of the door. "Now that he is gone, we can talk properly. Do you know what happened?". I didn't know how to answer, so I shook my head. "Well, you came into the castle like a badass and killed at least three squads of guards. And all you did to do that was wave your hand. So, lets discuss that.". I just stared at her. "I know who was controlling you. My question is what has she done to my master?". Once again, I didn't know how to answer this, so I just shook my head. "Corsa, you are quite important in my time. I can't exactly tell you why, but I will tell you that it's a good enough reason to keep that oaf, Tommer, from ever putting his hands on you. I didn't know who you were at first, but now that I do…", the girl named Lona was watching me very strangely. I felt like I had some connection to her, but I couldn't figure out or even imagine what it would be. "Listen, if you don't know what Trinity did to my master, it's fine. You're free to go. I'll have an escort prepared to take you back to Dasha.". I couldn't believe what I was hearing. "Why?", I said, with what I imagined was a very confused face. "Like I said, you are quite important.", "What about my sister? Or the king and queen? Or Nigel? You expect me to just leave them?!", I asked incredulously. "That is exactly what I expect you to do. You don't have to be a part of this. Go back to Dony and live your life.", "Why are you letting me go?". I couldn't understand what she was playing at. Claiming she won't let Tommer touch me, letting me go while keeping everyone else locked up. "Corsa, listen, I have to hurry up and take care of some things, but I need you to leave. And by the way…", she handed me the void disruptor, "…you'll need this to leave.".

As I was being escorted through the village, I felt guilty abandoning my sister and the rest, but I wasn't like them, I wasn't a fighter. My sister wasn't even normal anymore and now that all the adrenaline had gone, I understood what Nigel was saying about her, she wasn't her normal self. I looked around and noticed the small girl I had seen the night before. She was with her mother and she was once again holding onto her doll. I didn't know what interested me about seeing that little girl. One might say that I felt a sort of premonition from her. When I was coming close to the exit, I noticed Tommer was waiting there, but he hadn't seen me yet, "I have to use the quarters.", I said, leaving my escort and finding somewhere private to hurry and activate the disruptor. As soon as I had, I hurried towards the exit. "Do not let her leave. Wait, here comes her escort.", Tommer said, hurrying towards the men that were walking with me. "Where is she?", "Sorry, sir, we have orders to let you nowhere near her.", "WHAT?!", yelled Tommer, as I slipped right by. I hurried into the country and tears started to fall. My sister didn't know if I was alive or not, and even worse, she will feel like I betrayed her by not coming to tell her. I proceeded into the forest and found a log, where I just sat and cried for a long time. After a while, I heard voices headed my way, "…to look for a way in. If they have the front covered, and Lona is already there. It would make sense. Plus, it's what I would do.", "I agree, but one of us should go in first to make sure that everyone is okay first and that nobody has been killed.", "IF, Lona has harmed Mileeda or Nigel, I will rip her head off myself.". I hid, even though I recognized the voices. Amana was coming through the trees, along with Ko-e, and Calypsa. It was the first time I had seen them all together. Ko-e was wearing silver plated armor, and Calypsa had the same, while Amana's armor was red and had the Kindy plant symbol on the front. As I watched them walk through the area I had just been sitting in, I wondered why I was hiding. Just then, Amana stopped. "What is it?", Ko-e asked, looking somewhat concerned. "It's the energy in the air. Someone is nearby, and they are hiding.", "How can you tell?", Ko-e asked, looking around. "This allows me to know if someone is disrupting the particles in the air.", said Amana, taking out a device that looked similar to the void disruptor. Once again, Amana was looking around, trying to find me and I knew it was me she was looking for because I had a void disruptor. I was curious as to how this thing worked and how it was able to make me invisible. I thought it was magic, but now I understood there was some science I couldn't understand. I once again tried to find a new place to hide but having stopped paying attention to the sisters for a split second, I felt something touch the side of my head, "Move, and I blow your head into pieces. Deactivate the disruptor and show yourself.", Amana said, holding a strange device to my head. I pushed the button and showed myself. "CORSA!", Ko-e yelled, coming to me, and hugging me. "You know this girl, Ko-e?", "Amana, Corsa is Mileeda's sister.", Ko-e said, helping me to my feet and looking at the state of me. "Wait, something is very wrong, how is it that I can feel Trinity emanating off of you, Corsa?". I told them the story of Trinity possessing me and how Lona allowed me to leave after I did something to Tig. "Tig was possessed by The Unknown?", "Who is that?", I asked, confused by why someone would go by the name, The Unknown. "Well if we knew who he was, we wouldn't call him The Unknown, would we?", Calypsa asked impatiently, "We are wasting time, we need to hurry to Nasher and kill Lona.", "Yeah, but I'd like to know why Lona let Corsa go, but kept her sister there. Corsa, what aren't you telling us?", Amana asked. I chose to leave out the part that Lona said I was important in her time. I didn't know what that meant and was afraid it could mean something bad. "Do you think that the same thing is happening to Corsa?", "Scion is different from Corsa, she actually had her essence inside of her.". Ko-e and Amana were discussing my situation as if I wasn't present. "Scion has been entirely infected by her energy. It's changing his cells on a highly unrecognizable molecular level. I'm afraid that Scion is beyond help, but Corsa, if I can get her to my lab, I'm sure that I can remove the excess energy left over by Trinity.", Amana said, looking more through me than at me. "WE DON'T HAVE THE TIME, AMANA! WE NEED TO GET TO NASHER!", Calypsa yelled, once again, impatiently. "Someone should take her to Scion, he is working on something. Ko-e, why don't you take her? Calypsa and I will proceed to Nasher.". Ko-e nodded and motioned for me to come with her. I turned and watched, as Calypsa, my former princess, and Amana, the princess to Kindy departed for Nasher, to go fight Tommer and Lona, the strange girl, who for some reason, needs me alive.

SCION: Amana's words were still fresh in my mind. "Scion, it appears that being within close proximity of Trinity's real form has changed you. It's altered your biology. I honestly don't know what to say right now.", "Amana, just tell me what you are trying to tell me.", "Scion, you will die if you don't remove this from your body. But it is a strange disease that you have gotten. It is eating your cells and slowly taking your strength. Soon you will be too weak to lift even that gauntlet you wear on your hand. But in the meantime, it's also strengthening certain parts of you. You're able to use the godly items due to this, cancer, which is the best word I can think of.", "How long do I have before I die?", "Judging by the rate this cancer seems to be eating you, I'd say you have less than a month. Maybe a few weeks at best.".

I walked around the garden of Dasha, looking at the plants, and trying to admire all the beauty in life. "Sir, we need you in the castle.", "Trus, I would very much like to just enjoy my time right now. Please leave me alone.", "But sir, it's your mother!". I turned to go see what was going on. As we entered the castle, my mother was waiting for me in the throne room. "Hello, Scion.", my mother said, once she laid eyes on me. I realized her eyes weren't normal and knew right away. "Trinity. I'm glad you're here. We need to talk. I directed her to my meeting chamber. "So, lets talk about how you're killing me. Probably killing my mother just by being present in her.". Trinity looked at me for a minute before finally speaking, "You realized what is inside of your body? My energy has affected you. Yes, you do not have long to live, Scion, which is why it is important that you listen to me.". I couldn't believe the stones on her. "Listen to you? You truly are as Amana said. You don't care about any of us!", I yelled, losing my composure. "Scion, would I have made you King Of Dasha, if I was going to allow you to perish after only a few weeks' rule?". I considered this for a minute. That's what I figured before, but Amana and Ko-e made it sound like she wouldn't give a damn. "Okay, I'm listening now.", "You have a great mind, Scion. It's one of the reasons you were chosen by Sebastian to look after the planet. You have been chosen to gather the rest of what's left of Sebastian's items here on Plinth. Doing so will aid in the endeavor of your immortality.", "But what of the Tree Of Curses?". Trinity looked at me for a minute, then from thin air, a paper appeared. She handed it to me and I looked it over. "But this is just the same drawing of the tree.", "It is more than that, Scion. The Tree Of Curses does not exist, but what does exist is the machine. It is hidden well, between the kingdoms. You will need this map to find it. Once you do, it will be then that Amana will need you, Scion.", "Amana? But what does that mean? How will she need me?". Trinity didn't answer and instead left. My mother was now sitting in a chair sleeping. Trinity left me, once again, leaving me guessing on what she actually meant.

After a certain point, I had found myself locked in my chambers, trying to decipher the map Trinity had left me with. I tried with all my might to figure out how to take control of the situation, and put Lona and Tommer down, but it seemed that there was nothing I could do, and this one mystery that Trinity has left me with is the only option. I fawned over its content's night and day. I ran my fingers across the page. I remembered when Ko-e said that I found the tree. Now I understood. Trinity had told me the truth. That it wasn't real, but I kept the mystery as to hide how I truly gained my immortality. More and more I was starting to understand my future-self and why he didn't tell me everything. I even realized that parts of the future might be different now because of my knowledge. I wondered if future-me had also met his future-self and knew that I would be coming. I also thought of the ramifications of that. That would mean that there are parallel dimensions out there, all set around different timelines. In the one me and Alexa were in, my daughter was being kept alive by machines that were helping to control her power, but she couldn't wake up or else she would destroy a good part of the galaxy. How could such power exist inside of somebody? I thought about what Sebastian actually was, and what my mother saw when she saw Trinity's true form. I vaguely remember what I had seen when she showed me her true form. I saw Alisa, Micka, and Alex, all combined into one being. But they were more than that. They were other worldly. I couldn't quite explain it. I somehow knew that it had to do with finding this machine. I looked at Micka's ring on my finger. I wondered if it would transport me to this machine. I closed my eyes and focused. I soon felt a breeze on my face. As I opened my eyes, I was somewhere I hadn't been before, and before me was something I'd never seen. Lots and lots of water. No matter how far I looked, it was nothing but water ahead. I looked down and I was standing in some kind of soft ground. My feet seemed to be sinking in as I stood there. When I moved, it was with some difficulty, pulling my feet out of the ground each time. As I moved down the way, there was a strange child. A young girl sitting on a rock looking at the water. "Excuse me! Do you know where I am?". The girl looked in my direction and I knew who she was right away. But it was impossible because she should be dead and not a child. Falsa was somehow alive. She climbed down off the rock and came to me. "Scion, I have been waiting a long time for you. It's time to do what I was truly made for.".

CHAPTER 14

The Unknown's Truth

SCION: I was more confused than all the times that Trinity has left me confused all put together. Falsa was supposed to be dead. She was killed twenty years ago. I took a piece of her dead flesh. She was Ko-e's, and Caprius' mother. And yet, now she stood before me, no more than fourteen. "You look lost, Scion. May I ask why?". I stared into her eyes. "You. Your name is, Falsa, right?", "I was her, for a time. I go by my original name. Falta.". I looked around us, "Where the hell are we?", "This is called a beach. The stuff you are standing in is known as sand. It is a lot of rocks finely grained. You can barely tell with your naked eye. The water that you see before you is known as the ocean.", "I didn't know any of this was on Plinth.". Falta gave me a smile, "That's because we aren't on Plinth. We are on another plane of existence. But you have come for the machine.". I felt my excitement when she mentioned the machine. "Wait, are you Trinity?", I asked, starting to guess on the impossibility of Falta being here. "No. Trinity is my creator. She is the ultimate female-being. She made us in her image, just as Sebastian has made you in his.", "Wait, are you saying Sebastian created men, and Trinity, women?". Falta laughed, "Trinity has explained this to you already. She created the goddesses, so that she may be reborn. She split the best three parts of herself and waited till they came together again. As for everyone else, they are the creation of Sebastian.", "When you said we are on another plane of existence, what did you mean?", I asked, looking at the ocean and realizing its beauty. "This plane of existence was created by one similar to Sebastian. But he has overexerted himself, and now sleeps. Woe to those the day he awakens, for this place shall destroy itself. If it survives till then.", "What is this place called?", "Earth. It is very far from our plane, and we usually don't travel between like this, but this was the best place to hide it. For it is a machine of epic proportions. And after you use it, you must destroy it. For you shall be the last one.", "The last one to what exactly?". Falta grabbed my hand and started to lead me, not answering my question. We walked for long minutes, Falta getting ahead, and slowing down when she realized she was too far ahead. "Not much longer now, Scion.". I was still confused about how she was alive. Trinity obviously had something to do with this, but I didn't understand what she did. "Falta, how are you alive?", I finally asked, after what felt like two hours of trekking through the sand. "Well, that is sort of hard to answer. Are you familiar with reincarnation? I was reincarnated before. That was when I became Falsa. But somehow, when Desian killed me, I found myself here. Sebastian told me to wait here. He said that one day there will be a man from Dasha, who will need me to show him something.", "But how long have you been here?", I asked, still confused. "Well, it has been twenty years.", "Then why do you have the form of a child?". Falta laughed again. "I have been this way since I arrived here. I believe once I've served my purpose, I shall return to the Great Collective.". I'd never heard of this 'Great Collective' and wanted to ask more questions, but wherever we were headed, we had finally arrived. One could see that something strange indeed was inside of this thing. It had the body of an animal but the face of a man. It had some kind of head dressing, and it towered over me and Falta. I then noticed, next to it were three triangular shaped monuments. It was the most incredible thing I had ever seen. "Sebastian placed these here a very long time ago. We shall reach behind the right ear of the Sphinx and open the chamber to the machine.". I followed, unable to speak, due to my amazement. Sebastian became more and more interesting the more I learned about him. "You said, Sebastian didn't create this plane, right?", I asked, still taking in the wonder of the massive statue. Even my father wouldn't have the capability to craft something this awesome, but did Sebastian build it? "The Pyramids and the Sphinx served a great purpose once, but that was when the gods all lived together.", "Falta, do you think you can be a bit straighter? What do you mean the gods all lived together?". Falta, for the first time, looked annoyed, and stopped moving towards the Sphinx, "Scion, I feel like you are asking the wrong questions. There is a word for people like you. Nosey.", Falta sniggered, but then gave me a more serious look, "Listen, there isn't much that I know. I only know as much as I've been told, and I've only been told about what I need to show you. Which is to teach you about this machine.", "And you don't know anything else at all? What about the gods living here? What is all that about?", "If you want those answers, I suggest you ask Sebastian, in the meantime, do you mind?", Falta said, signaling for me to give her a boost. I did. As we climbed up the Sphinx, I saw the Pyramids from a different angle and was even more amazed. There were signs that there may have been an outer layer on them, meaning something even more magnificent took place here. "Where are the people of this 'Earth'?", I asked, noticing we were the only two for miles. "Oh, they are here, but they rarely visit this part of the desert. But everyone knows the gods once lived here, but nobody knows exactly when or how they lived here.". Now I understood what she meant. "So, have you just been waiting for me in the desert? How did you know I would show up?", "I didn't, Scion. I wasn't even expecting you. I have been living secretly amongst these people, keeping a very low profile. I often would relax where you found me, but perhaps it was Sebastian leading my will.". I thought about this. "Can he do that? Lead you into something?", "He can put the idea in your head. Make you do something without thinking. Perhaps I went to that spot everyday subconsciously, because I knew you would arrive sooner or later. But I didn't know that personally. Understand?". I nodded. As she was reaching up to touch the lever behind the Sphinx' ear, I realized right then and there that this was the place I was talking about in the Milky Way galaxy. This is the little planet with life. It was amazing how much mystery surrounded my future but was now unraveling.

We proceeded to climb down a ladder that had appeared at the top of the head of the Sphinx. As we walked into the chambers, it was nothing but empty tunnels. I was almost close to asking what she was showing me, when I started to put my hands on the walls, "This isn't normal stone. This stone can attract P.E.", "Here it isn't called that. It's called electricity. And yes, it is the planet's energy. I see now why Sebastian chose you.". As I was starting to let excitement fill me, I saw something that didn't make a lick of sense. My daughter, Cophone, was standing at the end of the tunnel and had taken off, running in deeper. I followed her, chasing her, with Falta right on my heels. We ran for what felt like a good thirty minutes, until we found a strange room that had what looked like a star-chart on the ceiling. As we walked into the room, I looked around and realized it was more than that. It was a chart depicting this planet's star system, along with its planets. Falta had found another switch and it illuminated the room, making the stars and planets on the ceiling glow, and giving them a very realistic look. "Oh my god.", I said, looking at all its splendor. Cophone was standing in the corner watching me, smiling. I touched a pedestal that seemed to just be in the room, but it was some kind of activator. The room started to shake, and I noticed that I was suddenly alone. "Falta!", I called out, but she was nowhere in sight. Cophone had disappeared as well, and an even brighter light filled the room. Before I dozed off, a man in diamond armor was walking towards me.

KO-E: As me and Corsa arrived in Dasha, it was to a very somber community. When I first came here, there were mixed emotions of who was in rule. Now, it seems Scion, in the short time that he has ruled, has brought something to Dasha that has never been seen, a chance. A chance to live life without fear of persecution from its government. "I can't believe how much has changed.", Corsa said, looking around. People were working on their homes, and it seems they were improving it beyond reason. They had made them wider as well as taller. The streets had people who were actually cleaning it. The even stranger part was that a group of soldiers were passing us by, and Hoss was leading them. "HALT!", Hoss yelled, and he directed his men to wait. "Ko-e! It is good to see you. And Corsa as well. Scion might be a bit busy for the time being, but I can take you to him if you like?". As surprised as I was that Hoss of all people was showing us such kindness, I remembered the man I had seen in Callista who looked like him. "Hoss, who is Tommer?", I asked, knowing slightly, but wanting more info. Hoss gave his men the order to continue patrolling while he escorted Corsa and I to the castle. He didn't even answer me. Once we had arrived, Dony was there helping Scion's mother eat. "What has happened to her?", I asked, startled by this. "Trinity has done something to her. I don't know what she has done, but Scion won't tell me, and neither will she.", Corsa said angrily. "Well it is beyond us, but she is getting much stronger, but her vision is still gone.", Dony said, and Lona nodded in agreement. "Has my son returned, Dony?", "Not yet, mam. Are you done? Should I escort you to your chambers?". Lona nodded, and Dony helped her up and directed her away. "Where is Scion, Hoss?", I asked, wondering why he wouldn't be here. "He has been in his chambers examining something.". I thought about what it could possibly be and then remembered that he is dying. "Thank you, Hoss. Corsa, wait here while I go speak to Scion.". I started towards his room, now starting to feel the gravity of the situation. He's dying. The man I love is dying. I felt tears starting to come, but when I walked into his chambers, he was sitting in a chair at his desk. I walked around to face him, "Scion, I must speak with you.". I looked at him and realized he wasn't awake. "SCION!", I yelled, trying to shake him, but he wouldn't wake up. I checked to see if he was still breathing and he was. I grabbed his face and I kissed him, and he suddenly started kissing me back. When I backed away from him, he looked confused, "Ko-e? Where...?". He stood up and looked around, "Oh...", he said. "Scion, are you okay? I feared...", "I'm fine, Ko-e. I just took a little trip. What's happened?". I quickly explained what Corsa had told us, "Hmm. And she allowed Corsa to leave? This doesn't seem right, Ko-e. Corsa is hiding something. Perhaps the best person to ask would be Corsa.", Scion said, with a more serious tone. "I feel like she has been through enough. I don't want to give her more reason to feel bad.", "Ko-e, we don't have time for games. Whatever she knows must come to light, now. Especially if Lona allowed her to leave.". Scion stormed out of his chambers and marched straight to the castle royal hall, where Dony and Corsa were catching up. "Corsa, we must speak about why Lona allowed you to leave.", Scion said without hesitation. Corsa looked frightened, like someone had told her she dies in an hour, "Scion, I don't know why she let me go.", "What did she say?". Once again, Corsa looked scared and began to bite her nails, but still spoke, "She let me go, because she said that I was important to her in the future.", "Why?", Scion said, looking more serious. "I don't know! She never said!", "Well, I'm afraid I have no choice, I'll have to lock you away until I know what is going on.", "Scion you don't have to! I would never join her!", Corsa yelled, becoming more and more frantic. "Scion, you aren't being fair. Corsa has done nothing.", I said, standing in front of her to defend her. "Ko-e, Lona is our most dangerous adversary. If she has a use for Corsa, it would be wise to keep Corsa from her. I know your connection, so why don't you go with her? You can watch over her.".

I thought about this, and looked to see if Corsa agreed. Corsa slowly nodded, and then we proceeded to follow Scion out of the castle.

Scion had led us to the vault where Mileeda had been locked away. "You should be safe in here. I can't imagine Lona being aware of this place.", "But what about the fact that she is a goddess, Scion? She will be able to open the vault.", "True, but she doesn't know about it.", "Tommer is with her. You don't suppose he's mentioned it?". Scion thought about this, then turned around, walked into a small corner, then he came back with a strange machine. "You know the void disruptor? The thing I gave you?". Corsa nodded, taking the little thing out of her pocket. "Imagine that this is a much bigger version of that. It will conceal the room completely, making it seem as if it isn't here. Even more interesting, I have another tool you could use to defend yourselves.". Scion took out a small hand glove. It was similar to the one he wore that he called his gauntlet. "This packs a lot of energy, and can channel that said energy into one place, and it is a very dangerous creation. Micka made almost everything in here. Or should I say, Trinity made it through Micka. I don't really know how that works, I'm still learning, but I can tell you, that you are indeed safe here. Ko-e, a word?". I nodded and followed Scion out, leaving a very curious Corsa alone, with a lot of godly weapons. As soon as we were out of sight or earshot of everyone, Scion grabbed me and kissed me deeply. "You have no idea how much I have missed you.", he said, softly into my ear. "I've missed you as well, but we don't have time for this, Scion.", "We may never have again if we don't take advantage now.", "What does that mean?". Scion told me about his trip to a place called Earth, and how my mother was there in a teenage form, and how she showed him this great machine that had been left on Earth by Sebastian and a group of other gods. I was so intrigued by his story, I wasn't paying attention to the fact that he had slowly been undoing my dress. "Scion...", "Please, Ko-e, I need you...". We had fallen and began to make love.

Much later, I found myself in the Dasha garden, admiring the statue of my mother. I wondered if on Earth, she knew that I was here. I felt a small pang of sadness, as I thought about the fact that I had never met her. She was alive, but so far away. I told Scion that he couldn't have left, because when I found him, he was disoriented in his chambers. But, Scion claims he felt the sand on his feet, the ocean on his face, and that he climbed a large statue called the Sphinx. I tried to understand completely what he had told me, but it seemed so far-fetched. Yet, my whole life was far-fetched. Looking back on my own childhood, I was raised in what these people of Plinth would consider to be a fictional kingdom. I lived so close to the heavens and the power that it bestowed, that I was able to have anything and everything I wanted. In truth, coming here was my biggest mistake. Perhaps if I had stayed, Calypsa and Amana would never had been infected by The Unknown. If I had stayed in Alexandria, perhaps my brother wouldn't have been hurt. Maybe coming here had something to do with my brother's child wanting to kill my sister. I kept trying to find the answers, but everything was all jumbled and mixed up. I finally left the garden and went to a more secluded area, where I found myself looking at something even more interesting. It was a small pond. In this pond I saw my reflection, but for the briefest of moments, I saw another woman. A young girl. She looked a lot like me. "Ko-e, I was looking for you. Scion has brought us some food to the chamber. I didn't know if you were hungry.". I turned, and Corsa was standing there with a basket of stony. Then I felt even more guilt. Corsa and her family have suffered even more due to my arrival. Her parents have been executed for harboring me, her sister isn't even Plinthinian anymore, and just looking at her, and knowing everything else she has been through, I began to understand why Father wanted me to stay away. "Ko-e, why are you crying?". I hadn't noticed that tears had formed in my eyes. "Corsa, you must hate me. If you do, I don't blame you.". Corsa put the basket of stony down, and came up to me, and gave me a hug, "I don't hate you, Ko-e. None of what has happened is your fault. You can't blame yourself for these things. Life is what it is.". I looked into Corsa's eyes, and saw that she had indeed strengthened her resolve. "But, what happened to your parents was…", "NOT YOUR FAULT! Ko-e, when Mileeda and I first met you, you saved us from a terrible fate. I can't be angry at you for what happened to my parents. And my parents wouldn't want you to be sad. They were proud to aid a child of their god, and that was all they lived for. Trust me, you did them a favor.", Corsa said, tears coming to her eyes as well, "Look, let's not think about that, lets just eat. It's been a while since I had stony.". After we had finished eating, we spent the rest of the time abusing Tommer, and the idea that he was trying to force Corsa to marry him. We talked about what was going to happen in Nasher with Tig, Tisiphone, and Nigel all locked away, and we discussed Scion. "You do know, Mileeda once had a thing for him?", Corsa was asking, sort of in a mocking tone. "Yes, but I'm quite sure she has forgotten all about it, or just chooses to ignore it.", "Do you think Tommer will actually come back here for me?". It was obvious that Corsa was really scared of Tommer. "We won't let anything happen to you.", "Lona said she would kill him if he tried anything.", "Why does Lona care so much about you? I wish we knew the connection.". I ran it over in my head. First of all, Scion had warned Amana about Lona, but didn't realize she was a servant of The Unknown Entity. Then, when Lona actually arrived, she tried to kill Amana while also trying to recruit Calypsa. Why would she make these attempts? The future that Scion spoke of is so far from here, how we could have the answers seemed impossible. Then to make matters worse, Lona was smart enough to recruit Tommer into her crusade, who now she has helped to overthrow the Nashin Royalty, making Tommer the king. There wasn't a lot of solutions that presented themselves, but what made me even more confused was the fact that Corsa had some connection to Lona, and as of right now, it seemed like everything else in my life, far-fetched. That night, we had fallen asleep. Two cells in the vault had been made into rooms for sleeping. I laid awake in mine, still trying to piece everything together miserably. Tommer was Hoss' father. Hoss hates his father. He hates him so much that he has joined our cause. Hoss was an idiot. He tried to hurt Mileeda. He was killed, and brought back to life by Calypsa, and as of now, he seems to be a completely different person. I thought of my brother, who at one point in time, was known as the Rapist Prince. But he has changed dramatically. It got me thinking that people change. Sometimes they change so much, you don't recognize them from when you first met them. Amana is headed to Nasher now with Calypsa, who Lona claims Amana will kill. Amana loves Calypsa, and I couldn't imagine a reason why she would kill someone she loves. Then I remembered, people change. I sat up immediately. Calypsa had been possessed by The Unknown and wasn't in control of her actions. What if the same thing happened, and that's how Amana killed her? Because of The Unknown. I became more frantic.

By the morning, sleep had never come, and I was still wracked with guilt over what happened to Mileeda and Corsa's parents, and what was happening with my sisters. Even the fact that I had taken Scion as my lover hurt, because he was with Calypsa. And when Calypsa hurt him, it wasn't really her. Corsa was knocking on my door, but I couldn't bring myself to open the door for her. I was still crying, when finally, I heard, "Ko-e, what's wrong in there?". I slowly moved out of the bed and went to the door. I then opened it and saw Scion standing there, with a very worried looking Corsa. "Corsa, why don't you go into the town with Dony?". Corsa gave me another look and left. "What is wrong with you? Corsa said you've been feeling guilty.", "Do you even remember what you felt for Calypsa?", I asked him. His facial expression didn't change. "Ko-e, we've discussed this…", "No, we really haven't. What about the fact that she wasn't herself when she hurt you? Does that make you want her back?". Scion looked at me for some time. I was feeling so sad, and angry, and looked back at him with a look of anger, and self-pity. "Ko-e, listen, Calypsa and I, we discussed this. We know where we stand. She isn't angry with you. And as for me, there will always be a part of me that loves Calypsa.". I looked at him, almost heart broken. "But you are the one who has the full contents of my heart. You are the one who will bear my children someday. I know it seems tough now, but I will always be here for you. I love you, Ko-e.". Although I knew he was tasting my tears, I couldn't help but smile and laugh, and feel somewhat relieved that Scion has given me his heart. I felt compelled to make love with him again, but then we heard a loud noise. We proceeded out of the vault and ran into the village. It was there that we saw the most unexpected thing. Dony was crawling on the ground, while a crowd of onlookers gasped and screamed for the guard. We ran straight into the center of the scene, and were shocked to see Corsa, standing over Dony, with a bloody knife in her hand. She reached down, and started to stab him several times. "CORSA!", I shouted, running towards her, but when I got close, she smacked me, and I flew into a house. "Shit, she's possessed!", Scion yelled, and he took out his gauntlet and shot at Corsa. Corsa was hit, but barely seemed fazed, and now had her eyes set on Scion. Scion shot again, but she continued moving towards him. I quickly got back on my feet, and went at Corsa full force. I punched her, and then tackled her to the ground. I looked into her eyes, and her pupils had been dilated red. "Corsa, what's happened to you?!", I shouted, trying to help her, but she threw me off, almost with ease. And then, to our amazement, floated into the air, and flew off. "We have to warn Amana!", Scion said, running in the direction toward the castle. I just sat in disbelief. How could I have let Corsa get possessed on my watch like that? I felt even more guilty than I felt earlier, and slowly followed Scion back to the castle.

AMANA: As we arrived in Nasher, we were greeted immediately by Tommer. Calypsa rushed at him, but he held his hands in front of him, "WAIT! JUST WAIT!", he yelled, and Calypsa stopped just short of punching him. "Wait for what? After what you did in my kingdom?", "LISTEN! We must talk. Now.". He motioned that we follow him. Seeing as how he was just a Plinthinian, we decided we would oblige. We followed him into an alley. He looked around cautiously before saying, "Look, I may have made a slight mistake joining Lona. She is…really something. But I'm starting to think she doesn't have my best interests at heart.", "And you think we will?", I asked. "I don't expect you to believe me, but I want to help you. I want to make it right.". I pondered on what he was really up to. "Tommer, what is it you really want?", "Look, I overheard Lona speaking with someone. They are on their way here. From what they were discussing, I think they want to harvest souls, or whatever that means.". Calypsa had a look of understanding on her face, "No, they can't!". I was confused. "Calypsa, what does that mean?", "You know how some souls that live in the wood were once dead? Well I brought their souls back and gave them new bodies to live in. It wasn't an easy science, but it wasn't the first time they had been brought back. If Lona succeeds and harvests souls, the souls they take will be lost. They have to go somewhere, and that will be wherever Lona sends them. It is worse than dying.". I understood now. "Where is Lona?", I asked Tommer. "She is in the castle right now, still speaking with that voice.", Tommer pointed us in the direction of the castle, "I'm going to go underground and make my way to the dungeon. It's time someone freed the proper royalty.". Tommer ran off, and me and Calypsa rushed to the castle. As we started to get close, we looked up, and saw a figure flying ahead of us. It flew straight into the castle. We rushed inside and found Lona was facing us, while whoever flew in had their back faced towards us. When Lona gave a small nod in our direction, the person turned to face us, "CORSA?!", both Calypsa and I said at the same time. "Yes, it is me.", she said, slowly moving towards us, "Calypsa, it is good to see you from the outside. You, too, Amana.". I suddenly felt like my arms and legs had lost all substance. Looking into Corsa's eyes, I saw they were her regular eyes, but behind those were hidden eyes I was familiar with. An entity that had taken over me before. "No…", I said, becoming more and more frightened. "You are not taking souls.", Calypsa said, moving towards Corsa. "You don't get it. These souls belong to me already. You're lucky I let you have yours back, but that can change.". Calypsa grabbed her head and fell to her knees. She let out a blood curdling scream, then remained motionless. "WHAT DID YOU DO TO HER?!" I yelled. "She is only sleeping. But what should I do with you, Amana?". I took out my blade and rushed at Corsa, who was deflecting my blade with her hand. "What have you done to Corsa? How are you even possessing her?", "I'm not possessing her. Sebastian was the one who made it easy to take Tig's mind. He instilled him with…", Corsa was cut off. She had been hit with some kind of beam. I looked to see who was firing it, and it was Tig. "AMANA! TAKE CALYPSA AND GO! GO FIND NIGEL AND HIS MOTHER, AND GET THEM OUT OF HERE!". I looked at Corsa, who looked like that beam wouldn't hold her long. Lona was moving in slowly towards me, and I quickly shot her with my cannon, and she was once again blown back. "Tig, I can't leave you! She'll kill you!". Tig turned and smiled, "Well I had to go sometime, Amana, might as well die saving my best-mates children.". The beam was still going, but Corsa was now moving against it. "TIG, COME ON!", I yelled, but Tig turned and pointed another weapon he had concealed, "GO, AMANA!". I felt myself crying, as I lifted my sister on my shoulders, and ran out of the castle. I turned and saw the beam of light cease and knew that I had to keep moving.

As I rushed to the gate, a figure flew over my head, it was Lona. She landed in front of me. "You're not going anywhere. Today, you finally die.". But as she said this, Mileeda came up from behind her, and stabbed her, twisting the blade, "Now, how does this feel, bitch?", Mileeda said, taking the blade out. Lona, who was surprisingly still alive after this, crawled on the ground towards her sword, leaving a trail of blood. Mileeda came up and stabbed her again. This time, Lona didn't move, she was dead. "Where is my sister?", Mileeda asked, looking at me and Calypsa, who was still passed out. "The Unknown is possessing her. There is nothing we can do, Mileeda, we have to go.", I said, seeing that Mileeda was ready to run back in.

"But…", "She is too powerful! We can't stop her!", I yelled, grabbing her and leading her away. Once in the wilderness, we found Nigel and Tisiphone. "Tig. Where is Tig, Amana?", Tisiphone had grabbed me, once I set Calypsa down. "I'm sorry, Tisiphone, I tried to tell him to come but…", I had gotten choked up, not even being able to look her in the eyes, as I told her that her husband is dead.

We were all weary and frightened. At any moment, we imagined that Corsa was coming for us. But she hadn't. I had begun to wonder what her intentions were. Now that Lona was dead, how was she going to get souls without her help? Tisiphone was quiet, and hadn't said anything since I told her about Tig. I glanced at her, and saw in her eyes how broken she was. Tig was her husband, of course, but I also remember hearing Micka killed her father. Now, Micka was more powerful than ever, and Tig was dead, and Calypsa still hadn't awoken. Nigel was as quiet as his mother, but both him and Mileeda were finding comfort in each other. I felt alone in this group. I kept thinking about how scared I was, once I realized who was inside of Corsa. But what did she mean she isn't possessing her? "We should rest.", Tisiphone said, catching up to me. I nodded in agreement. We had been walking for a day and a half. Tisiphone had started a fire. "Mother, I didn't know you had these kinds of skills.", "I wasn't always a queen, Nigel, at one point in my life, I was just a normal girl.". I watched Tisiphone for some time. She was holding it together, but was becoming more and more unraveled. Eventually, she got up and walked away from us. Calypsa was still out, and I knew now that there was a possibility she wouldn't wake, unless Corsa wanted her to. "Amana, it's time you explain to me what is happening to my sister.", Mileeda said, watching me closely. "I don't know if I can yet.". I replied. "YOU BETTER TELL ME OR…!", Nigel stood up and grabbed Mileeda. She sat back down, watching me with anger. I decided to follow after Tisiphone. As I proceeded into the woods, I realized I didn't see where she had gone. I continued to walk through, and I saw something that I couldn't believe. There was a small girl staring at me. She didn't really fully seem to be visible, but was more like an apparition. She watched me, as I stood and watched her for some time. As I was about to speak, she pointed behind her, and I saw Tisiphone. I looked at the girl again, before I proceeded towards her. When I looked back, the girl had gone. "Sebastian, I stopped praying to you a long time ago. You never answer me, and now I've lost Tig. Please, I miss you, and I miss him. Please talk to me, please…". I watched as Tisiphone looked up towards the sky, expecting a miracle. When it didn't arrive, "WELL, FUCK YOU, THEN! YOU'VE TAKEN EVERYTHING FROM ME!", Tisiphone yelled, standing up and throwing the nearest rock at nothing. She continued screaming and yelling until she fell to the ground. I approached her and placed my hand on her shoulder. She quickly reacted by grabbing me and trying to throw me down, but I was too strong, and she realized who I was, "Amana. How much did you hear?". I didn't say anything. "All of it, huh? Well I'm sorry for that. Your father, he doesn't care about us. At all. It's funny, because that isn't the Sebastian I knew.", "And who is the Sebastian that you knew?". Tisiphone told me how my father saved her from Caprius, and how he made her and Tig the Queen and King of Nasher, because his grandmother was the queen, but didn't want to go back after everything that had happened. As I listened to her story, I, too, became confused about the person that she was referring to. Sebastian in her stories sounded like a hero, but I had only met him once, and he told me to kill Calypsa. Calypsa, as far as I knew, was still passed out, and wasn't waking due to something that Corsa had done to her. But on the other hand, Lona did say that I was going to kill her, and she was from the future, so she would know if I did or not. At first, I thought she might have been lying to turn Calypsa to her side. Now I know there is probably some truth in what she said. Ko-e was with Corsa before she showed up in Nasher, so my guess was, maybe Ko-e was hurt, or maybe she was just too ashamed that this happened while she was protecting her.

TOMMER: I knew I couldn't go back to the castle, so I made my way towards the exit of Nasher. Once I was in the field, I found Lona's dead body. She had been stabbed through the heart. I looked at her for some time, trying to understand how she was so strong. After a while, I figured there was no point in hanging around trying to understand what happened, so I was about to proceed, when I heard, "…wait…". I looked around, and Lona was moving around. She was weak but alive. "You…betrayed us.". I knew I had to act right away, so I took out my blade and rushed at her. Before I could stab her, Corsa landed in front of me, and that was the last thing that I remembered.

When I came to, I wasn't in the dungeon, but rather, I had been tied to a bed. Lona and Corsa were standing over me. "Master, or you sure? You don't need to do this.", "Yes, I do, Lona, for this body must be preserved, I need an extra vessel to contain my power, you know this.", "I do! But must it be him?", "I see no greater punishment.", Corsa said, laughing. "What have you two done to me?", I asked, struggling against the restraints. "Well, nothing, yet.", Corsa said mockingly. "Corsa, what's happened to you?", I asked. "You desire this girl?". I didn't answer. I knew right when she looked in my eyes what happened. It was the same entity that was in Tig. It seemed to be flourishing inside of Corsa, almost like Corsa was who it was all along. "Corsa, you can fight this, Tig did it, I saw him!", I shouted, trying to get through to her. "Lona, leave us.". Lona left the room and that's when fear settled in. "I'll ask you again. Do you desire this girl?". I nodded. "She doesn't desire you. She loathes you. You disgust her. The idea that you even believe she could love you is preposterous. But let's make this simple, I can give her to you. Even she agrees to this.". Now I was confused. "What is it she is agreeing to? I thought you said she hates me?", "Oh, Corsa does hate you. I hate you, Tommer.", she said. "You see, me and Corsa, are one and the same. We are Corsa and we don't like you, but we will give you what you want.". Corsa climbed on top of me, but I knew it wasn't what I thought. She started to remove her clothing, but not in a way that you would think was sexy. Once she was fully naked, she placed her hand over my eyes, "Now you shall see.". As she said this, at first, I saw darkness, then I saw what I thought was just a big wall, but it moved. I didn't know what I was seeing. The wall seemed to be moving in a rhythmic way. I looked around at my other surroundings and realized there was nothing but darkness and smoke. Smoke that was starting to rise in my nostrils. "WHERE AM I?!", I shouted, hoping to get an answer. Instead I heard loud breathing, and the distant sound of wailing and moaning. I looked around, but it was all just blackness and nothing else. "WHERE THE HELL AM I?!", I shouted again. This time there was an answer, "You are dead, Tommer, and I now have your soul and body.", said a voice so unlike anything I'd ever heard before. It was at this point that the wall that I had been looking at, started to move more noticeably, and I looked at what was completely before me. A creature, unlike anything I've ever seen. A creature so massive, that it occupied the space of where I was, and with it facing me, there was an illumination that allowed me to see it clearly, "AHHH…!", I screamed, because it was a monster. It's wings, which I thought was a wall, were massive, and its face was terrible to behold. It had eyes where a nose and mouth would be, two sets. And its teeth were wrapped around what would be a normal person's face, and the most frightening part was its body, which looking at it, suggested that it was bloated somehow. The monster turned towards me and I couldn't scream anymore. "GOT YOU!", it yelled, as what was a giant nasty claw seized me. I realized I wasn't wearing any clothes and that my body was different. It was skinnier. "No, no please, please no!", I pleaded and begged, but to no avail. It consumed me and all I felt was pain. Pain that wouldn't stop. Then I found myself back where I was before, looking at the wall that was actually the monster's wing. I looked around, and started panicking, and then the monster turned towards me again, "I'M COMING AGAIN, DIN!". I tried to run, but I couldn't move, and once again, the monster consumed me, and I felt the pain. Then I was looking at the wall again. "WHAT IS THIS?!", I screamed, unable to contain myself any longer. I was going insane. What was this place, and why did this event continue to repeat itself? As the monster consumed me again, I felt the pain and agony, and this time I finally understood what happened. Corsa killed me. My soul was being tortured. Then I was in a room, where I was finally whole again. But even though I was whole, I still couldn't move. I saw my son, Hoss, standing in a room. He was a fat embarrassment I always thought. But now, Corsa was in the same room. The two began kissing. While my son and Corsa were having sex, he was watching me. I couldn't turn away. While at the same time, I felt a hand on my shoulder, and it was Corsa. "Look at how she embraces him. Listen to her soft moans. Look at the way he…", "Stop this…please, I don't want to see…", "I DON'T CARE WHAT YOU DON'T WANT TO SEE! THIS IS WHAT YOU WANTED TO DO WITH ME, ISN'T IT?!", Corsa shouted at me, while I was still watching my son screw Corsa. Now all of a sudden, it was my dead wife, Tariet. She was Hoss' mother, and died when he was seven. It was the reason he became so violent and perverted. He had no mother to teach him, I didn't care. But it wasn't my son that came in to screw my dead wife, but rather, Godrick, the old King of Dasha. He grabbed her, and took her into a room, and closed the door, where all I could hear was the muffled crying of my dead wife. "PLEASE, I'M BEGGING YOU, NO MORE!". Corsa looked me in my eyes, "Would you rather I continue to eat you for eternity or this? You can only choose one.". I felt myself crying, and knew that I would never see hope or happiness, and I knew what I had done to deserve this. But it was too much. "CHOOSE!", Corsa yelled at me, "FINE, I'LL CHOOSE FOR YOU!". I found myself naked again, and the creature was before me again. This time when it ate me, it didn't return me to where I was, but instead, I proceeded all the way into its stomach, where tubes came and filled every hole on my body. Then a liquid began to fill up into me, but it was a liquid that didn't fatten me, but rather, it exited out of my eyes. It was a hot liquid that burned as it entered and seared as it exited. I kept hoping it would return me to it's outside, but to no avail. After what felt like hours, I was finally back in the room where I could see Tariet on the other side and she was naked. This time, instead of Godrick raping my dead wife, it was Scion, then there was a line of men. All faces I was familiar with. Corsa stood next to me, smiling evilly at me. "When does it end?", "IT NEVER WILL FOR YOU!".

SCION: Ko-e was completely distraught. She wouldn't even talk to me. She was so upset about what happened to Corsa, that she felt like her life meant nothing unless she could save her. I had gotten word from Amana already about what had happened in Nasher. I knew right away that if Corsa is really that powerful, then how could we stop her? I knew that Trinity knew we would, but how? I tried praying to Trinity, but no answer. I tried praying to Sebastian, no answer. I tried praying to anything higher than Sebastian, still no answer. I tried using my ring again to take me to Earth, but that didn't work. Right when I started to lose hope, that's when I had the dream.

It was dark outside, and I couldn't see very much. There was a small cottage in the center of what looked like nothing but woods. I proceeded into the cabin and Cophone was sitting inside. "Father, you're home!", she said, rushing to me and hugging me. In the corner of the cabin, sat Ko-e, who was holding another baby. "Scion, your daughter made you something, come look.", Ko-e said, standing up and leading me. As we walked into another room in the cabin, I saw a painting. It was me with my gauntlet, and in the background was what I recognized as my Spaceship. "She is trying to tell you something with this one.". The message, if I had to assume, was that she didn't want me to go back to Space. "Ko-e, you know why I must return, but does Amana have any idea about this?", I said, pointing at the painting. "Amana doesn't know where we are, and not only that, but I'm quite sure that she doesn't know about the ship.", "Make sure she never does, you may have to destroy this.", "Scion, that would hurt your daughter!", "Amana will do far worse if she finds her. And him.", I said, pointing at the other baby in Ko-e's arms. She swallowed, and then there was a loud noise outside. Something had flown over the cabin. I looked outside and there were men landing in the clearing. They were weaponized and were definitely here for us. "Scion!", Ko-e called, but I had already gone outside and started activating certain points I somehow knew were in the ground. Amana was coming through the clearing, and when she saw me surrounded by her men, I quickly activated whatever I was doing and that's when I woke up.

"Scion, what are you doing?", Ko-e asked me. She had just got back from checking on Dony, who was unfortunately alive, and aware that the girl he loves is possessed by an evil creature. "I've got it, Ko-e. We have to leave. This is it. I'm building my ship now. I know what I use to build it. But first, there are some things I'm going to lay around the city. Things that will help protect Dasha and give us the power that we need to leave the planet. Second, we have to go help Amana. She needs us. I understand now. That thing that is in Corsa, can only be stopped if we destroy its main tether here. And I believe that's Tommer.", "How can it be Tommer? That doesn't make any sense.", "Think about it, Ko-e. First, Calypsa was possessed, and it made her stronger and infected her mind. You carried it here, but it was only a small trace amount of essence, that's why you didn't lose your mind like Calypsa. Then it was able to go to Amana, but by this time, it was gaining more power.". I could tell that Ko-e was still confused. "Okay, look, why do you think it's sent Lona here? Lona wants to kill Amana, but it wants her to do it, BECAUSE for whatever reason, it needs Amana dead, but whatever it's planning, Lona is here to ensure it happens. It needs me dead, too. So now that Tommer is with it, it has gained more strength. I believe that it has been slowly sinking its teeth into Tommer, gaining more and more strength with different hosts. After Amana and Calypsa, it was way more powerful because it took some of their essence. Because they aren't Plinthinian. They are something else entirely, but you have something different in you. Something Trinity made herself that stops it from completely consuming you. That's why you weren't affected the same way I was when Trinity showed you her true-self.". Ko-e gasped, not realizing that I could somehow see that she had seen the real Trinity. "And, as for me dying, I'm not. My body has indeed been altered, but do you remember that time in Callista with Calypsa? At that time, it was possessing me and Calypsa back and forth. It even took Hoss for a bit and may have learned of Tommer from that moment. Probably intended to use Tommer as it's main tether. You see, now that it is in Corsa, somehow, it's thriving. And the influence of power has made Corsa its main host. But even with that, it needs to place parts of its soul here. That way, they can be used as gates anytime Corsa wants to travel between dimensions.". Ko-e was starting to slowly understand. "So, what you are saying, Scion, is that The Unknown has left traces of itself inside of its host so that it can exist on this plane?". I nodded, "It isn't unknown anymore, Ko-e. I think…Corsa is somehow connected. It's why Lona allowed her to leave. Because in the future, Corsa is who she is now. But I believe she has two main tethers. Before Tommer, its main tether has been Calypsa, but now it probably sees fit to make more. Corsa's mind is completely gone. When it possessed Tig, there was enough of Sebastian in him that it made Corsa weaker inside of Tig. That's why it seized the Corsa we know when it saw the chance. Now it makes even more sense why Lona let her live. Because in the future, Corsa is her master.". Ko-e sat back, thinking about all these things. "But if we have to kill Tommer, because he is a tether, you also said, Calypsa is a tether.". I swallowed, "I did say that.". Ko-e stared for a minute with understanding in her eyes. "You have to tell Amana… that Calypsa has to die. It's the only way to stop Corsa from existing here.", she said, now tearing up, and placing her face in her hands. I nodded. I felt a tear, because after everything that had happened with Calypsa, I didn't want her to die like this.

CHAPTER 15

The Ascension Of Scion

AMANA: It had been a long week. Scion hadn't responded back to me since I had written to him a few days ago. While I was patiently waiting for his response, we made our way back towards Kindy. It was the only thing I could think to do. Calypsa, who had been in a coma for the last few days, started to wake up. We were all happy she was awake, despite everything else. Especially me. I hugged her and held her for a long time, "Come on, Amana, we need to keep moving, I'm okay now, I promise.", "I thought you weren't going to wake!", I yelled, with tears coming from my eyes. Calypsa lifted her shirt and wiped my face, "I'll not leave you so soon, Sister.". Although Calypsa said she was okay, I could tell something was off. She seemed to keep looking into the distance and wasn't there a lot of the time. Mileeda, who had every reason to hate Calypsa, was also happy she was awake. It was clear her, Nigel, and Calypsa had formed a very strong bond. We started to feel somewhat better, despite the darkness surrounding us. Corsa hadn't attacked yet, but I was expecting her to.

We had stopped right outside Kindy, and was resting, when Mileeda decided to drag up the situation, "So, is there anything YOU can tell us, Calypsa? About what has happened to my sister.". Calypsa looked like she was trying to swallow a pine cone whole. She looked Mileeda in her eyes when she spoke, "Mileeda, this is going to be hard to hear, but your sister isn't dead, she IS the thing that is trying to kill us. She isn't what she was, and I don't know how else to explain it to you.". Mileeda looked taken aback but didn't say anything else. I was wondering how Calypsa could know that. She had the same knowledge I had, right? And I didn't really know anything about it. What I knew is that this entity had been the start of this. It was inside of Ko-e, who then passed it to Calypsa, who then passed it to me, who then went from me to Tig, and then from Tig to Corsa. But what I didn't understand was what exactly Calypsa had meant. Later that evening, I decided to ask. We were finally back in the castle of Kindy. Some people who remembered Calypsa's attack on us, were stunned to see me holding my sister. As we got into the castle, I told Calypsa she could share my room. Once we were all showered, fed, and tired, we decided to rest and plan tomorrow. "Um, Calypsa, what did you mean earlier by Corsa is the one attacking us? I thought she was just possessed.". Calypsa took a breath, "When it was in me, I remembered feeling its power and realizing I could do what I wanted. My first thought was to kill my mother. But from there, I didn't know why I wanted to do all those other things. I hurt Scion, and I didn't want to. I was okay with my mother, which I couldn't understand, because I always hated her, and then I almost...", she broke off, because I knew what she was going to say. "You almost killed me.". Calypsa began to cry, "Amana, there is something I must tell you but...", as she began to speak, two people materialized in my room. "Scion! Ko-e!". We jumped up and hugged them. "Listen, Amana, I've come to help you. But I can't stay long, so I'm going to just give you this.". Scion handed me a small blade with a serrated edge, and a blue and gray hilt. It was glowing bright purple. "This can hurt Corsa, might even force her to never come back to this dimension, but there will be more you must...", "We will, when we arrive there, Scion.", Calypsa said, cutting Scion off. The two looked at one another, and some kind of understanding was in their eyes. "What are you hiding, Scion?", I asked, feeling left out, but he nodded, looked at me, and disappeared, leaving Ko-e with us. "So, sister sleepover?", Calypsa said, obviously avoiding the subject. I decided not to press the matter and dropped it.

Over the course of the next few weeks, all we did was strategize and plan on what we were going to do. Corsa still hadn't attacked, and at this point, I was getting edgy. I sent scouts to find out what the word was in Nasher and I couldn't believe it, but Corsa wasn't there, and Lona, who we thought was dead, was ruling over Nasher. Alexa, who knew of Lona but didn't know Lona was here and trying to kill us, tried to ride to Nasher immediately, "There won't be anything you can do, she isn't going to listen to you.", I tried telling her. "BUT SHE IS MY DAUGHTER! YOU SHOULD HAVE TOLD ME, AMANA!", she said, riding off. I decided to tell Caprius, who sought counsel with Sebastian, and ended up being told by Trinity to go and collect Alexa, but that's all. She said to leave everything else to us. US being me, Calypsa, and Ko-e. It was with great effort, but Alexa finally decided to leave, being convinced that the smart thing was to wait out the situation. After all, she hasn't given birth to her yet, so Lona isn't really HER daughter. Caprius was worried when he learned of Lona and wanted to approach her as well, but knew better than to disobey Trinity. I kept looking at the blade Scion gave me. It wasn't glowing at the moment, but I quickly learned what it reacted to. "Amana, I think I have the formation of a plan.", Calypsa walked into the room and stated. As she did, the blade began to glow. Calypsa looked at it, and then our eyes locked. "No. I'm not doing it. I'm not.", I said, as I finally understood, and threw the knife, "You knew. The moment you woke up, you knew.". Calypsa didn't say anything. Instead she looked down at her feet. Ko-e walked in, followed by Tisiphone. "YOU KNEW ALL THIS TIME!".

Ko-e rushed to me, but I pushed her away, "AND YOU! YOU KNEW, TOO, DIDN'T YOU?!". Ko-e saw the blade and looked to Tisiphone, "I'm sorry, Amana. But, Calypsa is…", "NO! I won't hear it!". I started to back away from them. I looked at Calypsa, who walked up to me, and placed her hands on my shoulders, "Amana, if I must die to stop Corsa, then so be it. I would rather die a hero's death, than be the reason she manages to succeed.". I shook my head at her, tears coming, "Calypsa, please, there has to be another way. I don't want to lose you. I love you.", I said, falling before her. "I know. And I love you, too, Amana. Look at everything we've done together. But it's for the best. I'll never be able to live happily, Amana. I have to die. I just want you and Ko-e to live happily. I just want you to be…", I broke away from her and ran. I heard footsteps coming after me, but I didn't turn to see who it was. I wasn't going to kill Calypsa. I didn't care about the future or even this planet. I only cared about my sister, who was so ready to die for everyone, I couldn't forgive her.

I found myself in the Kindy garden, crying my eyes out. I lost both my mothers, and now, the one thing I had left, wants to sacrifice herself. "Amana.". I turned to see Calypsa standing there. She was crying as well. "Do you think I want to die?", she asked me. "I know you don't…", "Amana, if you were in this situation, I would do the same. But we need to understand that Father created…", "WHO CARES ABOUT FATHER?! HE DOESN'T CARE ABOUT US! HE TOLD ME TO KILL YOU!", I shouted, realizing Calypsa didn't know that. "Father wants me dead? Well, he probably knew this would happen. Can't blame him. I'm dangerous, Amana. Me and Tommer. We are Corsa's tethers. Take us away and she can't hurt Plinth.", "But, Calypsa, I don't want you to die for this.". I started to cry into her chest. Ko-e came up, tears in her eyes as well, "Amana, it is my fault, kill me. Please, I deserve to die, too!". Ko-e handed me a blade, with a pitiful smile on her face. "Ko-e, I'm not going to kill you. I'm not killing either of you. Please let's try and find another way!", "Amana, there is no other way. Me and Tommer have to die.

It's the only way to trap Corsa back where she came from. If we waste anymore time trying to work out this situation, it will be too late. She wants to make more tethers. We can't let her. We have to protect this planet, Amana, because WE are all it has. We are its most powerful protectors. I know right now feels like we can't do anything, but gain never comes without loss, Amana. You and I know that too well.". This was true. To learn the truth of our father, this was the price. We knew it was a risk when we started this journey, but we didn't know, couldn't know, that THIS is how things would end up. That I would have to kill my best friend, my sister.

SCION: It was the greatest endeavor ever embarked upon. We were taking amazing strides. The citizens were all excited. I had spread the word. Dasha was leaving. The amazing ship I rode in the future was filled with Dasha's lineage. It made sense who the people on the ship were now. We all put in the effort, despite everything that was going on outside of Dasha. Corsa was somewhere biding her time, Lona was ruling Nasher in her stead, and Amana, Calypsa, and Ko-e were all in Kindy. Alexa had returned with Caprius to Alexandria and was told to stay until Corsa had been dealt with. I on the other hand received my orders from Sebastian. He didn't tell me in person but instead had sent a boy with vibrant, short, pink hair. "Well, it's nice to meet you, Scion, I'm Brixin, son of Sebastian.". I stared at the boy, unable to contain myself at his appearance. He wore armor similar to his father's, except it was closer to Caprius' Alexandrian armor. He had a handsome face, which of course he had gotten from his father, but what was really intriguing was how readily he accepted Trinity. "So, you're the son of Alex?", "Well, technically I'm the son of Trinity. Alex was only a piece of her.", "So, you're not like Amana on the subject, then, huh?", I asked, thinking the whole situation over. "No, she couldn't even begin to understand.". Brixin and I walked until we came to another end of Dasha, where there was another entrance/exit gate. This was being torn down because we were building a great wall around the city. I had workers underground, fitting out a platform that could carry the entire village of Dasha. Brixin looked over the work, kept tabs, and reported to Sebastian. Brixin was good company. He was funny when he wanted to be and told me that he would be preparing me for what's above. I decided that Brixin was like the best friend I never had. I hadn't really made friends, not counting Amana, Calypsa, and Ko-e. Brixin told me of Space-women, and how some of them were very different but very similar. I had gotten the idea of that during my trip to the future. Brixin also explained the war to me. "You see, Scion, the reason Father hasn't come here himself, is because he is quite busy trying to keep the other four races out there from destroying one another. So, there is no reason to feel like he has abandoned this planet or his children. It's the reason that I'm here.", Brixin was explaining, as we rode on my underground track-cart to check on the underground workers. "How is everything, Trus?". Trus turned out to be quite the engineer. It was funny, because he was under-used during Micka's rule. "It is going AWESOME, Your Highness! It's almost hard to believe that we are actually doing this.", Trus said, excitedly looking between me and Brixin. "And you feel you've outlined most of the kingdom?", I asked. "Yes. We have already done a whole outline and have put the rotors exactly where you specified, Your Highness. Now all we await is your orders and the workers from the top.", "Trus, I need you to make sure that everything is in order. Come the day when we ascend, I don't want any accidents. Everything has to go as planned.". Trus nodded. "Okay, men, our king needs us to quadruple check and make sure that the entire underground is complete. We need to test the rotors, the wires, and all of the reserve power units. We must ensure that when ascension comes, we ALL make it to the heavens.".

As Brixin and I left Trus, we proceeded to the side builders. The sides all had to connect with the underground complex. These workers were working with a crowd of people that were easily taking care of the inside of the kingdom. "How is this project going?", I asked the main leader of the project. All the leaders of the projects were people who I had chosen personally. Most of the leaders were people who worked in the computer shop with me. The others were people who had proven their worth once the news started to get around. Some of Dasha's citizens didn't like the idea of ascending, so they departed for Kindy or Callista. Callista surprisingly had made a small name for itself. It was big enough that people from Kindy and Dasha were departing for Callista. I myself had allowed the citizens that wanted out to leave, warning them that it was entirely dangerous outside of Dasha at the moment. "Sir, we may have a slight issue. If you can come check this out please?". I looked and saw the issue immediately. There was a part coming from the underground that wasn't connecting to the side. I was going to have to inspect this one personally. "Brixin, I have to go underground, do you mind waiting up here?". Brixin just nodded and I went back to the descender and went back underground. Upon walking and arriving on the spot that I saw was out of place, I was shocked to find Corsa in here. "So, you did this.", I said frustratedly. "Well, I just thought we should talk. After all, you and I have a very important future, don't we?". I had no idea what she was talking about, considering I never saw her in the future. The look on my face must have presented this, because Corsa looked hurt. "Well, this is awkward. So, you don't know about us…". I just stood transfixed. "There can't be an us!", I yelled. "Sure, there is. You need me, Scion, but you don't realize this yet. Don't worry, I'm not here to kill you or even ruin your precious Spaceship. I just wanted to see if you knew.", "YOU ARE TRYING TO KILL MY CHILD!", I yelled. "And why do you think that is exactly?". I told her about Lona wanting to blow up Plinth using Cophone, and Corsa just laughed, "You really think I would do that? Please be reasonable, Scion. Cophone is my greatest asset. But I can't tell you why now, because then you'll never realize why you belong to me.", Corsa said, moving towards me. She placed her hand on my face and I looked in her eyes. "Corsa, you have to fight what is inside of you.". Corsa raised an eyebrow, "You still don't get it, Scion. What is inside of me, isn't controlling me. You've been three-thousand years forward and you still never even realized what Cophone was showing you…”. I started to think back to when Cophone led me to that church, where I met that priest that told me he knew Ko-e. Ko-e was upset that Amana allowed Cophone to die. Now that I started to think about it, I was seeing her here. But I didn’t understand why, now something was dawning on me. “Cophone, you’ve gotten to her?”, “You don’t see? Okay, Scion. Let me tell you this; Why do you think that Sebastian has chosen you? What does he see in you that you are worthy? What of Trinity? She made you a god, and the King Of Dasha. But why did she do that? Because she is setting up a curse.”. This didn’t make sense. “What do you mean?”, “Almost every mortal has something in them that connects them to the All. Sebastian calls it the Cosmos. Trinity has activated you and it’s changed you. It’s made you immortal. Like me, and your girlfriend Ko-e. Now, your daughter will explode, and she will aid me in harvesting souls. The only way to stop it, would be to kill your daughter. And well, this is why Ko-e and you want to keep her from Amana. Because Amana is going to stop every god or goddess from being born. That’s her role. That’s why I am at war with her. But she isn’t the only one with knowledge.”, Corsa said, pointing at me. “I don’t believe you.”, I said, not sure if I really didn’t. “You will.”, Corsa said simply. She then walked up to me, and kissed me on my cheek, “Till we meet again, Scion.”, Corsa said, putting a sexy tone to my name. She disappeared, and I fixed the issue. As I made my way back up, I ran what Corsa had just said in my head. I still didn’t fully understand what she meant. Then, it dawned on me. She only knows of her future, not the one I’m about to change. As I was making my way back towards Brixin, I saw Cophone’s spirit watching me. “Is it true?”, I asked her. Cophone shook her head. She then pointed into the sky. I looked up and all I saw was the sun. When I looked back down, I saw that Cophone was gone, but something had been left behind. It was a flower bracelet. I had seen it before, on Calypsa’s arm. Starting to focus on it, I also saw it on Amana’s arm. As I bent to pick it up, it wasn't really there, and it just disappeared. I couldn't figure out what that meant.

"Took you long enough.", Brixin said, as soon as I returned. I decided not to mention Corsa to Brixin, and instead just continue focusing on the building effort. After we had made sure the side now connected to the bottom, we rode on to check the other areas. From the looks of everything, things were going smoothly now. "Brixin, what are you going to do after we leave?", I asked curiously. "Well, I plan on returning home to help Father with the war effort. My sisters can handle what's going on here, I'm not needed. So, let's just make sure everything is good to go so that we can get a move on.". After checking everything else, and making sure everything was connected, and that all the components had been put in the right place, I knew it was time to start on the interior, which was going to be a much harder project. This was going to take more than just engineering, I needed a good architect as well. This took a lot of great design and a lot of try and fail. At the announcement of the fact that the sides and bottom were finished and that now we were starting on the interior of the ship, it was time to own up or jump ship. We had closed off the exits, but now there was a mechanical metal door that opened diagonally when you wanted to exit. It would be one of the many exits to the Spaceship. The interior was much more difficult because we had laid down metal throughout the streets which took us weeks to accomplish. We had one accident where an individual had accidently burned his whole ankle off due to his foot being caught in the hot metal in liquid form. But other than this incident, it turned out great. Finally, we were now setting up the cockpit, which was large. I had the castle torn down to build this area of the ship and also to build my chambers and royal room where I had met myself thousands of years in the future. I was now seeing the corridors I had grown familiar with when I was in the future, as well as rooms and homes of the citizens. I was so proud of what I had done that I had completely forgotten about Corsa and what she told me. That was until I saw Cophone again, who this time when she showed up decided to do it in her older form. "What are you trying to tell me?", I asked her, starting to become frustrated when she would show herself. She pointed up again and I looked up and started to finally realize what she was telling me. "You're up there? I'll meet you once I ascend?", she nodded, smiling. "Is what Corsa told me true?". Cophone shook her head and pointed at me, then she pointed down and I saw the flower bracelet again. I was trying to understand what the flower bracelet meant, but then I remembered, "Your mother had one of these! She was wearing it before I left her in Kindy. Use my imagination. That's what you're telling me?", I asked. Remembering that's how I thought of the computer. This bracelet would help me save her. Cophone nodded, smiling. She held her hand out for me to grab it and I did, but it went straight through. She mouthed the words, "Corsa cannot be trusted. I love you, Father.". And with that, she disappeared. I felt a bit at ease knowing that Corsa didn't know that I was going to change things. Whatever that thing is inside of Corsa, it isn't Corsa. I knew that my part in the battle was done and so did Corsa, which is why she didn't attack me.

It was finally the day of ascension, and I was excited, along with the rest of Dasha. I had my team of pilots, who had gone through flight simulations that I programmed into my more advanced computer system. It seemed like everything was ready. Out of all the test pilots, of which there were over two-hundred, only fifteen of them made the cut. Neither had actually flown into Space. Hell, I hadn't even flown, but I got an idea of how to. I proceeded to allow myself to do all the work possible I could, and that's when I realized it was really time to go. I wanted to see Ko-e before I left, but learned I wouldn't be able to see her. As I checked my digital map, which I configured to react to the energy that the Sphinx back on Earth was putting out, I saw that Space, as of right now, was going crazy. There was a certain blip that appeared on my map that seemed to be firing something. My team had assembled in the cockpit and all the other engineers were where they needed to be. Everyone was prepared. So, I sat in my Captain's chair. "Sir, we think we're ready to depart. All the systems are connected, and all the gas mains are filled, and now there are complaints coming from below to get a move on.". I laughed a little bit, "Alright, lets ascend.". As the engines fired and I felt the ship lifting, I considered that all that was going to be left of Dasha was a giant hole where it once stood. I remembered where this all started; With me falling for Calypsa, then I met Ko-e, then Amana. Things got out of hand for some time. Then, Alisa, Micka, and Alex, whom I hadn't met or seen before, all turned out to be sisters, that fused into one ultimate being, who even now, hasn't been back here since she had possessed Corsa. I tried to think about what Amana was going to do, and what was going to happen with Lona. I thought about the fact that she is the child of my cousin, Alexa, and I knew I should be trying to do something, but this is what Sebastian wanted me to do, and I had seen the future and know that I would do this. This was just the beginning. I'm immortal, and while everyone else on this ship is going to die at some point, I will live. And in three-thousand years from now, I might end up meeting my past-self again, and showing him everything I was shown. But I questioned what was going to happen in these next two-thousand years. What was going to be taking place and when would I be meeting my daughter, Cophone?

CHAPTER 16

Calypsa's Ultimatum

KO-E: I tried convincing Amana that she should just kill me as well. After all, if I had stayed in Alexandria, this wouldn't be happening. But, Amana got angry with me, "I AM NOT GOING TO KILL YOU, NOW PLEASE STOP ASKING ME THAT!". In truth I understood. She didn't want to kill Calypsa because she loves her, and I know that. But what I didn't know was that she loved me as well. I just couldn't see that because I came into their lives when they were already fully grown, and they didn't know who I was. But I was able to tell them about Father and how we are goddesses. I was devastated watching Amana trying to come up with ways we could possibly win without killing Calypsa. Amana was putting all efforts forward, and was upset that the rest of us agreed with Calypsa and saw no other way. Tila, who had been avoiding Shay, found it even more disturbing, but accepted the truth and spent time with Calypsa. Amana just stayed shut in her lab, never coming out. I had decided to try and speak with her. I knocked on the door, but I knew it was a large lab and she probably didn't hear that knock. I opened the door and found the place almost empty aside from what looked like multiple different projects. Amana was way in the back, sleeping. I approached her. She was draped over a desk and was laying on top of a paper titled; ALEXANDRIAN BASE. I tried to figure out what that meant, then she awoke with a start, "CALYPSA!", she yelled when she woke. She looked around and saw me and relief spread on her face. "Are you okay?", I asked her. "No, I'm not.", she said flatly. She stood up and rolled up a scroll. "What do you want, Ko-e?", she asked me in an impatient tone. "I'm just checking on you. Everyone is worried about you.", "Well, they should invest their time in worrying about Calypsa. Am I the only one that doesn't think she has to die?", "Amana, none of us want her to die, but you heard what she said, and so we truly are wasting a lot of time.". Amana shot me a nasty look, "Ko-e, if you aren't going to help me, then get out.", she said, planting both hands on the desk and giving me an irritated look. "Amana, I just…", "LEAVE!". Without another word, I looked at her, then turned and left.

I ran into Calypsa later, who saw I had been crying. "What's wrong?", she asked. It was strange seeing this kinder, gentler Calypsa, and I had to keep reminding myself that the Calypsa who I originally met was infected by Corsa. "It's Amana, she still won't come out of her lab.". Calypsa looked at me with pity, "Ko-e, Amana and I have known each other since we were little girls, and the truth is, she can't imagine life without me. She doesn't want to believe what we've told her, and so I've done some thinking, and maybe I should just leave. Leave and let whatever is going to happen, happen. This way, I take the choice from Amana.", "You'll kill yourself?", I asked, shocked at this. "I was going to do it when you first met me. My mother made me so miserable, now, here I am, in Kindy. I have my own Kingdom, which is thriving and…", she got choked up, "…I have my sisters, and I love you both, but I love this planet and its people and I don't want them to suffer.". I stood, looking Calypsa in the eyes that are so much like my own. I hugged her and we embraced each other for a long time. "Please, you can't tell Amana that I'm leaving. I'm going to Nasher to face Lona and Corsa. I will have Mileeda and Nigel accompany me, and perhaps, Nigel can win his kingdom back. I must ask though, Ko-e, why isn't Scion helping us?". I knew the answer to this, but knew I couldn't tell her. I just shook my head and decided it best to not focus on it. "We don't really NEED his help, do we?", I asked Calypsa, who smiled. "No, I suppose we don't. We are the children of Sebastian.", "You are the child of Sebastian and Trinity.", I said, and Calypsa hugged me again. "I truly do appreciate you, Ko-e, and please stop feeling guilty, for none of this is your fault.".

I proceeded to look for Tila, since we had a lot in common. Tila was like my mother, an experiment. Falsa believed herself to be an all-powerful goddess, but really, she was just a vessel to hold Trinity. But her body's physiology wasn't designed to hold something like her. Falsa knew this, and this is why she first had Caprius. She thought maybe her child would be a piece of Trinity. After thinking carefully for a long time about my mother, I came to the conclusion that she was loyal only to Trinity. It actually fit into everything she did. She probably needed Sebastian in his full form or maybe not. In truth, why she forced Father back into his full form made no sense and was the only confusing thing to me. But when I look at the actions of Alisa and what she was capable of, it makes even more sense. Alisa was able to enter into the dreams of others and she had the ability to foresee things. Micka became powerful after she had met my mother, who informed her of her true lineage, leaving out the fact that she was actually a Princess of Kindy, and that Alisa is her twin. She didn't tell Micka about Trinity, and I'm quite sure she knew Micka was a part of Trinity. Micka was evil, but Trinity said we just didn't understand her. Alex grew up in Alexandria, and I'm sure Falsa knew she, too, was Tila's daughter. How come there were never any other goddesses? Of course, the answer was because Trinity was already here in the forms of Alisa, Micka, and Alex. Falsa had indeed known a lot, but didn't tell all she knew. But in the end, she sacrificed herself to save Micka, which makes more sense now that I know why she did it. Tila was like Falsa, but was a successful candidate to carry Trinity. I realized that there was some kind of connection to my sisters being born. But I couldn't understand what it was. Alisa had Amana, Micka had Calypsa, and Alex had Brixin. Falsa impregnated herself with me. Perhaps she had hoped for me to be a part of Trinity. But that can't be right, because she had to have known what Alex and the other two were, so then what am I, and why did Falsa have me? My father could answer these questions, but since the last time he spoke with me, I haven't heard from him. I finally found Tila, who was resting in the garden. "Ko-e, how nice of you to join me.", she said as soon as I joined her. We sat just looking at our sun. Its bright yellow light shining down upon us. "So, what brings you here?", she asked me. "Amana and Calypsa. Amana is still trying to find a way to save Calypsa, but Calypsa has decided to leave and go to Nasher, and confront Lona and Corsa.". Tila looked like she was thinking about this. "You know what, Ko-e? I've been so afraid of coming back here because of how the prince just left with me. The effect that we have on men, it's quite funny really. But who would have thought that our children would be goddesses? Or the ultimate goddess? The way Shay looks at me, the anger she feels, how she treated Micka just because she looked like me…", Tila said, fading out on the last part. "Yes, we can agree Shay was wrong, but look at how everything has turned out. I want to help Amana, but I don't know how. Tila, can you tell me why my mother made me?". Tila gave me a pitying look, "Falta was sick. She was upset that she wouldn't bear Trinity, and that she was destined for misery. I felt bad for her but didn't know how I could help her. She did ask how she could help me, though. I told her of my children and how they need her help.". Once Tila said this, it was like a bright light had gone off in my head. As evil as my mother was, could she had actually been working for Trinity the whole time? The possibility was there. Lona was from the future, but so was Corsa. What if Trinity was telling Falsa what to do from the future? "Do you think that Amana, Calypsa, and myself are all accidents?", I asked Tila, hoping that I was right about my mother. "No, I don't think so. I think, on some kind of subconscious level, I believe it was all intentional. Maybe the girls didn't realize it at the time, but they wanted to have you children. Falsa was different. I think you were her last chance at Trinity, and well, now she has to deal with the fact that you simply aren't.". I thought about how weird it would have been to be my father's daughter and somehow his wife. I shuddered. "Listen, Ko-e, I think it's time I showed you our birthplace. Trinity has shown me the truth and it's time for you to know where you come from.". I nodded.

Calypsa was getting ready to leave. Amana was so distracted trying to save her, that she didn't know. Calypsa, after being fully ready to leave, turned, and saw I had been watching her pack, "Calypsa, I just had a thought. Please don't go.", I said, realizing what Amana was feeling. Seeing Calypsa ready to sacrifice herself for everyone, including me, gave me an admiring feeling towards her that for a long while, I didn't think was possible. "Ko-e, you know I have to, you understand.", "I understand, but I've changed my mind. Calypsa, don't do this, or at least tell Amana. Don't leave her like this.". Calypsa gave me a look, "You're leaving, too. Tila told me where you two are headed. So, you don't want me to leave, because then you'll feel even more guilty about Amana.". I couldn't deny she was right about this. "We should tell her.", I said. "I can't. You know she won't let me leave. I have to go, but you tell her where you're going.". I ran to my sister and hugged her, tears falling from my eyes, "I'll never forget you, Calypsa! I promise, I will avenge your sacrifice!". Calypsa broke apart from me, tears in her eyes as well, "Ko-e, when you finish your journey, can you do me a favor? Can you please be the queen to Callista?". I was so taken aback by this request, that I didn't answer right away, but then slowly nodded. We hugged again and then, Calypsa left. I watched her go.

AMANA: I was in a strange room, where it seemed like I was watching something on the other side of a glass window. I didn't know what I was looking at, but then it started to become clear. It was Tommer. He was tied to a chair and wasn't going anywhere. He looked like he was beaten, and blood was dripping from almost every angle of his body. As I wondered what did this to him, a soft voice whispered into my ear, "He suffers now, he suffers.". I looked around, and it was Calypsa. She was watching Tommer, who whimpered and cried. "Calypsa, where are we?", I said, looking around more, trying to get an idea of my surroundings. "We are in it's cell.", Calypsa said, unlike herself. I looked through the glass and realized he wasn't alone. Corsa was there as well. She was naked, and walking around with a small blade in her hand, and cutting at random places on Tommer, who just continued whimpering and crying. The scene in the glass had changed, and it was Calypsa now who was in the room. She was tied up to the ceiling with her hands above her head. She wasn't crying, but rather, she had a brave face on. Scion was there as well, and Ko-e. They were kissing and obviously getting ready to do more. Calypsa watched with her eyes wide open. It was then that I noticed that she couldn't close her eyes. There was something forcing her eyes to remain open and watch the scene before her. "CALYPSA!", I shouted, but she couldn't hear me. I looked around, and this time, it was Trinity who was in the room with me. "What are you doing to her?", I asked. "Nothing, this is not my doing.". Trinity stood and walked towards the window, "My daughter suffers. Although she is awake, her body is without essence. What you see on the other side of the glass is her essence. The entity that you call, Corsa, is an old enemy of mine, and she cannot hurt Calypsa, because her essence is too strong. Part of her essence is mine. So, this is the best torture it can come up with. You wish to end your sister's suffering?", Trinity said, pointing through the glass. "I'm not killing her, there has to be another way.", "There is no way she lives without sacrificing who she is.", Trinity replied. "What the hell does that mean?", "You will see when the opportunity presents itself to you.". I suddenly woke and was back in my lab. Seeing Calypsa suffer like that, made me want to see her. I opened the lab door and found Ko-e outside about to enter. "Ko-e, where is Calypsa? I wish to speak with her.". Ko-e looked as if she had seen a ghost and turned completely red, "Calypsa is gone, Amana. She's left. And me and Tila are leaving as well.". I felt hit by a thunder horse. "HOW COULD YOU LET HER LEAVE?!", I yelled at Ko-e, who surprisingly didn't buckle down, but rather stood her ground and became angry. "SHE TOLD YOU WHAT YOU WOULD HAVE TO DO, AMANA! SHE TOLD YOU AND YOU DIDN'T WANT TO ACCEPT IT!". I looked at Ko-e, who was now crying as well, "I don't want to leave, Amana, but Tila and I need to leave. There are things we must learn about ourselves and they cannot wait. I'm sorry.". Ko-e outstretched her arms to hug me, but I just stood there, still in shock she had let Calypsa leave without talking to me first. "Put your arms down, Ko-e.", I said coldly. She slowly lowered her arms, as I turned my back on her, and started to gear up, and grab my weapons. "Amana, what are you doing?", she asked, walking towards me. I turned and slapped her, and she fell to the floor. "You were right, Ko-e, I should have killed you. Now I have to go after Calypsa. I'm not going to let her kill herself like this.". I stepped past Ko-e, who stood up looking hurt. "Amana, I'm sorry.", she said, as she looked at me one last time, then stormed off. A part of me knew what I told her was wrong, but I didn't care. Calypsa was going to die and I wasn't about to let that happen.

I rushed to my stables and took one of my thunder horses. As I was getting ready to depart, my grandmother, Shay, was blocking my path. "Move.", I commanded. "So, is that how you treat your grandmother now?", she asked me, approaching the horse. "I don't have time for this. Just leave me alone! I have to go save my sister!", I yelled at her. I could feel my face was wet, but I wasn't thinking about that. I kept seeing Calypsa in that room, being forced to relive her nightmare. "Amana, I watched you grow from a small girl to the woman before me. I was always angry at Tila for taking my son. I kept from Micka that I was her family. I never told her the truth. Alisa was raised as if she was my daughter. I know that I was wrong. Derrek and I were wrong. But I can't let you go. I've lost your mother, Micka, and Alex. Now I'm supposed to lose you? How much more can be taken from me by a goddess?". I looked at Shay, who obviously was hurting horribly. I never met my mother's real father and I never knew that Shay even had a son. "So what? I'm supposed to lose my sister, my BLOOD, to your guilt? Perhaps if you had told them who they truly were, they would have left sooner. The truth is, this is how Trinity wanted it, you just can't see that.". Shay stood before me, watching my face. She then hugged me and ran her hand through my hair, "Amana, I don't care what else happens, I love you, and I love Calypsa, but I know that you two are something that I can't comprehend.", she said, releasing me and standing aside. "Please don't die, Amana. Please, come back here.". I rode out of Kindy in hot pursuit of Calypsa. I didn't know how far she had gotten. She had the ability to fly and may already be in Nasher. Whatever the case, the thunder horse would get me there quickly, and hopefully, it will be in time to save her life.

CALYPSA: As me, Mileeda, and Nigel arrived in Nasher, we noticed that things were downtrodden. Tisiphone had stayed in Kindy, because she wasn't fully over Tig's death and needed time to heal. I promised her that I would protect Nigel. So, my plan was to somehow defeat Lona, then Corsa, then kill myself, so that Corsa can't exist in our dimension anymore. My essence was being tortured. Every time I closed my eyes, all I saw was that damn room, where I was forced to watch Ko-e and Scion make love. Where I had to watch my mother beat Amana, and anyone else I loved. I had stopped crying a long time ago, but now I wanted payback. "This way.", Nigel directed us, and we followed him to a deserted area, where we began to plan. "So, what do you think?", I asked Nigel. "Well, can't be easy. She has guards all over the place, and even worse, is now she has a special group. I've been hearing all about it. They are some kind of elite soldiers, and from what I know, maybe you two stand a chance, but not me.", Nigel laughed this off. "It isn't funny, Nigel. And what about Corsa? How do we save her?", Mileeda asked. I hadn't told this to Mileeda, but Corsa was beyond saving. I knew that her sister was just a vessel. A vessel created by the real Corsa. "Mileeda, I don't know if we can save Corsa. We can try, but please don't get your hopes up.". Mileeda looked saddened, but none the less, ready to try something. We heard a commotion and went to see what was happening. Amana had arrived and was jumping off her thunder horse. Some guards had attacked her, but she made short work of them. Then, Corsa came down from the sky, and landed right in front of her. "You should have stayed in Kindy.", she said, as she snapped her fingers and Amana keeled over. "AMANA!", I yelled, trying to rush forward, but Nigel and Mileeda held me back. "We can't let her know we're here yet! We need time, Calypsa!". I watched as Corsa ordered some men to take Amana, and carry her up to the castle. "We have to move. Now.", I said, becoming more frantic. I knew what happened. Ko-e left and told Amana I had left, and Amana charged out of Kindy after me. I wasn't about to let her die for me like this. We moved stealthily throughout Nasher, keeping mostly to the shadows. We had made our way towards the castle. As we stepped inside, all at first seemed quiet, but then slowly, men had come from out of the cuts. They had us surrounded in the entrance hall. "Well, this is expected. I knew once Amana was brought in, somebody would be right behind her. Where is my dear old auntie?", asked Lona, as she haughtily stood before us. She was wearing a different type of armor this time that seemed to actually fit the era. "Where is Amana? This is the only time I'll be asking you this.", I said, looking Lona hard in the face. "Amana is being taken care of nicely. I wish Master would just let me kill her, but she claims she has a need for her, so…". Now I was feeling my blood boil. The thought that she was playing with me about Amana's whereabouts made me so angry, I lost all thought and attacked her. Lona and I started going at it, while Mileeda and Nigel were fighting off the Nashin soldiers. Nigel, who had taken one of the men down without killing him, recognized something, "Calypsa! They aren't themselves!", he yelled. I looked into their eyes, and sure enough, they were all black. These soldiers were being controlled by Corsa. Lona, who I had taken down, had gotten back to her feet and flew at me hard. We ended up going through the ceiling of the castle and were fighting in the air. Lona was holding me by my throat while I was punching her. Eventually, my punches caught up to her, and she let me go, and I flew at her hard, but back into the castle. We hit the ground, and then she stood up, a bit broken. I looked at Mileeda, who was making short work of all the men she was fighting, but Nigel had gotten surrounded. I quickly flew in his direction and aided him. Then I felt my hair being pulled, "We aren't done.", Lona said, throwing me. "I don't know why you want to protect Amana! She is going to kill you. I've told you this before.", Lona said, as she leaped at me. I quickly dodged, "I know my reason for needing to die, Lona, and I've accepted it. It's Amana that hasn't.", I said. Lona and I stood face to face for a brief moment. "Why are you doing this, Lona? What is in it for you?", I asked. "I just want to kill Amana.". I rushed at her, and took out my hidden dagger. I quickly reached to stab her, but she grabbed my hand. I was edging closer and closer to her chest and she was watching me, and the dagger at the same time. Finally, it pierced her skin and she let out a howl. She quickly pushed me away. The dagger was glowing green after it touched her. It was her essence that I was seeing on the dagger. Mine was already attached, thanks to my mother. I rushed back at her, and she moved out the way, holding the spot I had stabbed, and trying to hold in the blood. Mileeda, who had finally finished fighting the men, and had helped Nigel, rushed to me, and came from behind Lona and held her, "NO!", Lona shouted, as I rushed, and stuck the dagger in her chest and twisted it. I watched as life left her eyes and she uttered one final word before she fell, "...again...". Now, with Lona down, and the soldiers down, Nigel looked around, "My father has a vault here and it has weapons that Sebastian gave to him. I'm going to go get one of those weapons.".

AMANA: I woke up and found myself tied to a chair. Gold chains had been tied around me. Calypsa was standing before me. "Calypsa, thank goodness you aren't dead yet!", I exclaimed, just in time to watch blood fall from her mouth and she collapsed. "CALYPSA!", I screamed. I immediately started crying and trying to break the chains. Then, Calypsa was gone and had been replaced by Ko-e. "Ko-e?", I questioned. "You hate me, don't you, Amana?", she asked. I shook my head no. "Ko-e, I'm sorry for what I said, I don't want you...", but before I finished, Ko-e took out a sword and stabbed herself. "KO-E! NO!", I yelled, trying with all my might to break the chains. Then I watched as Scion stood before me and killed himself. Then I watched as Shay and Tila killed each other. Then I watched as my mother, Alisa, was killed by Micka and Alex. Alex had a look on her face that didn't fit her character. "This isn't real.", I said, starting to brave up. The scenery changed and I was sitting in a chair, but I wasn't tied up, and Corsa was just standing in front of me, "You are tough, Amana. I knew you would put up a good fight. It's hard to find people like you. Willing, capable, powerful.", Corsa was saying, as she looked me up and down. "Where is Calypsa?", I asked, hoping she was okay. "Depends on what you mean. You see, her essence is here...", Corsa said, pointing at her temple, "...but her physical form is no doubt by now killing Lona. I warned Lona she wouldn't be powerful enough to face her.". I looked at my surroundings and tried to figure out the best way to come at Corsa. I wasn't tied up but realized I couldn't move. "You are under my control, Amana, just like before.", she said with a nasty smile. She then made me stand up, and then punched me, and I flew back and hit the wall. She walked up to me with an expressionless face, and then, kicked me in the face. I felt my nose crunch under her foot. "Amana, I wish I could kill you now, but I need you alive. So, you will remain alive for some time, but do know, when the time comes for you to die, I will be the one killing you. It's our destiny. You'll see soon enough. When Mileeda and I were children...", she said, now pacing back and forth in front of me, "...Father used to make us sit in church and listen to him talk about how great Sebastian is, and how we have to love and appreciate everything. Now, I realize that Father was wrong.", she said, turning towards me and kneeling in front of me. "You aren't Corsa.", I said weakly, spitting out blood. "You still don't get it? Corsa…is exactly who I am. Trinity used me, then she used you. But you don't see how she is using you. It's okay, though, one day you'll see it and you will hate her even more for it.". I tried to stand but couldn't and fell back against the wall. "Amana, let's say, you and I have some fun.".

NIGEL: I proceeded through the castle, looking for any sign of Amana or Tommer. Mileeda and Calypsa were searching for Amana and I knew that I would be better off on my own. I proceeded up into the upper parts of the castle and then I saw the most frightening thing. My father's body had been nailed to the wall. There were strange circles carved into his body. He was almost unrecognizable. I knew he was dead and had accepted it, but this was more than that. Angrily and hurt, I took out the nails keeping him pinned and took him down. I looked over his body and felt my eyes begin to water. Then he breathed. "Father?", I said, unable to believe this. "Nigel…", he said, barely able to speak. He reached up and touched my face, "Listen…to me. There isn't much…time.", he said, trying to sit up. "Father, please, let me find you help or…". He put his hand up with great difficulty, "NO! Listen to me. The thing inside of Corsa, it is Corsa. It's hard to explain. But she is from the future. She is possessing herself. I don't know how to tell you other than you have to kill Tommer and Calypsa.", he said, coughing blood. "We know, Father. We are here to do that.", "It's more than just that. You must warn Amana! Even if you destroy her tethers here, she is still out there!", my father said, starting to breathe really hard. "Father, let me find you help!", I yelled, becoming frustrated. I thought he was dead, yet here he is talking to me. "I wish I could see your mother, but she would die if she saw me like this. Best keep this to yourself, Son.", he said, as he reached up to wipe the tears coming from my face. "Father, please, you don't have to die!", "I'm already dead, Son.

I'm barely being kept alive. You have to take your blade, Son, and cut into the circles. Break the circles, Son. Free me!". I stood above his body, him looking me in my eye with a weak smile. I looked at the circles carved into him and realized he wanted me to mutilate him. "What are these circles doing to you?", I asked him. "It's a curse, Son. Break the circles, break the curse.". I took out my sword and placed it on his gut, right on the inside of one of the circles. I cut across the circle and from inside of my father, a bright light erupted, filling the whole hall. As the light faded, I realized my father was truly dead now. I felt anger that I had never known my whole life. I became fed up with Corsa and the thing inside of her. She had to pay for this. As I moved through the rest of the castle, after leaving my father's body, I found another tortured soul. Tommer had been treated the same. Nailed to the wall and carved into. His carvings were squares, rather than circles, and he was fully wide awake. "You, seed of Tig.", he said to me as I stopped and looked at him. "You have to get me down from here! Please!", he yelled desperately. I remembered he freed us when we were in the dungeon, so I decided to pay him back for that. I took out the nails and he fell to the floor in a heap. He was whimpering and moaning. "Son, now I need you to kill me. That bitch is using me. I can't die unless...", he didn't finish. He froze up and then suddenly attacked me. I quickly stuck my blade in his heart, but he didn't die and instead, tears of blood flowed from his eyes, as he continued to come at me. I jumped out of his way as he dived at me, then I went for his head. As I slashed at his head, it came off, but his body was still moving. It punched me and I realized he was really strong. The body went to the head and picked it up and placed it on its neck. From there, the skin reattached, and he was no longer headless. As freaked out by this as I was, I remembered my father, who I had to cut into the circles on his body. I quickly placed my sword in the center of one of the squares on his body and slashed downward. The spell was broken, and a blackness filled the whole hall. When Tommer fell, he laid on the floor, breathing heavily, then looked up at me and thanked me. He then turned his head and he was dead.

MILEEDA: Calypsa and I kept moving through the castle until we finally heard voices, "…have some fun?". We kicked in the door and found Amana bleeding from her face and being held up by her neck by Corsa. "CORSA!", I yelled, rushing at her. She quickly turned and grabbed me. "Mileeda, you really shouldn't have come.", she said, as Calypsa rushed to Amana's side. She helped Amana stand up, who was relieved to see Calypsa. "CORSA, YOU NEED TO STOP!", I yelled at my sister, who had taken on a whole new appearance. She had a crown on with snakes to either side. She wore a red dress with gold lining going from the top part of her dress to the sides and all the way past her hips. She had taken to wearing purple lipstick and hardly looked like the sister I knew. She punched me and I flew into the wall behind me. "Mileeda, why would you try to stop me? Look at these two. Our parents our dead because of them. They are the reason that I have become what I am. Thank you for that.", she said, nodding towards Calypsa and Amana. "I don't know what you are, but you aren't my sister. Please, let my sister go.". Corsa looked at me, and in her eyes, I saw something. She walked up to me and placed her hand on my face, "Mileeda, I love you. But I can't let you stop what's coming. I need soul's, Sister. I must have Plinth's essence. Because, it is rightfully mine.". I didn't know what that meant, but Calypsa flew at Corsa, and flew out of the castle through the ceiling. I rushed to help Amana, who was having a hard time standing on her own. "Mileeda, do you blame us?", she asked me. "Never.", I said. "Good, because after this, I will have a great need of you and Nigel.", Amana said. She saw the blade she needed to use on Calypsa on the floor. She picked it up and looked at it. Then she threw it. "Mileeda, I need you to knock me out.". I was confused by this. "Why?", I said. I looked at her as if she was sick. I thought that must be why she is asking me that. But she looked me in my eyes, "Because I can save Calypsa, but you mustn't tell anybody what I'm about to do. Promise me!". I nodded. I took her arm from my shoulders and I didn't hold back as I punched her. She fell out. I looked up and saw Calypsa still fighting Corsa in the sky. Nigel ran in, blood all over and tears in his eyes, "Tommer is gone.". The look on my face obviously said what I was thinking, "I found my father. He was still alive.", Nigel said, trying to not look at me now, as he approached Amana. "Was?", I said. Nigel looked at me, "I had to kill him.". I felt completely horrible. Whatever Corsa was now, she was never this. I went to hug Nigel, but he put his hand up, "What's happened to Amana?". I explained that Amana wanted me to knock her out, but left out the part about her saving Calypsa. I didn't understand how she was going to do that. Especially if she is unconscious.

CHAPTER 17

Corsa's Void

AMANA: I was back in that room. On the other side of the glass, I saw Calypsa. I was free and I wanted to be with Calypsa. I closed my eyes and I was there. "Calypsa, can you hear me?", I asked. Calypsa looked at me. Her eyes had threads in them to force them to stay open. She couldn't speak, but nodded that she knew I was here. I took out a knife and cut her down. She rubbed her wrists and threw her arms around me. "WHAT HAVE YOU DONE?!", I heard from what seemed like everywhere. Then, Corsa's face appeared. It was huge and frightening, but I handed Calypsa a blade and we both stabbed her through her face, "AHH!", she yelled, and then I found myself back in the room with Mileeda and Nigel, and blood all down my front. I stood and looked up. Corsa fell through the ceiling, and Calypsa landed next to her but she was passed out. "Calypsa!", I called out, shaking her, but she didn't move. "You've freed her essence, but now her vessel is empty.", said Corsa, with an evil smile, "You still have to kill her, Amana.", she said, getting to her feet. Mileeda rushed at her, quickly, and then, Nigel helped her. Corsa was weaker. I tried shaking Calypsa some more, who finally gave a small moan, "Amana, now, you have to.", she said, turning over to look at me.

"No, I don't. Calypsa, I can save you.". She shook her head frantically and tears rolled out of her eyes, "NO, AMANA! WE ARE OUT OF TIME! DO IT NOW!", she yelled, handing me the blade. I looked at Mileeda and Nigel, and they had been tossed aside, and now, Corsa was coming for me. I looked at the knife in my hand, glowing more brightly purple than before. I looked into Calypsa's eyes, as she nodded towards me reassuringly. I continued to shake my head no. Mileeda had gotten back to her feet, and rushed at Corsa, and tackled her down. Nigel piled on the top of them, "AMANA, NOW!", Nigel yelled. My eyes were so blurred with tears I couldn't see straight. "Calypsa, please? I don't want to! I love you so much!", I yelled at her. Calypsa grabbed my wrist, "I love you, too, Amana.", she said, then she forced my wrist down into her heart. Calypsa glowed, a bright light emanating from her. The light filled the whole room. At the same time, Corsa, who once again had thrown Nigel and Mileeda to the side, was rushing towards me, when another bright light appeared, as if someone was unveiling something. "NO…!", Corsa yelled, as she was sucked into the bright void. As she was engulfed, and the white void closed, there was a force that hit all three of us. When I came to, there were Nashin soldiers all around me. My face had been cleaned, and I seemed to be in some sort of med bay. I tried to move, but as soon as I did, I felt a hand on my shoulder, "Whoa, Princess, you need to relax. You aren't really capable of moving yet.", said a woman with bright blue hair. I sat up, and then the woman pushed me back down, "Princess, I said you need to stay down.", the girl told me again. "Where am I?", I asked. "You are in Nasher. In our medical bay. We're using medicine you've given to us. You're my role model. By the way, my name is Dalia.", the girl said, then smiled at me, then walked away. I tried to move again, but I was starting to realize, Dalia was right, I was really sore. Nigel hobbled into my tent. His leg had been mended. He saw me looking, "Landed on it wrong when we were fighting Corsa.", he said, sitting down. "Where is Mileeda?", I asked him. "She is mourning. I've given her some time. She is going to Dasha.", "What about my sister? Where is

Calypsa?". Nigel looked sick now, "She is dead, Amana. I'm sorry.", he said, a small tear coming down his handsome face. "But where is her body?", I demanded. Nigel pointed at the tent across from mine, and I could see her now. I leaped off my bed and started to make my way to Calypsa. Nigel aided me, seeing that I could still barely walk. As we entered her tent and I looked down upon her face, I recalled when we first met. She was so beautiful, and she had my eyes. We knew we were related right away. I placed my hand on her face, which looked so peaceful, and began to cry. Nigel had left me with Calypsa's body for some time. I continued crying over her and recalling old memories. I bowed my head and decided to talk to my father, "Sebastian, please, if you can hear me, please bring Calypsa back to me. I can't live like this. Please.", I said, looking up into the tent canvas. But nothing happened. Then I tried the other one, "Trinity, please answer me. YOU TOLD ME I COULD SAVE HER, DAMN IT! ANSWER ME!". But there was no response. I stood up, forgetting the pain, and Dalia came into the tent with some men, "PRINCESS! I told you to stay put! How did you even get here in your condition? Look, these men are here to take this body, so…", "NO!", I yelled, infuriated. Dalia looked frightened, "Please, Princess, she is starting to decompose, and we need to…". I put my hand up, "I'm taking her with me to Kindy.". Dalia looked livid, "Look, you are my role model. You're the reason I became a med person. But I can't knowingly let you take this body. If you do, it will be almost unrecognizable by the time you get to Kindy.". Dalia was now directing the men to take her body, and I threw myself on top of her, tears flowing out of my eyes, "PLEASE, SHE IS MY SISTER!", I yelled. Dalia looked surprised, "HALT!", she yelled, and the soldiers turned towards her, annoyed. "Leave this tent.". Dalia ordered, and the men left at once. "I didn't know you two were related. I thought her mother was Queen Micka, and yours Queen Alisa?", she asked me. "We share the same father.", I said, irritated that she hadn't left me yet. Dalia looked at Calypsa, then looked at me again, "I will prepare a cart for you.". She left without another word.

It hadn't occurred to me how long I had been out, but when Mileeda had returned, it was with a sour face full of confusion. "What's happened?", asked Nigel, embracing her the moment she was within reach. "Well, I don't exactly know how to say it.", Mileeda said, looking at me, "I've just got back from Dasha, and there was no Dasha.". Both me and Nigel looked at each other. "What the hell are you talking about?", I asked her, unable to process this. I imagined there was a giant hole where it used to be, but that's just silly. There were whole villages and not to mention the shops and nice homes. But more than that, the castle. "Can you be more specific?", I asked, because I couldn't picture it in my head properly. "Maybe you should just see it.". We rode out of Nasher, Nigel leaving Dalia in charge. Dalia was the Head of Medical in Nasher, and had been appointed by Tig, who had apparently forgotten this. Tig had seen her grow into a very smart woman, and she had a small fling with Nigel. But in the end, she decided that she didn't want to be royalty. I was riding with Calypsa's body in a cart, covered, and surrounded by dry ice to keep her body from decaying too much. I kept trying to imagine what Mileeda said, but it seemed impossible. But before we even reached Dasha, you could see the crater. There were no villages, no lights, no homes or shops, and the castle itself was all gone. I jumped off my horse and was shocked. "Where did it go?!", I exclaimed, looking at Nigel, who looked just as frightened. We sat around trying to figure it out for a while, until we decided, what was the point? As we started to ride back, something fell from the sky that it seemed like only I had noticed. I went and picked it up, and then I realized it was a communicator. I had started working on this when Scion was in Kindy. I looked around, then I looked up and could have sworn I saw something, but then it was gone.

Over the course of the next few days, things were finally starting to die down. I was feeling like I was being mowed over. While everyone else was adjusting to things, I found it quite hard to do. Mileeda, who wasn't entirely over what happened to her sister, a few weeks later announced she was carrying. Nigel, now the King of Nasher, had sent for his mother, who was staying in Kindy. Tisiphone had arrived, and was overjoyed to learn she would be a grandmother. I tried to be happy for them, but kept finding it difficult. I needed to be alone. "Amana, why haven't you returned to Kindy? Your grandmother is worried about you.", Tisiphone said to me. "I don't want to return yet.", I said. I was sitting in the Nasher garden, located behind the castle. I was staring at a large tree with a carving in it, claiming that this was the resting place of Sebastian's parents. I quietly cursed Sebastian. "I know what losing Calypsa did to you, Amana.". I looked at Tisiphone with nothing but anger, "HOW COULD YOU UNDERSTAND?!", I yelled at her. Tisiphone was patient with me and replied, "Amana, my sister committed suicide, and my father was murdered by Micka. And now, my husband is dead. I believe I have some idea of what you are going through.", she said, giving me a pitying look. I had forgotten that Tisiphone had suffered all of that, and I began to cry. I fell into her arms, and she was stroking my hair, and patting my back. "I…just… didn't want it like this!", I yelled into her shoulder. "I know, Amana, I know. I'm so sorry this had to happen.", Tisiphone said, continuing to stroke my hair. We both sat in the garden for some time, then we decided to head back into the kingdom. My face was still wet when we reached the front of the castle. It was at this time, though, that I knew what I had to do. I spent the rest of the evening with Tisiphone, Nigel, and Mileeda, as we just sat around, listening to the sounds of the instruments that were being played, and enjoying each other's company. After I had locked eyes with Tisiphone, I stood up and walked out of the hall. I made my way down to the dungeons where I was storing Calypsa's body. I found Dalia standing over it, looking down. "WHAT ARE YOU DOING DOWN HERE?!", I yelled at her, rushing to my sister's body, and pushing her away. "I'm sorry! I didn't mean to frighten you or give you the wrong idea!", she said, looking shocked and hurt. I remembered her telling me I was her role model. "I'm sorry. I shouldn't have reacted like that. What are you doing here?". She brushed her front off and then walked next to me and looked down at Calypsa's body, "I was just so shocked to learn you two were related. How long did you know this?", she asked me with a confused but curious look. "Ever since I was five years old. It's when we first met.". She nodded and looked at Calypsa again, "And who did you say your father was? Have you two ever met him?". I found it annoying that she was asking me all this. It was after all, none of her business, but I kind of found her interesting. "Not really. But we did find out who he is. But you wouldn't believe me.", I said, smiling a little bit now. "Try me, you'd be surprised what I believe.". I told her mine and Calypsa's story. Dalia was very somber. She was a really good listener. She didn't say a word until I had finished. "So, this thing that was inside of her wasn't controlling her, but somehow causing her to act on certain emotions? And it's done the same thing to Corsa, our new queens' sister? This is all very interesting, Amana. I really wish I had more time with Calypsa. Her body must be filled with all kinds of special things.". I didn't understand what she meant by this. "What does that mean?", I asked. "Well, you are the daughter of Sebastian, and he is our creator. So, if Calypsa is his daughter, how do you know that she has truly died? You said she could bring people back from the dead, right? Well if she had that ability, how is it she was able to perform that feat?", she said, giving me a puzzling look. I knew that she had a point, though Calypsa never told me how she raised the dead, and how she rid their bodies of the decay, and how she was able to control people. Calypsa was powerful, but never told me how I could become powerful like that. "Did you have another sibling? I believe I've seen her before.", said Dalia. "Yes. Her name is Ko-e, but she is gone for now. She is with my grandmother.". Dalia thought all this through. "Amana, what do you intend to do with Calypsa's body?", she finally asked me after some time. "I want to bring her back.", I said. Dalia looked at Calypsa's body again. "How can I help you?", she asked me with a serious face. "I can't ask you for help, Dalia. I barely know you.", "True, but in the end, I don't think you can do this on your own. You need somebody.". I looked at my sister, who still wore that peaceful face and looked like she was just taking a nap. "I'm going back to Kindy. If you really wish to help me, then return to Kindy with me. There I'll tell you what I need from you.". Dalia nodded and left to go pack.

I had some guards get Calypsa's cart out by the gate. Dalia had packed a moderate sized bag and loaded it onto the cart. I was looking at the sun and trying to imagine how my father created something like that. "Amana, can we speak?". Tisiphone came up next to me. We walked towards my cart, "Listen, I know that you are hurting, but you still have a responsibility to Kindy. You are it's queen.". I hadn't even been thinking about this. "I don't think I can be queen now.", I said, "It isn't the same, knowing Calypsa isn't in Dasha.". Tisiphone looked at me with pity again, "Amana, I know she was more than just your sister, but you can't let this become an obsession. It will if you allow it to.". I knew she was right, but all I could think about was how Trinity lied to me. She said I'd be able to save Calypsa, but I couldn't. She didn't deserve to die like this. I hugged Tisiphone, only nodding to her words and went to the cart. "So, you're leaving with Amana?", asked Nigel of Dalia, who nodded. "The princess will need my help. You know I've always dreamed of working with her.". By the time I had hugged Nigel and Mileeda, and waved bye to them, we set off and headed for Kindy.

Once we had reached Kindy, I was immediately escorted to the castle. My grandmother and grandfather rushed to me and embraced me. I quickly regaled them with the story of what happened in Nasher, finding it extremely difficult to talk about the part where Calypsa forced me to stab her. My grandparents decided to have a funeral of their own for Calypsa. After all, she was also their granddaughter. My mother, who was now gone, and I didn't know when I'd ever see her again, would have loved this. Purple drapes had been thrown over almost everything in honor of my sister. I remembered Callista was still in the woods and wondered if it had a new ruler. Calypsa was smart, and of course if she knew she was going to die, she would ask someone to take over. At the funeral, I was approached by one of the Royal Congressmen. The Royal Congress was a group of seven people who aided my mother in certain decisions that had to do with the kingdom and its citizens. I never cared, nor trusted either of them. "Princess, or maybe I should call you, Queen? Either way, we will need to prepare for your indoctrination. Are you prepared for that?", a man named Seamus asked me. "Seamus, I would rather not talk about this at my sister's funeral.", I replied, not even looking at him. I was watching a group of kids reenact the attack on Kindy and pretend to be fighting. I noticed some of the people present at the funeral looked confused. No doubt wondering why we would be having a funeral for the woman who killed Queen Sheena. "This isn't something you can just ignore, Amana. Your mother tried this as well, you know? You have responsibilities to your kingdom.". I turned in Seamus' direction, "The rules say if I don't want to rule, I can appoint the throne to somebody of my own choosing.", "Technically, yes, but…", "So I have someone else who will be doing the queenly duties.", I said, turning away from him again to watch the children some more. "YOU CAN'T JUST APPOINT SOMEONE WITHOUT CONSULTING THE CONGRESS!", Seamus yelled, and some people turned to look. "Yes, I can. I've already done it. I will be introducing her tomorrow. I'm sorry if that is unagreeable for you, but I myself will be too busy to deal with these things.". Seamus looked livid but walked away. Seamus was the head of the congress and I knew he would be trouble.

Over the next few weeks, I spent time in my lab with Calypsa's body. I had been trying to figure out how to bring Calypsa back for so long that I started talking to her dead body, "…the nerve. I mean, they still keep asking me, even though I already appointed a new queen.", I was saying to my sister's corpse. Calypsa said nothing, but continued to lie there as if she was only sleeping. The very next morning after the funeral, I had announced to the kingdom that

Dalia was its new queen. Dalia wasn't happy about this, mainly because she truly wanted to help me bring back Calypsa. I explained that she was helping me by taking over Kindy. She felt betrayed, but none the less, rose to the occasion. She was very good. She had put Seamus in his place at their very first meeting. I had given her the protection she would need to keep herself safe from anything the congress might try against her. "You don't think I was wrong for putting so much on Dalia, do you, Calypsa?", I asked. Calypsa said nothing, but I pretended she answered. "I know. It's just so strange now. I really miss my mother. I bet you don't miss yours. Do you…?", the lab door opened, and it was Tisiphone. She looked around and then stared straight at me. She was closely followed by Dalia, who looked terrified. "Amana, if I had known this is what you were going to be doing, I would never have let you leave Nasher!", Tisiphone said in disgust. I looked over what she was looking at and understood what she was freaking out about. I had wires connected to Calypsa, and I was monitoring her vitals, which at the moment were flat. I was constructing tubes that were big enough for a person to fit in, and had already begun filling it with corpse fluid to keep Calypsa's body fresh while I put different chemicals inside to see what worked. "Tisiphone, I wasn't expecting you.", I said embarrassed. Dalia stood over Calypsa's body and then looked at me. "Amana, look at yourself! You're filthy!", Tisiphone yelled, handing me a mirror. I looked at myself, and sure enough, I was dirty. My face had dirt marks, and my eyes had bags. To be honest, I couldn't remember the last time I slept. "And before we came in here, were you talking to Calypsa's corpse?", Dalia asked me. I didn't answer. Instead, I handed Tisiphone back her mirror and went back to what I was doing. My grandparents came in and were just as horrified. "Okay, look, I need to work, so I need you all to get out.", "NO. Amana, you are going to cease this. You are going to bury Calypsa and end this.", Tisiphone said with such finality, that I almost considered it. But one look at Calypsa's face, "No, I'm afraid I can't do that. Trinity said…", "Amana, you told me Trinity said she wouldn't be herself anymore. Maybe that was her way of telling you that you can't bring her back.", said Dalia, with a hint of fear. Dalia was a tough girl and I could tell she more than worshipped me. So, to see me like this was probably destroying those admiring thoughts. Shay approached me and placed her hands on my face, "Amana, please, we all love and care about you, but this isn't you.". I felt my eyes begin to water, "But, I don't know who I am without her.", I said, with sadness in every syllable. Everyone looked at me with pity, then the last person I expected to walk in, came in. It was Alexa. She came with a clutch of men, and a round belly. "Amana, I'm so sorry. Come here.", she said, holding her arms out. I went to her and began crying intensely.

I don't know how long I was crying into Alexa's bosom, but eventually, she was sitting with me, patting my back, along with Dalia, who was resting her head on my shoulder. "Listen, Amana, Caprius and I were thinking, Calypsa never got to see Alexandria, and well, she should be buried there, don't you think?". I didn't answer. I knew she was right, and that Calypsa would love to be buried there. "Have you heard from Ko-e?", I asked, thinking about the sister that was still living. "No, she hasn't said anything or come to Alexandria since I found out I was carrying.", Alexa said, still looking at me sadly. I felt myself breaking down again, and Alexa must have noticed. "Come on, Amana. Let's go and prepare Calypsa's body for the trip.". I followed her, giving Dalia a curt nod that I would be okay. She then went to deal with other things. As we found our way back into my lab, the men were already loading Calypsa onto another cart. I watched, as she was still motionless and unmoving. For the briefest of moments, I found myself back at the lake with her when we were children. "We are sisters, aren't we, Amana?", I remembered her asking me. I remembered that sweet innocent face that had been through so much at the hands of her mother. How badly I wanted to save her from that. And in the end, I couldn't save her life.

We had reached Alexandria and were headed into the Royal Village. All I could think about was the fact that I wasn't ready to put Calypsa down yet. I looked at her body, which was still on ice. When we had stopped, and everyone was stepping down from their carriages, I went to her and placed her hand to my face. Alexa watched me and then, Caprius came. He took one look at Calypsa, then me, "I don't know what to say, Amana. I know how close you two were. I'm sorry.". I nodded, "Let's just get this done.". The funeral here was ten times the funeral we had in Kindy. People actually mourned because she was a child of Sebastian. We sat for some time very quietly, and then they lowered Calypsa into the ground inside of a glass coffin that was very intricately carved. I watched as she was lowered, and felt the urge to jump in with her. I turned away quickly and ran off. I had run all the way onto the other side of the garden. Caprius caught up with me. "Amana, are you alright?". I shook my head, "I can't do this. My mom, and now, my sister, too? I can't do this, Caprius. I can't live without them.". Caprius gave me the same pitying look everyone else had. "Can I tell you something? Something about you, Amana.", Caprius said, changing his tone, "I'm sure you were told of Desian.". I had been. I nodded. I then told Caprius what I knew about him. How he forced my mother to sleep with Sebastian. "What if I told you Desian had nothing to do with that?", "What the hell does that mean?", I asked, confused by what he was trying to tell me. "I mean, Desian told me himself that he had nothing to do with what happened in the cave. He said Alisa did that to herself. I didn't understand at the time. I thought he was trying to manipulate me, but he was telling the truth. Alisa had Trinity in her all the time. Trinity was what forced Alisa. He was telling me the truth. Amana, my point is, you weren't some accident. None of you girls were. Even my sister. There are times I even wonder about myself, and why Trinity allowed me to be born. But I think I understand now.", Caprius said, reaching into a pocket on his armor and handing me something. I stretched out my hand and it was a ring. It had a green stone on it. I looked at Caprius, confused. "The thing that took over me and Calypsa, it's inside of you, Amana. It can take you at any time. But if you wear this ring, it will protect you. I have a feeling, Amana, that you will rule over Alexandria one day.". Caprius held out his hand for me to shake it. I looked him in his eyes, "Do you think Calypsa will ever come back? What about my mother?", I asked. "Alisa is one of the strongest, bravest, and smartest women I have ever known. She is only a part of Trinity. I'm sure you will see her again someday.".

I had found my way into my chambers I stayed in last time. I had no idea how long I was staying in Alexandria this time. I kept trying to make sense of what Trinity told me, "There is no way she lives, without sacrificing who she is.". What did that mean? Did it mean there was a chance to save her? Or did it mean what Dalia said, and that I should just leave her dead. I tossed and turned, unable to sleep. Every time I closed my eyes, all I saw was Calypsa, smiling, and laughing, and holding her hand out for me to take. I did and we ran. I didn't know where we were going, but every once in a while, Calypsa would look back, just to see if I was still there behind her. I squeezed her hand to let her know I was still here. She smiled at me and continued to lead me. We were in front of a strange lake that was purple. She jumped in and then waved for me to join her. I did. At first, we were just swimming. Suddenly, we were children again. Calypsa swam to me, frightened. I noticed that I wasn't a child but my adult self instead now. Micka's face rose from out of the water. She looked angry and was gazing down on us. Calypsa put her face in my chest, too afraid to face her mother. "GO AWAY!", I yelled, but Micka started to come towards us. "AMANA! PROTECT ME!", Calypsa screamed, and I wrapped my arms around her and closed my eyes. Next, I was being woke up by Casian, who was licking my face, and Alexa, who was entering my room, followed by Caprius, and Penelope. "Amana! What's happened?", Penelope asked, falling on the bed and wrapping my head in her arms. I realized I was sweaty and breathing hard. "I...don't...know.", I said out of breath.

I couldn't breathe. It was like something was holding me. "I…had a nightmare.", I managed to say. "I'll say you did. You were screaming for Calypsa in your sleep.". Once again, everyone was giving me that pity stare. I was so tired of it. "I want to go back to sleep.", I said, looking at them all. Casian nestled herself into my blanket, stating she wasn't going anywhere. I found it funny sometimes how smart this little creature was. "Amana, I can stay with you, too, if you like.", Penelope said, already preparing to lay with me. I nodded, and Alexa and Caprius went back to their chambers, while I laid back down with my grandmother and Casian. This time when I closed my eyes, it wasn't Calypsa that I saw. "Amana, it's time to let this go.", Trinity was saying to me in her sing-song voice. "Where is my mother? I want to see her!", I replied. Trinity closed her eyes and a white light engulfed everything. The next thing I knew, I was standing in the center of Micka, Alex, and my mother, who held her arms out for me. I quickly fell into her arms and the other two wrapped their arms around us. "Don't you understand, Amana? We don't want this either, but it had to happen.", my mother said, placing her hands on my face. "We know it is hard to understand, but you must leave your sister where she is. If you try and bring her back, Amana, you will regret this.", said Micka, who was also looking at me with pity. "Calypsa was a strong child, but alas, her creation was meant to be a sacrifice.", Alex said. This piqued my curiosity. "What does that mean?", I said, feeling myself grow angry. "Calypsa was our daughter, and ours to choose how her life will be.", my mother said, in a tone that didn't match her personality. I looked at her and saw my mother, Alisa Tia, but felt something colder. "Is this, Alisa telling me this, or Trinity?", I asked, becoming angry. "We are one, Amana. We are the same. Trinity is your mother. We are your mother.". It was that strange crap she kept saying this whole time. I quickly backed away from them. "So, what you're saying is, you wanted me and Calypsa to be close, just so I would kill her when the time came? You knew all this would happen?", "Does this anger you?", they all said at once. I couldn't believe they thought they could just tell me that and everything would be okay. "WHAT THE HELL DO YOU THINK?!", I yelled at them. They didn't seem fazed, and at once, formed back into her. She held her arms out and directed me to come to her. "No. You stay the hell away from me! You could have saved her!". I felt lost. Betrayed by my mother. I backed away and backed into something solid, or someone. I turned, and my father, Sebastian, was standing behind me. "Amana, listen to her, she doesn't take Calypsa's death lightly. We mourn for our daughter, but now she is at peace. She doesn't want to return to this plane. If you bring her back, there will be consequences. Do you recall what I told you? I told you someone worse will kill her if you don't do as I say. I tell you again, leave Calypsa where she is. Live your life, Amana. Guard this place and protect it. But bring your sister back, and it's over. Yes, it is possible, but you endanger everything by doing it. We leave it up to you now. If you wish Calypsa to return, so be it. But remember, the cost.". I stared into my father's eyes, which were of course like mine. I saw Calypsa in his eyes. I knew I would ignore his warning. I didn't care what it took. But before I woke, I saw in his eyes, he knew I wasn't going to listen. He knew and so did Trinity. The question is, what is it that they truly wanted?

KO-E: It had been months already since Tila and I departed. We hardly found it strange that we hadn't heard from anybody, seeing as how we were traveling to where she had been hiding. She told me of the Yindin, the people that lived in this far away land. Warned me that they were dangerous and had tried to prevent Trinity from forming. But when we arrived, the Yindin had packed up and moved. There was no trace of them or their leader, Coxtil. Tila and I camped in this land and while we did, she explained to me more about her and my mother, "...there were never really any other goddesses. Just synthetic ones, like myself, and your mother. We of course were created so that Trinity can exist again, but at the same time, Ko-e, we were also made for another reason. When I first came to this land, it was to learn more about myself, for my daughters' sake. Trinity led me to this land because I was the perfect carrier. I was able to hold two of her selves at the same time. She used me to create Alex. It was different from how the other girls were born. Trinity put the rest of her essence into me when I was carrying Alex. So, you see, they truly were all sisters.". I was so amazed by this information. We all had always wondered after all. Even Alex herself. "But, Tila, I don't understand why they didn't know. Shouldn't the three of them coming together have told them something?", I asked. "Well, sure, a great many things happened. Alisa and Alex shared a connection right away. And Micka and Alisa being twins, I imagined that is what sparked their hatred towards one another. But rather, Micka realized it or not, she was always protective of Alex and Alisa. She was always looking after them. And, Alisa was the same way with Micka. All three girls were always connected. But it was the fact they were all carrying your father's children that proved without a doubt that Trinity was controlling them.". I thought about Alisa and that she had married a woman. "Do you think Amana prefers women? It's just that I've never seen her even consider a man.", I said. I knew it was weird to ask, but now that I was thinking of her mother, I couldn't help but wonder. "I knew it right when I met her. I noticed how she looked at Mileeda.". I hadn't noticed that at all, or maybe was too busy to notice. Once again, I felt that guilt over what happened to Mileeda's family. I felt terrible that I didn't at least stay to help deal with Corsa. After all, she was taken on my watch. "Tila, what do you think has happened to Corsa? Do you think it is over?", "That's what I want to talk to you about, but we will wait till tomorrow.". We both decided to sleep.

I felt like I was awake but knew that I wasn't. I looked around but didn't understand my surroundings. A woman was sitting across from me, who looked remarkably like, "Hello. Me.". I felt my heart beating extremely fast and felt a head rush. "Relax, Ko-e, you knew I'd do this eventually. It's happened so many times now, I've lost count. But this is it. I know it is.". I had no idea what I was talking about and continued to stare mouth agape. "Okay, I'll make this easy. We are a few thousand years from your time. Scion has been here, and Alexa as well.". I started to calm down at the mention of Scion. "Why have you brought me here?", I asked her to try and remain calm. "Ko-e, you aren't a mistake. Falsa knew what she was doing. You are stronger than Calypsa or Amana. Hell, even Brixin. You have something special those three don't. You're a creation of synthetic essence and the true essence of Sebastian. Why do you think Corsa couldn't take you? She never held influence over you. She took Calypsa, Amana…but not you.", "You keep saying Corsa… Am I supposed to believe that Corsa was possessing herself?". Other me nodded. I had somehow passed Corsa's essence to Calypsa when I first met her. "So, what are you saying?", I asked, confused by what she was getting at. "Ko-e, you can save this world, and all the other ones. You are what Trinity and Sebastian have been looking for. Trinity is glad to call you her daughter as well because technically she made you.". I looked at my doppelganger and began to cry, "Calypsa is dead? Isn't she? Amana has killed her.", I said, finally feeling it. "Amana…", the other Ko-e said with unpleasantness in her voice, "Remember when Micka warned us? She said we would hate each other.". I nodded. "She was right.". Before I could ask why, I was woken up. Tila was waking me and pointing at a fire she had started, "…are you hungry, I asked?", she said, and I realized she had already put something on the fire. I nodded.

After Tila and I fed ourselves, we decided to continue our journey. We finally had found the strange building left behind by the ancients and we entered. We walked to the back, where there was once a pond filled with Trinity's essence, now gone because Trinity has reformed. "This is where Trinity was all this time. She was here. Waiting.", Tila said, looking around. "Why was she here in the first place? Why did Trinity have to split herself apart.", I asked, looking around at everything. I could feel the old coming off of everything in this place. It was so strange and yet so fantastic.

Tila had already told me this place is over forty-thousand years old and if that is true, then who the hell put this stuff here? Of course, she proceeded to explain that Sebastian and Trinity are a lot older than people today actually know. I wondered if they had children prior to Amana, Calypsa, and Brixin. But what I learned in that place, I can't speak of yet. Processing it was too much. Tila and I journeyed back to Callista, where I had taken Calypsa's place as it's queen. The people all mourned, and we had a funeral of our own, which apparently, in Kindy, they had done months ago. All the news I was hearing from the other kingdoms could hardly be called good, but it also wasn't bad. In Nasher, my best friend had given birth to her first child, Vicdor, who she was very proud of. Vicdor was now the Prince of Nasher, seeing as how Tig was dead, and Nigel was the king. Tisiphone was still living in the castle but taking a small role in the head of royalty. Mileeda still mourned for Corsa and her parents. She often goes into the garden, where a memorial had been prepared to honor the Queen of Nasher. A carving had been made out to look like her father, Taxin, her mother, Floris, and her sister, Corsa. In Kindy, a new queen had taken reign and she was not to be trifled with. Her name was Dalia. I actually remembered meeting her. She was the nurse that aided my brother, Caprius. I wondered how she was appointed queen, but then started to hear rumors that Amana would often travel into the kingdom, and pretty much, all of the castle knew what they did behind closed doors. Speaking of Amana, she was no longer staying in Kindy, which told me she was staying in Alexandria. Calypsa had been buried there and so I imagined that is the reason she stayed. Alexa had given birth to Althea, her daughter. She didn't name her daughter Lona, obviously, but this didn't mean anything. For I had become well versed in the language of Praxima and Peroxa, and Lona was a Peroxian word for vengeance. Lona's real name was Althea. Something that I learned from my future version, who I had communed with only once more. The conversation's we had prepared me for what was to come. Mostly, I feared what was coming. Althea will become Lona, and another war is on the horizon in the next sixteen years. This would be the war that Althea would turn. Or perhaps she would have anyway. To be honest, some of the future is confusing, but at the same time, some of it is very enlightening. There were parts my doppelganger left out. Telling me that to reveal too much could mean dire consequences and what not. I stayed well away from everything, because in Callista, I had everything. The love of the people, and of course, my own love, who at this moment, was running late. I had been waiting in the garden for what felt like hours. I had gotten tired of counting the same petals on the same flowers, then the light came down, and there stood Scion. Handsome, and holding a basket. "What's in the basket?", I asked with a cocky smile on my face. "Just, a little something special for someone special.", he replied, emptying the contents of the basket. It was a bottle of spirits, two glasses, and some fancy new thing called cheese that Scion had picked up on. We sat, eating the cheese, drinking the spirits, and staring into the night. "Scion, I need to ask you something. Have you gone yet?", I asked again for the one-hundredth time. "Ko-e, I could ask you the same question. But I suppose I'll answer you. I have. I was almost seen, so I didn't stay long. She looks beautiful. If of course you haven't been yourself.". I hadn't been to Calypsa's grave, because I was too afraid of going to Alexandria. I was afraid of facing Amana, because I didn't help. I was afraid of seeing my sister in the grave, and I was afraid of facing my niece, who I knew was going to do evil things. Evil things I had to let happen. "I understand, Ko-e.", Scion said, wrapping his arm around me and kissing the side of my head. Scion, of course, understood. He'd been to the future. We both knew Alexa was kidding herself if she thought naming her daughter, Althea, would stop her from becoming Lona. "Ko-e, you shouldn't stress yourself out about these things. You know what you have to do, and I know what I have to do. Do I worry about everyone? Yes. But I can't and don't have the luxury of ignoring my duties. And one day, neither will you.", he said, fully wrapping me in his arms. I didn't want to think about it, so I kissed him to shut him up.

As usual, Scion was gone by morning, and I knew I should wake and get back to my mansion. When I did, it was to find a most curious situation. A young girl was standing before me. She was dirty and looked like she may have had an accident. "What's the matter, little one?", I asked her. She pointed at her leg, which had a bad cut on it. "I…was…climbing the tree…and, and, and…", she was having a hard time telling me, but I could see what happened. "Come here, child, I will help you.". I took her to my mansion and sat her down, while I had some servants fetch me a medikit. I started to dilute her wound, then dress it, "Thank you. Everyone says you're so nice!", the girl yelled at me. "Okay.", I said amused. "Queen Ko-e, what happened to Queen Calypsa? I miss her.", the girl said sadly. "I miss her, too, darling.". The girl got off the chair and winced a bit on her leg, "Is it okay?", I asked her. "Yes, mam. Thank you! My name is Clarise, by the way.". The girl walked out of my mansion, and I walked to the front and looked out. Callista was truly a marvel and I thanked Calypsa every day for it.

CHAPTER 18

Aftermath: Enter Dalia

KO-E: It had been a long twenty years. Amana was now a ghost. Nobody knew where she was, and most people hadn't really been looking for her. Dalia had abandoned the throne right when the war started. She had handed over the kingdom to Salana, the second born of Mileeda. Salana fought against her mad older brother, Vicdor, who had joined Althea, of course, after she murdered her mother, and took control of the Alexandrian forces. I had longed to enter into the fray, and so, I left Clarise in charge of everything and rode to Nasher, where Nigel, too ashamed to do anything about his son, was allowing his youngest, Tiber, to handle the situation for Nasher. Mileeda, who was also ashamed, spent most of her time praying and still mourning her family. While she was happy to see me, she was also very saddened by the actions of her first born. I, too, had a large stake in this war, because I knew what Althea would become, but she hadn't started to call herself Lona yet, and I didn't know why she would. We fought for almost two years, with massive losses on each side, until one day, it was said that Vicdor had been found hung from a post in the middle of Kindy, and that his queen, Althea, the one who committed evil deeds with just whispers, was nowhere to be seen as well. Many of their loyal soldiers went all out trying to locate her but to no avail. And most of those loyalists were put down by me. So, things did seem somewhat strange that she just disappeared. Then I got news from Alexandria of a new queen. But she had dismantled the royalty of Alexandria and now there was none. I went to go find out what this was all about. It was the first time in over twenty-two years that I had set foot in Alexandria. I looked around and everything was different. The grass wasn't as green as it was before and even the royal village looked down trodden. I saw a woman walking up to me and knew something was off right away. "Ko-e, it has been a long time. I'm sorry you've come at this time, though.", "What the hell is happening here, Dalia?", I demanded. Dalia didn't look a bit different from the last time I saw her, and even more, she was wearing Alexa's crown. "We've discontinued the royal system here. It's going to start happening to other places, too.", "Where is Amana?", I asked. I figured she had to know, after all, she was her lover. But Dalia looked sad, "I have no idea. I haven't seen her in over eighteen years.", "Then how did you end up here at the beginning of the war?", "Salana. She said I should come here.". I looked around a bit more. "Can you take me to…Calypsa's grave?", I asked nervously. Dalia bit her lip, "That's going to be a problem. You see, she has been taken.". I knew by who. "To where?", "Well remember, we don't know where she is. She just wouldn't let it go, Ko-e.", Dalia said, looking sadder now. "What of Alexa?", I asked. "Follow me.". She led me to both Alexa, and my brother's grave. My brother had died around the time Althea was five. It was a strange and sudden death that never made sense to anyone but me. And probably Amana. I stood over them for some time, mourning. Penelope, who was somewhat aged now, came to me. "Ko-e, why haven't you been to visit?", she asked, hugging me. "I'm sorry, Grandmother, I wanted to, but I couldn't. There are things I've learned.", "Your sister has learned much as well.

I only wish she would have let us help her.", "She has taken Calypsa's body. Why?", I asked. I somewhat knew why, but also thought, she is wasting her time. Calypsa would not want to come back.

I had left Alexandria and made my way to my own kingdom, Callista. As I arrived, I was greeted right away by Clarise and a good healthy clutch of soldiers. I had been away for two years, and much had changed, but much remained the same. As I found my way into my home and into my room, I was startled to find a girl all chained up in gold chains. She had faded green hair and a smug face that's features were being contorted by the fact she was gagged. Althea was on my floor. Nobody had told me, so that meant nobody knew she was here. Then, from out of a dark corner, stepped Amana. There were dried blood stains on her face, and she was filthy, but through all that, you could see her face was still beautiful. She still had the scar on her face where Micka had slashed her. She walked up to me and held out her arms to hug me. I embraced her. When we broke apart, we looked into each other's faces. I know that I had been in battle as well, some very fierce. But Amana looks like her battles would give my battles a zero on the scoreboard. "Amana, what has happened to you? Where have you been all this time?", I demanded. "Ko-e, listen to me, I need you to do me a favor.". I nodded. Amana placed her hands on my shoulders and looked me in my eyes very seriously, "No matter what, and I MEAN that, no matter what, do not take that gag out of her mouth. Do you understand?". While I didn't appreciate Amana talking to me like a child, I none the less nodded. "And also, do not remove those chains. Althea is dangerous in ways you can't imagine.", "I think I can imagine quite well since she murdered her mother.". Amana said nothing to this, but continued to look me in the eye. "She is tricky. She will convince you, Ko-e, I'm telling you, just lock her up and leave her until I get back. You have strong magic here, I can feel it. And some of Calypsa's old stuff is here as well, so you can use that. Please, take care to do this, Ko-e.". I did as Amana said. I had Althea locked away. She kept trying to speak, but I kept the gag in her mouth.

Days had started to turn into weeks and Amana still hadn't returned. I decided that I needed to understand why Althea did these things. Why she killed her mother, why she started a war, and why she murdered innocents. I proceeded into my cells. I knew my magic would be strong enough to keep her inside. As soon as I saw her, she was leaning in a corner of her cell, depressed, but then looked up and saw me. She started trying to speak immediately and I snapped my fingers and the gag fell out. "Anything out of the ordinary and that goes right back.", I said. She nodded. "I have some questions for you.", "I know what your questions are, Auntie. You want to know why I killed my mother.". I nodded. "Well I didn't want to. But, Amana made me do it.", she said with a small simper in her voice. "And why would Amana want you to kill your mother?", I said, already feeling angry that she would lie like this. "You see, Amana is a killer. She will stop at nothing to gain what she wants.", "And that is?", I said, starting to grow impatient. "What do you think? Why do you think she brought me here and has been gone for weeks? Nobody had seen her before then, right? She has been gone for many years! Where do you think she has been?". I put some thought into her words, "Calypsa…", I said. "Yes.", Althea replied rather hastily, "She wants to bring her dear old sister back, damn us all. She made me kill my mother for her twisted plans and now look where she has put me!". I considered what she was saying. "Is this why Amana wanted you gagged? So, you wouldn't tell me this?", "That is the precise reason.", she replied, starting to believe I believed her. "And do you think this excuses your actions?", I said viciously. "Listen, Amana made me. What don't you understand? It's all about Calypsa! Amana taught me all the things I know. She wanted me to help her!", "I do not believe you, Niece. You are lying to me.", "It was worth a try, but if I can't convince you, then…LALAVBENDA!", she shouted, and the chains fell off of her. Before I could make a move, she had already started chanting another enchantment that removed her cell door. She blasted me out of the way with green energy, "I don't have a problem with you, Ko-e, but I will kill Amana, no matter what it takes.", she blasted me while I was down.

I woke up to Amana and Clarise sitting over me. Clarise was wiping my head. "I need the room with your queen, please?". Clarise looked at Amana like she didn't trust her, but I nodded and Clarise stepped out. "Damn it, Ko-e, I gave you one job!", she yelled at me. "I don't work for you, Amana!", I yelled, getting to my feet, although I was a bit shaky. "I told you, she is more dangerous than you could know. Now she is…", "Was she telling me the truth, Amana? Are you trying to bring back Calypsa?", I asked her. She swallowed, then replied, "That's not the point. I told you that she is tricky. You can't believe anything that girl told you. She is a liar. And by the way. She isn't calling herself, Althea, anymore. Can you guess what she goes by these days?", "Vengeance?", I said. She looked at me for a minute, "Ko-e, what the hell do you know? You better tell me.", she said, coming closer to me. "I don't know why she calls herself that, though.". Amana soon lost her tough demeanor and descended into sadness. "IT'S ALL MY FAULT!", she yelled, looking to me for sympathy. She told me the entire story. She was staying in Alexandria until she couldn't take it anymore. She had removed Calypsa's body from the grave, and took her into a secret part of Alexandria. Althea discovered her little hideaway and soon had become something Amana hadn't expected. A replacement for Calypsa. Althea was very smart and reminded Amana so much of Calypsa, that she convinced her to keep her a secret, and continued to teach her things. Amana taught Althea magic and thought that Althea was in no way shape or form the girl from the future that wanted her dead. After all, Amana hadn't learned the language of the Praximites and Peroxians yet. But apparently, this was something she studied with Althea. It was how they learned to use the hidden pathways of energy, or in other words, magic. She taught her for many years in secret, until one day, she learned what Althea wanted. "Althea wants vengeance for Caprius. She was angry that Micka was the reason he died. She knew Micka gave me this scar and assumed we were of the same mind. I didn't tell her of Trinity until a few years ago. Since then, she has been trying to summon her. But it's more than that, she wants to split her into three again, just so she can kill Micka. I told her it was impossible, but she proved it wasn't. She found the requirements.", Amana said, taking a swig of spirits. She looked at me, tears reforming in her eyes, "I should have seen it coming, Ko-e. I met her before. I should have known she would do this. She killed Alexa right in front of me. I was too late to try and...", Amana broke off, unable to finish her sentence. "Amana, when did she start calling herself Lona?", I asked, more curious as to when the change came. "Right after I killed her...right after I killed her unborn child.". I was shocked. "She was carrying?", "Yes, Vicdor's child. I couldn't let that child be born, Ko-e. I know it seems harsh, but she was going to give birth to a monster.", said Amana, convinced she was right. "YOU DON'T KNOW THAT, AMANA! HOW COULD YOU DO THAT?!", I yelled, losing myself in the anger I felt. I could hardly believe she would think that was fine. "You think I wanted to kill that child? Ko-e, Althea is a different type of goddess and mixed with whatever blood made Vicdor so strong, I couldn't chance letting that child be born. I'm afraid all of Mileeda's descendants will be different. I'm afraid what that will mean for the planet.", "But how do you know what Althea's child would have been? This is why she wants to kill you! She wants to kill you because of what you did to...". Before I could finish, Amana got to her feet, "YOU THINK SHE DESERVES TO HAVE A HAPPY FAMILY?! SHE KILLED HER MOTHER AS A SACRIFICE TO UNDO TRINITY!", Amana yelled angrily. Now I understood better. "That little bitch took everything I taught her and used it against those poor bastards she killed. She killed children, women, and elderly. Just for her own vengeance. I had to punish her, Ko-e. I wish I had the strength to kill her, but...". I knew what she was going to say, "You still love her, almost as if she was Calypsa.". Amana buried her face in her hands. "Amana, you need to learn, you can't fix everyone. Sometimes that's just how it is.". Amana didn't look at me anymore, but instead said, "I should get going, I have to find her.". Amana turned to leave, and I grabbed her wrist, "Amana, don't go. Please, lets figure this out…together?", I asked her. My sister turned towards me and shook her head, "Like how you helped me figure out how to save Calypsa and Corsa? I don't need you, Ko-e. I don't need anybody.". She snatched her hand from me and walked away. Only turning to look at me once she had gotten a bit up the path from the mansion. I didn't know what Amana was planning or what she intended to do once she found Althea. I only knew what I knew, and that is that one day, a long time from now, this planet will be in grave danger. All the stages were set. Scion was in Space above us, watching us. Amana was on course to begin her military unit in the sky, and Nasher, Callista, and Kindy were soon going to end it's royalty system. What happens after that, is all up to faith.

DALIA: It had been over five-hundred years. I watched from my perch in Alexandria, as Plinth descended into hell. First, Nasher, which is filled with the descendants of Tig, the blessed one he is called now, attacked without precedence. They had come after Kindy, which was also ruled by Tig's descendants. The Nasher/Kindy war lasted for almost one hundred years, only ceasing when Dol, the great-grandchild of Nigel and Mileeda, sacrificed herself to end the fighting. Dol was a peace seeker and ruled over Kindy for over thirty years. After this, Callista had finally gotten involved and had dissolved the royalty system in both kingdoms. They instead came up with a congressional system where, no one person, contained too much power. Two hundred years after that, there were what was now known as life canners. These scums went around killing for fun and made it into an obsession. While there were people who started to hunt these folks, it started as a volunteer thing. Then it turned into an actual job to have, with the congress offering actual shills now. Shills were the new currency and could actually be tracked in a system so that you didn't have to physically hold them. These systems were known as shill placement centers, or SPC's. Most SPC's were owned by some rich asshole who obviously belonged to the Royal Family. The Royal Family were Tig's descendants, and now, most of them run the whole planet. There were seven main members who all had their own armies. This is how the great separatist war began. Although family, they felt that they had rights to Plinth that other members of the RF didn't. So, it was only a matter of time until a whole different war happened. This war would continue for generations and end with the complete dissolution of all the kingdoms. Now, certain areas of Plinth were being named after certain RF members. Vicdor had landed his name where Kindy and Nasher used to be. Vicdora was a city filled with mixed citizens. Some were all about advancements, while others were about that one-time advancement. This was the beginning of gang violence. It had been twenty-seven-hundred years, and a man named Eddie Folto, who had no ties to the RF, or anything, suddenly found himself in a turf war with Tiggy Dat, who was a member of the RF. Tiggy, although he had shills from the day he was born, found a new lucrative business, drugs. Kind flowers were rare to find, seeing as how the kind field had been razed over one thousand years ago. But this stuff was made from mixing deadly chemicals, and if taken in small doses, can have small, but major effects on your mind state. Many had overdosed and died from these drugs. Kids were even managing to get their hands on it. I felt I could no longer sit by and watch these poor kids kill themselves. At the time, I had left Alexandria over seventeen-hundred years ago, and had been living and training with Ko-e. When I came into Vicdora, which is now called Edge, it was to heal. Unfortunately, I came at the wrong time. Eddie was dealing the same drugs, but just on the other side of town. When Tiggy found out, he shot up the block. This of course meant war, and the next thing anybody knew, blood was running all over the streets. I tried to help as best I could, but things only started to get worse when Tiggy had his money invested into coming up with a better drug. This is when Lilac was created. Lilac was the new drug, and it held hallucinogenic properties. People would actually go crazy using this stuff and it was becoming such an epidemic that I couldn't just hide myself anymore.

One night, when Tiggy and his crew were closing up shop, I was waiting to get Tiggy alone. But that was proving to be hard. Tiggy never was by himself, which made sense, since he was the leader of his little gang, and was involved in open street warfare. Tiggy was a creature of many habits. Many times, he would change his routine. It was an immediate guess that he does this to keep his enemies confused. But I was a different type of enemy. I had been trained by a goddess and had made myself immortal. Or if not immortal, something close to it. I knew what I would have to do just to get close to Tiggy. As soon as he had found himself in his home, he started to get ready for bed. His men were all throughout his house and it was obvious why. Earlier, there was a woman who had been led here. She was obviously drugged up and I knew what the intention was. I figured I would make a better replacement. "What the hell happened to the other girl?", one of the men asked once I had switched her out, sending her home, and saving her life. "She was too tired, and I'm fresh but looking to score. I'll do anything for some lilac.", I said in a sexy tone. One of the men was looking at my ass. I was wearing a small skirt that I made sure was high enough to leave some interest. And with the skirt, I wore a tank-top that was pink. And I had long since dyed my hair tan and kept it that way. It was sort of bushy at the moment. The men all looked at one another, "Right this way, chickee.", a big man said. I followed, and the men behind me started to push me roughly. As we had arrived in what was a basement, I saw the lilac on the table. It was a white powder that was left after boiling very hazardous chemicals. The air was thick with the smell of burnt chlorine and glass. One man grabbed me and tried to kiss me. When I didn't let him, another man grabbed my head and tried to force it on the table. When I didn't budge, but instead, smiled, and knocked the man upside his head, sending him flying into the wall, the other men rushed at me. I quickly subdued them. As I was wiping my hands and dusting myself off, a girl entered the room. "Dalia, I really wish you would have told me you were going to do this.", said Amana, looking at the scene, impressed. I hadn't seen or heard from her in hundreds of years, and yet, I felt like a school girl whose crush just entered the room for the first time and I was barely laying eyes on her. Amana didn't look different. She was cleaner than the last time I saw her, and she was wearing an interesting uniform. "How could I have told you? I haven't had any knowledge of where you were.", I replied, telling myself not to let her suck me in. "Would you like to join me upstairs?", she said, already turning to walk up there. As I followed her, we were standing outside of what I had to assume was Tiggy's room. Amana kicked in the door and Tiggy had already been subdued. There were a couple of men in here wearing black uniforms, with the same emblem as Amana's. Tiggy was sitting on his bed with his hands cuffed in gold cuffs. "DO YOU BITCHES HAVE ANY IDEA WHO I AM?! YOU HAVE NO IDEA THE MISTAKE YOU'RE MAKING!", he yelled at us. Amana just smirked, "Tiggy, you have no idea who you have been messing with. All your shills, and you're wasting them on what exactly? Killing people? Your family isn't too happy with you by the way.", said Amana, looking around the room now. I was going to join in looking, but, Amana held her hand up and reached in her pocket and handed me a pair of gloves, "Don't touch anything with your bare hands. I need to find something with his prints or any DNA.". She was walking around the room not really touching anything. "Mam! Look what I found.", said one of the men in uniform, rushing to Amana, and showing her the inside of a box. "Well, this is funny. Tell me something, Tiggy, is this your idea of a joke? Or is this your sick way of getting off? I'll go with the second choice.". Tiggy said nothing, as Amana took the box and threw it at Tiggy, who looked guilty, but continued to say nothing. I looked at what Amana was talking about and there were memory sheets. They all showed young girls in various positions. Some of the young girls were children and some had no clothing at all, while other sheets showed Tiggy in the photo, doing unspeakable things. Tiggy started to shake his head, "You know who I am, don't you, Tiggy? Do you know how much it upsets me, that you have been named after a great man?", said Amana with pure disgust in her voice. Tiggy looked down at the photos, "I DIDN'T DO THIS! IT WAS LO! I want a GP!", Tiggy shouted. GP's were guard protection. Basically, they defend those that have been taken in by the guard force for crimes they either did or didn't commit. Amana smiled, "These photos are too incriminating, Tiggy. You don't get a GP. You my friend, get locked away, with the key thrown in the toilet.", said Amana, directing the men to take Tiggy. "Also, don't forget his men in the basement. Make sure to not damage the lab down there, though, we'll need evidence.". I had no idea what was going on. I hadn't heard from Amana in years, and yet here she is, like she was never hiding. Once the men walked out the room, Amana grabbed me and kissed me. I felt my heart jump, I missed her, but I couldn't allow this. I pushed her away. "What? Oh. Let me guess; You are upset that I haven't been around in a while.", "A while? Amana, it's been two-hundred years.". Amana looked a bit guilty, then she changed her demeanor, "I know. And every day I have thought of you. But I had to disappear for a time. Have you seen or heard anything from Ko-e?", Amana asked me. "No, I haven't.". Amana watched me for some sign I might be lying, but then decided I wasn't. "Do you want to come with me, or not, Dalia?", she asked, getting impatient with me. She was always like this with me. Even when she left me in Kindy, and I didn't see her for a long time after that. "Amana, you do not get to just show up and demand I go with you!", I yelled at her frustratedly. "Okay, that's fine. Go back to Ko-e. Yes, I know that is who you have been with. I don't have time for this crap anymore.", Amana said, turning her back on me and walking out the room. I could hear her giving orders down below and I wanted to go with her badly. But she was right. I had been with Ko-e this whole time. Ko-e, after she left Callista, decided to help defend the streets of Plinth. She had trained many soldiers to aid us. Most of the people Ko-e and I had trained were learned in the way of hidden energies. We taught this because it was crucial in the major fight. Ko-e had told me that her and Amana weren't on good terms, and that by joining her, I'd be betraying Amana. I didn't see how at the time, since I hadn't heard from her in centuries. Mileeda, who was supposedly still alive somewhere, hadn't revealed where she was. No doubt she was sickened by what her children's children had become. The RF were filled with people like Tiggy, but a majority of them were heavily involved in the politics of the planet. I didn't want to let Amana walk away from me again. So, I came up to her and grabbed her in front of her men, who were packing up the lilac lab. They looked confused as to what they should do. Amana held up her other hand, "I'll deal with it. Just take care of this and get all of it, and I mean ALL of it, to Base.", she said, taking her hand from me. She led me upstairs back into Tiggy's room. "What the hell was that? Who the hell do you think you are?", she said to me, folding her arms. "I think you owe me some kind of an explanation, Amana! Tell me where the hell you've been!". She thought for a minute, "I've been in Alexandria. Yes, even while you were there. I've been building up my army. Thanks to your departure, I was finally able to come out of hiding and lead.". I felt my blood boil, "So, you mean all that time that I was looking for you and hoping you'd come back... All those times I laid up crying, wishing you were in my bed, you were just ignoring me?", I asked. "Not really ignoring you, just too busy to sleep with you. That's all it has ever been, hasn't it? We don't really love each other, do we?", she asked, still looking at me with her arms folded. "HOW CAN YOU SAY THAT TO ME?!", I demanded, feeling more hurt than I've felt in three lifetimes. "So, then, come here.", she said. I listened and she embraced me and began kissing me.

After we had made love on Tiggy's bed, Amana got up and started to dress. "Where are you going?", I asked her, sitting up myself, and holding the blanket up to my breast. "My men are going to worry. I need to get back to Base.", she said simply. "And what about me?", "Well, are you coming or not? I'm not fighting you on this, Dalia.", she said, irritated. "I thought we were having fun, Amana?", "We were, now you're messing it up.", she said, zipping up her leather uniform, and checking a device in her hand. "Listen, if you aren't coming with me, I suggest you refrain from doing this kind of stuff in the future. There are laws meant to be followed.". Amana turned and walked out of the room, not even giving me another glance. I was furious with myself. Amana always takes me in like this, and then leaves me feeling stupid. I got out of the bed and got dressed. I returned to mine and Ko-e's house. It was magicked to be hidden in plain sight. As I went inside, Ko-e was sitting with one of our disciples. When they noticed I was walking in, the disciple got up and left. "Dalia, I assume you've seen my sister.", Ko-e said. Ko-e was always pretty intuitive. In truth, Ko-e may know more than Amana does. I nodded. Ko-e held out her arms for me and I fell into them, "She did it to me again.", I said, angry and hurt. "I'm sorry, Dalia. I know it's hard for you to say no to her. Come though, I have something to show you.", Ko-e said, standing and leading me. What she led me to, was a map that was sitting on our dining table. "What is this, Ko-e? Why is this important?", I asked. "This is a map of Alexandria now. Amana and the others have changed some things, but this is what I am most worried about.", she said, pointing to a part of the map that was blank. "How did you even get this?", "I have people everywhere, just like them.", she said with a smile, "I believe it is a cell, and I have no doubt who is locked up in there.", "So, what is your point? What do you intend to do?", I asked, feeling tired and still hurt after Amana used me. "Well, lets see, I'd say nothing. I believe that this is it, Dalia. I'm going to need you to split from me.". I looked at her, feeling lost. First, Amana abandoned me, and now, Ko-e, who has been almost like a sister to me herself? Something in my face must have shown because she quickly said, "Don't worry. We'll stay in contact, but I mean you will have to go off on your own now. This is the point where you and I put my plan into action.", she said, rolling up the map and getting out the old book me, her, and Mileeda started four-hundred years ago. "Ko-e, where am I supposed to go? Amana told me not to interfere with the criminal activity anymore.", "Then don't. Find something legit. Settle into it and stay there. I promise you, you are destined now for things involving us and our problems.", Ko-e said jokingly. I smiled and then went to my quarters. I figured that I would figure out how to do this, and that I didn't need to be afraid. The future was before us and Plinth was going to see some dark days.